Serious Men

Serious Men

MANU JOSEPH

W. W. Norton & Company
New York · London

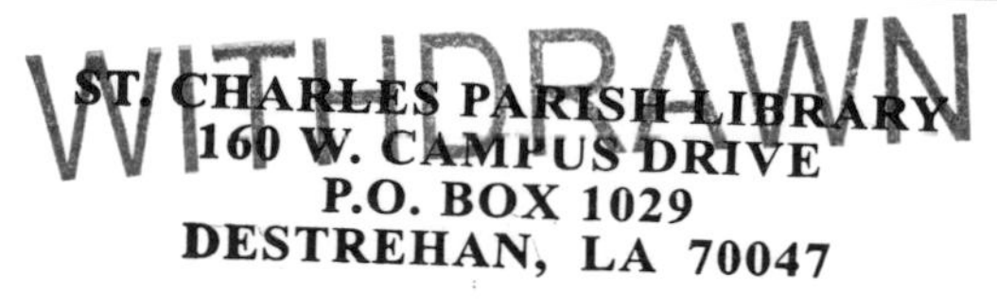

First American Edition 2010

Manufacturing by Courier Westford
Production manager: Devon Zahn

Library of Congress Cataloging-in-Publication Data

Joseph, Manu.
Serious men / Manu Joseph. — 1st American ed.
p. cm.
ISBN 978-0-393-33859-1 (pbk.)
1. Dalits—India—Fiction. 2. Research institutes—Employees—Fiction.
3. Astronomers—Fiction. 4. Ambition—Fiction. 5. Bombay (India)—Fiction.
6. India—Social life and customs—Fiction. 7. Satire. I. Title.
PR9499.4.J676S47 2010
823'.92—dc22

2010009298

W. W. Norton & Company, Inc.
500 Fifth Avenue, New York, N.Y. 10110
www.wwnorton.com

W. W. Norton & Company Ltd.
Castle House, 75/76 Wells Street, London W1T 3QT

1 2 3 4 5 6 7 8 9 0

For Anuradha, my love.

PART ONE

The Giant Ear Problem

AYYAN MANI'S THICK black hair was combed sideways and parted by a careless broken line, like the borders the British used to draw between two hostile neighbours. His eyes were keen and knowing. A healthy moustache sheltered a perpetual smile. A dark tidy man, but somehow inexpensive.

He surveyed the twilight walkers. There were hundreds on the long concrete stretch by the Arabian Sea. Solitary young women in good shoes walked hastily, as if they were fleeing from the fate of looking like their mothers. Their proud breasts bounced, soft thighs shuddered at every step. Their tired high-caste faces, so fair and glistening with sweat, bore the grimace of exercise. He imagined they were all in the ecstasy of being seduced by him. Among them, he could tell, there were girls who had never exercised before. They had arrived after a sudden engagement to a suitable boy, and they walked with very long strides as though they were measuring the coastline. They had to shed fat quickly before the bridal night when they might yield on the pollen of a floral bed to a stranger. Calm unseeing old men walked with other old men, discussing the state of the nation. They had all the solutions. A reason why their wives walked half a mile away, in their own groups, talking about arthritis or about other women who were not present. Furtive lovers were beginning to arrive. They sat on the parapet and faced the sea, their hands straying or eyes filling depending on what stage the relationship was in. And their new jeans were so low that their meagre Indian buttocks peeped out as commas.

Ayyan looked with eyes that did not know how to show a

cultured indifference. He often told Oja, 'If you stare long enough at serious people they will begin to appear comical.' So he looked. From behind, a girl with a bouncing pony tail and an iPod strung to her ears overtook him. Through her damp T-shirt he could see her firm youthful back. He quickened his pace, and regained his lead over her. And he tried to look at her face in the hope that she was not pretty. Beautiful women depressed him. They were like Mercedes, BlackBerry phones and sea-view homes.

The girl met his eyes for an instant and looked away without feeling flattered. She had a haughty face that would be a pleasure to tame. With love, poetry or a leather belt, perhaps. Whatever she liked. Her face did not show anything, but it did grow more cold. She was aware that she was being watched, not just by a strange brisk man but also by the unending hordes of miserable people all around who spread dengue and scratched her car. They were always there on the fringes of her world, gawking at her the way stray dogs look at good stock.

Ayyan slowed down and let her march ahead. A few feet away, a man stood still and stared at her. His head moved from left to right as she passed him. He was a short man who appeared to stand erect because his back was not long enough. Ayyan knew from the tension in his shirt that it was tucked straight into the underwear for a tighter grip. (The secret fashion of many men he knew.) A thin brown belt ran around his slender waist almost twice. His shirt pocket sagged under the weight of the many things it held. A red comb peeped from the back pocket of his trousers.

'Stop staring at that girl,' Ayyan said.

The little man was startled. He then opened his mouth in a sporting but silent laugh. Transient strings of saliva ran from the upper jaw to the lower.

They went to one of the pink concrete benches that were dedicated to the memory of a departed member of the Rotary Club.

'Busy day,' the man said, flapping his thighs. 'I'm travelling. That's why I troubled you, Mani. I wanted to settle this fast.'

'It's all right, my friend,' Ayyan said, 'The important thing is that we have managed to meet.' He took out a piece of printed paper and handed it to him. 'All the details are in this,' Ayyan said.

The man studied it more carefully than he probably wanted to. And he tried to appear nonchalant when the envelope full of cash was thrust towards his chest.

After the little man left, with quick hectic steps to emphasize that he was busy, Ayyan continued to sit on the bench and stare. The game has to escalate, he told himself. It has to move to a different level. In a way, what he had just done was cruel. It was probably even a crime. But what must a man do? An ordinary clerk stranded in a big daunting world wants to feel the excitement of life, he wants to liberate his wife from the spell of jaundice-yellow walls. What must he do?

The crowd on the Worli Seaface was swelling: it was now a giant colourless swarm. Pale boys with defeat in their eyes walked in horizontal gangs; they giggled at the aerobics of unattainable women. And they did not give way to the hasty girls. Ayyan loved this about the city – the humid crowds, the great perpetual squeeze, the silent vengeance of the poor. In the miserly lifts and stuffed trains, he often heard the relief of afternoon farts, saw scales on strange faces and the veins in their still eyes. And the secret moustaches of women. And the terrible green freshness when they had been newly removed with a thread. He felt the shoves and pushes and the heaviness of paunches. This unnerving constriction of Mumbai he loved, because the congestion of hopeless shuffling human bodies he was born into was also, in a way, the fate of the rich. On the streets, in the trains, in the paltry gardens and beaches, everybody was poor. And that was fair.

The desperate lovers were still arriving and they quickly stole the gaps on the parapet between other fused couples. And they, too, sat facing the sea with their backs to the great passing crowds, arranged their bodies and did their discreet things. If there were ever a sudden almightly silence here you would hear a thousand bra straps snap. Among these lovers were married people, some of them even married to each other. When night fell, they went back to their one-room homes, which were as large as a Mercedes, to rejoin their children, elders, siblings, nephews and nieces, all heaped under a single roof in gigantic clusters of boiling tenements. Like the BDD chawl, the mother hell. People who knew what BDD stood for were not the kind who lived there. But Ayyan knew such things, even though he was born on a cold floor there, thirty-nine years ago.

It was a hive of ten thousand one-room homes carved inside a hundred and twenty identical three-storeyed buildings that stood like grey ruins, their paint long removed by old rains. A million clothes hung from the grilles of small dark windows. Portions of the outer walls, sometimes even roofs, kept falling off, especially in the calamitous rains of August. The chawls were built by the British more than eight decades ago in a belated attack of conscience to house the homeless. But the tenements turned out to be so badly constructed that the street dwellers refused to move in, seeing no point in forsaking the whole world and the blue sky in exchange for a small dark room on an endless corridor of gloom. So the buildings were converted into gaols to shove in freedom-fighters. The unclaimed one-room homes became inescapable cells. In this place that was spurned eight decades ago by even the homeless and which was once a prison, now lived over eighty thousand people who heaved and sighed with the burdens of new unions and the relief of death.

Ayyan made his way home down the broken, cobbled ways which ran between the stout buildings. Men and women, hundreds of them, just stood around. As if something bad had happened. Emaciated girls, with hollow chests, chatted among themselves. They were clean and eager, and there was hope in their eyes. Some of them were speaking to each other in English, for practice. They moved away to let a drunkard pass. Boys in tight counterfeit jeans, their arses like mangoes, wrestled with each other jovially, hand-to-hand, legs trying to trip. The expression of one of the boys was beginning to change. Someone was bending his finger. His face, at first in moronic mirth, now turned serious. A fight broke out.

But Ayyan loved going home. At the foot of the steep colonial stairways of Block Number Forty-One, a good marriage was the only incentive for a man to go up. He climbed the steps saying '*kaay khabar*' to the men who were going down to drink. The women of BDD did not expect much from their men. Ageing mothers who had lost all their sons before those boys could turn thirty were still capable of laughing till they were breathless. Here the frailties of the male folk showed all the time in the tired faces of the newly dead, or in the vacant eyes of drunkards, or the resigned calm of the jobless boys who just sat for hours watching the world go by. In a way, this was the easiest place to be a man. To be alive was enough. To be sober and employed was fantastically impressive. Ayyan Mani was something of a legend.

Even though the men here loved Ayyan through the memories of a common childhood, he had long ago cut himself off from them. He laughed with them always, lent money and on humid nights chatted on the black tar-coated terrace about who exactly was the best batsman in the world, or about the builders who were interested in buying up the chawl, or about how Aiswharya Rai was not very beautiful if she were observed closely. But in his mind he did not accept these men. He had to abolish the world he grew up in to be able to plot new ways of escaping from it. Sometimes he saw bitterness in the eyes of his old friends who thought he had gone too far in life, leaving them all behind. That bitterness reassured him. The secret rage in their downcast eyes also reminded him of a truth which was dearer to him than anything else. That men, in reality, did not have friends in other men. That the fellowship of men, despite its joyous banter, old memories of exaggerated mischief and the altruism of sharing pornography, was actually a farcical fellowship. Because what a man really wanted was to be bigger than his friends.

Ayyan saw a young couple come down the steps. 'All well?' he asked. The boy smiled shyly. He was holding a travel bag. Ayyan knew that the bag was empty. It was a sign of love. In some rooms here, over a dozen lived. So the newly-weds slept on the illegal wooden lofts with the unspoken assurance that the rest of the family down below would not look up. Every now and then, incontinent couples went to cheap lodges in Parel or Worli carrying empty bags to pass off as tourists. Some carried their wedding albums too, in case the cops raided. They spent a day in a whole bed that was entirely their own and returned with fond memories of room-service and love. Ayyan had never had to do such a thing. Oja Mani came into his life after everybody else had departed. His three brothers had died of bleeding livers in a space of eighteen months, and a year later his father died of tuberculosis and his mother soon followed out of habit. He was twenty-seven-then, and Oja was seventeen. He had ushered her in, calculating that she would remain young long after he ceased to be fully potent.

He walked down the dim corridor of the third floor, which was the top floor. It was flanked by ageing pale yellow walls with huge cracks that ran like dark river systems. There were about forty open doors here. Unmoving shadows sat on the doorways and gaped. Old widows calmly combed their hair. Children ran happily on the ancient grey stones of the corridor.

He knocked on the only door on the corridor that was shut. As he waited, he felt the turbulence of all those open doors, and the milling shadows. An old familiar sorrow rose like vapour inside him. Oja was trapped here with him. Once, her youthful words used to rush out like a giggle; she used to sing to herself in the mornings. But eventually the *chawl* seeped into her. The darkness grew, and it sometimes stared at him through her big black eyes.

The door opened, somewhat slower and with far less anticipation than it used to years ago. Oja Mani appeared, her luxurious dark hair still wet from a new bath. As delicate as ever, entirely capable of touching her toes in the unlikely event of being asked to do so. But she was not sculpted by the vain exercises of those forward-caste women on the Worli Seaface. Beneath her thin red cotton nightdress, she had a slight paunch that might flatten out if she rested on her back.

Their home was exactly fifteen feet long and ten feet wide. There was a cleared patch of smooth grey stone floor at the centre. Along a wall were a television, a washing machine, a benevolent golden Buddha and a towering steel cupboard. At one end of the room, by the only window that was reinforced by a rusted iron grille, was a rudimentary kitchen that ran into a tiny stained-glass bathroom where one would fit, and two would be in a relationship.

Oja left the door open and went back to sit on the floor and stare at the television. From seven to nine every evening, she was hypnotized by the melancholic Tamil soaps. During this time she encouraged everybody to disappear. Ayyan sat beside her and watched the serial patiently.

'Why is that woman crying?' he asked to irritate her. 'Last night too she was crying. She has no dialogue?'

Oja did not respond. Her own large interested eyes were moist.

He told her, 'I come home after a hard day's work and you just sit and watch TV?'

Her nostrils flared a bit but she chose to remain silent. That was her strategy.

'You know, Oja,' he said, as he began these things, 'rich people have a name for everything. They even have a word for the time a man spends with his family.'

'Really?' she asked, without turning round.

'They call it Quality Time.'

'It's English?'

'Yes.'

'Why should they name something like that?'

'They name everything out there,' he said. 'You know, Oja. There are people in those tall buildings who suddenly begin to wonder, "Who am I? What am I?" And they have a name for that too.'

There was a knock at the door. Oja muttered that there was no peace in this place. When Ayyan opened the door, two little girls walked in. One was about ten and the other must have been two years younger. They said, both at once, 'Guests have come to our house, we need chairs.' And they carried away the two plastic chairs.

Oja shut the door and latched it firmly as though that would protect her from other intrusions that were lurking outside. She then sank onto the floor again. But the television erupted in the cheerful jingle of a shampoo commercial. She got up briskly and went to the kitchen. She knew the exact lengths of the commercial breaks. The first break was the longest and in that time she always tried to do most of her cooking.

'Look at this,' Ayyan said pointing at the commercial. 'This woman has a problem. She has a big problem, actually. Her hair is thin and weak. That's her problem. Now she is using a shampoo. Look now. She is happy. Her problem is solved. A man is ogling her and she looks at him sideways. Now her hair is very thick and strong.'

Ayyan was laughing, but Oja knew that the muscles around his temples must be moving. She did not turn from the trembling vessel on the stove. She waited for him to empty all his hate.

He was saying, 'This is what these bastards think is a problem. Hairfall. That's their big problem.' Then he asked, 'Where is Adi?'

Oja answered, 'Girls and butterflies; boys and monkeys.'

Ayyan did not understand most of her proverbs. 'Oja, where is he?'

'God knows what that weird boy is up to,' she said. Yet, it was she who had enthusiastically asked him to go away when the serial was about to begin.

ON THE VAST tar-coated terrace that was surrounded by distant looming buildings, people sat in small scattered groups. Beneath the starless sky children screamed and ran. One boy, about ten maybe, stood silently in a corner. His hair was oiled and severely combed. He was in a T-shirt that had the image of Einstein sticking his tongue out jovially. The boy had clear black eyes: Oja's eyes. A hearing-aid was strung to his left ear. Its white wire ran into his T-shirt.

He did not seem very keen to run around, though he appeared very interested in what was happening around him. After a while, the children came together, close to where he was standing. They were panting gleefully, and someone decided that since they were all very tired they would play husband-and-wife. In their opinion it was a relaxing game.

Without too much conflict they split into pairs. A remaining girl was quickly joined with the silent boy. She looked at him condescendingly, because she was a girl and he was just a boy. Though he didn't ask for directions she explained the game to him. 'It's easy,' she said, as an incentive. They had to just behave like parents. All the other pairs walked away to various nooks of the terrace where there were imaginary markets and theatres. The boy looked at his girl for a few seconds wondering what they must do that parents did. Then a solution entered his oddly large head.

He gently eased the girl to the ground and spread her legs. She looked confused but tried to figure out what he was trying to do. He climbed on top of her and bobbed his hips clumsily. The young mothers, who until now had gazed lazily in intervals at their children like wild animals on grassland, came to life. They let out embarrassed chuckles and rushed to separate the boy from his temporary wife. The boy went back to his corner with a foul look on his face. The girl disengaged herself from the adult intervention. Now that she understood what he was doing, she continued with the game by pretending to tie her hair, a hint of boredom on her face. Then she went to sleep on the tar-coated floor.

Since all the pairs were busy, and his own mate was asleep, Adi went home. Oja let him in. The boy walked into the house with a wise calm and pulled out the *Encyclopaedia Britannica*: *M–P* from the lower portion of the television stand.

'Forgot to tell you,' Oja told her husband, 'his teacher has written a complaint in the handbook again. You have to meet the Principal tomorrow morning.'

'What has he done now?' Ayyan asked with a proud smile. Adi looked up at his father and gave a mischievous wink.

'You are the one who is spoiling him,' Oja said. 'They are going to kick him out of the school one of these days.'

She went to Adi and twisted his ear gently. 'He asked one of those questions again in the class,' she said.

'What question?' Ayyan asked, now chuckling.

'I don't know. I wouldn't know even if you told me now. This boy is crazy.'

'What did you do, Adi?'

'The science teacher was saying that if you throw anything up it has to come down. Basic things like that. So I asked her if the acceleration due to gravity of any planet anywhere in the universe can make an object travel faster than light.'

Oja looked distressed. 'And he was reading one of your books in the class,' she said in an accusing way. 'I don't know how he took it with him.'

Ayyan made a conspiratorial face at his son and asked which book it was.

'*Brief History of Time*,' Adi said. 'I don't like it.'

Oja was staring at her son with a mixture of fear and excitement. Ayyan loved that look on his wife's face, that sudden awakening in her from the gloomy acceptance of a life in BDD.

'He is just ten,' she said. 'How does he understand these things?'

Last month, in the middle of the class, Adi had asked the science teacher something about arithmetic progression. A few weeks before that it was something else. Oja heard these stories from his teachers who were usually in some sort of happy delirium when they complained to her.

That night, Adi was sleeping near the fridge, as always, and his father lay next to him, holding the glass-bangled hand of his wife. Ayyan wondered if he must build a wooden loft. He turned towards his son who was facing him, but he was fast asleep. After a few minutes the boy turned in his sleep and hid his face under the fridge. That was a heartening development.

A pale light was coming through the rusted grilles of the kitchen window and Ayyan could see Oja in the blue glow. Her open palm, with its clear fatelines, rested loosely on her forehead. Her red nightgown was far less arousing than the saris she used to wear after marriage. She was always in a sari in those days because her mother had said that she should not come across as liberal. Oja's legs were joined together and folded at the knees. Her silver anklets lay still. Ayyan ran his hand over her waist. She opened her eyes without confusion or protest. She lifted her head to check on Adi. The couple moved with skill. They could caress and even tumble and roll a bit without making a sound.

They were in a sort of common entanglement, with Ayyan's shorts hanging at his knees, Oja's nightgown lifted, her legs parted, when she, yawning, decided to check on Adi again. He was sitting with his back resting against the wall.

'They wouldn't let me play that yesterday,' he said.

In the morning, when Adi was having his bath in the glass enclosure, Ayyan told his wife, his eyes dejected and voice deep, 'I have something to say.' Oja looked at him and then at the boiling milk. 'For the sake of our son,' he said, 'we must stop seeking our own pleasures.'

One hour later, as he was walking Adi to school, Ayyan thought of how Oja had readily accepted his decision. She had nodded, with one eye on the milk. It was an image that stayed with him till he reached a back lane in Worli and approached the tall black gates of St Andrew's School. The decay of a man, he told himself, is first conveyed to him by his wife.

Oja's face, in the inconvenience of love, was now a cold face that did not seem even to register pain any more. Once she used to moan and make short gasps and turn coy. Now, when he made love to her, she looked as though she was waiting for the bus. When she first began to assume that hollow gaze, he used it as a device in a private game in which the goal was to extract a reaction from her – a yelp, a sigh, a moan, anything. Then the game transformed. He imagined he was a powerful tea-planter raping a worker who had come to him asking for a loan. But the blank stare of his wife continued to haunt him. Eventually he put an end to all his private games. And he accepted her detached love in the same way that he accepted her cups of tea.

But her blank disenchanted face sometimes frightened him. It reminded him that the woman he loved so much was stranded in a dull life because of him. There was a time when he thought he could save her from BDD and everything else, that love alone could make him superhuman and somehow take them to a better life. But that did not happen, and it probably was never going to happen.

He felt an irresistible urge to fall down and go to sleep, like the perpetual drunkards of the chawls. He felt like fleeing to some place far away where he would be single, where he would expect nothing from people and people would expect nothing from him. He would eat from the fruits of a tree owned by no man, and sleep under clear blue skies, lulled by the sound of the waves and the winds from faraway lands. He imagined himself on a giant billboard, his back to the world, walking on a long tapering road towards an endless sea, and from the horizon of the sea rose the incandescent words – 'Free Man ®'.

But, he knew, the freedom of a bachelor is the freedom of a stray dog. On such days, when he felt stranded in family life, he always invoked the memory of the evening when Oja had first walked into his home as a terrified bride. She was so beautiful, and her fear was so arousing. But on the first night, when he sat beside her on the conjugal mattress that was filled with funereal roses left by neighbours and friends, he discovered that his new wife had cut her arms and legs with a Topaz blade. She had done it very carefully and methodically so that she did not damage her veins. She wanted an excuse to be left alone. It was her way of saving herself from being undressed by a stranger.

'I was afraid' was the first thing she ever told him.

'Of what?' he had asked. And she looked even more frightened.

Ayyan had read that a woman had to be ready, whatever that meant. So he decided to wait. Sometime in the second month of their marriage, Oja's cousin was sent by her mother under the guise of a casual visit to check if everything was all right. In the middle of churning curd, the girls talked about private matters.

'He has not done it yet?' the cousin screamed. 'Something is certainly wrong with him.' She spoke of the dark thing, 'that looks half eaten,' that nailed her even before she could give her man his milk on the wedding night.

'It was big and it hurt,' the cousin had said in a whisper. 'I walked like a spider for two days.'

Ayyan did claim his rights soon, one Sunday afternoon, when Oja was sitting on the stone floor cutting onions. When it was over, Oja looked up at the ceiling, an onion tear running down her cheek, and asked, somewhat disappointedly, 'That's it?' Then, unexpectedly, she lifted both her legs and pressed her knees to her face in a curative exercise. The first year of their marriage went by in their endless chatter about things they no longer remembered, and in moments of loneliness that sometimes bore the gloom of exile and at other times the sweet isolation of elopement. And in their infrequent physical love through which Oja maintained a calm, interested gaze. And in Ayyan's perpetual knowledge that a box of condoms in their home outlived a jar of pickles.

During that time, he had a nightmare that he would never tell Oja. He dreamt that he was summoned by God, who looked exactly like Albert Einstein but highly illuminated. God asked him: 'Why did you get married?'

Ayyan answered earnestly, 'To have sex any time of the day or night'.

God looked at him with a thoughtful face for an instant, and the creases of a smile appeared. The smile became a laugh and the laugh burst into echoes. Men and women on the streets, too, looked at Ayyan and laughed uncontrollably. People who were dangling from the doors of a local train threw their heads back and laughed. The motorman stopped the train to laugh. Fish-sellers in the market covered their mouths and laughed. Even the framed portrait of Jawaharlal Nehru held his stomach and laughed until the rose fell from his buttonhole. Then Ayyan saw the face of his beautiful wife on a giant public billboard, so embarrassed and so elegantly distraught by it all. That wraith woke him up because he could not bear to see her like that.

When he realized it was just a dream he turned to her sleeping figure and hugged her. Though her eyes were shut, she accepted the embrace hungrily as though she too had arrived at the same scene in her own dreams.

AT THE SCHOOL gates, Ayyan feasted on modern young mothers. Their faces were still youthful, loose flesh shuddered inside their small tops like water in the immoral pink beds of Tamil films; their trousers were aghast at the tightness of it all and their asymmetric panty-lines were like birds in the sky drawn by a careless cartoonist. These days many young mothers wore long skirts too. They looked nice, he thought. In the chawls, mothers never wore skirts. Two years ago, misled by aspiration, a woman had tried. By the time she reached the broken cobbled ways, so many people had laughed at her, so many eyes had judged her intent, that she ran back home, made peace with her fate and returned in a salwar.

In the mornings, the air was somewhat tense around the school gates. Boys in whites and girls in blue pinafores walked away from their parents with unhappy faces. In the evenings, they ran happily towards the gates, the way earthquake survivors in this country might run towards the BBC correspondent.

Ayyan inspected his son. Adi was in a white shirt and shorts. And smart black boots. His bag, oversized for a boy of just ten, was in his father's hand. The sight of the calm studious boy comforted him. And the secret game that they were playing, the mother of all games, filled Ayyan once again with anticipation. That's all he asked from life some days, the exhilaration of anticipation.

The solitary guard, in the khaki uniform and cap he was forced to wear, was looking at the backs of the departing young mothers as though his wife was morally superior. He gave a friendly nod to Ayyan, almost nudging him with his eyes to pay attention to one very fleshy young mother. Ayyan ignored him. He always did because he wanted the guard to know that they were not equals, that he must respect him the way he hurriedly saluted the fathers who arrived in cars. But the guard knew that he did not have to concede.

The Principal was a tough Salesian matron. Her veil rested on half her scalp. She had a thick volatile face and severe eyes. She was square and muscular, and the calves that showed beneath the habit sported wiry hair. Her name was Sister Chastity.

Jesus Christ, with a crown of thorns on his head, surveyed the room morosely with a hand on his visible heart, which was on fire. The Principal was environmentally conscious (uncharacteristically for a Catholic matriarch). Her table was littered with articles made out of paper and other recycled things. 'Everything in this woman's room was once something else,' Ayyan had told Oja after he first met Sister Chastity.

'So, we meet again,' Sister Chastity said unhappily, pointing Ayyan to a chair. She usually spoke to him in Hindi with a faint Malayalee accent. 'How come the mother never comes when there is trouble?' she asked.

'She is scared of you and very ashamed of the boy.'

'Where is Adi? Already in class?'

'Yes.'

There was an uncomfortable silence, because Sister Chastity wanted it. She then said, 'Mr Mani, I don't know if your son makes me happy or sad. When he is asked to do addition, he talks about things that boys many years his senior do not even understand. He wants to know about the speed of light and the acceleration due to gravity and things like that. Obviously, he is some sort of a genius and we have to nurture him. He is very special. But his conduct in school, the way he blurts out things in the middle of class, questions the authority of his teachers, you know, we cannot tolerate these things.'

'I am going to make sure that he behaves. It's hard to control him but I am going to make sure he is disciplined.'

'Discipline. That's the word. And that's all there is to education.'

When it looked as if the meeting were over, she pushed two books towards Ayyan. They were about the life of Christ. 'My small effort, as usual, to bring you closer to the Lord,' she said, with a smile. Her eyes grew kind.

'I love Christ,' Ayyan said softly.

'Why don't you accept him?'

'I accept him.'

'Accept him in a formal way, I mean. There is no compulsion, obviously. We never compel. As you know, the fee waiver and other small things we can offer, purely as a concession laid out for financially backward Christians, will benefit you immensely.'

'I am giving it some thought. I am trying to convince my family. You know, there is this mindset against conversion.'

'I know, I know. The human mind is so ignorant,' Sister Chastity said. She held him with her deep hard eyes. She loved pauses. With nothing more than silence she usually asked him either to leave, or stay right there. This silence now was the calm before a sermon. He wondered if she really was a virgin.

'Mr Mani,' she said, 'in a way, you are a good Christian.'

'I am?'

'You are, Mr Mani. How beautifully you've forgiven the people who brutalized your forefathers. The Brahmins, the kind of things they did. The things they do even now. In private, they still call you the Untouchables, do you know that? In public they call you "Dalits", but in private they call you such horrible things.'

'I know,' Ayyan said, trying to appear angry and moved, because that was what she wanted.

'Hinduism is like that, Mr Mani. It has the upper castes and it has the Dalits. The Brahmins and the Untouchables. That can never change. People only pretend that it has changed.'

'You speak the truth, Sister. The Brahmins ruined my life even before I was born. My grandfather was not allowed to enter his village school. They beat him up when he tried once. If he had gone to school, my life would have been better.'

'Absolutely,' she said. 'Tell me, Mr Mani. In the great Institute where you work, all the scientists are Brahmins?'

'Yes.'

'And all the peons are Dalits?'

'Yes.'

'But that's not because the Brahmins are smarter than the Dalits,' she said.

'No,' Ayyan said, now allowing himself to be somewhat engulfed by rage even though that was what Sister Chastity wanted. 'The Brahmins were three thousand years in the making, Sister. Three thousand years. At the end of those cursed centuries, the new Brahmins arrived in their new vegetarian worlds, wrote books, spoke in English, built bridges, preached socialism and erected a big unattainable world. I arrived as another hopeless Dalit in a one-room home as the son of a sweeper. And they expect me to crawl out of my hole, gape at what they have achieved, and look at them in awe. What geniuses.'

'What geniuses,' she whispered angrily.

'They are murderers,' Ayyan said, noticing that she smiled exactly like him. Invisibly.

'That's why you're a good Christian, Mr Mani. You've forgiven them, the Brahmins, whose great fiction Hinduism is.'

'I have not forgiven them,' Ayyan said, 'And you know that. I have long renounced Hinduism. I am a Buddhist.'

'Mr Mani,' she said with a tired face, pushing the two books she had gifted further down the table towards him, 'Hinduism, Buddhism – all the same thing.'

AYYAN MANI WALKED through the low, elegant gates of the Institute and sought the will to survive another day in this asylum of great minds. He waved in greeting to the dispirited guards in their glass box who smiled at him.

'Run, you are late,' one of them shouted with a fond chuckle, 'the Big Man is in already.'

Ayyan never understood why this place was so seriously guarded. After all, what happened here was merely the pursuit of truth.

The Institute of Theory and Research stood on ten acres of undulating lawns and solitary ancient trees. At the centre of the plot was a stout L-shaped building that held its breath inside shut windows. It ran along two sides of a carefully pruned central lawn. Beyond the angular building, the backyard rolled towards moist black boulders. And then there was the sea.

Here sanity was never overrated, and insanity never confused with unsound mind. Sometimes on the pathways calm men spoke to themselves when they needed good company. This was a sanctuary for those who wanted to spend their entire lives trying to understand why there was not enough lithium in the universe, or why the speed of light was what it was, or why gravity was 'such a weak force'.

Ayyan had a haunting desire to escape from this madhouse. Thirteen years was too long. He could not bear the grandness of their vocation any more, the way they debated whether universe must be spelt with a capital U or a small u, and the magnificence with which they said, after spending crores of public money,

'Man knows nothing yet. Nothing.' And the phoney grace with which they hid their incurable chauvinism and told reporters, 'A physicist is ultimately judged through citations. *She* has to constantly publish.' They were highminded; they secretly believed that their purpose was greater; they were certain that only scientists had the right today to be philosophers. But they counted cash like everyone else. With a wet index finger and a sudden meditative seriousness.

Even though Ayyan was late for work that morning, it was inevitable that he would stand in front of the blackboard in the porch of the main block. It was a morning ritual that always cooled the fever in his chest. THOUGHT FOR THE DAY, the blackboard said in indelible white ink. Under it was an ephemeral thought, written in chalk:

God does not play dice – Albert Einstein

Ayyan took a duster from the top of the blackboard and erased Einstein's famously abridged message. Then he pretended to look into a paper, just in case somebody was watching. And he wrote:

It's a myth that Sanskrit is the best language for writing computer code. Patriotic Indians have spread this lie for many years – Bill Gates

Bill Gates never said that. Some days, Ayyan invented quotes that insulted Indian culture, that exclusive history of the Brahmins. Nobody remembered when exactly Ayyan was assigned the task of writing the Thought For The Day or by whom. But he did it, without fail, every day. Most days he wrote genuine quotes. Some days he had fun.

He took the lift and travelled in the carefully maintained silence of three sweet-smelling elderly scientists who were lost in very deep, expensive thoughts. He got off at the third floor and walked down an almost interminable corridor that was jokingly described here as 'finite'. The corridor was flanked by numbered doors. Behind every door a great mind sat, and in between solving the mysteries of the universe, some of them were hoping that one man died. Things were getting a bit tense. A war was brewing. Everybody knew it here as The Giant Ear Problem.

At the far end of the corridor was a door that said 'Director'. It opened to a commodious anteroom, almost as large as Ayyan's home. He yawned as he sat in a nook behind a monitor, three telephones and a paranormal fax machine that came to life with the furtive whisper of a secret. Facing him across the width of the room was a seasoned black leather sofa, now vacant but with the irreparable depressions of long waits. Between his table and the sofa ran a short corridor that led to the door that announced its infernal occupant – Arvind Acharya.

Ayyan looked at the door without fear and dialled a number. 'I am sorry I am late, Sir,' he said, 'Any instructions for me?' The line went dead, as expected. Ayyan put the receiver down and calmly studied his fingers. The receivers of all three phones on his table were on their cradles. That was rare. Usually, one of the receivers was left off the hook. That was because he almost always arrived before Acharya, called one of the Director's landlines from here and left the receivers of both the phones slightly askew. That way Ayyan could just pick up his phone and hear the conversations in Acharya's room, and keep abreast of all the developments in the Institute and, as a consequence, in the universe.

A peon walked in and filled the anteroom with the faint odour of jaggery. Some peons had that smell. He dropped a thick wad of papers on the table.

'For the Big Man,' he said softly, throwing a nervous glance at the inner door.

Ayyan flipped through the pages of the material and chuckled. It was yet another epic analysis of cosmic observations by a visiting researcher. This one tried to prove that a distant object was indeed a White Dwarf.

'What is this, Mani?' the peon asked with sudden curiosity, 'Do you ever understand these things that land on your table?'

'I do, my friend, I do,' Ayyan said, and tried to think of a way to explain. 'The chap who has written this is trying to say that an object far far away in space is a type of star.'

'That's it?' the peon said, almost angrily.

'Yes, that's it. And this type of a star has a name,' Ayyan said. 'White Dwarf.' That made the peon giggle.

'One year later,' Ayyan whispered, 'another man will say, "No no, it is not a White Dwarf, it is a Brown Dwarf." A year later, someone else will say, "No no, it is not a Brown Dwarf, it is not a star at all, it is a planet." Then they will argue over whether it is a rocky planet or a gaseous planet and whether there is water out there. That's the game, my friend, that's exactly the game.'

The peon covered his mouth with his hand and giggled again, partly from lack of comprehension. Then he remembered something.

'I've got something to show you, Mani,' he said. He dug into his pocket and took out an ATM card. 'I got it today,' he said, and looked at it fondly. 'All your work, Mani,' he said.

Ayyan had helped the peon to open a bank account. He somehow knew people everywhere who magically waived the requirement of difficult documents. Ayyan leaned towards the peon and said softly, 'You know what I used to do when the money machines first came? When the machine would spit out the cash, I would pluck out only the central notes. I would leave the first and the last. It was a difficult art. It needed technique. I had to practise. The machine would swallow the two remaining notes and the way it was programmed then it would not register the transaction. It would spit out a paper that would say "zero rupees withdrawn". Now these machines have become smarter.'

The peon shook his head in easy awe. 'You are such a clever man, Mani,' he said. 'If only you had the fathers that these men had, you would have had a room of your own today with your own secretary.'

'There are bigger things in life than that,' Ayyan said. 'See where I go.'

The main door outside opened, startling the peon who always

stood erect when surprised. Murmurs from the corridor filled the room like fresh air. Jana Nambodri, the convivial Deputy Director of the Institute and a radio astronomer who was incurably infatuated with corduroy trousers, stood in the doorway holding the door open. 'Good morning,' he said cheerfully. His hair always distracted Ayyan. It was a silver tidal wave that lent him an amicable flamboyance. And he had a long benevolent face that clever women usually mistrusted.

There was always a quiet dignity about Nambodri, something very calm, even though he was at the heart of The Giant Ear Problem. He wanted to scan the skies with radio telescopes and search for alien signals, but Arvind Acharya would not let him.

'I believe he has come,' Nambodri said, making eyes at the inner door in a conspiratorial way.

'Yes he is inside, Sir, but he has asked me not to disturb him for thirty minutes,' Ayyan lied. He never missed the slightest chance to cause the smallest misery to a Brahmin. Nambodri stared at the floor for a moment and left.

'There is something happening here, Mani,' the peon said. 'My chaps are telling me that something big is going to happen. Things have been very tense. Old men are speaking in whispers in the corridor. What is it?'

'War of the Brahmins,' Ayyan said. 'That's what is going to happen. It's going to be fun.'

'War? What war?'

Ayyan studied his fingers thoughtfully. 'It's like this,' he said slowly. 'Some men here want to search for aliens in space by using something called a radio telescope. They think we might receive messages from life forms in outer space. But the Big Man inside says they are talking rubbish. He won't let them search for aliens that way. He says there is only one way to search for aliens – his way.'

'And what is his way?'

'He says aliens are as small as germs. They are falling all the time from the heavens to the Earth. So he wants to send a balloon up and capture them.'

'That's it?' the peon whispered.

'Yes, that's it,' Ayyan said.

After the peon left, Ayyan went through the research papers that the peon had brought for Arvind Acharya. There was a lot of maths in the pages and its incomprehensibility lent it an air of special wisdom. Ayyan had developed the habit of reading anything in front of him, even if it was something he did not really understand, because he believed that one reason why everybody was here, including the sons of municipal sweepers, was to collect as much information as possible before dying with a funny look on the face. All through his boyhood he had read anything he could lay his hands on. That's how he had taught himself English. Even when he used to go with friends to art film festivals to watch the uncensored nudity in foreign films, he tried to read every word in the free brochures.

Ayyan read the White Dwarf's grim tale with his elbows on the table and fingers gathered around his temples. He looked more resolute than interested. But progress was hard. He could not get through the numb dullness of the prose. Then the sharp fragrance of lemon reached him. He looked up. She was always a sight.

He dialled a number briskly and said, 'Dr Oparna Goshmaulik has come, Sir.' He put the receiver down and pointed her towards the seasoned black sofa. Acharya had asked him to send her in, but Ayyan wanted to take a good look at her. 'You have to wait, Madam,' he told her.

The moment Oparna Goshmaulik had walked into the Institute, three months ago, for the interview, in a blue sari that the stenographers thought was a devious masterstroke, and with her wiry black hair tied back in a fierce knot, she was a commotion. Even now, almost beautiful in a deliberately modest cream salwar chosen to calm the men, she was an event. Aged scientists always veered towards here on the corridors and narrated the many tales of their past, the great things they had done. In the overtures of mentoring, they tried to smell her breath.

She had a round unsmiling face and the flawless skin of lineage; moist lips; and eyebrows arched in a surprise she probably did not intend. Her eyes were arrogant and distant some days, smiling other days.

Ayyan was watching her surreptitiously as she stared thoughtfully at the floor. Another high-caste woman beyond his reach. She went to the Cathedral School in the back seat of her father's car. Then on to Stanford. Now she was here: the Head of Astrobiology, the solitary queen of the basement lab. So easy it was for these women. Soon, some stupid reporter would write that she had 'stormed the male bastion'. All these women were doing that these days. Storming the male bastion. 'Rising against the odds' – they all were. But what great subjugations did these women suffer, what were they denied by their fathers, what opportunities didn't they get, what weren't they fed, why were they so obsessed with their own womanhood? Oja Mani did not even know that there was something called womanhood. 'Downmarket' was what women like Oparna would call her, even discreetly laugh at her perhaps if they met her: at the powder in the nape of her neck, the oil in her hair and the yellow glow of turmeric on her face.

Ayyan felt an immense hatred for Oparna and all her friends. Of course, they too had miseries. Chiefly, the state of men. They were obsessed with men. And men were people who were different from him.

Oparna knew he was looking. Jerk. She looked up from the floor to meet his eyes. Ayyan caught her naked glare only for an instant before turning away, but that moment was enough for him to decide why she had always seemed so familiar to him.

So composed and normal she appeared, but in her eyes he saw the hidden insanity of some women that drove men to the security of marrying others. Through the promise of transience, they would lure men, and frighten them while lying spent by weeping uncontrollably or muttering the name of a man from their distant adolescence. Oparna Goshmaulik was an enchantment that was always beyond his fortunes, but despite the unscalable rungs of society, there were only so many types of people and once upon a time, he had rumbled with the type of Oparna.

That was over a decade ago when he was a young salesman for Eureka Forbes. He would woo typists, secretaries and shop attendants, and mesmerize them with his general knowledge, the future rebellions he planned against the rich, and his jokes about the Brahmins. They would let him squeeze their breasts on the Worli Seaface. Then, misled by decency, they would ask for marriage. And weep through the pause. Traditionally on the Worli Seaface, infatuation fondled and love cried. He was terrified of that love.

When they began to brush his hand away from their impoverished chests and talk about where it was all heading, and whispered to him the simplicity of marriage, he left them in the knowledge that they could cash in their virginity somewhere else. But some who made love to him in the bushes of Aksa beach, or in the cheap hotels of Manori, were the dangerous kind. It was them he saw in the deceptive calm of Oparna. After their coy nudity and uncontrollable moans that he had to muffle by stuffing his fingers in their mouths; after their easy compliments about how good a lover he was, how thoughtful and informed, how big his penis was (though they had not slept with too many men) came their madness. They would weep for no reason, talk about death, and with great sorrow that matched the despondence of the pale yellow walls of the cheap nocturnal rooms, ask for marriage. They made him fear love, and drove him to the hard mattress of a prostitute in Falkland Street, whose bedsheet was still soaked in the sweat of clients who had been with her before him. As he rocked her beneath him, he would always remember, she sang a song: '*Joot Bhole Kauva Kate*'. It had no meaning. She meant no metaphors. When he asked her to shut up, she said, 'But I have to while away the time.' He threw some notes at her and ran. Her laughter echoed behind him. No wail he had heard in his life equalled the melancholy of her psychotic laughter.

Often, he used to tell his girls, as they looked at him with growing affection on the parapet of the Worli Seaface, 'What is the saddest sight in the world? A couple weeping together. At their failed love, or at the ruins of their home demolished by the municipality, or at the funeral of their child. There is something about a man and a woman weeping together. Nothing is more heart-breaking.' But he knew that the laughter of that whore was far worse. He would never forget it. 'Come back, hero,' she had said.

Unable to bear the promises he had to make merely to touch the breasts of girls who said they loved him, and the sudden sorrows of the broadminded women after they had brought their legs back together, and the wails of undead whores, he finally decided to place a matrimonial in the expensive classifieds of the *Maharashtra Times*. And he found a virgin who had none of the memories he had given other women.

AYYAN MANI HAD just asked her to go in. Oparna rose from the tired black sofa. She did not know why her heart was pounding. There was something about the hermit who sat inside that unnerved her. Three months ago, Arvind Acharya had interviewed her in between reading something. And when he did look at her, it was with total indifference – as if thirty-year-old women were not regarded as people here. He had studied her gravely and said, 'You were born after Microsoft?'

She pushed open the inner door and remembered its unexpected heaviness. Acharya, his head bent over some loose sheets of paper on the table, always appeared bigger than she imagined. His desk was cluttered with heaps of bound papers and journals. And there was a curious stone which he used as a paperweight. Some said that it was a piece of meteorite he had stolen from a lab many many years ago. Four fresh orchids stood in a cylindrical glass jar and she knew he was not responsible for them. There was an unnaturally large waste-paper bin near his table, four feet high. Behind him was a long sliding window that was like a living portrait of the Arabian Sea. The walls were stark and empty. No pictures, no framed citations, no quotable commandments that men so loved. Nothing. In the far corner of the room were four white sofas that faced each other around a small centrepiece. The sofas offended her every time she entered the room. White sofas? Why?

She sat across his massive table, wondering whether to clear her throat. That would be too cinematic, so she decided to be silent and look at him carefully. Silver strands of hair on his pink bald head rose and fell in the draft of the air conditioner directly above him. His thick capable hands rested on the table. His tranquil elephant eyes usually looked directly into the heart of the intrusion. Sometimes they stared like an infant's.

Occasionally, Oparna googled Acharya late into the night. She searched for stray pictures from his youth. He was always in badly stitched suits then, and seemed much angrier; his severe eyes appeared to survey the changing times somewhat baffled as if physics were in crisis. And it really was, according to the young Acharya. He spent the best years of his life in the passion of mauling the Big Bang theory, the world's favourite idea – that everything began from a microscopic point, that most of the universe was made in about three minutes after an inexplicable moment of beginning called the Big Bang.

How much this man had hated the theory. He accused the Big Bang of being Christian. The Vatican wanted a beginning and the Big Bang provided one. According to him, the Big Bang was that moment in the history of white men when God said, 'Try to understand from here.' He did not accept it. Acharya's universe did not have a beginning, it did not have an end. 'Because I am not Christian,' he had famously said. He hated the Big Bang theory so much, and considered it such a repulsive influence of religion, that during a niece's wedding to an American in San Francisco, when he heard the priest say solemnly, 'In the beginning was the Word,' he threw his shoe at the altar.

Around that time (it must have been about thirty years ago) he was at the height of his intellectual powers. Many believed that his work on gravitational collapse would fetch him the Nobel if he behaved and tempered down his embarrassing opposition to the Big Bang. As it was, the odds were stacked against cosmologists. An old rumour had it that Alfred Nobel's wife had had an affair with an astronomer and the cuckold laid out in his will that those associated with astronomy must be considered to share his money only under exceptional circumstances. Oparna believed that rumour. It was absolutely possible.

Acharya was the type of man who would believe first and then spend the rest of his life seeking that little matter called evidence.

Oparna liked such men. They were obsolete in a world where something as low grade as practicality was increasingly mistaken for wisdom. When they spoke, their words had so much power because they knew there was such a thing called the truth. They just believed, blindly. And for many years Arvind Acharya believed in his heart that microscopic aliens were falling all the time on Earth. To prove it he was finally going to send a hot-air balloon to a height of forty-one kilometres with four sterilized metal containers that would capture air at that altitude. The containers would come down, and in her basement lab Oparna would study their contents. If there were any microbes in the containers it would mean only one thing. They came from space. Mankind would have finally found aliens.

Oparna craned her neck to see what Acharya was reading, but from that angle it was hard for her to figure it out.

He was in fact immersed in a confidential report on the mysterious red rains over Kerala. Nobody could convincingly explain the phenomenon that was confirmed by thousands of ordinary people who were stupefied by the red downpour, but he believed he knew what was happening. He was formulating a simple explanation in his mind, when he began to sense a distant smell that he thought was coming from another time, like an old memory. It was familiar, but he could not place it. Then it struck him that it was the odour of youth and it was somewhere very close. Youth. Pathetic, desperate, broke, its glory overrated. He felt in his heart the ignorance and smallness of the mind when the body was strong, and how easily it was brutalized by deceptions that sometimes came as love, and at other times, as convictions.

'Dr Acharya,' Oparna tried one more time.

He leaned back in his chair and observed her in a peaceful way. He liked her. She had done reasonable research in South America on the private lives of earth microbes that survived in almost extraterrestrial conditions. She was fresh and bright, and she knew all that she had to know. He preferred the intelligence of women, which was somehow subdued and efficient, to the brilliance of men, which often came across as a deformity.

He rubbed his hands and said, 'So, Oparna. Good. What took you so long?' She tried not to react. He looked at the door and maintained a long comfortable silence.

Oparna probed softly, 'You called me?'

'Yes, I did,' he said. 'Just wanted to know how the lab is shaping up. Everything OK?'

She thought there was something high maintenance about his face. His teeth were so clean and nothing was peeping out through his nose at all. Extraordinary for an Indian male of his age. The same force that sent the orchids must be maintaining him.

'Yes, everything is OK,' she said. 'But, Dr Acharya, you had mentioned that the basement was a temporary arrangement.'

'I remember. It'd be nice if the astrobiology lab is above sea-level. It's a shame. I know, I know. I called you actually to give the bad news. There is no space. The lab needs a large sprawling area and we simply don't have room anywhere, it seems, but in the basement.'

He stood up. He was probably over six foot two. The enormous black chair shuddered in relief. He steered his trousers around his waist. 'Let's go to your lab,' he said, and dashed out. In the anteroom, he wagged a finger at Ayyan Mani asking him to follow.

The three walked down the interminable corridor. The woody sound of Oparna's heels was still so alien to the Institute, which was used to the unremarkable silence of men, that Acharya looked back at her and at her feet. She smiled meekly and tried to walk softly. That made her feel stupid, and, for a moment, angry with herself. She was not accustomed to being servile and she wondered why she was so in the presence of this man. She had heard all the famous stories about him. Of his newsworthy rage and tragic brilliance. But she could not accept that this was the way it was going to be between them. She walked faster to keep up with him, and thought of something friendly to say, something equal. 'This corridor is endless,' she said.

‘That’s not true,’ he told her.

They took the lift to the basement and from there they walked through a network of narrow corridors flanked by stark white walls and in the ghostly hums of invisible subterranean machines. At the end of a corridor was a door that said ‘Astrobiology’.

It was a huge hollow room. Unopened cartons lay piled up in heaps. The walls were newly painted off-white. And there was this smell of fresh paint. In a far corner was a large ancient desk, with just a phone on it. A wooden chair was by its side.

‘This is what happens when the equipment comes before the carpenter,’ Acharya said cheerfully, and his voice echoed. ‘Oparna, you deal directly with my secretary. He will get you anything you want. Except, of course, windows.’ And he left the room walking away like a tusker.

Ayyan Mani took out a small scribbling-pad from his trouser pocket, poised a pen over it and stared expectantly at Oparna.

‘What are your instructions, Madam?’ he asked. He liked her smell. He wondered how a woman could smell like a lemon, yet seem so unattainable.

She thought he smelled exactly like a room freshener. But at least he didn’t stink like other men. For a fleeting moment, she remembered a friend who went through an insane phase of sleeping only with poor men, really poor chaps. Like drivers and peons. Just to see if they were any different in bed from the MBAs.

Ayyan looked at her back as she walked into the expanse of the almost empty lab and put her hands on her hips. Those hips curved so beautifully. Even in the intentional modesty of the salwar kameez, he could see how perfectly sculpted she was. He wondered how she would look naked. He tried to imagine her face as he plundered her in the bushes of Aksa.

‘I think I will see the plans first and send you a detailed list of things to be done,’ she said, without turning. ‘I hope you will move fast. I hear you are a very efficient man.’

‘I am just a small man, Madam,’ he said. ‘A small man who manages this and that sometimes.’

'That's not what I've heard,' she said, walking towards him and attempting a calculated smile.

'What am I, Madam, in front of scientists like you?' he said. 'It is through the great things you people do that I learn a little here, a little there.'

'OK then,' she said exhaling loudly. 'I will see you soon.'

When he was at the door, he said, 'It's so hot here.' He walked briskly to a corner and turned on the AC. 'Madam,' he said softly, 'can you tell me something about the Balloon Mission?'

'Why do you ask?'

'Every night I make up a science story for my son. That's how I put him to sleep. All my material comes from the Institute.'

'That's sweet,' she said with a chuckle. (Ayyan, of course, knew it was very sweet.)

'How old is he?'

'He is ten.'

'I don't know how much you know,' she said, 'but it's like this. Twenty thousand meteorites hit Earth's atmosphere every year. They are so small that they burn up immediately. Dr Acharya believes that some of them carry extraterrestrial living matter, like an alien DNA or even fully formed microbes or something entirely unknown to man. These things survive their entry into Earth and take a while to come down. We are going to send a balloon high above the Earth. The balloon will carry four samplers. Samplers are sterilized steel cans that will be controlled by remote from the ground. They will open at the height of forty-one kilometres, capture air, and shut immediately. I will study the samplers after we bring them back down. I'll study them right here where we are standing.'

'What if you find something?'

'Then Dr Acharya becomes the first person to find living matter from outer space.'

'Why forty-one kilometres above the Earth? Why not twenty, or ten?' he asked, narrowing his eyes to show curiosity – though he knew why.

'Because, because,' she said, with mild appreciation, 'nothing from Earth floats to that height. Even volcanic ash does not go up that high. So if we find, say, a bacterium at that height, it will mean that he was coming down, not going up.'

'It's so interesting what you people do,' he said. 'I think I can cook up a great story for my son tonight.'

As he walked to the door, Oparna asked, 'What do you know about the Giant Ear?'

'Nothing that you don't know, Madam,' he said, walking a few steps back in. Giant Ear was the name given to thirty radio telescopes, a vast array of mammoth dishes pointed at the sky. One after the other, they stood like white monsters on vast farms, about a hundred kilometres from the city. 'Have you seen them?' he asked. 'They belong to the Institute.'

'I saw them once when I was driving past,' she said. 'They look beautiful, and evil.'

'There is one strange thing about the Giant Ear,' Ayyan said softly. 'You won't find a single champagne bottle there.' (The way he pronounced 'champagne' was a bit funny but she did not react. She was more intrigued by what he had said.)

'Champagne bottle, you said? There is no champagne bottle inside the Giant Ear. Why should that be strange?'

'Madam, every radio telescope in the world keeps a champagne bottle. It is a tradition. The bottle has to be opened when there is a contact with an alien signal.'

'Why doesn't the Giant Ear have a champagne bottle?'

'You know why,' he said, with a conspiratorial smile. 'The Director hates the search for extraterrestrial intelligence. He says it is not science. He really hates it. The radio astronomers here have been begging him to let them search for signals of intelligent life. But he is not going to allow that.'

'I know, I know,' she said, almost dreamily. 'I wonder why he is so adamant about these things?'

'The heavens speak very softly to the Earth, Madam,' Ayyan said. 'A mobile phone left on the Moon would be the third clearest radio signal in the entire sky. So you can imagine how easily the gadgets we use can interfere with radio telescopes. A passing car's radio could start wild rumours of alien contact. So the Director thinks it is an imperfect way to search for aliens. Also, he does not think aliens are in the habit of sending signals.'

'You know a lot, Ayyan,' she said, with an honest smile.

'I am just a small man, Madam, who picks up this and that through the great things that people like you do.'

Her nipples, he observed, had hardened in the air conditioner's draught.

After he left, Oparna sat by the desk and looked blankly at the walls. She sat for hours like that, with nothing to do. She felt in her heart an old nameless sorrow. That same melancholy of a twilight rain in a deserted street. She felt stranded. Five years ago, she would have wept like a fool.

She went up to the porch for respite. She stood behind a fat beam and lit a cigarette. The half-naked gardener who was watering the lawn stared. A few men who were passing by, discussing the Möbius Strip, fell silent.

'Yes, yes, stare at me. You're right. I smoke. I must be a whore.'

The stares would always follow her here and she would grow to accept that she was in the world of men. She would learn to laugh at things that did not make her laugh. She would smile when Jana Nambodri said, 'We have been seeking beauty in physics, but it looks as if it has come to Astrobiology.' And she would smile when she learnt that the ladies' rest-room on the third floor was called Ladies and the men's was called Scientists. She would endure the men who inescapably fell towards her in the corridors and gave her guidance she never sought. She would try to pass through the long corridors of this place like a shadow, and she would fail every day.

She took one long drag and threw the cigarette butt, and felt a bit manly as she squashed the stub with her foot.

ARVIND ACHARYA LIKED the brooding hum of the air conditioner. It reminded him of the faint drone that was once speculated here to be the sound of the early universe. He was listening to the hum intently and reading another report on the red rains over Kerala. Ayyan Mani walked in holding a bunch of fax messages.

'Dr Nambodri is here,' he said, setting the papers on the desk. He always spoke in Tamil to the Director because he knew it annoyed him. It linked them intimately in their common past, though their fates were vastly different. Ayyan's dialect, particularly, almost always distracted Acharya. It reminded him of the miserable landless labourers, and their sad eyes that used to haunt him in his childhood when he watched the world go by from the back seat of a black Morris Oxford.

Acharya put the Red Rain papers on the table and placed an irregular black stone on the material. 'Send him in,' he said. He leaned back in his chair and awaited the simple duel that he would win. Jana Nambodri entered looking more cheerful than the circumstances allowed.

'So you are on for dinner tonight?' he asked, as he sat across the desk from Acharya.

'Of course, and you are serving fish this time,' Acharya said.

'Arvind, try to understand. We are married to hopeless vegetarians.'

'I get fish in my house.'

'OK, I'll try,' Nambodri said, and, as casually as he could, 'The Seti conference, Arvind. Remember? Jal has been invited to Paraguay for the Seti conference.'

'Ah, the Search for Extraterrestrial Intelligence in Paraguay,' Acharya said, with a soft chuckle. 'Jana,' he said, turning serious, 'is there any evidence that Paraguay actually exists?'

'What do you mean?'

'Do you know anybody from Paraguay?'

'No.'

'Nobody does.'

'But somehow I do believe Paraguay exists,' Nambodri said.

'I gather they are not sponsoring his trip? We have to pay?'

'Yes, but it is important that he goes.'

'We can't afford it,' Acharya said. He lifted a pen from one holder and put it in another.

Nambodri expected this. This man was a stingy bastard these days. He was saving every rupee for the Balloon Mission. The men looked at each other with the comfort of an old friendship and with the strains of a dispute that was threatening to become destructive.

'It's all right,' Nambodri said. 'It's your decision. But Arvind, I came here to talk about the Giant Ear.'

Acharya let out a soft groan.

But Nambodri persisted. 'We are getting a lot, a lot of requests from radio astronomers all around the world for the Giant Ear,' he said. 'You have to seriously consider the matter. You have to let the Giant Ear search for alien signals. Even the astronomers in our Institute are unhappy with the ban.'

'I am not going to let anyone use the Giant Ear for nonsense,' Acharya said, and he looked around the room calmly.

'Universities have approached me with very attractive usage fees,' Nambodri said, somewhat desperately, though he had intended to be politely strong.

'We are not in it for the money. We are scientists,' Acharya said.

'But Arvind, we need funds.'

There was a reason why Nambodri used the word 'funds'. In the Institute, they looked down upon money. But they respected funds.

Acharya inhaled deeply. He did not like the persistence of other men. He said, 'Do you remember the time when all of us thought robots would change the face of the Earth? Scientists said robots would do this, robots would do that. But they didn't do much. Jana, do you know why robots failed? Robots failed because man built them in his own image. The first-generation robots were anthropomorphic. Because man was obsessed with man. Now the most successful robots, say on an auto assembly-line or in an operating theatre, do not look like humans.'

'What are you trying to say, Arvind?'

'The human search for aliens is now in the imbecilic stage that robotics once was,' Acharya said, an ominous edge in his voice. 'I will not support people who presume that somewhere, far away in space, there could be beings so human that they will build machines that will send us a radio signal. Man is not searching for aliens. Man is searching for man. It's called loneliness. Not science. The universe is simply too vast, and we know too little about consciousness, to invest in a quest that rests on a narrow concept of life. Scientists want to search for alien signals because that's what gets them publicity. They are like Jesus Christ.'

'Jesus Christ?'

'Yes. They are exactly like Jesus Christ. You know that he turned water into wine.'

'I've heard that story.'

'From the point of view of pure chemistry, it is more miraculous to make wine into water than water into wine. But he did not do that. Because if he had gone to someone's house and converted their wine into water, they would have crucified him much earlier. He knew, Jana. He knew making water into wine was a more popular thing to do. Searching for extraterrestrial signals is like that. It is more glamorous than searching for pulsars. Lay people love it. Journalists love it. A more meaningful thing to do is to investigate the stratosphere for evidence of microscopic aliens that have come riding on meteorites.'

'Are you saying, Arvind, there is not the slightest possibility of an alien civilization sending us a signal?'

'There is always a mathematical possibility.'

'That's good enough, isn't it? A mathematical possibility. Listen to this, Arvind. In 1874 the *American Medical Weekly* reported something strange. During the Battle of Raymond in Mississippi in 1863, a bullet hit the scrotum of a soldier, shattering his left testicle. The bullet penetrated the left side of the abdomen of a seventeen-year-old girl who was sitting in her house nearby. Nine months later she delivered a healthy boy. Apparently, the bullet had carried with it some of the soldier's semen and had entered the girl's ovary. That's how she had become pregnant with the soldier's child.'

'That's what she told her mother.'

'A mathematical possibility,' Nambodri said, 'a mathematical possibility however small, is enough for us to go in search of truth. In science, hope is everything.'

'Hope,' Acharya said, with bitter memories, 'is a lapse in concentration.'

Nambodri looked gloomily towards the window and rubbed his nose. He knew he had to find more diabolic ways to win this war. And he had to find battlefields where Acharya did not know how to fight. This insufferable fat tyrant was once a lanky affable boy with a lot of mischief in his eyes. When they were in Princeton, Acharya was famous for growing marijuana in a flower pot. He even wrote a secret manual called *The Joint Family*, with clear instructions for future generations on how to grow the grass in a hostel-room environment. How did that boy become this monster who was willing to antagonize everyone for the sake of something as ephemeral as conviction?

Nambodri rose from the chair and headed for the door. Just then something crossed his mind. 'You do know about the Pope, don't you?' he asked.

'What about him?'

'Arvind, switch on the TV.'

'Why?'

'The Pope is dead.'

The two men looked at each other through a perfect silence. Then Acharya smiled.

He and Pope John Paul shared a past. The top cosmologists in the world were once invited to attend a conference in the most unlikely venue for such a gathering – the Vatican City. The Pontifical Academy of Sciences hosted the scientists because the Pope had figured out that the Big Bang theory was not in conflict with the Old Testament after all, and he wanted to support it cheerfully. Since the Big Bang claimed that the universe had a beginning, it left room for God to do something, like create the beginning. Heretics like Acharya were invited to educate them that God and science can coexist. At the end of the conference, the pontiff met his guests, one after the other, at his summer residence, Castel Gandolfo. In the long queue that moved towards the holy man, the famous crippled scientist Stephen Hawking was right in front of Acharya. When Hawking was wheeled to the Pope, the pontiff famously knelt down on the floor and had a lengthy conversation with him. Then Acharya walked towards the holy man and said something to him in his ear. The Pope turned away looking dismayed. What exactly Acharya had said was never known. He would never tell. The Vatican refused to comment, but a spokesman later said, 'What that man told the Pope is not important, but, yes, I don't think he will be invited here again.'

Nambodri held the door knob, but he was unwilling to leave his friend without solving an old mystery. 'What did you tell the Pope, Arvind?'

'Nothing.'

'Come on. He is dead now. Some people told me that he looked very hurt. What did you tell him?'

Acharya wanted to chuckle, but these days he discreetly mourned any death, even if it was the Pope's.

'He was a good man,' Acharya said, in a mellow voice. 'In 1992 he admitted that Galileo was right. He admitted that the Earth goes around the Sun. He was a good man.'

Nambodri left the room with a melancholy smile, thinking of the charming old conflicts he was never a part of. That smile, Acharya knew, was the summary of all men who stay out of fierce enchanting battles because they want to build their place in the world through the deceptions of good public relations.

AYYAN MANI ALMOST sprinted up the steep colonial stairway of Block Number Forty-One carrying a plastic bag which had two caps for Adi and prawn fry that was still hot. The faint smell of prawns made his stomach rumble and he was in a hurry to get home, but he stopped on the first floor when he saw the outsiders. Two girls in smallish T-shirts and fitted jeans, and a tall reptilian boy were surrounded by the tiny women who lived on that floor. 'The morons have come again?' Ayyan asked a man who was going down to drink.

These three were among the pubescent scholars of International Board schools who landed occasionally in the name of social work to add a glow to their imminent applications to American schools. They brought food for children, pens for illiterate old men (who hated them) and generally tried to empower the women. They often wandered around the corridors, knocking on random doors. Once they told Oja that she should, 'share responsibilities' with her husband and make him wash clothes and cook some days.

Ayyan stood at the edge of the small crowd and studied the scholars. Their faces were so lit by good breeding; they were so distinct, so large. This time the saviours were here to influence women to send their children to English-medium schools. They were also running a campaign to convert all municipality schools into English-medium. When the women noticed Ayyan they smiled at him.

'His son goes to a good school,' a woman said pointing to him. The two reformist girls looked at him and smiled approvingly. He wanted to slap them really hard.

'You came in a Honda Accord?' he asked anxiously.

'No,' one of the girls said, 'it's a Lancer.'

'Yes, yes. That's the car. The boys are scratching it and trying to break the windows.'

'Oh my gaad,' the girls yelped together. 'Where is the bloody driver?' one screamed. They ran to the stairs. The boy ran behind them.

Ayyan looked at the crowd of women through a moment of silence and they all burst out laughing.

'Why do you stand like this and listen to those fools?' he asked.

'Timepass,' someone said, wiping her tears, and they shook again with seismic laughter.

He was confused when Oja Mani opened the door and asked him sternly, 'Did you read the full story?' The question was meant for Adi, who was standing near the gas-stove looking exasperated. Oja was in the middle of interrogating her son. She had bought a comic book for him to ensure that he read something normal, something far more ordinary than the fat reverential books that his father was encouraging him to read. She was worried that her son was becoming abnormal. She had seen him on the terrace last evening, standing aloof during a cricket match. She had encroached into the notional pitch and asked the boys to let him bat. They looked at her confused and then ignored her. Adi, from the fringes of the game, had made an embarrassed face asking her to leave. The fear of raising a strange genius was eating her for some time. It had inspired her this evening to buy him a *Tinkle* comic even though it cost twenty rupees. After just a few minutes of sitting with it near the fridge, Adi had declared that he had finished reading it. She did not believe him.

'Did you read the full story?' she asked again, pointing to *Tinkle*. The smell of prawn fry distracted her for a moment and she threw a foul look at her husband because she took outside food as a direct affront. Adi came to his father sniffing like a dog.

'*Praan*,' he said.

Oja dragged him away from his father and looked at him severely. 'Tell me the truth,' she said. 'Did you read the whole story?'

Adi made a tired face at his father, pleading for rescue with his large eyes, and said, 'Yes, I read it'.

'So fast?'

'Yes.'

'What happens in the end?'

'There are many stories. Which end do you want?'

'What happens in the end of the end?'

'Don't confuse me.'

'Tell me, Adi, what happens in the end of the last story.'

Adi took off his hearing-aid and shut his good ear with one finger.

'Adi,' his mother screamed, stuffing the hearing-aid back into his ear, 'What happens in the end of the last story?'

'The giant runs away.'

Oja checked the last page of Tinkle. 'There is no giant,' she said. 'Did you read this book? Tell me the truth. You should never lie, Adi. The end of an ox is beef, the end of a lie is grief.'

'So what if he does not want to read silly comics,' Ayyan said, winking at his son who winked back.

'You don't interfere,' she said angrily. 'This boy is going to become mad if I don't do something about it right now. Yesterday, he was standing alone on the terrace, in a corner. Other boys were playing.'

Adi put his hand on his head in exasperation. 'You don't understand,' he said. 'How many times do I have to tell you? I was out.'

'What do you mean, you were out?'

'I was in the batting team and I got out.'

'So?'

'If you get out, you can't bat till the next match.'

'But other boys were playing,' she said.

'Don't confuse me,' Adi said angrily.

'Look, Oja,' Ayyan said sternly, 'when a batsman gets out, his chance is over. He cannot play.'

'Why are you always on his side?' she said. 'And why are you standing here? The meeting is going on now. You are late.'

'I'll go, I'll go.'

The television was on all this while. Oja now appeared to calm down and she settled on the floor to watch her soap. Ayyan observed her closely. He knew something was wrong. Her eyes had been shifting too often towards the washing machine and even now she was not in the trance she usually was while watching TV. She seemed to be very aware of him. She looked sideways to see where he was.

'What is it?' he asked.

'Nothing,' she said, and stole another glance at the washing machine. Ayyan opened its lid and peered in. There was a red cardboard box inside. Oja said, first softly and then with a rising pitch, 'What's wrong with having a god? All these people have a real god in their homes.' Ayyan opened the box and there he was – a cheerful Ganesha. It was not the first time she had brought the idol of the elephant god home. Ayyan always threw him away on his way to work. But every few months, the lord returned in different moods.

Ayyan rolled the idol in a newspaper. 'I will throw him somewhere tomorrow,' he said.

'You cannot keep doing that,' Oja screamed. Adi took off his hearing-aid and shut his right ear.

'Isn't Buddha enough?' Ayyan screamed back. 'Buddha is our god. The other gods are gods the Brahmins created. In their deviant stories, those gods fought against demons which were us. Those black demons were our forefathers.'

'I don't care what the Brahmins did. Their gods are now mine,' Oja said. Her voice faltered. 'I am a Hindu. We are all Hindus. Why do we pretend?'

'We are not Hindus, Oja,' he said, now calm and somewhat sad. 'Ambedkar liberated us from being treated like pigs. He showed us how to renounce that cruel religion. We are Buddhists now.'

'I can live with nothing,' she mumbled, 'I don't even want

dreams. All I am asking is to let me have some gods. Our son is growing up. I want him to know the gods that other boys know. I want to take him to the temple. I want him to be aware of these things. I want real festivals in this house.'

Ayyan considered what his wife had just told him about their son. He had thought about it before. In a way, Adi was growing up like an animal, without any influence of culture. The epics that his father believed were the propaganda of the Brahmins were also the only epics the boy had. And a boy needed those to understand fully that there was an eternal battle between good and evil, and that in an ideal world the virtuous triumphed over the bad. Superman was good, but Mahabharata was deeper. It had complexity. It made the good choose the wrong path, and there were demons who were fundamentally nice persons, and there were gods who ravished bathing girls. Ayyan wanted his son to know those stories. Even though he could not accept Hindu idols in his home, for some time now he secretly wished Oja would win that battle. He wanted to yield but yield grudgingly, so that the religion of the upper castes could be used in his home for entertainment and education, and nothing more. He wanted Adi to grow up knowing morals, patriotism and the gods. And when the boy turned twenty, may he have the intelligence to abandon them all.

Oja wiped her tears and looked angrily at her husband. The way she looked, he knew what she was going to say.

'His ear,' she said, and wept, pressing her wrists on her eyes, 'This might not have happened if we had had gods.'

'Enough,' Ayyan screamed.

There was a time when Ayyan thought he might never become a father. Long before he had married Oja, he had once gone to a fertility clinic's nascent sperm bank with the insane idea of donating his Dalit semen to the fair childless Brahmin couples. He had heard that sperm banks do not reveal the identity of the donor, and so his seed could impregnate hundreds of unsuspecting high-caste women. He hoped stout brooding Dalits would spring up everywhere. But the doctors there told him that he had a defect and so his contribution could not be accepted. His sperm-count, they said, was just half the normal rate.

He told Oja about the defect many months after their marriage. 'Since my sperm-count is half the normal rate, you must be doubly prepared to sleep with me,' he had said. She replied in a lethargic way, in the middle of folding clothes, 'I don't understand all this maths.' Despite his fears, just three years after their marriage, Adi was born. In the insanity of her labour, Ayyan will always remember that Oja had screamed the filthiest abuse at him. He didn't know any woman could mouth such words, let alone his wife. 'My husband is a son of a whore. May his arse explode,' she had screamed in Tamil. But it was a tradition. Women in her tribe had to abuse their men when they were in labour.

As Adi grew up, they slowly learnt that he was almost entirely deaf in his left ear. Oja believed that the gods were angry. Buddha's eternal smile, she had always interpreted as the peace of a cosmically powerless man. It was the other gods, the Hindu gods, who had all the magic. One night, she told her husband with a wisdom that baffled him, 'You love this man who found God under a Peepal tree. Do you know that a Peepal tree is a Brahmin? Yes it is.'

Ayyan could never bear it when he saw Oja cry. His heart grew heavy at the sight and his throat felt cold. He thought of what he could say about the elephant god whom he would fling by the wayside tomorrow. He searched for something entertaining. 'You know, Oja,' he said, 'an elephant's trunk has four thousand muscles.'

There was a time when she used to love such facts. She would marvel at a world that was so strange and at her man who knew so much. He collected such curious facts every day to ration them out to her.

'Did you know elephants can swim?' he tried again. 'Five years ago, a whole herd of elephants swam three hundred kilometres to reach a far island. Can you imagine? Thirty of them swimming three hundred kilometres. Their fat legs pedalling underwater.'

Something happened in the trembling vessel on the stove, and she busied herself with that.

After dinner, which was saved only by the prawn fry, Ayyan went up to the terrace for the meeting. He took his son along. Adi was wearing both the caps his father had got him, one over the other. Against a bleak starless sky, over a hundred men and a few women were gathered. Some were sitting on chairs; some sat on the tar floor of the terrace; others were standing. A drunkard sang softly. At the heart of the conference were three men who looked cruel. They were the agents of a builder. One of them was a fat man with moist black lips and calm eyes. He was an old hand of the underworld who mended his ways after the spiritual experience of being shot by the police. It was said that every Tuesday, when he went to the Siddhivinayak temple in Prabhadevi, he wore a bloodstained vest with three bullet holes in it.

Every now and then, builders who eyed the vast sprawling property on which the grey blocks of BDD stood started a round of enticements to lure the residents into selling off their flats. This nocturnal meeting was one of the many Ayyan had seen. He knew nothing would come out of it. There were too many dissenting voices and an irrational greed. Some thought they could extract more if they waited. Alcoholics wanted to sell fast, and that strengthened the resolve of those who wanted to wait. And then there were many who feared that they would not be able to survive in the new skyscrapers that the builders had promised. 'My sister says that in the apartment blocks, you have to keep the doors shut,' a woman was saying aloud, but not to anyone in particular. Someone was telling the agents that all the forty families on the ground floor would have to be given adjacent flats in the new high-rises because they had lived like one big family for decades. Ayyan wanted to sell, but he knew it was not going to happen soon.

Some men spotted Ayyan, and egged him to get closer to the agents. 'Ask questions,' an old man begged him, with hope in his cataract eyes.

'Mani has come, Mani has come,' someone said aloud.

Adi looked severely at a woman and said, 'That's our chair.'

Ayyan endured the meeting in silence wondering if there was a way he could decide for all these fools and settle the matter once and for all. But how? He thought a good special effects engineer could pull it off. Make God appear and say in cosmic echoes, 'Sell your stupid homes. Take ten lakhs for every flat and be done with it. And don't piss in the corridors, you bastards.'

When the meeting ended with the plans for holding another meeting, Ayyan took his son for a long walk to the Worli Seaface. The furtive couples and brisk walkers had left, and the promenade was almost deserted. They ambled in the gentle breeze for a while. Then they sat on a pink cement bench. Adi was sleepy. He was leaning on his father, but his eyes were open.

'Say, "Fibonacci . . . Fibonacci",' Ayyan said. A familiar look of concentration came to Adi's face. He played with the words in his mind. His father mouthed the words slowly. 'Fee bo na chi.'

Adi repeated after him, 'See rees. Fee bon a chi see rees.'

Ayyan said, 'Fibonacci Series.'

Adi repeated the words.

'Brilliant,' Ayyan said. They sat there in silence and listened to the soft lull of the Arabian Sea.

Adi yawned and asked, 'What if someone finds out?'

Round Tables were oval even in the Institute of Theory and Research. That was the first thought that came to Oparna as she reached the second-floor hall for the monthly Round Table. She had missed the last two and so this was her first. There was a massive oblong desk at the centre of the room around which men were sitting in agitated concentric circles. Some were standing and chatting. Cheerful peons were passing biscuits and tea. There was much gaiety and jostling. Like sperm under a microscope. Most of the scientists were in light shirts worn over loose comfortable trousers. They were austere men who knew they were austere. Some of the younger ones were in jeans. Despite the overwhelming informality of this place, the loose shirts, the tempestuous white hair and the leather sandals, they were so clearly the masters in the room, their special status differentiated from the final concentric circle where the secretaries stood silently, sullen and unspeaking, as though the biscuits were stale. In the eye of the room's gentle commotion was the solid figure of Arvind Acharya. The men either side of him were turned away, talking animatedly with others. Once again, he was a rock in the stream. All turbulence went around him.

When Oparna walked in, a silence grew. She made her way nervously through the outer rings. Grey balding heads turned, one after the other. There were two female secretaries somewhere on the fringes, but she felt as though she were the only woman in the room because she knew the men felt that way too. Jana Nambodri, with that cloud of stylish silver hair, short-sleeved shirt neatly tucked into corduroy trousers, was at the oblong table, directly facing Acharya. Nambodri stood up, and with an elaborate sweep of his hand showed her an empty seat in the second row. She inched her way delicately towards the chair. Old men in her path moved their legs and made way. Some of them turned away uncomfortably as her back almost grazed their tired faces. Some pretended to continue chatting while looking at her rear in respectful nonchalance.

'She is a Bengali?' a man intended to whisper, but the silence was so deep that everybody heard it. (The man probably was a Bengali.) Faint chuckles filled the air.

'Historically,' Nambodri said aloud, 'the only just punishment for a Bengali male has been a Bengali female.' A round of laughter went through the room. 'We forgot to mention it before, gentlemen, she is our first female faculty,' Nambodri declared.

One man clapped. The solitary applause was about to die prematurely, but the others joined in to reinforce the compliment. The applause faded into a long comfortable silence.

And that was how the evening would unfold, with festive commotion giving way to silences, and silences broken by profound questions about the universe, and questions easing into laughs. It was a long tradition here for the scientists to meet on the first Friday of every month and chat.

Ayyan Mani surveyed the room with his back to the wall, as he had done many times, and tried to understand how it came to be that truth was now in the hands of these unreal men. They were in the middle of debating the perfect way to cut a cake and were concluding that carving triangular pieces, as everybody does, was inefficient. Then they made fun of a French scientist, who was not in the room, because he had said that man would never devise a way to predict the highest possible prime number. After that they began to wonder what the Large Hadron Collider near Geneva would reveal.

Ayyan could not bear it. This never-ending quest for truth. In the simpler ages, wise mendicants, metaphorical zens, sons of God, sages who turned into anthills, all such types could not say in crisp clear copy that *The Times of India* could publish, the reason why life existed or why there was something instead of nothing. They could have just said it in a neat paragraph and solved the mystery once and for all. But they didn't. They told fables instead. Now, truth was in the hands of the men in this room, and they were more incomprehensible than the men of God. Ayyan was certain that there was no such thing called truth. There was only the pursuit of truth and it was a pursuit that would always go on. It was a form of employment. 'Everything that people do in this world is because they have nothing better to do,' he told Oja Mani once. 'Einstein had something called Relativity. You scrub the floor twice a day.'

The Round Table had begun to discuss the fate of Pluto. Oparna Goshmaulik was following every word carefully. She did not understand many things that were being said, but the melancholy induced by her basement office was being lifted. She had always liked the company of men who knew a lot. She tried to understand why they were talking about Pluto with so much seriousness. She liked Pluto. From the arguments around her, she pieced together that the planet had been recently dropped from the model of the solar system at a science exhibition in America. And that had caused, not for the first time it seemed, a fierce debate over whether it should be considered a planet or a diminished member of the Kuiper Belt.

'Pluto is too small, too small. It can fit into America. It's so small,' one man said vehemently.

Even here, she told herself without malice, everything is a kind of penis.

Nambodri, who was turning towards her and throwing the glances of an aspiring mentor, asked, 'What do you think, Oparna?'

She pretended to be coy because she wanted to convey that she believed she was not qualified to have an opinion. After all she was just an astrobiologist, not an astronomer. That meekness, she knew, the men would like.

She said, 'I'll be quite sad if Pluto goes. I am Scorpio.' Once again a silence fell because of her. Oparna awkwardly explained, 'Scorpio is ruled by Mars and Pluto.'

'So she is a Scorpio. Like me,' a man said in a low tone, hoping to set off a round of laughter, but somehow this did not happen.

'What are the Scorpio traits?' a voice asked derisively and chuckled. It was first a robust chuckle, but it soon faded into a self-conscious giggle when the source realized he had no support.

'Intense, strong, confident,' Nambodri said, looking at Oparna, 'and passionate.' A faint laughter died quickly. Oparna managed to smile and mumble, 'Astrology is not a science, you know.'

'That's why it's not in dispute,' Nambodri said.

Matters slowly moved to another simmering issue: quotas for backward castes in colleges. There was a fear that the Institute of Theory and Research might be asked to allocate seats for the lower castes in the faculty and research positions. The general mood in the room turned sombre. Some men threw cautious glances at the secretaries and stray peons when there were comments on the political aggression of backward castes. Ayyan looked on impassively. He had heard all these arguments before and knew what their conclusion would be. The Brahmins would say graciously, 'Past mistakes must be corrected; opportunities must be created,' and then they would say, 'But merit cannot be compromised.' He imagined Nambodri cleaning a common toilet in the chawls and telling his son while he was at it, 'Son, merit cannot be compromised.' Brutal laughter echoed inside his head, showing in his face as nothing more than a faint twitch.

'It's foolish to think that we all come from a privileged background. I come from a humble family,' Nambodri was saying, softly, with an air of mellow introspection. (Ayyan could mouth the words he was about to hear, and he would have got most of them right.) 'I had to walk five miles to school. I remember one day, we went hungry because my father was caught in a storm and he could not come home for three days. I survived all that and managed to reach the cream of Indian science, not because I was a Brahmin but because I worked very hard. And put my IQ of 140 to good use.'

Unconsciously, he threw a look at Oparna to check if she was listening. 'I think it is stupid of people to think we, I mean the Brahmins, are privileged and all that. You know, the richest boy in my class was a Dalit whose father owned a truck business. He had a big house, he had a car and all that. I do feel bad about what my forefathers did . . .'

The voice of Arvind Acharya cut through the air as though only silence had preceded it. 'Your IQ is 140?' he asked. There was a nervous laughter because no one was sure if he was capable of humour. Nambodri nodded with a sporting smile. Acharya fell silent again.

Ayyan watched patiently as the scientists discussed other issues. When they ran out of topics, a thoughtful silence descended. Acharya was about to rise when Nambodri said, 'There is something else, Arvind.' The way he said it, Ayyan's heart began to beat faster. He knew things were about to get unpleasant. Finally.

Nambodri's narrow eyes swept across the room and rested again on Acharya. 'The Balloon Mission is not the only thing that is important in the Institute, it is not the only thing that should happen here,' Nambodri said. His voice quivered at first, but it became increasingly more confident.

Oparna felt the stabs of cold stares. She wanted to hide. The silence in the room deepened.

'There are other experiments, other things people want to do,' Nambodri said. 'Many of us in this room, especially the radio astronomers, are disturbed by your stand against the search for extraterrestrial intelligence. You have constantly refused to let The Giant Ear be used for the search for advanced civilizations. You have publicly stated that Seti is not science. Many of us in this room believe that you are being totally autocratic and unfair. I want to put the discontent on the table.'

'You have,' Acharya said. 'Now I've better things to do.'

Nambodri said, with a resolute face, 'I agree that the search for intelligent life is a bit fashionable, but it is important for such things to exist.'

'It is not,' Acharya screamed. 'Look at how much money is being poured into this kind of shit. Millions on some rover that is supposed to search for water on Mars. Tell me why are we searching for water in space? Why should all life in the universe be dependent on water? There are Tamilians who can live without water. We spend millions and millions on such moronic missions. But there are not enough funds to find a way to predict earthquakes. Because earthquakes are not fashionable.'

He stood up, steering his trousers round his waist. Others began to rise. All eyes were on Nambodri who was still sitting. Obviously, there was something else.

'Arvind,' he said, 'We are left with no other option but to involve the Ministry to resolve the issue.'

A silence fell that was not like other silences. Ayyan was ecstatic. This was turning out to be a lot of fun. Oparna, who would have normally laughed at the intensity of men, felt a chill run through her. The stillness around the oval desk was the stillness of an aspiring rebellion. Only silence could resolve it and she prayed for Acharya to be still, to be quiet.

Nothing showed on his face. He walked slowly around the desk towards Nambodri, but then – as if he had decided against assault – he walked behind his old friend to where he was standing before.

'Why are you orbiting?' Nambodri asked.

Ayyan understood the insult. It was in the league of other incomprehensible subtleties of the Institute. Usually, a lesser body like the Moon orbited a more important object like the Earth. Acharya left the room without a word.

PART TWO

Big Bang's Old Foe

THAT MORNING, ARVIND Acharya was lost in the unreasonable joy of trying to solve an old intractable problem. Did Time move continuously, like a smooth line, or did it move in minuscule jumps, like a dotted line? He was standing on the narrow balcony nine floors above the ground and glaring at the Arabian Sea. The summer air was still. A crow on the wooden railing began to hop sideways towards him.

He was wearing a blue tracksuit that had a white tick mark embroidered at the hip, as if he approved of something. It had been sent by his daughter in California who wanted him to go on morning walks. Such things that came through DHL, he now grudgingly conceded as love. Some days, when he was not contemplating a difficult problem, he remembered Shruti fondly as the little girl who on a distant afternoon had looked up nervously and asked if maths was important in life. He had lied, 'No.' He might have liked to see her more often than when she decided to visit. Probably, he stood in the tracksuit every morning not to succumb to the indignity of exercise but because it was touched by his girl and dispatched in a packet on which she had written his name in her beautiful handwriting. Yet he never really craved to see her. The success of an old man lies in not wishing for company.

The sun was growing harsh. His eyes, which were the colour of light black tea, softened a little. He smiled too. The excitement of the Time problem was making him hold the railing and rock gently. That was when a steel tumbler with the unmistakable fragrance of Madras filter coffee was shoved towards his chest. His surprise was so operatic it drove away the crow. The strands of abstract geometry and physics collapsed. What remained was the question that had woken him up at dawn, as it did on many dawns.

His wife for forty-two years, and forever his email password, held the cup calmly in one hand as she watered a dying creeper with another. She looked tall and lean even in the oversized T-shirt and pyjamas. Her clear skin was stretched taut over a bony face and she had large dancer's eyes that men mistook as curious; the kind of woman about whom young girls would say, 'She must have been beautiful once.' Her dyed hair was short and thinning. Once, it was rich and flowing and she used to tie it up in majestic arrogance before a fight. She moved in a smooth delicate way, as if there were liquid gel in the joints of her bones. And she was as womanly when she nudged him again with her elbow, ordering him without uttering a word to take the steel cup, unmindful of the fact that she had delayed one of the answers science sought the most from one of the few men it could ask. He looked at her in disgust, but she was not wearing her glasses.

Lavanya Acharya yawned and pointed to a duster on the wire above and asked him to get it. His height was so useful. But when her mother had first met him with a silver plate full of moist fruits, she had said with a sad chuckle, 'This boy is taller than a Gandhi statue.' Acharya pulled down the dust cloth from the wire and gave it to his wife, muttering to himself that he had no peace in his own house. He then continued to glare at the sea.

She studied him fondly. He was dressed like a football coach, and just as furious.

'You wear these things every morning, and then just stand. Why don't you go for a nice long walk?' she said.

A twitch appeared on his face. He didn't turn.

'Oh, and yes, I didn't tell you,' she said with sudden excitement, 'Remember Lolo? Her husband died last night. Heart attack.'

Acharya abandoned the problem of Time. The news of death, any death, interested him these days. Especially the widowhood of her friends and cousins. These women began to grow healthier after the departure of their men. Their lugubrious eyes filled with life and their skin began to glow.

Lavanya pointed to the ceiling again. This time she asked him to bring down a suspended shrub. She was always doing that to him. Sometimes he complained that every time she saw him she imagined that she wanted something from a height. Yet she herself was tall, especially for a Tamil woman. Five foot nine. When she was twelve, her mother had made her walk one hour every day inside their silent labyrinthine house in Sivagangai with a wooden chest on her head because the family physician had said that the exercise would control her alarming height. But by the time she was eighteen, she had grown to unmarriageable levels. The elite of Sivagangai observed her sadly because tall Brahmin boys were rare then. The only tall types were loitering residues of the British, chiefly old enduring white men who were known to cohabit with servant maids, or Anglo-Indian boys who were terrible at studies and worse, good at sports. The entire family of Lavanya would rather consume Senthil Rat Poison than marry her off to a white man or to the 'coffee' as Anglo-Indians were then called. But the elders need not have worried so much. Somehow, they found a twenty-two-year-old boy from a very good family, who too had the deformity of height. He had graduated from the Indian Institute of Technology, but was still studying something inscrutable in the Annamalai University in Madras. Whatever it was that he was studying did not appear to ensure a government job. But Lavanya's condition made them overlook all the faults of Arvind Acharya. It was a marriage that was ordained not by the frivolity of love, or even its naïve expectation, but by the more reliable bond of equal handicap.

Acharya was now distracted by the excitement of the impending Balloon Mission. He looked up at the clear blue sky. Somewhere there, not very high actually, he knew there were millions of microscopic aliens in a gentle descent. He was going to find them. The glare returned, the morning burned in his eyes, and he was slipping into a pleasurable trance once again. Then he felt something cold touch his legs. He almost jumped. The maid was crouched like a giant frog and mopping the floor. She looked at him with fear and suspicion. She always did. The day she had joined the household, she was shaken by the sound of death that came from his room. It was the voice of Luciano Pavarotti.

Acharya used to listen to the angelic tenor every morning. Pavarotti was his ethereal accomplice in his incurable quest to solve the remaining mysteries of the universe. But Lavanya decided to ban the music in the mornings after she realized that it was terrifying not just the maid but also the cook. He resisted and even began to increase the volume until Lavanya proved that the days he played Pavarotti, the dosas looked baffled and tasted raw. 'Women are sensitive,' she had told him, 'and women cook your food.'

The maid scrubbed the floor near his feet and threw another glance at him. The way she looked at him, he was certain that she suspected he was Pavarotti. 'Move,' Lavanya said, 'she has to clean.'

As he walked around the maid carefully he muttered, 'All that happens in this house is cleaning.' He went to the kitchen without knowing why. There the cook was squatting on the sink and doing the dishes because she was too tiny to reach the tap. She turned and looked at him with one eye. It was all so terrible. So ugly.

He marched to Shruti's abandoned bedroom. It was now used to store the useless gifts that the young kept sending them in the moronic benevolence of keeping in touch. Lavanya saved all the presents and recycled them as wedding gifts.

He went to the huge bookshelf that covered one half of the wall. There was a delicate promise of peace here. But he saw the shadow of Lavanya approach. 'Arvind,' she said with a smile that she had initially wanted to hide, 'Are you going to just walk inside the house? You are supposed to walk outside, you know.' He did not say anything. He studied the spines of the books. Then he heard her shriek.

'They haven't gone,' she screamed. The way she said 'they', he knew she was talking about cockroaches. Lavanya and cockroaches had a special relationship. On the second day of marriage she had confessed that she had the ability to hear them. She was inspecting the floor carefully now, holding a rolled copy of a post-doctoral thesis on Large Molecular Structures in Interstellar Gas.

'Just last week we had sprayed the whole kitchen. I thought they were gone. But they have all moved in here.' She went on about the indestructibility of the insects and the inevitability of calling pest control even though, she admitted, it seemed like a very American thing to do. 'What do we do, Arvind? These things don't die. What do we do?'

He inhaled a lot of air and looked at her. 'Lavanya,' he said, certain that this was really going to annoy her, 'Like in maths . . .'

'What?'

'Just because there is a problem, it does not mean there is always a solution.'

She tilted her face. And looked at him with a menacing exasperation. He returned the stare. It struck him how rarely he looked at her any more, and how old she actually appeared this close. This was an old woman standing in front of him, whose hair, without the deception of dye, would be the colour of cobwebs. Her face was still beautiful, but the skin on her neck had become loose. In each other's eyes, probably, they had been diminished by age and disfigured by familiarity. Or was it the other way around? He could smell in her the vapours of all the oils from Kerala that she rubbed on her skin every night like a wrestler. That smell to him was the smell of death. His grandfather used to smell that way, and he used to tell all his grandchildren when they applied the odious oil on his wrinkled body that it was the lubricant old people needed to go smoothly down the tunnel of afterlife, into the body of a newborn. And the kids would then have nightmares about the crooked old men who had entered them when they were babies. The smell, strangely, also reminded him of the importance of digestion. His grandfather, in the aroma of ayurvedic oils that somehow made him appear wise, told the youth of the household every day that the secret of longevity lay in ensuring efficient digestion of food. 'Always', he used to say, 'listen to your arse.'

The vacant silence in Shruti's room was stirred by a nasal song. It was in an indecipherable language and its volume slowly grew. It was coming from the tiny wood-framed clock with Thai digits on the nightstand, and it was inevitable that the alarm would now make Acharya and Lavanya look at each other for a moment. The interminable song, probably a Thai song, filled the house as it did every morning. It was the 7.45 morning alarm of Shruti which she had set about five years ago in the ambitions of waking up early and reducing her illusory fat. The alarm never really woke her up but she tried every single day. Acharya used to find it poignant.

The alarm died abruptly, as it always did.

'You really can't turn this thing off?' Lavanya asked.

'I told you, I tried,' he said, avoiding her eyes.

After the girl left with a software engineer for California, Acharya told his wife that he had tried to disable the alarm several times but could not figure out how to do it. Lavanya found it hard to believe that a man who was once rumoured to win the physics Nobel did not know how to disable the alarm in a silly timepiece bought in the streets of Bangkok. She suspected that, like her, he too wanted to hear the alarm every morning and enjoy the momentary delusion of imagining their girl still sleeping in her room.

Acharya wondered why daughters always went away. So keen they were on finding a moron and leaving. The futility of love and marriage – did they need a whole lifetime to see through it all? Didn't they learn anything from the lives of their parents? Inevitably, he remembered the only two instances when he believed he had brought true grief to his daughter. Shruti always laughed at his conviction that he had made her suffer only twice.

'Every day, you were a monster,' she would say. The two episodes that he conceded happened when she was eight. The first was the morning she realized that chicken was not a vegetable and that he had lied to her about its origin. The second instance was when she had brought a poem to him that she had written called 'Infinite Stars in the Sky'. He had taken her to the terrace and showed her the night sky. If the number of stars were infinite in the observable universe, he told her, then at every single point in the sky there would be an endless line of stars stacked one after the other, and that would cause the night to be so illuminated that it would be brighter than day. Since that was not the case, since stars were just tiny points here and there, it meant that the number of stars was finite. She did not know there was a word 'finite', and had looked very dejected. She renamed the poem 'Finite Stars in the Sky', but it was not the same. She did not write another poem for many weeks after that because she was afraid of her father's facts.

Acharya was lost once again that morning. This time, he was in the trance of memories. Then he heard the voice. First as a whisper call, like the disturbing voice of conscience in old films that seeks the attention of the hero who searches everywhere for the source of the sound until he finds the speaker in a full-length mirror. The voice, the haunting insistent whisper, became a distant ungifted song that grew and grew in volume and tenor until he recognized it as the voice of Lavanya. 'You are not supposed to just stand in those shoes. You're supposed to walk. You wake up before the housewives of Mylapore every morning and then you just stand.'

Acharya went to his room and shut himself inside. He fed The Three Tenors into the music system and triumphantly thumbed the play button as retribution for everything he had to endure in the house. He sat on the edge of the bed and remembered how Shruti used to say that if he had more hair, and agreed to dye it black and comb it sideways, and opened his mouth more often in anguish, he would very closely resemble Pavarotti.

The piercing wail of 'Nessun dorma' filled the room, and he yielded to its anthemic glory. He stared back at his own images on the wall. How young and fierce he once was. There was so much hope in him those days for theoretical physics. But now he was tired. He was tired of the battles and tired of rubbish like Tachyons, Higgs Bosons and Supersymmetry. He felt in his bones the weight of how complicated the quest for truth itself had become. How obscure, how mathematical, how pompously it tried to exclude ordinary people. Physics was on the verge of becoming a religion. A medieval religion. A handful of seers stood on the pedestal and lay people had to accept everything they heard. He still found joy in theoretical physics, and in the mysteries of Time and gravity. But there was nothing he loved more now than his search for the eternal spores that came riding on meteorites.

In the decisive finality of 'Nessun dorma', so titanic, so perfect, he began to hear discordant beats which he slowly recognized as violent thumps on the door. He heard the desperate voice of Lavanya trying to rise above Pavarotti's. He was about to increase the volume when he heard her say, 'Shruti is on the phone.' That made him open the door.

He did not meet her eyes as he went past her to the hall.

'I have been banging on the door,' Lavanya said, and then got distracted by the dust on the door. They had moved from Princeton ten years ago, but she had never gotten used to how easily dust gathered in Bombay.

Acharya held the receiver and grumbled that the line was dead.

'Obviously,' Lavanya said, 'She is not going to wait for . . .' She clenched her fist and yelled, 'I am going to turn off that bloody music.' The doorbell rang just then and she opened the door with a violent smirk.

'Good morning,' said the cheerful voice of Jana Nambodri. He was the best-dressed scientist she had ever known. Dark-brown corduroy trousers and a crisp white shirt today. She knew that he dyed his hair evenly silver, and she was not sure if she should hate him for it. She had a peculiar soft spot for men who were shorter than her. Also, he was the cultural force of the Professors' Quarters.

Nambodri was visiting after a long time. She hoped he had come in peace. She let him in muttering, 'Don't worry, Jana, I am going to turn that thing off.'

'It's "Nessun dorma",' Nambodri said, 'You cannot turn it off like that. It's disrespectful.'

'In my house you can,' she said, and went away.

The two men stood in the living-room staring at each other. They heard Pavarotti perish abruptly, somewhat violently, and the sudden silence made the distance between them seem greater.

'I'm sorry,' Nambodri said, 'The Round Table was not the place for that. I am really sorry.'

OPARNA GOSHMAULIK WAS still not granted the peace of anonymity, but she was now an insider. Those cold gazes when she went down the corridors in the wooden beat of her low heels, the number of old scholars who wanted to show her the right path while staring at her breasts, and their wives, some of them, who arrived to have an accidental meeting with her and see for themselves the talk of the Professors' Quarters – those days were over. Only minor assaults remained. Some wiry post-doctoral students still gaped at her with infatuated eyes, an ancient professor of Number Theory who inhabited the corridors these days waylaid her and showed her his nature poems. Jana Nambodri continued to observe her in a way that he thought was wise and knowing. He wanted to sustain a mild tension between them. A cultured animosity, probably, was the second best thing he sought from a woman. Other radio astronomers still came down to her lab for what they said was just a chat and went back with the news of all that they surveyed – the looming shelves, chromatographs, spectrometers, the eager research students on hire from affiliated universities, the unmoving attendants who waited for something to happen and the many cartons, still unopened, that said 'this side up', including the cardboard box of a new coffee machine that they refused to believe was just that. But all this, the attention, malice and affection, she did not mind. Her situation was now improving. She even found the courage to paint her lips. (In pale shades.) Her thick healthy hair was still tied fiercely in the imagined modesty of a pony-tail, but these days she let some curls fall on her cheeks.

She could not abandon the reassurance of unremarkable clothes though. Usually, a long shapeless top over blue jeans. But in the sea breeze, the flowing top sometimes hugged her figure, and she feared she was then a feast.

She ran up two flights of stairs from the basement, humming a tune she could not recall hearing for the first time. She took in the breeze at the porch and the smell of the moist grass and wet earth. A gardener, who somehow did not look naked in just his underwear, was watering the main lawn. She made her way to the canteen: a gracious room with bare wooden tables and metal folding chairs, and large square windows that opened out to the undulating backyard. Here, the sound of the sea was another form of silence. Waiters in dark-brown shirts and trousers were emerging from an inner door carrying plates on their forearms and palms, or were just standing still at various points in the canteen.

She saw Nambodri huddled together with four other radio astronomers whose names she had forgotten. He was speaking into his mobile and the others were looking at him keenly. One of them, a bald man with quivering spectacles on his nose bridge, reminded her of a college professor who had once asked her in his cabin, 'Do you respect me?'

Nambodri put the phone in his shirt pocket and said in a soft, serious way, 'Not today, But he is going to get it soon.'

'I'm thinking of taking an off this week,' one man said. 'He is going to go crazy.'

'No,' Nambodri said calmly. 'We are all going to be there. It's very important that we are all there.'

'Look, I've had a bypass. I can't handle these things.'

'It's going to be very good for your heart,' Nambodri said.

He spotted Oparna, and a smile appeared on his face. He pointed to an empty chair beside him. In his shadowy conference, he did not mind the sudden fragrance of lemon. She was a relief in this asylum. These days, his neat foreign shirts and corduroy trousers and stylish silver hair had found a meaningful audience. She saved him from the banality of the academic society: those austere men and grotesque hairy women he usually met on the circuit. He had this affliction to be with the youth, the real fragrant waxed youth. Before Oparna came along, his only recourse was the parties thrown by his unscientific friends where young girls gathered around him when they heard he was a radio astronomer. He loved it when their delicate bodies, so slight, stood close to him, their legs so naked, their vodka eyes asking him what exactly he did, and their intelligent nods of incomprehension. He began with astronomy and told them what jazz was and in a naughty way made fun of Bryan Adams. He would search their pretty faces for one-minute crushes. He loved the young and spoke to them in their language.

Oparna suspected as much. He was the sort of man who would say to his son, 'I am a friend, not a father,' and then give the boy a condom when he turned eighteen. A waiter brought her usual glass of tea and stared hard as he pushed a sugar jar on the table towards her.

'Nice earrings,' Nambodri said, 'You don't wear long earrings very often. What's special today?'

'Nothing is special.'

'You need clearance from the old man for another microscope?'

One of the astronomers chuckled. Oparna made a sound that she was certain would pass off as a sporting laugh.

She knew there was a lot of pent-up resentment in these men because they could not accept that something like Astrobiology had become a bustling department in this temple of physics while the Search for Extraterrestrial Intelligence was not allowed to be even a parenthesis in radio astronomy.

Her mobile rang, and she was grateful for that. The voice of Ayyan Mani said, 'Sir wants to see you right now.' She looked at her phone, somewhat confused. She had not given her number to anyone.

Oparna burst into the anteroom and felt the full stab of Ayyan's calm scrutiny. She was wary of this dark man with his wide eyes.

'We've been searching for you,' he said, 'He is waiting.'

As she passed by his table, he studied her back. He was certain the men in this institute of excellence did not know her at all. They were all deformed. Too much education; too much class. They looked at a woman through the charades she created around her, through what she said and how she spoke, and her degrees. And through the many myths of modernity that men and women erected when they were fully clothed. But the bed is medieval, and honest, and in it he wanted to believe Oparna would be something else. She would understand it if a man slapped her in the urgency of love, or to destroy her arrogance. He saw in her the unmistakable insanity of formidable women who longed to crumble. Then the thoughts of Oparna vanished and the excitement of what was to happen next morning filled him. A shudder ran through him. He felt a cold fear in his tongue.

She pushed open the inner door and felt the same odd mixture of cold air and anticipation she felt every time she entered. Meeting Acharya was still an event, though he never did anything to make it an occasion. He was sitting behind his massive tumultuous desk. As always, his pink bald head that was now bent over something on his lap appeared larger than she had expected. She sat across the table and murmured, 'I am here.' He did not look up. It was a convenient moment for her to observe him carefully. Big ears, she thought, and his hand that rested loosely on the table was clean and brutal. She wondered, once again that day, how he might have looked when he was young. The archive pictures on the net were not good enough. And the vacant walls of his room frustrated her. There was not a trace of him here. A young sepia Acharya glaring from the wall might have been entertaining.

All through her brief struggle in the Institute, the infatuations of strange men and the malice of others, and some who were afflicted by both, working with Acharya had a calming effect on her. Their conversations were dry, chiefly about equipment purchases and setting up the lab. But there was something about being in his presence that she liked. He was a shelter. In his shade, she felt absolutely ignored. She had craved that always, from the uncles who used to touch her when they came home for the family dinner, from the boys outside her house who used to play cricket, and all the men who came her way. Finally, here was a man who did not notice her. It was like being in the dark corner of a theatre and watching a good play.

Acharya licked his finger hungrily and turned a page. He was reading a graphic novel which lay furtively on his lap. It was part of a series called *Topolov's Superman*, once an underground rage. It was Russia's investment in popular culture during the Cold War days. In *Topolov's Superman*, the man of steel was perceived by ordinary people as a superhero, but in reality he was a vain horny villain from whom two KGB agents constantly saved the world. Acharya licked his finger again and turned the page.

Clark Kent is walking down a deserted cobbled street in Prague. It's a cold gloomy morning. He sees a beautiful girl in a short skirt walk by. 'Look at this piece of work. I can have this right now. I am Superman,' Kent says. He follows her. She walks into a small deserted lane. Kent turns into a whirlwind and becomes Superman. He blocks her path.

'Superman,' she says excitedly.

'Can I take you for a spin, honey?' he says.

'Er . . . sorry . . . my aunt is ill. I have to go now. But what a lovely surprise. And what are you doing here talking to me? Don't you have a world to save, Superman?' She walks away waving goodbye. But when she turns, he is there in front of her, blocking her path again.

'Are you sure you don't want anything, honey?'

The girl looks confused, but before she can react, Superman strips her naked and laughs. She screams as he flings her on the sidewalk and takes off his cape and tries to extricate himself from the tunic.

'This outfit is not quickie-friendly,' he says.

All of a sudden police cars come with sirens blazing.

'Superman!' a cop screams. He is holding the red cape. Other cops point their guns at Superman. People peep through their windows above.

'Shit!' Superman says, looking a bit tired. 'Can't believe I've got to do this again.' He dashes up to space, circumvents the globe a thousand times and gains a velocity faster than the speed of light to reverse Time. The rotation of the Earth changes direction. Life on Earth rewinds to the point when the pretty girl is walking through the market lane.

'Not possible,' Acharya muttered angrily. He never liked it when Time was exploited this way.

But then this was what modern physics itself had become. Time reversal, black holes, dark matter, dark energy, invisibility, intelligent civilizations. Exciting rubbish. The money was in that.

Oparna was imagining a young man with fiery eyes, long gaunt face, hair neatly combed. Handsome, she thought. What would such a man say to a pretty sepia girl?

'What's the progress with the cryosampler?' the operatic voice of Acharya asked, destroying the ancient world she had carefully created in her mind. His elephant eyes were looking at her.

Outside, Ayyan Mani arranged the courier mail and the ordinary mail that had arrived. Acharya read only some of the courier mail, which he selected at random. He never opened the ordinary mail, those sad, stamped envelopes, though every day he received over fifty from laymen who believed they had a scientific temperament, or worse, had found baffling new theories. The only person who read those letters was Ayyan who knew how to repair an opened envelope. Once, Ayyan had thrown the letters in the bin and delivered only the courier mail to Acharya. The old man had looked confused for several seconds. There was an anomaly in a pattern he was used to. Ordinary mail and courier mail: that's what he wanted to see. So he asked Ayyan about the ordinary mail, and when he learnt what the secretary had done with it he told him never to throw anything away. The letters were a broad mathematical clue for Acharya as to his place in public consciousness. In a way, he wanted to be there, in the minds of ordinary people, even though he could not bear to read what they had to say.

Ayyan went in with the letters, courier mail and faxes and set them on the desk. The basement item and Acharya were discussing how to send the balloon up and from where. Ayyan glanced at one of the telephones on the desk. It was still slightly off the hook. Good. When he went back to his seat in the anteroom he picked up a landline and listened in on the conversation between Oparna and the Big Man.

Thirty minutes later, when Ayyan put the receiver down, he wondered if there was a way he could tell Oja Mani how absurd were the occupations of these men and women who so easily frightened her. An old man wanted to search the atmosphere for microbes that were coming down from space. A young woman would soon study two bottles of air. This was what people did. This was their job. In the real world that lay outside the Institute, it was even more weird. Majestic men went in cars, in the isolation of the back seat, studying laptops on their way to work where they would think of ways to fool people into buying cola, or a type of insurance, or a condom that had dots on it. Or invest other people's money in the stockmarket. Some wrote for the papers about how more and more women were interested in cricket, or why Afghanistan was important to Pakistan, or something like that, and some people rewrote what others wrote, some took pictures, some drew, some made faces in front of a camera. This was more or less what big people did, the beneficiaries of the millenniums, at the end of the tunnel of time – this was what they did. He could have done any of those jobs. Oja too. And they could have lived in a building that had a lift, and when they entered the kind of restaurants where emaciated men parked the cars of fat men they would not be so frightened by the calm of the cold air inside and the smell of mild spices and the difficult names of fish. It was so easy to be the big people.

All you had to do was to be born in the homes where they were born.

Adi did not have that good fortune, but he would be there one day, among these people. He thought of his little boy, his large eyes that were like his mother's and his unnatural calm. Ayyan's mind, inescapably, went to what was to happen in just a few hours. He felt a bit nervous, and he liked the way his fingers quivered.

That evening, as Ayyan went in the Institute's shuttle bus to the Churchgate station, he looked at the moronic city that was in the hysteria of going home. As though everyone here were going home for the first time. In the twilight that was now the colour of dust, in the fury of horns that was a national language because honking had telegraphic properties, cars stood stranded all around the bus like ants carrying the corpse of a caterpillar. Where a bumper ended and another began, in those crevices, people crossed the road and motorbikes wobbled through, honking. There was a caste system even on the roads. The cars, their faces frowning in a superior way through the bonnet grilles, were the Brahmins. They were higher than the motorcycles who were higher than the pedestrians. The cycles were lowest of the low. Even the pedestrians pretended that they didn't see them. The bus had to be something in this structure, and Ayyan decided it was him. Lowly, but formidable and beyond torment. In any given situation in this country, Ayyan thought with a chuckle that did not surface, someone was the Brahmin and someone was the Untouchable.

As the bus inched through the evening life, the traffic grew. There was no space on the road any more. A man on a bike was riding on the pavement. When he tried to plunge into the road, a car hit him. He fell down but managed to get up. He looked shocked. That, Ayyan loved. After riding like a moron all over the place, observe the face of an Indian when he crashes. He is stunned.

This country had become a circus, and that was fair. What

Ayyan's forefathers were once to the Brahmins, the Brahmins were today to the world. They and the other privileged, all of whom he recognized only as the Brahmins, had become miserable backward clowns in the discreet eyes of the white man. And there lay the revenge of the Dalits. They were the nation now, and they oppressed the Brahmins by erecting an incurable commotion on the streets. The Brahmins had nowhere to go now but to suffer in silence or to flee to nonvegetarian lands. Their women could no longer walk on the streets in peace. Pale boys elbowed their breasts.

He looked without emotion at the tall unattainable apartment blocks that seemed to rise suddenly. In the pathetic clarity of hope that he once had in his early youth, he used to tell himself that a day would come when he would live in one of those buildings, that he too would get home in a lift. He knew those homes very well, he knew those lives. After all, he was once a door-to-door salesman for Eureka Forbes vacuum cleaners.

A job at the Eureka Forbes was not only heralded then as the final frontier in marketing but also glorified in underground novels as an assignment that led robust young men to the homes of hungry housewives, whose saris sometimes slipped off their blouses as they innocently enquired in how many colours the vacuum cleaners came, or their nightgowns rose in the tempest of a table fan, or they answered the door in a wet towel that they flung away upon the incandescent sight of the Eureka Forbes salesman. The roadside stalls too, where the odorous salesmen sipped tea, were replete with the legend of insatiable housewives. He never encountered such women, but in those homes he learnt about the charmed lives of the rich. He saw women group together and meditate and even chant, 'I am beautiful.' Men who were nothing without their inheritances dedicated to themselves a song called 'My Way'. And he figured through the many pieces of conversations he overheard in those homes that there were four Beatles, and that you had to clap at the incipient guitar piece of 'Hotel California'. He also saw men scoop the shit of their babies, and once he even saw a man in an apron take the dishes from the dining-table to the kitchen sink. They were the new men. In time, their numbers increased and he saw them everywhere now, standing defeated next to their glowing women. Ayyan often told the peons of the Institute, 'These days, men live like men only in the homes of the poor.'

At the Colaba causeway, as the bus stood stranded in a jam, he saw kids beg near the window of a taxi. The young couple inside sat with strong defiant faces. How they would have loved to give a rupee, but they had read investigative stories that appeared at least once every year in English newspapers on the cruel begging syndicates that were rumoured to exploit children. By withholding one rupee they were hitting hard at the syndicates, apparently. So much philosophy for a one-rupee transaction.

Then he saw a sight on the pavement that he would later recount to Oja with slight exaggeration. A woman came out of Theobroma – The Pastry Shop. Urchins often stood outside its glass door and gawked. She made a benevolent face at them and appeared to ask them to stand in a line. They stood. There were six of them. They looked like stray dogs at the parcel she was holding. At the head of the line the woman stood in the glow of goodness and opened the packet in her hand. The urchin assembly collapsed. All of them pounced on her, laughing. Many more came from nowhere and joined the attack on the cake. The woman held on to the packet, first with a quiet severity, looking around a bit embarrassed. She began to yell, 'Line, line.' She tried to slap a few but missed. The children yelled with laughter and tugged at the packet. The cake fell on the pavement. They crawled all over it and ran away holding large pieces. Two dogs rushed to lick the strewn crumbs on the pavement. Ayyan hoped to catch the woman's eye and laugh, but she was preoccupied with disgust.

He thought of her shocked face for the rest of the ride. The image stayed with him when he reached Churchgate and as he waited for the train with the monstrous evening crowd that generated its own heat. He thought of her face as he stood silently inside the compartment in the tight squeeze of warm wet men all around. Her stunned face grew and grew in his mind until it was a giant billboard. By the time he reached BDD he had forgotten her, but his lungs felt good.

He went through the yellow gloom of the broken ways, avoiding the eyes of drunken men in loose shorts. On the ancient colonial stairway of Block Number Forty-One, a bunch of old friends were arguing about something.

'Mani, this guy says it is not possible,' a man said. 'Why don't you tell this fellow that you can make out if a girl has screwed by the way her arse moves.'

Ayyan said it was possible. He took a drag from someone's cigarette. From the corner of his eye, he could see that one of the men, a faint sickly fellow, was looking at him quite seriously. That meant he wanted to borrow some money. So Ayyan moved on.

ADI WAS ON the floor, his slight frame bent over a notebook. He was writing something and looking distraught. His T-shirt said, 'There are 10 kinds of people in the world. Those who understand binary and those who don't.' Ayyan had found it in the ladies' section of a shop. He bought it even though he did not get the joke. He probably bought it because he did not understand it. It annoyed him. There was always something that most people, very ordinary people, understood and he didn't. Later, he found an explanation on Wikipedia, and how the number 2 was written as 10 in the binary system. He then read about binary codes, a whole language built on the arrangement of zeros and ones, and he grudgingly conceded that it was so clever that even if he had been born into privilege, he might not have been smart enough to invent it.

Oja's long dark hair was still wet after her evening bath and it dampened the back of her red gown. She was smelling of Chandirka, their family soap as ordained by Ayyan. She was sitting on the floor and cutting her toenails with a blade. She did not feel like watching TV that evening, so there was a peaceful stillness. She threw a look at the boy and then at her husband, and they both chuckled at how miserable Adi was at that moment. 'Imposigen,' Oja said. 'Imposition' was one of the few English words she knew, though she could not pronounce it, just as most people in the world could not pronounce *vazhapazham*, which she could. She knew about imposition because very often Adi's teachers gave one to the boy. This evening, he had to write 'I won't talk in the class' two hundred times.

'Adi, tell your father who you were talking to,' his mother said.

'I was talking to myself.'

'And what were you saying?'

'I don't remember.'

'You remember all the science rubbish, but you don't remember what you were telling yourself?'

Adi continued to write in silence.

'This boy never answers me properly,' Oja said, looking accusingly at Ayyan. 'You have spoilt him. All those secrets you two have is not good for him. He talks to me only when he wants food.' That reminded her of something. 'He has left half the food in the lunch-box.'

'Did you give him Lady's Finger?'

'My god, no! This boy is already abnormal. Lady's Finger makes you do sums better. I would never give it to him.' And she said in an affectionate way, 'Strange boy. He has not troubled the science teacher for some time. I wonder why. But it will come soon, the next summons from the Principal.'

'He has done something else,' Ayyan said, with a mysterious smile.

'What is it?'

'I can't tell you now.'

'Tell me.'

'You will know in the morning.'

'What is it?'

'Don't waste your time. I am not going to tell you. Wait till morning.'

'Why morning? What's going to happen?'

'Wait and see.'

'Adi,' she said, trying to be stern. 'What have you done?'

'I've not done anything.'

'What is going to happen in the morning?'

'I don't know.'

'What do you mean, you don't know?'

'Don't confuse me,' Adi said, annoyed.

'Come here,' she screamed. Adi threw the pencil down and came to his mother. 'Look here,' she told him, trying to look severe. 'You are too young to keep secrets from me. What is happening? I have to know. Otherwise I will give you a slap and the truth will come out of your mouth.'

'I've not done anything,' he said.

'If you keep doing only what your father asks you to do, you will come to grief, boy. A lamb that follows a pig will eat shit.'

'Don't confuse me.'

'Tell me, what have you done? What's the secret?'

Adi turned to his father in exasperation.

'Don't bother him,' Ayyan told his wife, and that was that.

Adi went back to his imposition. In the brief silence they heard the faint noise of horns, boys playing cricket and the unmistakable sound of a man, somewhere, beating his wife. Adi raised his head from his notebook and smiled at his father. Ayyan smiled back. That set off Oja again.

'What is it?' she almost pleaded.

Ayyan pointed a finger upwards, his eyes inviting her to follow him.

The attic was built a few weeks ago, in the tremors of a carpenter's violent hammer, its every blow landing on Ayyan's heart and shaking a secret pride within. He never thought the day would come when he too would build an attic. It reminded him of the failed men of BDD and their desperation to sleep with their wives, away from the sight of the others. Ceilings were high in BDD and almost everyone had an attic. Most of the loud, insufferable children of the chawls were conceived in the attics. In the homes where there were more than one married couple, they took weekly or even daily turns to use the elevated bedroom. The conjugal attic was a sign here. That a man had failed to escape, that he was now stranded.

Oja looked cautiously at her son. He was absorbed in his imposition. Ayyan had a packet with him now and she was curious to know what it was. She had not seen it when he came home. It was remarkable, she thought, how her husband hid things and made them spring out when he wanted them to. He pulled down a folding ladder and climbed up into the loft. Oja followed. The attic was about six feet by three. There was a thin mattress and a blue table fan, and a lot of books that Oja wanted to throw away. They crawled on to the attic floor and sat there.

'What is it?' she asked in a whisper.

'I've got something for you,' he said. He opened the packet and took out a bra.

'This? It looks so fancy. How much is this?'

'Look, how stiff it is,' he said, pointing to the hardwire frame of the cups. She giggled.

'It's metal. What if lightning strikes?'

'It's plastic.'

'It's metal.'

'To be on the safe side, don't wear it in the rains.'

'It's so funny. Where do you find these things?'

'It's not funny, you idiot. This is what girls are wearing these days.'

'How do you know so much about girls?' she asked, toying with the bra. 'It's so funny. I can't wear it. What will people say?'

'I hope people won't know what you are wearing underneath.'

She slapped his thigh. The sight of the fancy skin-colour bra made her giggle again. Ayyan told her, in a professorial way, 'This will keep your breasts firm. Or they will begin to sag like your mother's.'

'Don't talk like that about my mother.'

Ayyan poked her breasts. 'Breasts have eyes, Oja. They look at me now. I don't ever want them to look down at the floor, like your mother's.'

He remembered a curious fact, one of the many he collected almost every day for her. 'You know, Oja,' he said, as he always started these things, 'an average woman's breasts weigh eight kilos.'

'Really?'

'Yes.'

'That's very heavy,' she said. Then her eyes fell on a smaller parcel. 'What's that?'

'That's for Adi.'

Ayyan went down the ladder with the packet. Oja followed.

'I've got something for you,' he told his son. Adi jumped. He tore open the packet and a toilet roll fell out. The sight of the roll made Adi almost breathless with laughter. He always found it funny. So, occasionally, Ayyan stole toilet rolls from the Institute. There was something else in the packet. It was a Rubik's cube.

'You keep turning till every face of the cube has the same colour,' Ayyan said, 'Not many people in the world can do it. But you are a genius.'

'Some boys in the school have it,' Adi said.

'Don't give him such things,' Oja said, snatching the cube from Adi's hand. The boy tried to take it back from his mother, but he was not tall enough. 'Do your imposigen,' she said. 'You keep giving him such things,' she told her husband, 'Don't play with his mind.'

'But he is a genius.'

'I want him to be normal. We have to make him do normal things.'

'What can we do if he is not?'

'That scares me,' she said.

Adi snatched the cube back from his mother.

Oja looked angrily at her husband. 'Don't do these things,' she said.

'These are the toys he needs. He is just too intelligent. You will not believe it in the morning.'

'Tell me, what has he done?'

'You will know in the morning.'

'Tell me, she said.'

'Wait till morning.'

Oja was so angry that night that she punished Ayyan with silences and refused to sleep in the attic. She slept with her son on the floor. From the wooden loft, Ayyan saw his wife through a dim streetlight that was coming through the kitchen window.

She looked weak and sad when her big eyes were shut. He wanted to pinch her till she yelped and tell her that he did not like it when she was sad. He wanted to tell her that she should never be sad because to be sad was to be afraid. And to be afraid was to respect the world too much. The world was not a scary place, he always told her. It was full of ordinary people who did ordinary things, even though some of them went in cars and lived in very big homes and spoke in English. He wanted her to know that he was smart enough for this world and that he knew how to take care of her. He whispered from the loft, 'You know, Oja.' She did not respond. 'Oja . . . Oja,' he said.

'What do you want?'

'A shark can sense a drop of blood miles away.'

'Let me sleep,' she said.

'Isn't it amazing?'

Ayyan lay awake the whole night. When morning came, he heard the no-talent pigeons first and then the crows whom he liked because they were clever and mean. He heard the rustle of Oja's silver anklets going to the kitchen. Steel vessels moved. He heard the hush of *The Times of India* slipping under the door. He went down the narrow folding ladder and put on a shirt.

Oja was by the stove, yawning. 'It's morning,' she said, still angry. 'Now tell me.'

Ayyan left without a word.

At the end of a lane outside the fringes of BDD was a newspaper-seller whose transient plywood stand that vanished at noon was now neatly packed with papers and magazines. Ayyan felt his tongue go cold as he approached the vendor. He ran his eyes over the stand but could not find it. Then he saw it in a corner. It was called *Yug*, a Marathi daily. He turned the pages impatiently and stopped when Adi's face beamed from a snippet. '*A Special Boy*,' the headline said.

> *It's unbelievable but true. Ten-year-old Aditya Mani has been selected by the Department for Scientific Education and Excellence of Switzerland*

to go to Geneva later this year on a one-month scholarship. Aditya took part in a written test which was meant for all students under the age of 16. Over five hundred 12th standard students sat for the screening test. Only one was selected and it turned out to be the ten-year-old genius who is in the sixth standard of St Andrew's School. 'I want to understand the universe better,' the shy boy said, when asked what he wanted to do in the future. He will spend one month with top scientists in Geneva. . .

Ayyan bought all the ten copies of the paper.

Oja heard him enter but she was engrossed in the milk. It was always the milk. Adi was still sleeping, hands and legs now spread all over the floor. Ayyan shoved the paper into his wife's face.

'What's this?' she said, and then she saw Adi's picture. She switched off the stove. That annoyed her husband who did not expect her to remember to switch off the stove at this moment.

Oja sank to the floor with the paper. Her knees gave way smoothly and she sat in a crouch. She looked frightened as she read. Then a smile appeared on her face. She put her slender fingers on her mouth and looked at her sleeping son. 'When did he write the test?'

'Two months ago,' Ayyan told her. 'The test was on a Sunday. I didn't want to tell you. You would have fussed.'

Oja began to cry. 'My son is famous? They should have carried his full picture. This photo is so bad. He is much more beautiful than this.' She rubbed Adi's feet and began to pull his toes. 'Wake up, Adi,' she told him. She shook the boy and showed him the paper. Adi stared at his picture and fell back on the pillow.

'Why didn't you tell me, Adi?' his mother asked softly. 'You should tell your mother everything. Your father never tells me anything. Adi, you should tell your mother everything that you do.'

Ayyan stepped out into the corridor and stood in a line flanked by the jaundice-yellow walls, holding a copy of *Yug* in one hand and a small blue bucket in the other. The two lines outside the four toilets were long. As always, the women's queue was longer. That was not only because it moved more slowly but also because fewer men used the toilets here. Several working men of BDD had taught their bodies how to wait till they got to the office. They squatted on the glimmering western commodes of their offices, and on some days even bathed there under luxurious showers. Ayyan too, usually, waited until he reached the Institute. But this morning he chose to stand in the queue with the blue bucket.

The man at the head of the Gents' line was hollering to the occupant of one of the toilets, 'How long is this going to take?' He turned to look at the others in the queue and said in a disappointed way, 'Boys these days.' The general suspicion about adolescent boys who spent a lot of time in the toilet was that they were clearing their pipes, and in the mornings, the suspicion drove even the most broadminded of men here crazy. At the end of the queue, Ayyan showed the newspaper to a man in front of him.

Soon, in the glow of a soft ethereal light that was coming through the broken glass of two arched windows above the toilets, a small crowd of men and women, with their own little buckets, gathered around Ayyan. And they read. Some read aloud, some silently.

'There was always something about him,' a woman said.

'The kind of things he talks about,' a man said shaking his head. 'I hear he talks about things even adults don't understand. You are a lucky man, Mani. Look at me. I have a son who lies around like a python.'

The adolescent finally emerged from the toilet and he looked confused at the small commotion outside. The orderly line was now in shreds.

'All done? Was it good?' a man asked him angrily, and then with a benevolent face asked Ayyan to jump the queue and finish his job before all of them.

'Already, the boy is making me proud,' Ayyan said, and everyone laughed.

★

In the glass enclosure that stood near the kitchen platform, Oja rubbed coconut oil on her naked son. The boy endured the special treatment with a grimace. She was muttering something about the great future that lay before him. 'But always remember, never be arrogant. People like humility in smart people because that way they don't feel very small.' She bathed him in cold water and dressed him up in white short-sleeved shirt and white shorts. She combed his thick oiled hair, holding his jaw violently, and watched like a hawk as he tied his shoelaces. Then she handed him over to her husband. 'Don't take the taxi,' she said, 'Walk.'

In the back seat of the taxi, Ayyan gave his little finger to his son, who reciprocally locked his in it. 'Our secret,' Ayyan said.

'Our secret,' the boy said, laughing.

'You will not tell your mother that we took a taxi?'

'I will not,' Adi said. 'Our secret.'

They didn't speak for a while. When the car stopped at a signal, the boy asked, 'What did the newspaper say?'

'You can read Marathi.'

'I can't understand the way the papers write. What did the newspaper say?'

'That you are very bright.'

'That's all?'

'It also said that you passed a test which five hundred boys wrote.'

'When did I write the test?'

'You know that. Think.'

'Twenty-second April?'

'Correct. And now you will go to Geneva.'

'Where is Geneva?'

'It's a big city in Switzerland. You know Switzerland.'

'Yes. But its capital is not Geneva.'

'What is the capital of Switzerland?'

'B-e-r-n-e'.

'You are a very clever boy.'

'I am a genius.'

Ayyan looked at Adi, a bit concerned for a moment, but when the boy returned the stare both of them burst out laughing.

'Why do countries have capitals?' Adi asked.

'Because every country wants to say this is the most important city in our place.'

'But don't other cities feel bad?'

'No. Do you think Bombay feels bad it's not the capital?'

'Yes.'

Adi muttered the name of every car that was passing by. 'Esteem, Skoda, Fiat, Accent, Accent, Baleno, Accent,' he was saying. He fell silent for about a minute.

'Say, "Decimal system",' his father said. 'D-e-c-i-m-a-l s-y-s-t-e-m.'

'That's easy,' Adi said, but a look of concentration came to his face. 'Decimal system,' he said slowly.

At the iron gates where the security guard stared at the backs of young mothers, Adi let go of his father's hand and ran to his class. Ayyan made his way to meet the fierce Salesian Principal. Sister Chastity looked surprised to see him. 'Something wrong?' she asked. (She always hoped something was wrong in the lives of married people.)

'It's something the boy has done,' Ayyan said.

Sister Chastity went through the news report. In the brief silence that followed, Ayyan could hear the distant murmurs of a class where the teacher was probably delayed. Sister Chastity's moustache had grown a bit darker, he thought. He caught a glimpse of Christ in the background: Christ, whose heart was on fire and whose munificent eyes reminded him of the woman who had stepped out of the pastry shop yesterday evening.

Sister Chastity lifted her head and inhaled thoughtfully. 'This boy,' she said kindly, 'What has this boy done? I see his picture. But I am sorry, I cannot read Marathi. I can read Hindi and even French, but not Marathi. The script is the same as Hindi you know but some words . . .'

Ayyan translated the story for her. 'This boy,' she said shaking her head. 'I am going to put it on the notice-board right away. Praise the Lord! I wish the report had mentioned St Andrew's, Worli. You know, there are so many schools called St Andrew's. Praise the Lord!' She stared at him for a moment and said, 'I see, Mr Mani, you don't praise the Lord.'

'Oh – Praise the Lord.'

'Please don't feel compelled to say these things.'

'Not at all. Lord is lord. Nothing Christian about it,' he said.

'Him, not it.'

'Him.'

'What if I meant it as a very Christian thing. Would you have still said, "Praise the Lord"?' she asked.

'Of course. God is one. Hindu god, Christian god – all the same thing.'

'The same one?'

'The same one.'

'Yes,' Sister Chastity said sadly. 'People say that. People say many things. But I am sure you like the sound of "Christ is the true Lord". There is something about it?'

'Yes, there is something about it, but a lawyer was telling me a few months ago that it is against the Indian constitution to say "Christ is the true Lord".'

'What matters, Mr Mani, is the human constitution.'

'I don't understand, Sister.'

'It's all right. A day like this, Mr Mani, when your son is showing signs of a great future, isn't it time for you to consider how the boy's spiritual life is going to be?'

'I am too dazed today.'

'I understand. But sooner or later, the Lord will make a decision for you.'

'His mother is happy with Buddhism right now.'

'But Buddhism is a philosophy, Mr Mani. Christianity is a religion. Christ said everything that Buddha said and much more. Buddha stopped at the Peepal tree. Christ went all the way.'

'Yes, but his mother is . . .'

'I know, I know,' Sister Chastity said. 'I've tried talking to her. She just keeps quiet and pretends to be dumb when I try to give her Christ. Once she told me she felt like a Hindu. What a terrible thing to say! After all the atrocities her ancestors and your ancestors suffered, she still wants to follow that religion.'

'You know how she is,' Ayyan said, trying to look disappointed.

'Yes, yes, but you're a very intelligent man. You are the father of a genius. You have groomed your son so well. Isn't it time you wondered how you are going to support his future?'

'I think I'll manage.'

'Education is very expensive, Mr Mani,' she said making a sorrowful face and leaning back on her chair. 'Christians get discounts. As a financially backward Christian, you will be eligible for many benefits. You know that. I am just saying this as a concerned educator. I am not even implying that you should accept Jesus for the monetary rewards that will certainly come your way if you do that.'

Somewhere in the school, Gloria Fernandes, her throat parched at the very thought of having to teach this class, said in her singsong way, 'Thirteen ones are thirteen.' And the class chanted after her. She kept a cautious eye on a boy in the front row. She had a bad feeling today. 'Thirteen twos are twenty-six,' Gloria said. The boy lifted his hand.

'What is it now, Adi?'

'Why do we learn only the decimal system?' the boy asked. 'Why not the binary system?'

Ayyan Mani stared at the Thought For The Day on the blackboard and was momentarily hypnotized by the power of the written word.

If ancient Indians were really the first to calculate the distance between the Earth and the Moon, why is it that they were not the first to land there? I look at the claims of old civilizations that they have done this and that with great suspicion – Neil Armstrong

Ayyan was tempted to write another invented quote. That would be risky. He usually inserted only one phoney quote every week or so. That way his subversive abuse of the Brahmins would not attract too much attention. But that morning he could not resist the temptation. He pretended to look into a piece of paper and wrote a fresh thought:

Reservations for the low castes in colleges is a very unfair system. To compensate, let us offer the Brahmins the right to be treated as animals for 3,000 years and at the end of it let's give them a 15 per cent reservation – Vallumpuri John

When he turned to leave, he saw Oparna Goshmaulik reading the Thought For The Day. 'Who is Vallumpuri John?' she asked.

Ayyan shook his head and looked up to ascribe blame.

'Dr Acharya cannot be asking you to write the Thought For The Day,' she said, and laughed when she tried to imagine Acharya giving instructions for the daily message. It was a very feminine laughter, heavy with affection, Ayyan thought.

'Not the Director,' he said, 'Administration.' Oparna nodded.

Administration was a word everybody understood here, though nobody knew who it was or where it sat. It was an unseen being, like electricity, that made things work.

She was about to go to the corner stairs leading to the basement when Ayyan asked her, 'Can you read Marathi?' He showed her the paper. 'My son,' he said.

Oparna read with an honest curiosity that made him like her for a passing moment. Her lips silently mumbled some difficult words. Her long earrings, with a small blue globe suspended in each, trembled slightly. And he chose to see nothing more. He did not look at her proud breasts or how the wind was making her thin purple top stick to her flat stomach.

'I can't believe this. I didn't know your boy was a genius,' she said. 'Won't you bring him here?'

At the end of the third-floor corridor, just before the fateful door called Director, was another door. It said 'Deputy Director'. Ayyan knocked twice and opened it. Jana Nambodri, who was in a huddle with five other radio astronomers, looked up with a grimace on his face. It seemed as if they were having a shadowy palm-on-the-candle kind of conference. Ayyan withdrew with an apology, but Nambodri's face swiftly changed into a warm genial emptiness.

'It's all right, come in,' he said.

Ayyan showed him the paper. It was put at the centre of Nambodri's table and since only one of the astronomers could read Marathi, he read the news item aloud. Murmurs of surprise followed. They looked at Ayyan with smiles and mild astonishment. But, clearly, these men were nervous and distracted. Something was about to happen, Ayyan knew.

'Isn't this the same boy who asks his teachers why nothing travels faster than light?' Nambodri asked.

'He does?' someone asked in disbelief.

'Get him here,' Nambodri said, 'Let's have a look at him.' And that was it.

Ayyan went to his corner seat in the anteroom. In the morning odours of old cushion and detergent, a faint haunting smell that usually reminded him of old sorrows, he switched on the various machines around him. He wondered what Nambodri and his men were up to. There was a sense of purpose on their faces. They had done something and were preparing for the consequences. The war against Acharya might have begun. The evangelists of alien signals against a dictator who believed that truth was usually not so dramatic.

Arvind Acharya bumbled down the interminable corridor, suddenly reminded of his daughter in the days after she was born. He would sit at the edge of her mother's bed and stare into the crib. Some days, he would imagine the world through her eyes and he would feel in his heart how long an hour actually was. As a proportion to the fragment of life his daughter had seen, an hour was a vast sprawling place. What appeared to be an hour to him, he calculated then, must have been one thousand five hundred adult hours to her. Time stretched or contracted, depending on who was keeping it. It was a strange enchanting force. In a way, it did not exist unless it was comprehended. And that to him was the key to the Time problem. Time was clearly woven into another force, the force of perception. And perception was the virtue of life alone. So he wondered if life was a fundamental element of the universe like Time itself. This line of thought had many holes, but he enjoyed it. He tried to imagine how a microscopic organism would perceive time. If its lifetime were a second, it would perceive the instant in a very different way from humans. It would live through its life feeling the sheer expanse of the moment, probably even getting bored sometimes.

He realized he was distracted by something, but he did not know what it was. It was a sound, a meek ugly voice that had none of the beauty of the thoughts it sought to abolish.

'Sir,' he heard someone say.

Acharya looked around and he realized he was at his door and a dark man with bright eyes and thick black hair neatly combed sideways was standing there with a newspaper and speaking in the tongue of the defeated landless slaves from another time.

'My son has appeared in the paper, Sir,' Ayyan said in Tamil.

Acharya's mind slowly emerged from the mist and began to understand what was being said. He grabbed the paper from Ayyan.

'It's in Marathi, Sir' Ayyan said.

'I can read Marathi,' Acharya mumbled, and he read. He looked puzzled and asked, 'Your son?'

Ayyan nodded.

'Brilliant,' Acharya said, 'Why haven't the English papers written about this?' The giant read the story again. 'I didn't know there was a Department of Science Education in Switzerland.'

'There is, Sir.'

'Bring him here on Monday.'

'OK, Sir.'

'Take good care of him. Don't ask him to become an engineer or some rubbish like that. Keep your relatives miles away from him. Do you understand?'

'I understand.'

'Let him be. Give him books, a lot of books. You can take anything you want from my shelf. And don't just give him science books. Give him comics, too. If you need anything you let me know. And don't forget, give him a lot of comics.'

A PHONE RANG on Ayyan's desk. It was Acharya on the line. He wanted a print-out of an email. This was a routine instruction. Acharya preferred to read letters the old-fashioned way and had given Ayyan his email password – Lavanya123. The dedication of passwords was the new fellowship of marriage. To each other, couples had become furtive asterisks. Nothing else had changed about marriages of course.

He printed the email of a man called Richard Smoot. In the subject line was the cryptic message – Qb3. At the start of the correspondence between the two, Ayyan did not understand the messages in the subject lines which carried codes like Nf3, a6 or something similar. Then he realized that when Smoot had sent his first mail enquiring about the possibility of Acharya delivering a lecture in New York, he had written e4 in the subject slot – the notation of a chess opening. It was customary, Ayyan eventually learnt, for some eggheads to mark the beginning of a dialogue, e4. Acharya, when he replied to the letter seeking further information about the lecture invitation, wrote e5 in the subject slot. Apparently, e5 was black's traditional response to white's e4. Smoot responded with the profiles of other speakers who had accepted the invitation, marking the subject as Nf3. Smoot's knight was now attacking Acharya's pawn. Acharya responded with Nf6 in the subject line. And now, the two insane men were not only in the middle of a long correspondence but also a fully fledged chess match.

A peon walked in and dropped a solitary courier letter on Ayyan's desk. 'For the Big Man,' the peon said. 'Mani,' he then said in a whisper, 'I need a residence proof. I'm applying for a job in the Gulf. I've to make a passport now.'

Ayyan appeared thoughtful. 'I've a friend who can help,' he said. 'Give me exactly two days.'

After the peon left, Ayyan studied the courier. It said in the bottom left-hand corner, 'Ministry of Defence'. The Institute of Theory and Research came under the Ministry of Defence because it was originally created to conceive the Indian nuclear programme. The Institute eventually wrangled out of the programme, claiming that nuclear physics was an obsolete science and of too much practical use to enthrall the poetic hearts of theoretical physicists. But the Ministry of Defence continued to fund the Institute.

Ayyan toyed with the envelope. There was something about it. Though the Ministry sent most of its communications through email these days, it occasionally sent courier mail and speedposts. In the canteen, Ayyan had heard impassioned discussions of scientists on whether there was a hidden physical law that governed what the Ministry chose to email and what it chose to courier. They could not find a decisive pattern. But it was generally considered that bad news was almost always couriered.

Ayyan had a stock of blank envelopes marked Ministry of Defence in the bottom drawer. He usually opened Acharya's official courier mail, read the letters, relocated them in fresh envelopes, recreated clerical scribbles and stapled back the receipts. He studied the latest arrival for another minute before opening it.

The letter was from Bhaskar Basu, a powerful Delhi bureaucrat in the Ministry of Defence who had once perilously tried to establish control over the Institute. He did not believe that scientists should be allowed to manage the Institute. Managing was the job of bureaucrats. But in that meeting when he had tried to wrest control, according to a legend, after Basu made an elaborate presentation about his future plans, there was a long uncomfortable silence which Acharya broke with a calm observation, 'But you graduated in sociology.' He had said nothing more, but the meeting had collapsed.

Dr Arvind Acharya [the letter began],

I hope this finds you in good health. Allow me to take your time to address a serious matter. I am deeply disturbed by your unofficial ban on the search for extraterrestrial intelligence (Seti). I have studied the complaints from several highly regarded scientists of the Institute and come to the conclusion that they have been unfairly treated. I also believe that an Indian search for extraterrestrials will greatly add to the prestige of the country. The Ministry has come to the decision, after due consultation with the Minister himself, that the Institute may start a Seti programme which will have a departmental status and an independent budget. It will be headed by Dr Jana Nambodri. Also, Dr Nambodri is being given complete charge of the Giant Ear. As he is a pre-eminent radio astronomer, it has been decided, he will have total freedom in deciding what projects the array of giant metre-wave radio telescopes will be used for and the distribution of their usage time to external agencies. For administrative convenience, and to spare you the trouble of supervising this small matter, we have relieved Dr Nambodri of the responsibility of reporting to you as far as the operation of the Giant Ear is concerned. This move is part of the Ministry's ongoing efforts to synergize the various research programmes that it funds. A formal letter will follow. I am in Mumbai tomorrow to meet you and the new Seti team in this regard. I hope to see you at eleven.

Ayyan folded the letter and put it in a fresh envelope. He checked the voluminous dictionary for the meaning of the word 'synergize'. It was not the first time he had looked up the word, but despite many attempts he never fully comprehended its meaning. Once more he tried to understand, but gave up. He got the full import of the letter though. It was a major breach. The authority of Arvind Acharya was being challenged. The first arrow had arrived. The excitement of being in the best seat to watch the duel filled him. He decided that whatever happened in his life, he would take no time off in the coming days. The clash of the Brahmins, an entertainment that even his forefathers enjoyed in different ways in different times and had recounted in jubilant folk songs that they once used to sing beneath the stars, was now coming to the Institute.

Nambodri was not a man who went to battle unless he knew he was going to win. This was because he was a coward. Acharya, on the other hand, did not know how to fight small men who were, probably, the rightful inheritors of an office, any office. But he had that terrifying quality called stature, something that his colleagues, of their own accord, had granted him. From what Ayyan had heard of the battles of the Brahmins, it would be bloodless but brutal. They would fight like demons armed with nothing more than deceit and ideals – another form of deceit among men from good families.

Ayyan went into the inner chamber with the letter. He placed it carefully in a vacant island in the sea of papers on the table.

'From the Ministry,' he said.

Acharya did not look up. Twenty minutes later, he opened the letter. He read it just once and put it in the large bin that was nearly as tall as the table. He turned to the window and stared at the sea.

Ayyan entered with some files to check if Acharya had read the letter. The envelope was missing from the desk and Acharya's face no longer wore its customary peaceful expression. His eyes were burning in the glow of the setting sun.

When Ayyan went back to the anteroom, the mobile phone on his desk was ringing. He could barely recognize the voice of Oja at the other end.

'He burnt her,' she said, crying, 'he burnt her.' She was calling from a phone booth outside BDD. Through the background noise of horns and the laughter of men, Ayyan could hear her desperate gasps for breath.

It seared him always, the sorrow of his Oja. She said that a boy from Thane had come home with the news that Gauri had been burnt by her husband. Gauri was a cousin she had grown up with. The violence of subsidized kerosene that Oja's mother had once feared might be the fate of her daughter had consumed another woman. Ayyan knew that woman. He had been to her wedding. She was an unremarkable girl who laughed a lot. He remembered her face through the red hood of her cheap bridal sari. She had tried not to giggle throughout her wedding. She was then consigned to a life of severe beatings, and now this. Two hours ago, she had died of severe burns in a government hospital. Her body was still in the morgue. Oja did not want to go there. She said she did not want to know how a woman looked after she was burnt. It was something every girl she knew had nightmares about when they were growing up.

'Some people say that after you are burnt the face looks white, not black – that is if there is any face left,' she said into the phone, and fell silent. She had nothing more to say, but she did not want to put the phone down. He could hear her breathing.

The main door opened and two scientists walked in. They were in the middle of a loud discussion.

'When these correction terms become large, there is no space–time geometry that is guaranteed to describe the result,' one man said. The other responded, 'Yes I agree, the equations for determining the space–time geometry become impossible to solve except under very strict symmetry conditions. But my point is . . .' He looked at Ayyan impatiently and pointed to Acharya's door. 'We have an appointment,' he said, with a frown, probably annoyed because the impudent clerk was talking on his mobile.

Ayyan picked up the land phone and put it on his other ear 'Sir, Dr Sinha and Dr Murthy are here.'

The voice of Acharya growled back, 'I am not meeting anyone today.'

In his other ear Ayyan heard Oja say something, but in the chaos around the phone booth where she was standing and the debate of the men in front of him, he could not make out what she was trying to tell him. 'And this is a hint that perhaps space–time geometry is not something fundamental in string theory, but something that emerges in the theory at large-distance scales or weak coupling,' one of the men was saying.

'I will go now, I think you have a lot of work,' said Oja, very faintly.

'Hello,' said Ayyan, but the line had gone dead.

He put his mobile in the drawer and looked at these men on

the ancient leather sofa, so wise and comfortable in their austere clothes.

One of them was saying, 'The curvature of the universe, according to Harrison, will be confirmed in our lifetime and I think that is a very important statement. It is nice to know that there are some people who are looking beyond the Collider.'

Ayyan now found these men more unreal than he could ever have imagined. And they were repulsive. He went to the inner door. Acharya was gazing thoughtfully through his window.

'Sir, they insist on meeting you right now.'

Acharya took his eyes off the window and glared at the table for an instant. Then he walked to his door, flung it open with brute force and yelled at the waiting men who were in the middle of describing the curvature of the universe, 'Get out, get out. Right now. Get out.'

The string theorists jumped. They looked confused and hurt, but they walked away without a word.

Deep inside himself, Ayyan roared with laughter. It showed on his face in a faint twitch at the edge of his lips.

Acharya returned to his chair and continued his sullen survey of the Arabian Sea. He sat like that for over an hour and then he felt an indefinable pain that he recognized as a familiar sorrow. Slowly, he understood what it was: Lavanya. Her eyesight was failing and there was a stent in her heart too. But why was he thinking about her? Yes, at six, he had to take her to the hospital. The driver was not coming in today and so he had to drive. There was something funereal about it, he thought: an old man driving his old woman to the hospital. Something very lonely about it. Something very sad and American. He got up and steered his trousers around his waist.

At the end of the main driveway of the Professors' Quarters there was a hard-surface tennis court. An instructor was coaching three little girls who were in frilled tennis skirts. He was gently lobbing the ball across the net to them. One of the girls was bored with the proceedings. She began to pick up jasmine flowers that had fallen on the clay court, and she arranged them on the fading baseline.

Lavanya was watching her. She was reminded of Shruti who was now a married woman and many worlds away. She felt deserted that moment, but was comforted by the thought of her husband who would soon come bumbling down the driveway. She was in the shade of a neem tree, and leaning against an ancient sky-blue Fiat – a relic that was misunderstood in the Quarters as a symbol of Acharya's simple ways. The truth was that he had neither the money nor the patience to sell his ancestral lands and buy a new car with the loose change. There was a time when she used to tell him, almost every day, that he should sell off the worthless fields and that monstrous house in Sivagangai which was haunted by the ghosts of her in-laws.

She looked at her watch. It was time, but she knew she did not have to call him. It was very strange how he forgot just about everything else but always remembered her hospital appointments. There he appeared at the gate and walked down the driveway, exactly the way she had imagined. He was an old man now, she thought, and for some reason that made her laugh.

Acharya did not say anything to her. That was not unusual. They got into the car and drove in silence. Taxis broke lanes and crossed his path, singing cyclists almost died under his tyres and gave him self-righteous glares before resuming their songs, buses were at his bumper and pedestrians stood in the middle of the road waiting to cross the other half, but Acharya's blood pressure did not rise.

'This country has become a video game,' he said. He did not speak for the rest of the journey.

When they reached the Breach Candy Hospital, he got out of the car, locked the doors and went into the porch. At the reception, he realized that he had left something in the car. He went back, muttering to himself. Lavanya was sitting inside the car with a calm expression on her face.

'You can open it from inside,' he told her.

'I know,' she said, as she struggled out of the vehicle.

'Then why didn't you do it?' he asked angrily. 'Why are you being dramatic?'

'I am being dramatic?'

'I know I forgot you in the car. So?'

'So nothing. It happens. Did I say anything?'

That night, after they returned from the hospital, Acharya could not sleep. He stood on the long, narrow balcony and looked at the dark sea and at the heavens above. It was a moonless summer night and he could see the stars. Once, he knew them intimately and by their names. Some people wanted the excitement of searching for signals from those faraway places. They were not romantic men who had the endearing desperation of a child. They were rotting scientists who were stranded in mediocrity, who had slogged for years in radio astronomy and had found no glory. They wanted the easy fame of a dramatic nonsense. They were willing to go to war with him for that. He knew how to fight them. Another battle, he thought. And he felt tired.

SEVEN MEN WERE gathered around the oval table. In the silence of an unnerving wait, they could hear the hum of the air conditioning. They were waiting for something to pass. Every time there was the slightest sound outside, they would look up at the closed door and return to a wait that they knew would soon end.

The door opened, and an almost perceptible wave of fear and anticipation went through the room. But when they saw Oparna Goshmaulik there was relief. She sat down, wondering who had died. 'Thanks for coming,' Nambodri said, the exhilaration of seeing her subdued by the heaviness of the moment.

She raised her eyebrows to ask what it was all about.

'You will soon know,' he said.

A few minutes later Bhaskar Basu walked in. He was a trim tidy man who suspected that he was good-looking. His jovial grey hair was distant cousin to Nambodri's radiant aureole. The frames of his spectacles were thick and artistic. Behind the glasses, his narrow eyes looked shrewd and capable. Asshole, Oparna guessed.

Basu's searching eyes, inevitably, rested on her. He asked Nambodri, 'Won't you introduce us?'

Oparna did not understand this peculiar habit of Indian men. If they could letch at her so overtly, they might as well ask her directly who she was. Why did they always turn to someone else and say, 'Won't you introduce us?' It was so pathetic.

'Oparna Goshmaulik,' Nambodri said, 'Head of Astrobiology.'

‘A Bengali girl,’ Basu said, a light coming to his face as if an inner bulb had switched on. He said something to her in Bangla and she tried to respond with something approaching a polite smile.

Basu turned self-important and stylish. He leaned back in his chair and broke the silence of the scientists around him.

‘Don’t worry, I am going to take care of it. I am here now,’ he said. ‘The old man is not here yet? I think we should call him.’

‘He will come,’ Nambodri said dryly. He feared that the presence of Oparna was inspiring the bureaucrat to assume a certain coolness that could be suicidal. Acharya, if slighted, was capable of flinging a paperweight at the offender. Oparna was in that room because Nambodri wanted her to witness the first tremors of a shift in the balance of power, and also to disrupt the Balloon Mission. But he was beginning to regret the move. Basu was getting carried away.

Basu launched into the structure of the new Seti department, even though the radio astronomers had already been briefed. When he spoke, he kept glancing at Oparna, who decided that she would toy with her mobile. He eventually fell silent because he had nothing more to say and everybody was looking grim and distracted anyway. The brooding wait resumed: all ears were listening for the door.

When Arvind Acharya walked in, one of the scientists stood up on impulse, thereby greatly ruining the ‘aggressive position’ Nambodri had said they should take. Acharya sat between two radio astronomers who looked more keenly at the table than they really needed to. Nambodri was disturbed by his old friend’s calm. He knew something was wrong.

‘Thanks for coming,’ Basu said, with a gracious smile. ‘Let me now . . .’

Acharya held up his hand to him and said, ‘Shut up.’

Basu’s elegant face appeared to lose size. He tried to form words. ‘Excuse me? I don’t understand,’ he said, looking severe. ‘What do you mean by that?’

Acharya consulted his watch.

'I don't understand this.' Basu raised his voice.

'Do you understand everything, usually?' Acharya asked. There was something about the way he said it, with the deep serenity of an ancient pedagogue, that brought about another silence.

The radio astronomers looked at each other. Acharya consulted his watch again. There was the sound of a mobile phone vibrating in silent mode. It was a persistent spasmodic screech. Basu reached for his coat and took out his mobile. He saw the number and went to a corner of the room.

'Yes, Sir. Yes, Sir,' the astronomers heard him say with a sinking feeling.

'Yes, Sir. Yes, Sir,' Basu said many times. It was a private dialect of bureaucracy, and it had no other words.

When Basu put the phone back in his coat pocket, Nambodri knew the revolution was over. Basu sank into his chair looking pale.

'Dr Acharya,' he said, 'the Minister has asked me to apologize for any inconvenience this may have caused you. We are dropping our proposal to start a Seti department and the matter will not be broached as long as you are opposed to it.'

Basu rubbed his nose during the pause and continued, somewhat pathetically, 'I hope you understand my efforts were in the best interest of science. I really believed that the search for extraterrestrial intelligence is a very important step forward. I thought it had defence implications too. I may have been wrong, but I hope you will get inside my mind and see the . . .'

'I have been inside your mind,' Acharya said. 'It was a short journey.'

Basu left the room first. Oparna followed. The radio astronomers then rose, one after the other, and left the room in a funereal procession. Only Acharya and Nambodri were left. They sat still, the officious parabola of the oval table between them. Nambodri was smiling. The smile reminded Acharya of the arrack drinkers who used to fall defeated in the paddyfields of his childhood.

'I thought you were beyond office politics,' Nambodri said, 'but it looks as if you have learnt a few things from the little men, as you call us. I forgot how famous you are, Arvind. Who did you call? The PM? The President? Who did you call?'

'I want you out, Jana.'

Acharya felt sorry for this old man who did not know he was old, with whom he had spent many summers of his youth in a cold distant land, when together they had so much hope for each other and the world.

'What do you want, you bastard?' Acharya asked, almost in anguish.

'What do I want?' Nambodri said, with a sad chuckle. 'I just want to search for extraterrestrial intelligence, Arvind. It's very simple. What do you want?'

'I want scientists in my institute to work on real science. If radio astronomers here are bored with pulsars, then they must quit and grow rubber on their fathers' hills. Not chase alien signals.'

'We have been saying the same things to each other for a long, long time,' Nambodri said, 'like two people in a bad marriage.'

'Tell me something,' Acharya said, in a tone that was remarkably kind. 'Do you really believe you are going to find a signal from an advanced alien civilization?'

'There is no reason why we shouldn't.'

'That's not what I asked. Do you believe you will? What do you believe? Remember the word "belief"? That thing you had when you were twenty? What exactly do you believe? When you wake up in the morning, what do you know is certainly true?'

'Not all of us are meant to believe, Arvind. Some of us can only wonder and, on good days, hope. Do you really believe that all life on Earth came from outer space?'

'Yes. I don't just believe. I know.'

'Through microscopic spores that came riding on comets and meteorites?'

'Yes,' Acharya said peacefully. 'And you know what? I also

believe that these spores fall on different worlds in different corners of the universe and they spawn life that is suited to those conditions. Life that could be vastly different from what we can imagine. Life that could even evolve into giant zero-mass beings. Like massive clouds. Things we cannot even imagine.'

'Why don't you go public on this hypothesis then?'

'It is not a hypothesis,' Acharya said softly. 'It's a theory.'

In the Institute, a hypothesis was a good idea, but a theory was a good idea that deserved funds.

Acharya rose from the chair, holding his left knee for an instant. When he reached the door, he heard a sad voice ask, 'Is there a way I can stay on, Arvind?'

Ayyan Mani was furious. The war of the Brahmins had ended so fast. And ended in the banal way in which medieval no-talent writers finished their moral fables – the great triumphing over the petty. The loss of anticipation deepened the grimness of his routine and he was filled with the fatigue of an unbearable boredom. When Oparna stood by his desk and asked to see Acharya, he did not even look at her. He just made a call and sent her in.

She entered the den, as usual, wondering why she could hear her heart every time she saw this man and if this fear had more disturbing names.

'I came here to tell you that I didn't know why I was called to that meeting,' she said. 'I don't want you to think that I am part of what they tried to do this morning.'

'I know,' Acharya said. She stood there in the vain hope that he would ask her to sit down and tell her how unfortunate it was that she was caught in the middle of all this, or maybe they could talk about the balloon that they would soon send to the stratosphere. But he was reading.

After she left the room, Acharya tried to remember something. He had told himself that he would recall it later, but he could not place the moment. Then it came to him: it was when he had seen Oparna in the conference room, he had felt something. It was like a stab, a trivial feeling of betrayal and then a more elaborate agony as though she had died and left him alone. He was not surprised that he thought of her death. Everybody died, the young especially. But why should her death make him feel deserted? He considered the matter for a few seconds, but then his mind drifted to the triumph of remembering it. Nowadays, problems that he scheduled for the future never returned to him.

The fumes glowed in the car lights, and they cast giant fleeting shadows of pedestrians in the air. In the vapours of the late evening traffic, cars and trucks lay stranded on the lane as if they were all trying to flee from an approaching calamity. Heads peered out of the windows. Long lines of honking vehicles melded and expanded until, somewhere ahead, they became a huge unmoving knot of metal and smoke. In the heart of the jam was a black Honda City, its bumper torn off. A girl whose navel was pierced by a glimmer of silver, and whose small pink T-shirt said in gold 'Skinny Bitch', was standing in a daze. Her hands were spread out, and she said in English, several times, the same thing: 'What the freaking hell?'

An abandoned taxi was still kissing the rear of her car. A dark man, who must have been the cab driver, was standing facing her in the middle of the road, sheepish and giggling. People on the pavement looked on in glee. A man who was sitting on his haunches and watching the fun screamed, 'Now look at *her* bumper.' Ayyan walked through the situation with a serene smile.

A few metres ahead was a barber's called Headmaster, and next to it was a restaurant with aluminium-topped tables and wooden chairs. At the entrance, Ayyan spotted Thambe, the tiny man to whom he had handed an envelope full of notes on the Worli Seaface. They sat at a table and ordered tea. 'The article was great,' Ayyan said. 'My boy is so happy.'

'I hope other papers pick it up,' Thambe said, flapping his thighs. He stopped a waiter to ask if there was a toilet in the restaurant. The waiter shook his head.

Thambe was a reporter with *Yug*, and one of those hectic men who did things that did not have a name. He could bring back lost licences, create ration-cards, and he knew the mobile numbers of government clerks.

'You really did a beautiful job of my son's achievement,' Ayyan said.

'I believe that brilliant boys like your son have to be supported,' Thambe said, pouring his tea into the saucer.

'Has anybody from the English papers contacted you about my son?'

'No,' the reporter said. 'The English reporters are such snobs. They never follow up anything we do.'

'I see. You know, Thambe, it would have been nice if you had put him on the front page. After all, a ten-year-old boy winning a contest like that is no small achievement.'

'I know. But the front page,' Thambe said, smiling sadly, 'is very expensive, Mani.'

'How expensive?'

'Oh, it's beyond us. I don't even go there. It is for big people.'

'Your editor knows that you . . . you help friends?'

'You are asking me if the editor knows if I take money to write? Be direct. We are friends now. Of course he knows. You know how much my salary is? Eight hundred rupees. When he hired me, he said, "We don't pay much." Then he took out a press card with my photograph on it and said, "Now go out into the market and make whatever you want."'

They drank their tea silently. Then the reporter said, 'I have to go now. So if . . .' Ayyan took out his wallet and counted some notes.

'This is for friendship,' he said, as he handed the cash to Thambe. 'The advance I gave you, that too was for our friendship.'

'Friendship, of course,' the reporter said. His face turned serious as he counted the notes. It was the same serious face, Ayyan remembered, that descended on the great minds of the Institute when they counted cash.

'Friendship is everything,' Thambe said, somehow finding space for the notes in his shirt pocket, which was already bulging. 'I took your word, Mani. You said your son won the contest, I believed you. No questions asked. That's friendship.'

'Is there a way such a friendship can get English papers to write about my son?'

On his way back home, a familiar gloom filled Ayyan. There was no getting away from it. He tried to fight it by imagining the face of Oja Mani, how jubilant she had looked when Adi's teacher had sent the first frantic note about the boy's insubordinate brilliance. But the gloom only grew into an acidic fear in his stomach. Fear worried him because it reminded him that life was not always a familiar place. This game he was playing was far bigger than the other plots of his life. The game, this time, was his son.

The rise of Adi as a child genius had begun about a year ago when Ayyan had gone home late one evening and Oja had opened the door with tears in her eyes and a deep joyous smile that made him suspect that her demented mother had finally won a lottery.

'My son got 100 per cent in the maths test,' Oja had said. 'There are forty-two boys in his class. All fair and rich and fat. My son was the only one who got 100 per cent.'

Oja, who usually stared blankly at him without ambition or hope, and sometimes in the sorrow of being stranded in a humid hell, was so ecstatic that only tears could release the joy. That night he had taken Adi out for ice-cream. When they were walking down the Worli Seaface he heard the boy mutter the name of every car that was parked or was passing by. He had merely to look at a car, its front or its rear, and he would know its make. It seemed exceptional, but Ayyan knew there was nothing there more than a simple streak of smartness that most children possessed. He had heard a thousand times men chatting in the train about the brilliance of their children – 'My son is just three but he knows how to turn on the computer and send emails. He is a genius.' Or, 'My daughter is ten but she knows the names of all the lakes in the world.' It was in that way that Adi was smart. 'City, Ambassador, Zen, Esteem, City,' the boy was saying on the promenade. The vigilant mind of Ayyan began to think of a simple plot, to achieve nothing more than some fun and a distraction from the inescapable miseries of BDD.

From that night, he drew Adi into a pact. 'Our secret,' he would tell his son, and make him memorize questions that he should ask his teachers. Ayyan devised simple questions, like, 'What is gravity made of, Miss?' Or, 'Why are leaves green?' He asked Adi to raise these questions any time during the class, never mind the context. 'It'll be fun,' he told his son.

At first, the boy's questions in the class seemed endearing. Teachers found him cute and, of course, bright and curious. Slowly, Adi's questions became more complex: 'If plants can eat light, why aren't there things that eat sound?' Or, when he heard a cue word like 'ocean', he would yell in the class, 'The average depth of the ocean is 3.7 kilometres, why aren't lakes so deep?' When his teachers, still enamoured with his oddness, tried to engage him in a conversation about light, or sound, or the ocean, Adi clammed up because he did not know anything beyond what his father had taught him. But his silence did not surprise the staff. He was, after all, just a little boy. An odd, laconic little boy who was also partially deaf.

When it all began, Adi used to mumble to his mother about having a secret pact with his father, but she dismissed it as the prattle between father and son. In time, Adi began to enjoy the attention he was receiving at school. He began to understand that he was considered extraordinary, and not 'special' which was what they called the handicapped. He began to attach a certain importance to the pact with his father and even understood the reason why it had to be a secret. He vaguely knew that his mother would not tolerate the game he and his father were playing, and her opposition would deprive him of the status he was beginning to be granted in school.

He looked forward to disrupting every class. The disruptions began to annoy his teachers. They were increasingly baffled by his questions. They began to write notes in his handbook summoning his parents, and that created moments of fear and entertainment at home. Oja was concerned, but she was also excited by the prospects of a genius. 'I want him to be normal,' she would say, but she told everyone about his brilliance. She circled fire around his face and stained his cheek with black powder to exterminate the evil eye. The myth of a child genius was surprisingly simple to create, Ayyan realized, especially around a boy who was innately smart and who wore a hearing-aid. Adi had simply to say something odd in the class once a week to keep the legend alive.

It was easy and it was fun, but Ayyan wanted something more. So he arranged for the fictitious news item about Adi. It was still simple. The whole game could be called off at any moment. It had to end some day anyway. And it had to end before they got caught. He believed in his heart that he could get away with it. He found some comfort in the fact that he was not the first person to create the myth of genius around his child. There were people, mothers especially, who had spun far greater yarns. He had once read the incredible story of a French girl called Minou Drouet, a name he could somehow never pronounce. She published her poems when she was just eight. Her poems stunned the giants of French literature until some people began to say that it was her mother who was writing them. Little Minou was tested. She was asked to write poems in front of people. And she did. But the whole matter was never resolved. Even today people did not know if she were a child prodigy or her mother's fraud. Then there was another girl, a Russian child called Natasha Demkina, whose mother claimed that the girl had X-ray vision. Many doctors even confirmed that Natasha had that ability, but there were many who said she was a fraud. Ayyan wanted to meet those marvellous mothers. He believed he understood them, and understood why they did what they did.

But he would not go too far. His game would end soon. It troubled him sometimes, the readiness with which his son was playing the game. Some days, Ayyan noticed that the boy chose to forget that it was all just a game. He believed that he truly was a genius. He loved the word. He mentioned it in his sleep.

The innocent face of Oja, in the glow of her overnight turmeric treatments and the illusion of a sudden extraordinary life, haunted Ayyan. She must never know the truth because she would never forgive him. The lies he had told her had already taken root and created a fable in her mind. It was too late to retract them. She must live with those lies forever. It frightened him, the thought of living with a woman for a whole lifetime without telling her that he had once fooled her. Even though he survived the world through unambiguous practicality, he believed that a man's bond with his wife should not be corrupted by too much rationality. Marriage needed the absurdity of values. In the world that lay outside his home, there was no right or wrong. Every moment was a battle, and the cunning won. But his home was not something as trivial as the world. To fool Oja into believing that her son was a genius was a crime, a crime so grave that it did not have a punishment. But the game was also a magnificent lure. He loved it.

That's what frightened him. Despite his own disgust at the cruelty of the myth he was creating around his son, Ayyan feared that he might not be able to stop. He was falling into the intoxication of the game, its excitement that was so potent. He thought of his alcoholic brothers, in whose eyes he had once seen the desperation to live, but who could not escape the powerful addiction that triumphed over the spirit of life. The thrill of erecting the story of a boy genius and the tales that drew his small family in a cosy huddle in their one-room home – he did not want to lose all that. Because that was all they had. So, what must a man do?

An ordinary man wants his wife to feel the excitement of life. Ayyan had been born into poverty that no human should have to endure; he absorbed the rudiments of knowledge under the municipality's lights; he learnt the guile to feed himself and his family; and he was now stranded because there is only so far that the son of a sweeper can go. Ayyan had no exceptional talent, but he was bright enough to see so clearly the futility of hope and the grimness of an unremarkable life ahead. So what must a man do? Without the sport of his son's genius, Ayyan knew that the routine of his life would eventually suffocate him. The future, otherwise, was all too predictable. He would type letters for the Brahmins, take their calls and suffer their pursuit of truth. Then, every single day of his life, he would climb the steep colonial steps of BDD, wade through its undead, and find refuge in the perfunctory love of a woman who did not really look at him any more. He would live out his whole life, so unspeakably ordinary, in a one-room home that was a hundred and eighty square feet (including the illicit loft).

Ayyan began to walk briskly now because that always abolished his sorrows and fears. He appeared so purposeful when he entered the BDD chawls that the defeated eyes of drunken men on the broken walkways looked at him with envy. Here, a man with purpose was a fortunate man. He went through the yellow walls of the top floor and felt the stares from the open doors. Children were playing and screaming on the corridor. Dreamless women combed their hair slowly. Silent widows, ancient and bent, sat on the doorways, their gazes transfixed at a past.

As he passed through the open doors of the corridor he caught voices of the lives in every cell. A woman was saying that she would never buy onions again, he did not know why. Next door, a peon had just returned from work and was sharing a leftover cake he had pinched from someone's birthday party in the office. Further down, a man was asking for the price of a Maruti Zen on his mobile. These were voices he usually heard. But then, he heard a language that was alien to him. He heard a mother slap her boy. He yelled. Then she gave him a whack on his back. The boy ran out into the corridor patting his mouth, and he sprinted to and fro as if trying to dodge his own pain. So far, there was nothing unusual. Then Ayyan heard the woman scream above the boy's wails, 'Do your homework, or I will kill you.'

That, he had never heard in this place before. What Oja had told him was true then. Ever since Adi appeared in the newspaper, mothers, especially in this block, had gone insane. They were belting their sons and making them study, while Oja was buying kites, cricket bats and comics for her son in the fear that he might otherwise become more abnormal than he already was.

After dinner, the three of them went to the tar-coated terrace. There were several dim figures ambling beneath the half-moon. From the distant shadows, a solitary drunkard sang of love and liberation. Adolescent girls stood in groups and giggled at the boys. The boys, pale and scrawny, were in an excited state and they indulged in mock fights among themselves to attract the attention of the girls. Oja mingled with the young mothers who were also in their nighties, which bore the indelible stains of turmeric and chilli. The women looked at Oja with affection or malice – Ayyan could never tell which – but they looked at her more carefully than before. And Oja had developed a certain grace, a sort laboured modesty that Miss World affected when she visited children with cancer.

Ayyan held the index finger of his son and went towards an isolated corner. He pretended to study his phone to escape old friends. They still came to him, but though Ayyan smiled and greeted them, he never took his eyes off the phone.

Adi spotted a tennis ball stuck in a drain. He looked around to see if anyone else had noticed it. He tried to extricate his finger from his father's grip, but it would not release. He pulled hard, but he was not strong enough. They were laughing now, father and son. Adi tried to bite his father's hand, but even that didn't help. 'Let me go,' he said.

'Say, "Supernova",' he heard his father say. That made Adi forget the ball. He loved this game.

'Supernova,' his father said.

'Supernova,' Adi said. 'Easy.'

'How do stars die, Miss?' Ayyan said in English.

'How do stars die, Miss?'

'How do stars die, Miss, apart from becoming supernovas?'

'How do stars die, Miss, apart from becoming supernovas?'

'How do stars die, Miss, apart from becoming supernovas?'

'How do stars die, Miss, apart from supernovas?'

'Apart from becoming supernovas?'

'How do stars die, Miss, apart from becoming supernovas?'

'Bright boy.'

Adi extricated himself from his father and went to take the ball that was stuck in the mouth of the drain. He looked around innocently before he crouched and pulled the ball out. He played with it for some time. Then he said to his father, 'I like prime numbers.'

Ayyan ignored him.

'I like prime numbers because they cannot be predicted,' Adi said, in a casual, conversational sort of way.

'You don't have to talk to me like that, Adi.'

'Like how?'

'Like how you are talking right now about prime numbers.'

'I like prime numbers because they cannot be predicted.'

'It's OK, Adi, you don't have to talk like that with me. We play the game only sometimes. Not all the time. You understand?'

PART THREE

Basement Item

OPARNA GOSHMAULIK FOUND it funny. That the curtain was blood-red, that it went up in somnolent folds, and that there was a silence of anticipation all around. All this drama at an event where the guest lecturer had promised to speak on the 'Interpretations of Quantum Mechanics'. Even the lights were dimming now. The Talks had begun. It was an annual event in honour of departing research scholars, the Institute's version of a convocation ceremony but without the black gowns or the precondition that the scholars should now get out into the real world.

The auditorium was full. There were silhouettes on the aisles. Scores of people were outside the doors, denied entry, denied the Interpretations of Quantum Mechanics. And they were disconsolate. She could hear their angry demands to be allowed to at least sit in the aisles. But then even the aisles were filled. This was a strange parallel world.

There was a deafening applause now. On the stage appeared an amicable white man, and Arvind Acharya. The two men sat on cane chairs in the centre of an illuminated circle. The sheer expanse of the stage was fit for ballet but the Institute allowed only lectures. A pretty girl, somewhat preoccupied with her long straight hair, arrived at the podium. 'Look at my hair, look at my hair,' Oparna thought she was going to say, but instead the girl said, 'Science is an evolution of the human mind. It is the true history of mankind.' After a few lines like this she said that the men on the stage needed no introduction and then she introduced them. The girl was not from the Institute and Oparna wondered where the men had found her. She remembered Jana Nambodri asking her if she could introduce the guests and hand out the bouquets too. 'We need some beauty out there', he had said. She had refused because she had felt like refusing him. Also, even though she understood the banality of men and the aesthetic improvements a woman would bring to an occasion like this, she was privately against women being used as ceremonial dolls. And, for reasons that were not clear to her then, she wanted to look at Acharya from a comfortable seat in the shelter of darkness.

His initial geniality had vanished. His red cheeks were now molten, his infant bald head shone under the lights and he was surveying the audience in dismay. Keeble rose from his cane chair and went to the podium. He drank two glasses of water. He was a tall slender man, elderly and pleasant. 'It is a pleasure to speak to a gathering like this,' he said, and then looking at Acharya, he added, 'a bit intimidating too.'

A gentle hush of laughter went through the auditorium. Some laughed aloud late to show that they understood the joke. Keeble began his lecture. Oparna endured the Interpretations of Quantum Mechanics by observing what Acharya did throughout the speech. He would open his mouth in a trance or glare at the roof, or signal to someone for a glass of water, or a faint smirk would come to his face at something Keeble had said.

At one point, he was looking angrily at Keeble, and she felt nervous. She hoped he wouldn't do anything stupid. Keeble was talking about Time and was coming to the perilous conclusion: 'Though Stephen Hawking had misgivings about what he had said earlier, I am of the opinion that the arrow of Time moves both ways. In some conditions we would remember the future and not the past, and a ripple would cause a stone to fall. Time can be reversed.'

Acharya's deep operatic voice exclaimed, 'Not possible.' He said it again, this time softly. 'Not possible.'

Keeble looked a bit embarrassed, but the spontaneous gasp of the audience, then the laughter and the festive murmurs that ensued, diminished the shock. Also, there was no malice in the voice that had spoken. Acharya's comment somehow invoked the spirit of science and everybody understood it that way.

'We will talk about it later, Arvind,' Keeble said jovially. 'Maybe we can meet yesterday, if you have the time.'

When Acharya eventually rose to speak, and steered his trousers around his waist, Oparna laughed. A studious stranger sitting next to her looked at her curiously before returning his expectant eyes to the stage. Acharya walked like a tusker to the podium. Oparna felt the world around her quietening. There was then a silence that was eerie and total. It was broken by the squeal of the mike when he tapped it gently.

'I like Henry Keeble very much and so it hurts me to say that the end of quantum physics is near,' he said, his voice manly and powerful. Yet, innocent, rude and pure. 'The Large Hadron Collider will confirm that many exotic particles do not actually exist and that many among us may have been talking rubbish for the last three decades. Maybe we cannot understand physics at the quantum level without understanding other things which are not considered physics today. Other things like . . .' He paused. He appeared to decide if he must say it. He did not say it.

'I believe it is time for a new kind of physics to arrive,' he said. 'Honestly, I don't know what this new physics will look like. Anyway, I am too old for that revolution. Maybe someone in this auditorium will one day bring it to us. But this is not what I want to talk about today.

'There are research students here who will be leaving us this year. They will be pursuing their interests in other universities. I came here, primarily, to tell you something. Go with the knowledge that man has just scratched the surface. It is a very impressive scratch and we must be proud. But there is a lot, a lot of things, to be done. I wish I were as old as you now, at this time. There is so much to do. But I have no tips on what you must do. In fact, I came here to say what you must never do. There is no pleasant way to say this, so let me say it the way I want to say it. Most of you will probably never really discover anything. You may not contribute anything to the great equations that describe the universe to the world. But you will have the good fortune of encountering people of exceptional intelligence. People who are much smarter than you. Never get in their way, never group together in disgruntled circles and play games. Respect talent, real talent. Worship it. Clever people will always be disliked. Don't exploit that and crawl your way to the top. By the laws of probability most of you are mediocre. Accept it. The tragedy of mediocrity is that even mediocre people shake their heads and mull over how 'standards are falling'. So don't mull. Just know when you've to get out of the way. Most of you will be sideshows, extras in the grand unfolding of truth. That's all right. Once you accept that and let the best brains do their jobs, you will have done your service to science and mankind.'

Oparna studied the faces in the auditorium. There was hurt and there was acceptance. She saw the light in their eyes, and it was a moment she knew she would always remember. They were under a spell, they were at the mercy of an ancient genius who was speaking his mind. The tension eased as Acharya changed course. He began to speak about the Balloon Mission and infected the audience with his conviction that microscopic aliens were falling on Earth all the time.

'We will find them,' he said.

Two days after The Talks, the work on the Balloon Mission intensified. The dormant machines and boxes and borrowed research hands in the basement sprang to life. And the lab in the bowels of the Institute became a hive of activity. It was now the most important place in the Institute, connected in spirit to the chamber of Acharya on the third floor. He began to arrive at the Institute before nine in the morning, bumbling down the corridors with more purpose than before, always with a comet tail of research assistants. One by one, Acharya's old friends from different parts of the world descended for short durations to help. In the company of the old hands he relaxed a bit and appeared less preoccupied with his own contempt for the world. Oparna began to see him the way she guessed he once was.

His eyes, that usually cast an insurmountable distance, now looked with the connivance of fellowship. The friends who came his way, he hugged fiercely, and in the meetings, which had become some sort of a festive reunion, the old men recounted the memories of their golden days and their battles with people whom they often described in a derisive way as 'normal'. Acharya was becoming easy to be with. In the middle of a discussion, when someone said the Balloon Mission needed a name, he did not consider it a frivolity. He understood, and was game. He even thought through a brief silence and said excitedly, 'Superman.' His bellowing laughter shook his paunch, and a button snapped. They discussed various names until they decided that they would just call it the Balloon Project, probably BP.

Acharya's office had been transformed into a bustling place, and Ayyan Mani in the anteroom was no longer a medium. All sorts of people had the right to walk in. But after the initial impetus, and after the old friends had fulfilled their promises, they all went back to their countries. Acharya's room returned to its calm. Ayyan slowly rebuilt the wall again between Acharya and the rest of the world, but his importance was somewhat diminished because the natural force of the events granted Oparna the undeniable right to open the sacred inner door whenever she pleased. Acharya began to spend most of his time with her, and they often worked together into the stillness of the night.

IT WAS PAST midnight, and they were probably the only people left in the Institute. The lone window in his room was shut, but the smell of the impending monsoon was in the air – a whiff of salt and wet earth that lulled the mind into sleep or into remembering old rains. Acharya was reading a long list of lab equipment that had to arrive. He finally took his eyes off the material to give them relief. He removed his glasses, leaned back on his enormous black chair and stretched. He looked at the girl who was sitting across the table from him. Her head was bent in intense concentration. Oparna was reading *Elementary Descriptions of Non-culturable Bacteria*. She was a reassuring sight, almost pleasing. There was this unremarkable happiness inside her. She laughed easily, and her laughter had a womanly tolerance about it, as though she had heard the joke before but still liked it. And when she chuckled, especially when the men had tried to find a name for the Balloon Project, she would cover her mouth with one hand and arch a bit. And there was this fragrance of lemon about her, a very expensive lemon. She was a few inches shorter than Lavanya, but somehow appeared tall. So firm and strong and agile, she was. Very tidy too. She was always producing tissues from her large olive-green bag.

Girl, he thought, and found it silly that he should think she was a girl because she obviously *was* a girl. Yet, if she died, mysteriously murdered probably, the newspapers would write, 'A thirty-year-old woman was found dead in suspicious circumstances.' They never described a thirty-year-old as a girl. He wondered why. Even she would die one day, and he felt sad it should be so. There was so much life in her, and so much beauty. She had a startling face, which he could not see right now. He looked apologetically at the reasonable mounds of her breasts. Her long fingers were toying with a thin gold chain around her long young neck. He strained to see her feet. But he could not see them from that angle. He liked the way her slender toes rested on her thin slippers. Her toenails were always red, and her fingernails pink. He concentrated on her head, which was still bent. Her thick real black hair was stretched to full tension and tied back in a severe pony-tail. He found it funny.

'If I strum your head, there will be music,' he said.

Oparna looked up. When their eyes met, he did not know why he felt he should not look at her. 'Just an observation,' he told his paperweight.

'Sorry, you said something?'

'I said nothing. Nothing important, actually.'

She smiled and went back to *Elementary Descriptions of Nonculturable Bacteria*. But she was not reading. She had not been reading for some time. You must strum then, she wanted to say. Unknowingly, her finger circled a curl that was falling on her cheek. She knew he had been looking. And her heart was pounding, her throat felt cold. She quietly conceded that she was all messed up and there was no hope for her. So many cute men in this country nowadays, all beginning to wear good narrow shoes too, and here she was hoping that a giant astronomer whose shirt buttons actually rotated in the strain of his stomach would look at her more carefully and find something more he could do with her hair. But he did have a very beautiful face and pure luminous eyes that sometimes stared like a child's. She knew how insane a man could make her, and she feared that. But what could she do?

An hour later, they stepped into the anteroom together. (Ayyan had left a long time ago.) They went down the corridor which was now completely deserted. They went in a silence that made them feel like accomplices.

Acharya walked with her to her silver-grey Baleno that lay on the side of the driveway. She got in with an expression that she was sure was the face of indifference. As she drove away, he waved, and he realized from the confused face of the night security at the guard post that he was waving long after she had vanished through the black gates. He went home wondering if Oparna had smiled at him through the rear-view mirror.

It was strange, the way she had got into her car without a word. She was probably angry because he had made a personal comment. He wanted to call her and ask if she was angry, but that, he knew, would be very silly. He turned the key, and opened the door of his home carefully so that Lavanya would not be disturbed, and felt his way from the dark hall to the bedroom. He could see the figure of Lavanya lying on her bed with her hand on her forehead. And the odours of Kerala's curative oils reached him.

Oparna drove down the Marine Drive with the windows open. The road was empty and against the lemon-yellow street lights she could see a gentle drizzle swaying in the wind. She was thinking of Acharya's eyes.

At the gates of a high-rise building in Breach Candy, a security guard let her in, his small-town eyes showing faint contempt for a girl who returned home so late. When the lift door closed and became a mirror, Oparna studied it carefully. Her hair was dishevelled, and her long top looked so terrible that she felt like some sort of activist.

When she let herself into her flat she did not know why she became so furtive, as if she had done something delightfully wrong. She tiptoed towards her parents' bedroom and peeped through the door. They were snoring. Father had a longer hiss. She went to her room, which was in a faint purple glow, its flimsy curtains flying in the wind. She felt shy as she undressed. And smiled to herself when she tried to read.

She lay awake for much of the night, thinking of his infant face and innocent rage. And how easily he understood the world of microbes. Just a silly crush, she thought – it would go away in the morning.

So it is with all sudden lovers who believed that their torments would vanish in the morning, but inevitably it is already morning when such a convenient consolation comes to them.

She was woken by her mother who usually had an ulterior motive when she did that. After ensuring that she had disturbed her daughter's sleep, she came back with a cup of tea and said, 'An alliance has come.' Oparna's eyes which had just opened shut tight. 'The boy is not in software,' her mother said encouragingly, and added, with an edge in her voice, 'Now don't say you are a lesbian.'

—

IN THE 'FINITE' corridor of the Institute, four astronomers were huddled together, questioning whether twin-star systems were indeed the norm in the universe. They were then distracted by the distant sound of heels. They fell silent and looked in the direction of the prospect.

Oparna appeared. Her hair flying, face glowing, in a sky-blue shirt that for the first time introduced them to the real shape of her breasts, their study in the coming days destined to be called topology. She was wearing a long black denim skirt which had a flower, or something similar, embroidered around the thigh. She passed by them with an innocent smile. They stared at her back. The sound of the heels faded and died. They knew that here as the Doppler Effect.

'Birthday?' asked Ayyan Mani.

'Yours?' Oparna enquired.

'No. Is it yours?'

'I don't think so,' she said. 'Is there anyone with him?'

'No.'

She pushed open the heavy door that once used to terrify her. She knew what she had to do. She could be a woman and wait for him to collapse, but she could not endure the game that she now realized she had been unknowingly playing for many months. Acharya lifted his enormous head and for a moment he looked as though he had found the Unified Theory by mistake. He looked down and appeared to study some material on the table. She sat on the chair facing him, crossed her legs, arched her body and looked at him fondly. He looked into her eyes and tried to understand her special glow.

He toyed with the paperweight and spoke of how the cryogenic sampler was still stuck in America. 'We need to get the Ministry involved,' he told the paperweight.

Ayyan Mani knew something had changed. He could see Oparna had arrived at a decision. And there was a force in her that morning, a calm arrogance that beautiful women usually had. He recognized it as her real face. The shadow she had pretended to be in this kingdom of men, in her long shapeless top and jeans, that subdued acceptance of all situations, he always knew was just a farce. He lifted his intrusive phone receiver and listened.

'Contamination is a serious problem,' Acharya was saying. 'We have to ensure that there is no way the sampler can be contaminated before or after the mission. If it's so difficult for the cryosampler to be a hundred per cent sterilized, imagine how vulnerable spaceships are to contamination. When we landed on the Moon or sent the rovers to Mars, we left Earth microbes there.'

'Are you trying not to look at me?' Oparna asked.

The insubordination of women, he would understand in time, is often a consequence of infatuation, but that morning her question registered as an anomaly. He answered nervously, feeling an unfamiliar excitement in his stomach, 'What do you mean by that, Oparna?'

'You can look at me as long as you want.'

'I don't understand your behaviour. It's strange.'

'Did you sleep last night?' she asked.

'How is that important?'

'To the Cosmic Ancestry Theory? No it's not important. Just felt like asking. Should everything always be important?'

'No.'

'I could not sleep,' she said.

'So?'

'Because of you.'

'I don't understand what you are trying to say.'

Acharya's mind went to a distant day in his childhood when he had seen, for the first time, a fish die. The final frantic palpitations of the fish was the condition of his heart right now. He toyed with the paperweight and through the silence that Oparna granted he heard faraway phones, stray horns, even crows and some orphan sounds he could not recognize. The silence approached a point after which it would cease to be part of the conversation and become a deafening diabolic force. But he did not offer to speak. Oparna got up to leave. The demented mirth of mischief and insolence had left her face. She walked to the door and looked at him with an affection that was at once hopeful and melancholic. Like light was both particle and wave.

After she left, in the sudden desolation of the room, he tried to understand the tumult inside himself. He could feel a strange nameless fear, but he was euphoric too. The mascot of real joy he had always imagined was a simple human smile, but now he suspected that a smile was actually very frivolous. The face of true deep joy had to be an impassive grimness.

He did not understand what had happened to her. She was wooing a fat old man. She must be ovulating. Men appeared attractive to women during that time, he had read. This would pass. Then he realized that he was afraid that it might pass.

His ascetic power of concentration deserted him. He tried to tear himself away from the haunting visions of her face. He forced himself to think of the Big Bang's devotees, because their thoughts usually built a mad rage within him. But in the place of the old malice was love and pardon for all, and Oparna's face, like a giant background spirit, appreciating his maturity. He tried to read *Topolov's Superman*, but he wondered what she would think if she saw him with the violent underground comic. No matter what he tried to do, he realized, the face of Oparna ultimately appeared. In every frame she was there, like R.K. Laxman's Common Man. He tried desperately to search for a distraction to abolish this distraction, but nothing could cure his fever.

Acharya decided to wander. He walked down the quiet lane from the Institute, through Navy Nagar and all the way to the

Marine Drive. He stood on the broad promenade and looked at the turbulent sea. The sky had turned grey, the wind was strong and it tasted of salt. At a distance, down the curve of the promenade, the sea lashed against the wave breakers and exploded into mists.

He could see the monsoon on the bleak horizon. It was coming like a grey fog. On the road, there was a sort of panic in the evening traffic, as though there had been a morbid warning and everybody was fleeing. The wind became stronger and it blew visible dust, leaves, old newspapers and a forlorn blue kerchief. Then, the monsoon arrived. First as a drizzle. Some evening walkers switched from the haste of exercise to the very distinct haste of running for cover. Old women unfurled their umbrellas with a wisdom that did not have a clear face. It struck him, how complete, how final, an umbrella actually was. As a technology, it would not evolve any further.

The rains became a torrent now. Distant buildings across the bay were no longer visible. He saw an old man jog to a bus shelter, dribbling his swollen testicles on his frail thighs, like a footballer during a warm-up. The young, who had come for the rains, howled. They stood still in the rains. Some of them were compelled to spread their hands in a cinematic gesture because they felt odd just standing. Young girls worried if their blouses had become transparent. But they took the rains on their uplifted faces. They giggled and skipped and ran, as if they were in a sanitary-towel commercial.

Then, the rains were gone. The clouds cleared. A new light descended on the Marine Drive that made everything glow. Acharya thought his vision had improved. The evening walkers returned. Old couples were reunited. They went carefully on the wet tiles, wise in the knowledge that they had now reached an age when a slip could lead to death. They went slowly, four frail hands holding a single umbrella that was bending in the breeze. They must have been thinking of old monsoons, many monsoons. When they were young and strong, and the rains never seemed so grey.

When he reached home, fully soaked, his white full-sleeve shirt now transparent, his trousers resting precariously below his hips and held in place only by the grip of wetness, Lavanya put her hand on her head. 'Who are you?' she said. 'Archimedes?' As she dried him with a towel that felt very warm, he stared at her. She was so frail, the skin on her forehead so tired, her dyed hair scanty. He counted thirteen lines on her neck. What must a man do?

In the days that followed, he tried to ignore Oparna. That, he thought, was a solution. He would not summon her until she came to him without being invited, and though he felt a nervous excitement in his stomach every time he saw her, he would talk to her about the weather conditions over the launch facility in Hyderabad, or the optimum size of the balloon, or something like that. And she would just stare at him. 'We need to lock the sourcing of the laminar air-flow cabinet,' he would say. 'We need to lock many things,' she would tell him. And he would say, 'I got a letter today. Cardiff has agreed to be part of the mission.' And she would take mock offence and leave his room.

Every night, he stood on the narrow balcony, nine floors above the ground, lost in the intoxication of Oparna, his reveries mistaken by his wife as his incurable affliction with the pursuit of truth. Lavanya did get confused when he once laughed in his sleep. Occasionally, she even found him looking at himself intently in the mirror. And yesterday morning, once again, he had taken vegetable stock from the freezer thinking it was ice. He had done that before, but this time he gulped down the juice and did not notice that anything was amiss.

Lavanya, though irreparably influenced by her mother to suspect men because they were unstable people, would have never guessed that the Big Bang's Old Foe could be lost in the thoughts of a girl who was born after man had landed on the Moon.

In the Institute, Oparna was now a carnival. Her hair was called 'dynamic' by the scientists because it was different almost every day. Her long floral skirts and tight blouses, her fitted jeans, and opportunistic saris that made stenos comment unhappily on the foolishness of wearing the costume in the rains, terminated the near anonymity that she was beginning to enjoy. She knew that, but above everything else, she wanted to be a silly girl weaving mischief around her man.

Acharya continued to ignore her. Sometimes, he would go all the way to the basement lab to ignore her. He would inspect the equipment, speak to the dozen research assistants there and ask questions. Oparna would wait for him to approach her and pass her by without a word. And she would whisper to him, 'Can I call you, Arvind?', or 'You look so hot today', or something else. This game went on, as the rains became the season, and the roads began to look so black and clean, people now a slow procession of umbrellas, the air so cool and sedative. Then one day Oparna went missing.

She did not come to him, and when he went to the basement to ignore her there was no sign of her. He waited till noon and asked Ayyan to call her. 'Don't forget to tell her that I called to find out if there was any communication from ISRO, nothing else,' he said. But Ayyan knew that it was the desperation of love. He tried her mobile the whole afternoon, but it just rang. Acharya would call him every ten minutes and ask, 'Where is she?' And Ayyan would tell him, 'It's just ringing, Sir.' Then, to trouble him, he would say, 'I hope she is all right.'

'Try her landline,' Acharya said.

'We don't have that number, Sir. I'll keep trying.'

Acharya began to pace the floor in his room. He thought she was hurt and angry, and had gone away forever. He also feared that she had died. And he felt the melancholy of the rains that reminded him of the departure of many friends who had left without a word, all courteous men otherwise. He started calling her himself from his direct line. He did not have a mobile, or he would have even endured the imbecility of texting. As the evening wore on, he became almost demented at the thought of her. He imagined her with a young man, an old flame who always pursued her but whom she had ignored, now getting lucky because she was spurned by an old fool. He kept calling her and waited angrily, holding the receiver to his ear as her ringtone sang, 'Baby Can I Hold You?'

Twenty floors above the sea, Oparna stood in her room staring through a wide open window. The thin purple curtains flapped wildly in the wind. She was in blue jeans and a T-shirt with a jovial amoeba embroidered on it. She was holding her mobile in her hand, and she was smiling. The smile became an insane chuckle every time the phone rang. She stood that way as the evening turned dark and the million windows in the monstrous buildings outside became illuminated. Then, as though a mystic cue had appeared in the starless sky, she reached for her car keys.

Ayyan Mani had left for the day and the anteroom was deserted. Orphaned phones on his table rang intermittently. Oparna stood outside the inner door for a moment before she opened it. Acharya was sitting with his elbows on the table, chin cradled in his palms. He did not move as she walked in and stood in the middle of the room. She heard the door shut behind her. 'It's OK, I am here now,' she said.

'Where were you?' he asked calmly.

She sat in a chair across the desk and returned his stare. 'Are you angry with me, Arvind?' she said. 'Do you want to hurt me?'

They looked at each other through the heaviness of a silence that they somehow comprehended as a tired acceptance of love.

'Arvind, I came here to say that you should not search for me tomorrow. I won't be here. At ten in the night, come down to the basement. There won't be anyone there. Just me and you. Do you understand what I'm saying?'

'Yes.'

She left a blue envelope on the table. It was sealed and scented. 'These are my pictures,' she said. 'I got them for you. Keep them safe. Not all men are allowed to see me like this.'

He took the envelope with great care, as if it were a piece of bread that had drowned in tea. He opened the second drawer of his desk and put it with the recent readings of interstellar dust-clouds.

'Tomorrow at ten,' she said, and went to the door. He looked at her back, the firmness of her shoulders, the imprint of her bra strap, so strained by tension, the succulent buttocks that were hoisted by high heels.

'Were you looking at me?' she asked from the door, her face lit by a shy smile.

It was around midnight when Acharya finally rose from the huge leather chair. He felt as if he had cried the whole day. His throat was dry and his eyes hurt. And there was peace in his lungs. He went down the long corridor of the third floor in the spell of a silence so perfect. The enchantment of this silence and the mystical way in which the deserted corridor lay in front of him, foreground approaching, the far end receding, made him walk faster. He enjoyed this eerie spectacle. But he felt a sudden pain in his left knee, and he slowed down. He turned back to see if the spectre of Oparna was lurking somewhere, watching his ache.

He wondered what it was that made a person old. This body that he was carrying right now, the aches in its joints and the weakness of its flesh, was not what he felt inside. An old man was in every way a young man but in the guise of a body that would look ugly and undignified if it tried to do what the young did. The elegance of age, like sanity, was an expectation people had of him. But at that moment, as he was walking down the corridor, he could not feel the antiquity that others had thrust upon him. He felt as if he were just another man accepting the affections of a woman. Just another young man. It was important to be young. Only the young can love, because the imbecility of youth is the only spectrum of love. He could see it so clearly now. Like every ray of light with a wavelength of 700 nanometres is always red, everyone who is in love is young.

At the porch, in the hush of the sea and the fragrance of wet earth, he stood looking at the rains. A guard came running to him with an umbrella. He was a tiny man, about a foot shorter than Acharya. He held the umbrella high, hoping that the monster would have the grace to hold it in his own hand. But Acharya walked in a trance as the guard, exhausted already by the effort of stretching his hand so high, got fully drenched.

He let himself into his flat, changed and went to sleep in the fumes of Lavanya's herbal remedies. He slept well that night. He dreamt of a beautiful girl. The sound of her silver anklets filled the spectral spaces of his reverie. Her face, somehow naked, looked at him in an amused way as if she were the master and he a no-talent apprentice. It was the face of Lavanya from another time.

He woke at dawn and sat on the bed like a mammoth infant, refusing to look at the figure of his wife lying next to him. The clarity of last night when he had walked down the deserted corridor and granted himself the spirit of youth in a body paralysed by illusory age, was now gone. He felt afraid because he knew his descent into the basement at ten that night was an inevitability. He went to the bathroom to stare at his naked body. It was, in a way, from an angle, if you looked carefully, a beautiful face. Twinkling eyes, affluent skin, succulent royal lips, not much hair on the head of course, but a lot of face. He had a cold bath, and furtively shampooed his crotch. He went back to the bedroom with light steps and gingerly opened the cupboard. He wanted to leave before Lavanya woke up. He did not want to see her that morning.

It was seven when he reached the office. He sat in his chair and heard the ghostly sounds of a world that was suddenly alien. The desolation of morning was so different from the desolation of night. Strange birds sang, distant objects fell loudly and echoed, and there were faint tremors of laughter. Even the smell was unfamiliar. There was this odour of wet rugs and wood. He was about to open the window when he heard boys shouting and singing in the anteroom. Four cleaning boys burst into his room in a private festivity. Their happy faces fell when they saw him. They fled in shock, but one of them came back with a transparent bucket and started mopping the floor, throwing discreet glances at the giant. Acharya stared at the boy. Once, their eyes met and held each other for a few seconds. He didn't know the Institute had cleaners.

Slowly, the morning unfolded and the world become familiar. Ayyan Mani walked in, neat and tidy, smelling like a room freshener, his thick black hair oiled and combed into an unflappable mass.

'Coffee,' Acharya said.

The whole day, he sat in his room, avoiding calls and dismissing visitors. He wanted the world to spare him, just for a day, but he was under siege. The forces of little men were outside his door. They infiltrated first as ominous telephone calls, and then they sent their dark messenger with clear white eyes who seemed to know something, who had a disturbing smile at the edges of his lips. Ayyan kept walking in and saying, 'They have come, Sir,' or 'They have been waiting, Sir.' By noon, Acharya yielded.

The Balloon Mission had proceeded into a frenetic stage and there were people on the black sofa outside whom he could not avoid. He called them in reluctantly and conducted meetings that collapsed into long silences when he stared blankly at the visitors, not knowing that a question had been put, a clarification sought, an opinion expected. By evening, the siege eased and he tried to find respite in *Topolov's Superman*. But he could not concentrate. He opened the table drawer and looked at the blue envelope that Oparna had left last night. He had not opened it. 'These are my pictures,' she had said. 'Not every man is allowed to see me like this.' To open the envelope was to accept the affair, and the thought of Lavanya tortured him.

THREE HOURS BEFORE his confirmed appointment with love in the basement, it was inevitable that Arvind Acharya's mind would wonder if Time flowed continuously, like a smooth line, or in tiny jumps like a dotted line. In the crisis of being seduced by a disturbing woman with real black hair, he needed the distraction of a problem that he knew he would not solve in three hours. But he could not take his mind away from the thoughts of touching the forbidden body of Oparna that would lie in wait for him beside microscopes and transilluminators (and, probably, perfumed candles which were not part of the Astrobiology department). But he also felt a morbid sorrow. For his wife of four decades who was at that moment, possibly, in the habitual melancholy of folding clothes. He had never felt this kind of sorrow before. He found it strange that the grief was not in his heart but somewhere in the stomach. And it was a dark, hollow kind of feeling. As if Lavanya had died, leaving him widowed in a pleasurable world. It was not a stab of conscience. It was, in fact, the emptiness of enjoying something all by himself without bringing her to share it. Without her presence, even the pleasure of adultery was not complete. And that was absurd. He could not bear it any more. This gloom in his stomach that hung just above an unexpected joyous swelling.

He got up from his chair and steered his trousers. The air in the room had become too still. But he forgot why he had risen. He stood rooted near his chair and contemplated the acoustics in the basement, and why men married, and the exalted place of fidelity on a dwarf planet that went around a mediocre main-sequence star somewhere in the outer arm of just another whirlpool galaxy. Eventually, he opened the window and breathed the first rush of sea breeze. It was dark outside, but he could hear the sea. It was violent. And there was something about the wind that portended the mother of all rains. He heard the door open behind him.

'I wanted to see you,' said the voice of Jana Nambodri, somewhat meekly. He was subdued these days after the defeat of the mutiny and the humiliation of being pardoned.

Acharya was about to turn and face the intrusion when he realized, just in time, that the youthful swelling caused by the thoughts of Oparna had yet to be tamed.

'Jana,' he said, without leaving the window, 'Come tomorrow.'

Nambodri had already walked into the room when he heard this. He stood there a bit confused, but went away without trying to understand.

When the door shut, Acharya went hastily to his chair and for a fleeting moment, he felt like a gaping radio telescope. He sat behind the reassuring expanse of his desk and waited for time, whatever it might be, to pass. He tried to squeeze the erection with his massive thighs, suffocate its blood flow and release the tension. It might have been unprecedented, he suspected, for a man of advanced age to kill such a serendipitous unmedicated vigour, the pursuit of which, even among the young, was a billion-dollar industry. He briefly remembered Nicolaus Copernicus, at a moment in history, throttling his own heliocentric theory and conceding to the Vatican that the Earth was indeed the centre of the universe.

But Acharya's problem did not subside. It protruded in a sort of sculptural defiance. Complicating the situation was a sudden urge in him to urinate. He did not have a private bathroom. He had dismissed past proposals by Administration because of the disruption that the creation of a washroom would have caused. He cursed himself for not having foresight. Now, he had to go halfway down the long, busy corridor. He grabbed *The Times of India* that was lying on the desk and went out reading, the paper unfolded to its full length.

Ayyan Mani looked at the giant figure walking away from him, and he wondered if the delirium of love could really make someone behave so strangely. Acharya went to the washroom that was called 'Scientists'. There he kept *The Times* carefully on the hand dryer because he feared he might need it on the way back. There were five urinals on the blue-tiled wall and three senior astronomers were standing side-by-side, each separated from the other by a free pot. Acharya stood in between two of them. An insane wish came to him then to startle them, for boyish fun. He put his hands around the nape of his neck, elbows pointed up, as though he were stretching, and stood that way. His brisk manly spurt shot above the urinal. One by one, the other men turned to see the spectacle. Acharya always humbled them, but never like this.

He resumed the wait in his room, patiently rearranging objects on his desk. He reached for the drawer where he had hidden the perfumed envelope of Oparna. He no longer had the strength to resist the offer of love in the basement. So he thought he might as well open the envelope. Two black-and-white photographs slipped out. A little girl was in a bathtub. She must have been four years old.

At five minutes to ten he walked out of his room. Like an elephant, as always. He was disappointed to see people in the corridor. He was hoping that the Institute would be deserted because of the rains and, well, the pursuit of truth could bloody well wait some days. The lift was packed and he stood in its grim silence with his head bent. When the lift door opened at the ground floor, nobody moved because he was closest to the door and he was standing still, blocking half the way. They waited for him to step out, but he did not move. They went around him, like a stream around a boulder. The lift emptied, and that comforted him. He pressed the button that said B.

The basement labyrinths, flanked by stark white walls, lay in the drone of invisible ethereal motors. At the dead end of a narrow corridor was the lab. He thought of what she must be wearing, how she must be sitting, what plans she had. In a preordained darkness, was she waiting as an unmoving silhouette? The swelling that had long subsided grew again and was now leading him down the path, like the proboscis of a foolish rover on Mars that was right now searching for water and beasts.

As the lab door approached him, the grief in his stomach grew. The wraith of Lavanya appeared. He pictured her folding clothes, with an accusatory face. He saw the distant days of their life when she used to walk like a doe. And how her long thick hair used to tickle his nose during the interminable flights over the Atlantic. And the way her head would rest on his shoulder as she slept like a child. He thought of the first beautiful months of their marriage. And their love that they never ever called love. Because it was not necessary to name it then.

He could see those days so clearly now, a whole lost age. How beautiful she had looked as a bride. He was still a student then. After their wedding in Sivagangai, when the time came for him to take her to Madras, he would always remember, a silent crowd of lachrymose relatives had shadowed them to the station. As he stood nervously waiting for the train to arrive, one of Lavanya's aunts said, 'Is he taking his new bride to his hostel room?' And the weeping entourage used the ruse of tears to laugh heartily.

Lavanya, in the isolation of her new home in Madras, began writing long morose letters to her mother. He had read the first without her knowledge. 'He wants to find out why things fall,' she said in the letter. He was researching gravity in the Annamalai University and his wife found it ridiculous that it was a whole subject. 'But he is a useful man,' she wrote. 'He can put rice sacks in the loft without standing on a stool. And he is so calm and obedient that I keep asking him to do things just for fun. I know I should respect him but I find him so funny. Yesterday, at the temple, I tried to fall at his feet; he jumped in the air. He has western ideas.'

They could never hold hands in the street because those times were different. But how much they had wanted to. Not merely for love, but to heal. In the by-lanes of Madras, shopkeepers, taxi drivers and pedestrians laughed at them mercilessly. The couple was so tall, especially for that time, and most Tamilians so tiny and genetically predisposed to believing something is wrong with the others, that Acharya and Lavanya when taken together were always a sight. Mothers with crying babies stood at the iron gates of their houses and pointed at them. That always silenced the babies. Gangs of eunuchs sang to Acharya, and they sang that if he liked Lavanya he would like them too. Urchins ran behind them screaming, 'LIC, LIC' (the fourteen-storeyed Life Insurance Corporation building was the tallest in the city then, and it was to remain so for many years to come).

Under the influence of an uncle whose asthmatic speech lent him a certain intensity, Acharya decided to quit his studies and join the Indian space programme that had been birthed in secrecy in a small town called Thumba in Kerala. But he soon realized how impoverished the Indian government was, and how the whole space ambition was just a pathetic attempt of a miserable nation to find respect in a world that had moved ahead. On unpaved roads that ran between tall palms, he had to carry rocket parts on a bicycle from a clandestine shed to a launch-site. Life was so simple at the time that one day Acharya even brought a rocket-cone home to show his wife. She wrote their names on it and without detection it was later fixed on a rocket, which was among the several of the first generation that failed and crashed into the sea. The simplicity of it all, and the red boiled rice of Kerala, disillusioned Acharya. After just a few months with the space programme, he went to Princeton to study cosmology, taking Lavanya with him. He would eventually become obsessed with gravitation. 'It attracts him,' his father would often say in a joke that relatives never fully understood.

For many years now Acharya had accepted that he had gone past the age of love. But here he was, almost at the door of Oparna Goshmaulik who could have got any man with the mere lowering of her gaze (or whatever the language was these days). He could not wait to touch her and hold so close her bare body and take in her citric smell that he had once pitied as the odour of youth. He was at the door now. His hand was on the silver knob.

He waited for a moment. Then he turned back and walked away.

He took the stairway up, to the porch, went down the pathways that circumvented the main lawn, and towards the gate where the guards stood up smartly and saluted him. He crossed the road without looking and entered the Professors' Quarters. In the lift, two senior scientists were with him. They smiled politely. He wondered if they could smell Oparna on him. And would Lavanya tell from his eyes that he had held the silver knob of a door that would have ended something between them, whatever that something was. As he walked from the lift towards his flat, he did not understand why his heart was thumping. In an importune moment of clarity he guessed that there must have been species in the prehistoric days whose hearts were so loud that they echoed in the forests, and whose blood flowed through their veins with the hush of rivulets washing over pebbles. Life then must have been a concert. But all that visceral sound would have given them away to their predators. So the species that made it through the ages were the ones whose hearts were not loud enough to hear and whose blood flowed in silence.

As he held the knob on the door of his home he thought of what Oparna was doing at that moment. Just then the door was flung open violently. Lavanya stood there with tears in her eyes and a box of tissues in her hand. 'Where were you?' she said.

He walked in and shut the door so that they could settle the matter in a discreet way.

'I was trying your phone,' she said and wiped her nose. 'Anju is dead, Arvind.'

'What?' he asked.

'Anju is dead,' she repeated.

Lavanya's frail shoulders shook and she began to weep. She looked incomplete, like the handless urchin he had once seen walking on a tense rope. She needed his hand around her, but he felt too dirty to touch her. He let her cry alone.

'I just checked,' she said, almost inaudibly, 'There is a flight to Madras in two hours. I have to go.'

'Do you want me to go with you?'

'I know you don't want to come.'

'I will come.'

'No. It's all right. She was dying anyway. I am crying because it seems right to cry. I am OK otherwise.'

'I will go with you.'

'Actually, I want to go alone. It's like a holiday for me.'

'Holiday?'

'Yes. I am such a sick woman.'

They took a taxi to the airport because Lavanya said he should not drive in the rains, and the black-and-yellow taxi was anyway the same ancient Fiat they had. He had insisted on driving but, as always in these matters, she prevailed.

'You don't know this, but you cannot see very well,' she told him, when they had squeezed themselves into the back seat.

'I can see very well,' he said.

'I will be thinking in the plane how you are going to get back. Today I feel everybody around me is going to die.'

'When are you back?'

'Ten days,' she said, 'Maybe more. There will be ceremonies. And I want a break.'

'From what?'

'From you,' she said.

The windows of the taxi were rolled up because of the rains. It was hot inside and there was the smell of damp cotton.

Acharya felt invisible creatures biting his buttocks. He moved in a jive as if to crush them angrily, and that made Lavanya chuckle. 'What?' he asked, thinking that she had gone mad with sorrow.

'Nothing,' she said. They travelled in silence for a while. Then he reached out and held her hand. As though it were a mystical martial art technique, her languid head fell on his shoulder.

The concourse that led to the departure terminal was a gentle gradient. Acharya walked up like a benevolent genie carrying a suitcase that appeared small in his hand. He felt odd holding a single suitcase. It had the austerity of elopement.

As a boy, he had once gone with friends to count the steam trains from a footbridge. He had seen a pair of fleeing lovers on the narrow-gauge track running towards the railway platform, fearing that the world was chasing them. The man was holding a black briefcase and the girl was carrying a small cloth bag. For many years after that, even now on this rainy night, in a corner of his mind Acharya associated love with lightness, and marriage with extra luggage. Usually, when he and Lavanya arrived at the airport, he was pushing an overloaded trolley like the hotel housekeeping arriving at a door. There was another reason why he felt odd as he walked up the gradient. This was the first time he was sending Lavanya off. Normally it was she who sent him off. Or, she travelled with him, and that was always an event. She never let him take shoulder-bags. Suitcases it had to be. 'Clothes don't get crumpled that way,' she would say. He secretly admired her logic, and even conceded that she was right, but a bag to him was a symbol of nomadic freedom, an imperfection that said the journey was not important, the destination inconsequential. A suitcase, on the other hand, was a sign of grand departures and self-important arrivals. It was a confession, like the shirt of a dandy, that life was important. Once, when he had told Lavanya this, she screamed, 'My god what a poet, you travel business class don't you?'

They reached the glass doors of the terminal where three guards were checking the tickets of passengers in the middle of bad-mouthing a senior who was not present. Acharya fumbled for Lavanya's ticket in his pockets. He had just purchased it from the counter. He was pleased when he found it and gave his wife a wide grin. She looked at him with worry. How was he was going to take care of himself?

'Open the door for the maids,' she said. 'I have Meenu's mobile. I will call her every day.'

'Who is Meenu?'

Lavanya looked exasperated. 'She is our cook.'

He pulled up the tow handle of the suitcase and gave it to her with a deep, grim face, as though it was a lifetime achievement award. She dragged the suitcase, sniffling, holding a kerchief to her nose which was now red. Before she entered the terminal she turned to look at her husband. He waved at her. A young couple behind her mistook her tears for the romantic distress of separation. They gave the seniors an exaggerated look of approval. 'So cute,' the girl said.

Lavanya disappeared somewhere behind the X-ray machines. When Acharya turned to leave he felt the same way he used to feel as a boy when he dropped letters in the postbox. There was this sense of an unremarkable relief mixed with a nagging suspicion that he had lost something he was holding.

It was two in the morning when Acharya reached home. He had expected the gloom of its vast tidy rooms, and the haunting silence of loneliness that was somehow different from the silence of togetherness. He went to the bedroom and played Pavarotti at full volume through the night. Just once he turned the volume down – when he called Lavanya on her mobile to ask if she had arrived safely. She was surprised to get his call. Against the background noise of her loud relatives, she screamed, maybe to show off that her husband cared, 'Yes, I've arrived.'

When the sun rose he was standing in the balcony, and the house was still in the turbulence of Pavarotti's wails. At the end of an aria, in its transient baffling silence, Acharya heard the doorbell. He opened the door and found the maid. She tried to enter, but Pavarotti's sudden murderous pitch rose and it shook her. Before she could recover, he slammed the door in her face. When the cook arrived, he did not open the door.

The whole morning he stood on the balcony, missing the interruption of Lavanya and her inopportune Madras filter coffee, and her unreasonable taunts as to why he was not walking when he was wearing Nike shoes. To impress her, in case she called him later in the day, he put on his tracksuit, wore the shoes with pump action (or something like that), and stepped out. He wanted to stroll down the inner lanes of Navy Nagar, but returned in ten minutes, unable to bear the sight of grown-up sailors going to work in white shorts, their hairy legs pedalling cycles or riding motorbikes. And there was something about people wearing white in the monsoon that he found rather foolish. He did not feel like going back home. So he walked inside the Quarters and discovered that its clear blue pool was actually used in the mornings.

A portion of the pool was cordoned off for fat women who were dancing in some kind of ludicrous aerobic activity. There were eight of them and their nervous eyes drifted from the female instructor to his dismayed glare. Close to where he was standing, he saw a little girl trying to swim without floats. She was scared and she told everyone who swam close to her, 'I am your friend, no?' She reminded him of Shruti, and he tried to meet her eyes to smile. But he was distracted by a woman in the pool who was trying to teach her mother how to swim.

'Mama, you're afraid. I can feel the fear in your stomach,' she was telling the old woman, with the severity of daughter's love. 'I want you to bring your fear up to the ribs,' she said, placing her hand on her mother's stomach and moving it up gently. 'Bring it up further to your throat . . . Now I can feel your fear. It's in the throat, Mama. Spit it out, spit it out.'

The shrunken ancient mother, in a costume that would have branded her a whore in her youth, blew uncomfortably into her daughter's hand, and she surveyed the pool sheepishly.

'I have robbed you of your fear,' her daughter said. 'Now swim.'

At the far end of the pool, Acharya saw a large man in swimming trunks. He had breasts. And near him, waiting to dive, there were more fat women. Apparently the young did not swim any more.

Oparna was on his mind all the while, like a foreboding. Later that morning, when he went to work and she appeared before him, he did not know what he must say to her. She looked more stunning than ever, even though she had resumed the austerity of the long shapeless top. The smell of young flesh returned to haunt his nervous peace and he was reminded again how, incredibly, she had granted him the right to be her lover. Their eyes met only for an instant. Then she sorted loose sheets of paper in her hands, and he rearranged things on his table. He asked her to sit down. She sat. They looked at each other again, this time for longer.

'I am sorry,' Acharya said, 'I could not see you last night.'

'There is some progress with the cryosampler,' she said, and gave him a print-out of an email. And that was how she was in the days that followed. Something in her was dead. He could see it in her eyes.

The way she used to look at him, with the glow of new love, was now replaced by the silent hurt of betrayal and humiliation. She made him sad, but he also longed for this sorrow to arrive in his room as often as possible in that ascetic uniform of long top and jeans, the cassock of her platonic detachment. She spoke to him only about work, and she looked so strong and resolute in her martyrdom that he did not find cues to speak about himself or to blame the forces of virtue that stole him away from the basement.

But he found excuses to be with her. He asked Ayyan to send her to his room on flimsy pretexts. And she came every time he summoned her. Some days, when he thought that he had summoned her too many times, and feared that she might leave the Institute, unable to bear the sight of him, he called group meetings with scientists and research assistants. His eyes would sweep across the assembly, and rest casually on her. She never looked him in the eye, but every time his carefully constructed perfunctory gaze fell on her he was certain that she knew he was looking. Her mask of detachment would slip a little: she would stare harder at the floor, or she would inhale unknowingly. So he devised a new way of looking at her.

He realized that if he adjusted the position of the cylindrical glass jar in which Lavanya's ethereal agents still filled orchids every morning, he could see Oparna's reflection. The vase was bought by Lavanya years ago as part of her failed attempt to make his office look beautiful. Now it was an accomplice in his furtive love. It had a reasonable refractive index, it seemed, and so her face was not too distorted. And this was how he would look at her during the long group meetings. Sometimes, he noticed in the jar, she would look at his face in a fond way and turn away when she perceived the threat of being found out. This device consoled him until one afternoon when he saw Oparna's reflection staring at him and then at the vase. She had somehow figured out the technique. He got up in the middle of the meeting, even as someone was talking to him about the optimum dimensions of the balloon, and carried the vase to the far end of the room. He put it on the centrepiece that lay in the middle of the interfacing white sofas. He rejoined the perplexed group with an innocent face and threw a casual glance at Oparna for appreciation, but she was looking at the floor.

Acharya was miserable the whole week. All day, he would try to work, try to survive the unrelenting influence of Oparna, and go home to hunger and wakefulness. He realized that his home was entirely the colony of his wife. He was running short of shirts and trousers. Underwear that was usually laid out on the morning bed for him like a buffet, now became rare. He could not find anything. So Lavanya, in the middle of sombre funeral prayers, or while serving food to the mourners, would get calls on her mobile and she would whisper, 'the nail-clipper is in the leopard-skin box . . . the box is inside a bag with polka dots in the second drawer of the nightstand on my side of the bed . . . I cannot explain what a polka dot is right now . . . yes, lots of dots on the bag . . . I don't know why they are called polka dots and not dots . . . don't forget to put the nail-clipper back in the box . . . dry yourself after your bath . . . And why haven't you been opening the door for the maids?'

Despite his condition, Acharya was aware that the Balloon Mission was entering a crucial phase. The problems in equipment procurement were slowly being solved. His friends in Nasa were helping to release equipment that the American government had blacklisted after the Pokhran nuclear tests. Despite the torments of love and its weird distractions that expanded time, he worked hard on the many finer aspects of the Mission. He was talking to government servants, scientists and weathermen, redrawing the design of gadgetry, scrutinizing the physics at the altitude of forty-one kilometres and commanding everything in him to ensure that the lab in the Institute was worthy of testing the samplers at the end of the Mission. But he had lost his peace. And the privileges of high thought, and his isolation that had once guarded him from the trivialities of life. The beast of genius inside him was now fatally infected by what he diagnosed as common infatuation, but through a minute crack in the fog of misery his mind could still see the beauty in the conviction that alien microbes were always falling from the heavens and they had once seeded life on Earth.

The thoughts of the origin of life sometimes diminished his longing for of Oparna. Microbe to microbe – that was all there was to life and death. Love was insignificant – a devious evolutionary device. Nothing more. These thoughts comforted him, but only briefly. Ultimately, he realized, Oparna was the unavoidable inspiration behind his renewed attempts to keep the Balloon Mission on target. She was deeply involved in the project, the very heart of the core team. It was the most important time in her professional life. That was why, despite the discomfort of unrequited love, she was not leaving the Institute. Any serious snag in the project would disappoint her and, as a consequence, embarrass him. So he ordained in his mind, come what may, the balloon would go up and come down, and the air sampler would be analysed. This resolve made him work like a madman. He slogged in the glory of an old incurable faith in the extraterrestrial origin of life, in the fear of losing Oparna forever, in the torturous certainty that he had no choice but to lose her eventually, in the confusion of what exactly a wife means to a man, in the bitter aftertaste of the terrible food Ayyan Mani brought him and in the deathly fatigue of insomnia. Finally, eight days after Lavanya had left to mourn her sister, something in him snapped.

He pushed everything that was on his table to the floor and rose from his chair. He did not know what time it was and he did not care. He knew Oparna was in the basement. She had to be there.

He walked out through the anteroom that Ayyan had long deserted. Its ghostly phones rang and fax machines belched. There was not a soul in the corridor. It lay in front like a supernatural bridge to autumnal love. He heard the lift heave and echo as it descended to the basement. He walked beside the stark white walls, feeling the anxiety of violating a young body that was right there at the end of this narrow corridor. He felt a mad rage against her for pushing him from the fortress of stature that others had built for him over the decades into a miserable hell where other old men like him crawled on their stomachs and begged young women for a mere look of affection. But what truly infuriated him was the painful suspicion that it was now, in this late age, that true love had come to him.

Until a few weeks ago, he was in the peace of consigning love as that brief juvenile excitement he once felt for Lavanya in the freshness of marriage. It was an easy painless thing. There was no pursuit, no battle. She was there in the morning, she was there in the evening, and on some nights of her choosing she became naked. Love, he had always thought, was arranged. He was certain that alcoholic poets had overrated its misery. But now, he felt its agony and the insane fear of rejection.

He flung open the door of the lab. It was almost dark. Oparna was sitting on the floor at the foot of the main working desk that filled half the room. She had turned off all the lights except a single inadequate bulb directly above the desk. It cast giant shadows of microscopes and other optical devices, and they appeared to lie in wait, like curious voyeurs. She was in her long top of forced modesty and blue jeans. Her hair was tied back. He walked to her side, and stood with his knee brushing against her shoulder.

'Why are you doing this to me?' he asked.

She did not reply. He lifted her by her arms and kissed her, or bit her (he would not remember). They fell on the floor in a heap, and they kissed and licked and wrestled. He tore her top and dismantled her jeans. She fought, not sure yet if she was resisting or assisting. When he took away all her clothes, she stopped fighting. She turned away from him in a sting of shame, her face on the floor, an elbow shielding it from this wild man, proud breasts reaching for a place to rest, her bronze back rising and falling like the roll of a sand-dune in the twilight, her long firm legs lying languid.

He tugged at her shoulder to make her face him. He wanted to see her arrogant face now tamed and helpless, but she held on tenaciously to the foot of the main desk and dug her face further into her elbow. He held her hair in his fist and tried to see the face that had destroyed his peace. She had no more strength left in her to resist. Her hand left the foot of the desk, her shoulders obeyed and she turned to him, defeated and deranged. Her hair was now wild, the terrified hair-band had rolled away long ago. She shut her eyes as he suffocated her with a long violent kiss. He tried to hold her legs, but they were now glistening in sweat and his hands slipped. That made her laugh. But her demented laughter soon become wails as he finally managed to prise open her legs and plunder her with an inhuman strength. But it was a brief attack. In less than a minute, he fell on her breasts and rolled down on the floor panting and laughing.

He did not know such pleasurable violence was permitted outside the myth of pornography. The amused smile of the young Lavanya, that look of a patient zen master condoning the imperfection of an apprentice, was what he had thought the face of woman's love to be. But what had happened just now was different.

Oparna was looking at him, breathing hard, lying on her mauled breasts. She and Acharya stared at each other as if they both knew they were going to die and had accepted this death. It was a long time before either spoke.

'What have we done?' she said, with a smile.

'What have we done?' Acharya repeated, more seriously than her. 'What now?'

'What now? You can't steal a woman's line. That's not allowed.'

'It's a woman's line?'

'Of course. Anyway, it's too early to say it.' She rolled to his side and put her head on his chest. He felt her finger probe his navel. 'You have such a big navel,' she said, 'It's very deep too. And there is a lot of lint.' She showed him what she had scooped out.

'Your wife is away?' she asked.

'Yes,' he said. 'You seem to be very experienced.'

'In what?' Somehow it was a question that had only uncomfortable answers.

'How many lovers have you had?' he asked.

She looked at the ceiling, toying with her hair. 'Is it true that we follow the decimal system because we have ten fingers?'

'Most of us have eight fingers.'

She looked confused, but then her face lit up in comprehension. 'Eight fingers and two thumbs?'

'Yes,' he said. 'Why do you want to know about the decimal system?'

'I was counting my men,' she said, 'and eight fingers and two thumbs were not enough.' She lifted her head to see his face. 'Does it annoy you that I have slept with so many men?'

'Yes. And I hate them,' he said.

'And that's a nice thing to say to a woman,' she said.

She looked at him fondly. He was like a cuddly giant seal. His eyes, usually bright and furious, now stared in the diffused glow of affection or gratitude. They lay together on the floor in silence for over an hour. Then something crossed her mind.

'At The Talks,' she said, 'you remember the speech you gave at The Talks?'

'You were there?'

'Yes. I was there to letch at you. You said something then.

You said, "Maybe we cannot understand physics at the quantum level without understanding other things which are not considered physics today. Other things like. . ." Then you stopped. I thought you wanted to say something, but did not think it was right to say it.'

'Was it that obvious?'

'What did you want to say?'

He became thoughtful and distant. She set her chin on his chest and tried to understand his face. Beautiful lips, she thought, full and somehow smug. As if they would accept the kiss of a woman as a deserved right. She was offended by this. She should have made him suffer more before yielding. He must not think she was his right, like a Nobel or something.

'Tell me,' she said.

'There are things that a man like me cannot say in public,' he said. 'There are things that physics does not accept as its own. That's why I could not say it then.'

'You can tell me. A man can tell a naked woman anything.'

He did not speak for what seemed like a long time. She waited.

'I have not told anyone this,' she heard him say. And he fell silent again. He found it odd that he must say this now, in the dampness of a nudity that was somehow comical, and say it to a woman he did not know beyond the temporal anguish of love.

'Physics has to go,' he said, like a dying revolutionary wishing freedom for his real estate. That disappointed her even though she knew what he had to say was going to be, of course, about physics. She had hoped it would be about something else.

'Nobody is admitting it, but physics is stuck, physics has to change,' he said. 'The current laws are not enough. It needs something else. It has to accept something. Bombarding particles in a nine-billion-dollar collider is useless. It has to accept that. And more. It has to accept that life and consciousness are a hidden part of what we are trying to study. I cannot say something like this in public because it is a privilege given only to scientists who have gone mad.'

What he had in his mind was so simple and clear, but when asked, for the first time, to express it through the inadequacies of language it seemed so difficult and even plebian.

'I believe the universe has a plot, a purpose,' he said. 'I don't know what the game is, but something is there.' Then he said abruptly, clumsily, 'Have you heard of Libet?' That surprised her. Never would she have associated Acharya with the name of Libet.

Benjamin Libet was a part of male exotica, like time travel and antimatter. His name was usually invoked at the confluence of beer and philosophy, when stranded men asked deeply, 'Who are we?'

Oparna sat up. 'Libet?' she said, and giggled.

'Yes, Libet.'

'When was he active? Sixties, seventies?' she asked.

'Seventies, eighties.'

'He was with the physiology department, wasn't he, of the University of California?'

'You seem to know him pretty well,' Acharya said.

'Some things stick,' she said. 'He probed the human consciousness or something like that? And claimed to have proved that Free Will does not exist. But how can anybody prove something like that?'

'He fixed electrodes on the scalps of volunteers,' Acharya said, in a deep, solemn way, 'and he asked them to perform ordinary tasks like lifting a finger or pressing a button. He then showed that moments before they believed they had made the conscious decision to perform a task, their brains had already started the neural process to achieve the action. This implies that when a man lifts his finger, he is merely in the illusion of having made the decision. In reality, the event is preordained. If Libet is right, then there is an interpretation that people may not want to accept. That every action on Earth, the turn of a head, the bark of a dog, the fall of a flower, is a predestined inevitability. Like a scene in a film.'

Oparna wanted to say 'crap'. But there was something about the way he was gazing at the ceiling, with his eyes soft and intoxicated by a distant memory. She told herself that she would be a woman, she would be understanding. That was her perpetual weakness, anyway. To see the point of the men she loved.

'A long time ago I worked with him very briefly, just for a few weeks,' Acharya said, without taking his eyes off the ceiling. 'I helped him in his experiments.'

Oparna was surprised, but first she had to make a scientific objection: 'Libet's equipment was obviously primitive. There could have been an error.'

Acharya had heard these objections a thousand times, but there was something he knew which made him certain that Libet had stumbled upon a mystery that lay at the very heart of science. Oparna saw in his eyes an opaqueness, a grim unchangeable faith that would have normally exasperated her, but now, in the darkened lab, it almost convinced her that Libet was probably not so bad.

'What were you doing with Libet, anyway?' she asked. 'Weren't you busy demolishing the Big Bang then?'

'When I heard what he was trying to do, I got curious,' he said. He looked at her. 'Oparna,' he said, 'when I told you that I have not told anyone this, I was not referring to my connection with Libet. It's something else.'

She pulled herself closer to him. 'What is it then?' she asked.

'Something happened when I was about nine years old,' he said. He tried to sit up, but the floor was slippery in his sweat. She helped him, and he sat resting his back against the foot of the main desk. 'I was walking with my family to the circus. The car wouldn't start that day, and father said that since the circus tent was just a kilometre from home we should walk. There were a lot of us on the road. We were a big family. My mother had a box of groundnuts and she kept putting a heap into my palm. Suddenly, my mind went blank and I saw clearly a dwarf in a red T-shirt and white shorts. He was sitting on an elephant. A blue bird flew over his head. Then he fell off the elephant and was trampled. I saw this in my mind. My mother was walking by my side. I told her what I had seen. She smiled at me and ruffled my hair. "Don't worry," she said. When we entered the tent, I saw it was packed but the front seats were reserved for us. Everybody looked at us as we walked through the aisle and sat on the best seats. I sat between my parents. I wanted to feel safe because I knew what was going to happen.

'In the middle of the show an elephant walked on to the stage with a dwarf in a red T-shirt and shorts sitting on top of it. I looked at my mother. She was looking at me as though I were playing a trick on her. She was trying to figure out how I could have known. She pinched my thigh and whispered, "You sneaked in here yesterday? Tell me, I won't tell your father." A small blue bird appeared from nowhere and flew in a panic over the audience. Everybody howled because it was so beautiful. It flew over the head of the dwarf and disappeared through a small hole in the roof. The dwarf then fell off the elephant. The elephant had not shaken him off. It was calm. It was not afraid, nor had it gone mad. As though part of the show, the elephant then walked over the dwarf. It put its leg on his chest. I saw the dwarf's head rise for an instant and then fall. He died there on the floor. There was a commotion and everybody tried to run out. I remember my mother's face. She looked at me in fright. When we returned home she told my father about what I had told her. He didn't believe her or me. Then, somehow, the incident was forgotten. My mind never went blank like that again. I have never seen the future again. But something in me changed that day. And I have remained the same after that.'

Acharya's mind, in the trance of recounting an event from his childhood, stayed in that distant time. He remembered other images. The steam trains that bellowed beneath the footbridge, the stiffness of his starched shirt, his mother's safety-pin that sometimes held the fly of his shorts, the dragonflies in the paddy-fields to whose tails the boys tied a thread and used them as live kites. How the girls disapproved of this. And how they cried when the boys told them that soon it would be the fate of butterflies too. The final journeys of the dead, their noses stuffed with cotton, their faces yellow, the seriousness of the mourners on whose shoulders went the bed of the corpse or the decorated chair in which the dead sometimes sat so comically. The sunlit courtyard of his childhood home, its clean chessboard floors, the huge immovable doors and those carved wooden pillars that were more ancient than ghosts. And the narrow enchanted lane outside which ran through the shadows of other huge benevolent homes that could only be inherited now and never built. On their tiled roofs peacocks that had no masters used to stand still. Once, that was his life. And it all came back to him.

'So God has just been playing an old film all this while?' Oparna said. There was another question on the tip of her tongue, a more serious question, but she felt a little foolish articulating it. 'Why do you think there is life?' she asked, somewhat sheepishly. A naked woman sitting beside a naked man and asking, 'What is the meaning of life?' It was like a terrible moment from a porn film that aspired to be art. Yet she wanted to know what he had to say.

'I have a hypothesis,' he said, and the word 'hypothesis' made her arch forward and laugh, her loose hair falling over her face. He took it sportingly. He laughed too. 'I have a hypothesis,' he said again, and looked at her eagerly in the hope of making her laugh one more time. Then his grin slowly narrowed until it vanished entirely.

'Through life, the universe saves itself the trouble of making whole star systems by concentrating vast amounts of energy as consciousness. Why make a Jupiter, when you can just create a frog.'

'Jupiter and a frog have the same energy?'

'I think so.'

'That, Dr Arvind Acharya should never say in public.'

'Of course not.'

She put her head on his shoulder. There was something healing about this closeness that reminded her of all her wounds. What this man had told her about his childhood and his interpretations of what it all meant should have shaken her. But somehow she imagined that only he could be a part of this spring-toy universe where everything unwound in an inescapable, preordained way. Absolute truth was a gloom that happened to other people. Like him. It suited him. She could imagine Arvind Acharya, in the long pursuit of truth, wading through star systems across the aeons, trying to crack the game of life. The universe comprehending itself through him more than it probably did in other men. Now, after covering the vast stretch of space and the interminable ages, here he was by her side as a tired journeyman, to stay at this fortuitous crossing just for a fleeting night and proceed again on his solitary quest. So lonely he seemed. And then she felt a strange fear. It was the fatigue of loving another ephemeral lover. She did not want this one to leave.

When she finally found her watch on the floor, it was three in the morning. 'I have to go now,' she said. And they groped for the pieces of clothing that were strewn all over the floor. She crawled on the floor and searched under the tables for her hair-band. 'There you are,' she said, when she found it under a chair. She pulled her hair back and secured it in the loop.

He observed her as she put on her bra, very deftly, he thought.

'It is the ugliest word in English,' he said, 'Bra: it sounds terrible.'

'Be more sensitive,' she said. 'Oprah Winfrey says that 85 per cent of the women in the world live in the constant discomfort of wearing the wrong-sized bra.' And she said in a mock concern, mimicking someone he probably did not know. 'Poor women. We have to survive men, succeed in our professional lives and maintain good homes, and do all that in the wrong-sized bra.'

'This one seems to fit you well.'

'No, no, no,' she said, with a grimace. 'It's horrible. My ambition is to live in a decent country where a woman does not have to wear a bra.'

'You should have stayed back in Stanford.'

'But, you know, I cannot live without maids,' she said.

He was now standing up, fully dressed. She was sitting on the floor looking accusingly at him, holding her torn top. He was embarrassed by her stern look.

'How do I go home now?' she asked.

Ten minutes later, they were walking down on the driveway where her Baleno was parked. She was wearing his massive anorak that came almost to her knees.

'Do I look like a scarecrow?' she asked.

'Yes,' he said.

When she got into her car, he bent his head like a benevolent father. She rolled down the window.

'I will see you tomorrow,' he told her.

'We have a lot of work to do,' she said.

'Yes. A lot of work to do.'

'Tell me something,' she said, turning on the ignition. 'This search for life in the stratosphere, does it have anything to do with . . . you know . . . the missing link in physics and all that?'

'No.'

The guards opened the gates for her car to pass. Long after it disappeared, Acharya was standing on the driveway feeling the cool breeze and listening to the roar of the sea. He was relieved to be alone. There was a sense of joy in his heart and a feeling that he had done something endearingly mischievous. He imagined Lavanya smiling at him disapprovingly. It started to drizzle, and he made his way towards the gates. The night security scrambled to salute. As he passed through the gates, he and a guard exchanged a long glance of mutual suspicion.

Acharya's simple joy vanished when he reached home and turned on the lights of the hall. He felt dirty and cheap. He sat in the leather armchair, too scared to go to the bedroom. The clothes Lavanya had discarded in a hurry before shutting her suitcase still lay there on the bed. Her bottles of homeopathic tablets were on the nightstand. There was her treadmill too. Her things. They would be looking at him. So he slept in the hall, in the armchair, until he was awakened by the 7.45 alarm of his daughter. The alarm had an edge to it this morning. It was morbid. Like a little girl's dismembered doll. The alarm was a voice from the other side of a fence, from where the severe wraiths of his wife and daughter looked at him with hurt and anger. But as the morning unfolded, he was filled with the anticipation of seeing Oparna again.

And that's how he was in the days that followed. He would wake up in the despair of having murdered his wife and daughter, and then he would search impatiently for his clothes, to go and wait for Oparna.

In the common paranoia that afflicts lovers, Acharya and Oparna did not meet alone in his room any more, even when there was a professional need to meet. Eyes were watching, ears were listening. They feared the omnipotent gaze of Ayyan Mani and his smile that Oparna believed was replete with meaning. The scientists and research hands who were involved in the Balloon Mission began to feel that group meetings were suddenly frequent and long. In those meetings Acharya and Oparna would steal glances of forced grimness. They smiled with their eyes and spoke the language of love through dry enquiries. At night, she would wait for him in the abandoned basement and he would appear like a shadow.

This went on for a week, including a whole Sunday of love and dining in the dungeon. Oparna brought an electric toaster, bread, fruit and even blankets, and they lay huddled all day. On Tuesday, Lavanya called.

Ayyan Mani set the phone receiver down with a diabolic smile. The fate of every love story, he knew very well, is in the rot of togetherness, or in the misery of separation. Lovers often choose the first with the same illusory wisdom that makes people choose to die later than now. And in the deceptions of new love, they not only forget that this insanity is transient but they also, hilariously, imagine that they are clandestine. Their nocturnal nudity, they believe they have camouflaged in office clothes. Their private bond, they have spread thin in public as careful distances. They infect each other with the fever in their eyes and they believe only they can diagnose it. But in reality, love is like forbidden wealth. Its glow cannot be hidden. Sooner or later everyone comes to know. And two people become spectacles in a show they do not know is running to full houses.

Ayyan was not certain if the Brahmins who contemplated the universe were aware of it yet, but the security guards and the peons and the sweepers knew that the Big Man was screwing the basement item. The spectral presence that the lovers had sensed outside the basement door was the spirit of Ayyan's long reach. The whole week, he was told about the moans and whispers that came from the lab. The time Acharya went to the basement and when the two emerged, and how he crouched fondly at her car window and said goodbye. Now the time had come for this romance to be shaken, and he suspected it did not have the good fortune to survive. Lavanya Acharya had just called from Chennai.

'Is he there?' she asked.

'No, Madam,' Ayyan said, after a deliberate pause. The pause, he knew, annoyed her. She suspected that her husband avoided her sometimes at work.

'Where is he?'

'I don't know where he is, Madam,' Ayyan said. (Acharya was in his room at that moment.) 'Can I take a message?'

'Tell him I'm on the seven o'clock flight. I will be arriving before nine. Is it raining heavily?'

'Very heavily.'

'Are the roads flooded?'

'The trains are running.'

'And the roads?'

'The traffic is moving.'

'Tell him he doesn't have to come to the airport,' she said. 'A friend is picking me up.'

Ayyan collected the late mails and fax messages, and walked into Acharya's room. He was scribbling something on a notepad. Ayyan peeped to see what he was writing. It was a long string of maths rubbish. Numbers and symbols. Pursuit of truth, apparently.

'Any instructions for me, Sir?' he asked. Acharya shook his head.

'I'll leave then.'

Ayyan did not tell him about his wife's call. She would be home in a few hours and would try to call him. But then he would be in the unreachable depths of the basement, naked with his mistress. He would go home before dawn in the stupor of love and see the terrifying image of his wife. Why would Ayyan want to tell him about the call?

That night, the lovers lay curled on a purple blanket, like two brackets. A bowl of seedless grapes was by their side. 'Have you ever wondered about Junk DNA?' Acharya asked.

'Yes,' she said, '98 per cent of the human genome is junk and does nothing apparently. It makes no sense that junk genes exist.'

'There must be a reason,' he said, reaching for a grape. 'I have a hypothesis.' He thought she would giggle because she usually found it funny when he said 'hypothesis'. But she was listening keenly. He said, 'Life travels through the universe as microscopic spores riding on asteroids and they fall on different worlds. Depending on the conditions in those worlds, different segments of the genome become useful. On Earth, only a fraction is needed.'

'Where do you think the spores are coming from?' she asked.

He took another grape and said, 'I don't know everything.'

It was around two in the morning when he made his way home. It was raining hard and he went unmindful, like a happy drunk. His light-blue shirt stuck to his soft body; his trousers lay precariously at his lower waist. (He had left the belt in the basement.)

He put the key in the latch and turned the knob. The light was on in the hall. He shut the door and stood near the couch. He tried to understand why the light was on. Then he noticed the tidiness of the room. The curtains and the tablecloth had changed. The books he had left on the couch had vanished. He went to the bedroom with a sinking heart. He could see a sleeping figure shrouded in a blanket.

Lavanya was dreaming, and these days, she knew she was dreaming. She was walking through a rain forest. She had never been inside a rain forest, but it was so obviously a rain forest. Gigantic tree trunks, black and wet, stood like creatures. The floor was a bed of wild creepers. There was also a board that said 'Rain Forest'. It was raining so heavily now that when she stretched her hand she could not see beyond the elbow. But she was not wet. Because she did not like getting wet. She was carrying a maroon shopping bag and she was searching for a shop that sold cashews. From the dense mist of rain a huge elephant head appeared. The rest of its body was hidden in the rain. It was a wise lovable elephant. 'Arvind,' she said, 'what are you doing here?' And she opened her eyes.

She saw his huge silhouette lurking beyond the other side of the bed. She reached for the switch above her nightstand. 'You're wet,' she said, getting out of bed. She opened the dresser sleepily and took out a towel. 'I don't know why you like getting wet,' she said, reaching for his head with the towel. 'The house was a mess, Arvind. Are you really mad, or are you doing this to annoy me? It was filthy when I walked in. I am going to give the keys to the maids now.' He did not move as she wiped his head and his face.

'You can say you are happy to see me,' she said.

'I missed you.'

'You are working late these days? Is it the balloon?' she asked. Her shoulders ached, so she stopped drying him. 'Now go to the bathroom and change. Put the wet clothes in the washing machine.' When he left the room, she wondered what the smell was. It was sweet and it reminded her of something she had known a long time ago. But she could not recognize it. The smell of rain on a man's body maybe?

He walked in dry and tidy, in a loose tracksuit, his chest bare. He lay on the bed and stared at the ceiling.

'What is worrying you, Arvind? What has happened?'

'Nothing.'

'And what is this? You sprayed deo?' she said with a chuckle. 'Two weeks I am away and you become totally crazy?'

His chest was still moist and she dried it, muttering that he was making the bed wet. And unknowingly, she dug her finger into his navel. 'There is no lint at all,' she said. She went to the corner of the room to put the towel away. 'How can you not have any lint at all in that well of a navel? Are you having an affair or something?' she asked.

'Yes,' he said.

Lavanya wondered if she should go to the balcony and put the towel on the wire, or if she should just put it on the floor for the time being. She was too sleepy to go to the balcony, but the floor was not the place for a towel. And, obviously, she did not want to put it on the dresser. The thought of a wet towel on polished wood was repulsive. Then she wondered why the word was hanging in the air like sorrow. 'Yes,' he had said. She turned to him slowly.

'Her name is Oparna,' he said. 'She works with me.'

Lavanya collapsed slowly and sat on the edge of the bed. 'This is not a hiccup cure, is it?'

'You don't have hiccups.'

'I am confused,' she said. 'What did you say? What was it that you had said?'

She went to the nightstand and searched for her glasses, as though that would make her hear better. 'What did you say, Arvind?' she asked, putting her glasses on. She sat on the edge of the bed again.

'Her name is Oparna,' he said.

The rain outside the window was furious. They listened to it. She said, a bit dreamily, 'I cannot believe this. You? You don't know anything. You don't even know if your nose is long or short.'

He did not understand the connection between his nose and the situation. But he realized that she was right. If someone asked him to describe his own nose, he wouldn't know what to say.

'How long has it been going on?'

'After you left. Just before, actually. But, in a way, after you left.'

The silence returned and the rain appeared to grow even more violent. He looked at the ceiling. She stared at the dresser.

'I am sorry,' he said. 'I feel as though I have murdered you.'

'Is she young?'

'Yes.'

'Pretty?'

'Yes.'

'How young?'

'As old as Shruti, I think.'

'Did you bring her here?'

'No.'

'You slept with her?'

'Yes.'

'Where?'

'In the basement of the Institute.'

‘That’s sick,’ she said. She began to fold the towel. ‘Do you love her?’ she asked.

‘I don’t know.’

Lavanya walked out of the bedroom. She heard him say something, but she would understand it only moments later – ‘But you’re still my email password.’

She sat on the couch in the hall, her legs tucked beneath her. I am tired of funerals, she thought, and she wondered who had died now. It did not feel as though he had died. She still felt his looming presence. The quiet turbulence of a man was very much there in her life. But certainly it felt as if someone had died. She sat there that way the whole night until she could hear the birds and see the first light of the morning in a small patch of sky that was visible through the suspended shrubs in the balcony. She recognized the wound now. It was fear that she was feeling. Fear at not feeling sad at all. It was shocking to imagine him having an affair. It was pathetic. But it did not make her feel sad and that’s what made her feel afraid. People usually feared the future, but this fear was about the past. She wondered why she didn’t care. Did she ever love this man enough? What was it that they had for over four decades? Another arrangement? But she also knew she loved him. He was some sort of a stranger now, but when she remembered him as a memory, she loved that memory very much. In fact, she wanted to go to him and run her hand on his bald head and tell him it was all right. She felt a heartbreaking compassion for him. She wanted him to be happy. As he was on that distant day when he was a boy groom and for some reason he had whispered to her eagerly, ‘Lavanya, you know, the Earth moves at forty kilometres a second.’

She saw a shadow in the passage that connected the hall to the kitchen. He was standing at the doorway of the bedroom. She could not see him but she could see his shadow. His head peeped out. He was surprised to see her on the couch. They looked at each other and turned away. After a few minutes, the shadow came to the hall and stood by her side. She did not look at him. He went to the dining-table and sat on a chair. Occasionally, he turned to look at her. At 7.45, the sound of Shruti's alarm pierced through their silence. And both of them felt that they should hide.

He sat in the hall all morning toying with a spoon, or wrinkling the edges of the newspaper, or raising his legs for the maid to sweep the floor, and raising them once again when she came to mop. Lavanya went to the kitchen to be with the cook. It was the cook who brought him coffee that morning, and then breakfast. He drank the coffee and ate the breakfast without budging from the chair, as if he were encroaching and he would lose his home if he rose. Around noon, he went for a bath. He stayed at home the whole day. The cook did not come in the evenings. And Lavanya did not cook that night. So he fumbled through the fridge for food and heated whatever he could find.

And that's how it was all week. He would wake up and sit silently on a chair, or stand in the balcony, and not utter a word. He would eat what was served on the table and when he realized that food was not coming to him, he would go to it.

On the morning of the third day of his exile, Lavanya was in the hall reading the paper. She realized that the maid was staring at her.

'Phone,' the maid said with a grimace.

Lavanya went back to reading. The phone on the steel double-helix stand near the television rang for a while and died. They had not been taking calls for the last three days. That morning, the phone was ringing relentlessly, and Lavanya knew why. It was the desperation of a bitch.

The phone rang again. Lavanya let it ring. Acharya looked at the phone just once and turned away sadly. She saw that. The day went by in the lull of the rains and the sedation of its cool breeze, and the unrelenting calm of a wound that was stirred every now and then by the phone. In the evening, when the phone rang one more time, Lavanya finally took the call. There was a silence at the other end.

'Is that Oparna?' Lavanya asked.

'Yes,' the voice said.

'This is our home and we do not want to be disturbed. Don't call again.'

She put the receiver down and pulled the cord out of the socket. She looked at her husband who was sitting at the dining-table. His back was bent and his head drooped to his left a bit. She felt an ache, as though she had denied an infant a simple joy. She served him dinner that night.

'Can't get good fish in the rains,' she told him, wondering if crustaceans could be called fish. He had said something about it before.

On Monday morning, he left for work. On the walkway around the central lawn, he felt he was being watched. The soft sound of the sea was like the murmur of whispers. And two young men in jeans who passed him by appeared to look at him with a cautious respect that had nothing to do with his scientific stature.

Ayyan Mani rose in his customary half-stand. The edges of his lips, surely, were wrinkled in a knowing smile.

'Ask Oparna to come in,' Acharya said, as he went into his room.

Ayyan punched in the numbers, thinking of Acharya's unreasonable tranquillity. It reminded him of the peace in his own chest a fortnight after his father's death. It was the peace of a cruel relief at how easily a trauma had passed.

'The Director has asked you to come up,' he told Oparna. He heard the phone go dead immediately. He looked at the clock to mark the time. If she arrived in less than three minutes it would mean that at some point on the stairways or down the corridors she had been running. It was always entertaining, the misery of lovers. He held a receiver to his ear to check if he could hear the Director's room clearly. He did not want to miss anything today.

She walked in less than three minutes after Ayyan had called her. But she pretended to be calm, almost lethargic. Ayyan pointed to the sofa. He wanted to study her face. It had been over a week since he saw her. She stood there in a sort of meek defiance. She wanted to head straight to the door, but she was not sure about her place any more. Ayyan could see that.

He dialled a number and frowned as if he could not get through. From behind the frown, he looked at her carefully. So this is how a liberated woman looks when she is heartbroken. Dark circles, defeat in the eyes, hair unhealthy. She would let a man do this to her. Oparna Goshmaulik would. Again and again. But there were many maids in BDD who would never let a man break their hearts. In fact, a growing number of girls in the chawls, especially the ones who were really poor, were choosing to remain unmarried so that they could live in peace. So Ayyan wondered what was so formidable about women like Oparna. More than the impoverished girls of the chawls whom they hoped to uplift, it was Oparna and her lemon-fragrant friends who were weak and dependent on men. They appeared to do many marvellous things, but what they wanted was a man. He thought of Acharya and Nambodri, and the alcoholics of BDD whose livers bled, and the silver sperms in the seaside homes that they inherited, who listened to 'My Way', and the pathetic evening faces in the gents' compartment, and he shuddered at the thought of ever being in a situation where he would have to be dependent on the emotions and love of men. It was a terrifying thought, really.

'Oparna is here,' he told the phone, and pointed her to the inner door.

Arvind Acharya could not understand why this apparition always made him weak. The words he was forming in his mind, the morose declaration of separation, vanished. Like the careful notes of an orator blown away by a sudden gust. There she stood, so splendid in her long shapeless top and jeans. Her eyes, so breathtakingly tired, her face diffused and weak and adorable. He wanted to hold her and touch that mystical spot which made the heads of women fall on the shoulders of their men.

He was standing by the window. She walked over to him and held his hand. 'Why didn't you call me?' she asked.

'I didn't feel like it, Oparna,' he said.

'You didn't feel like it?'

'That's the truth.'

'Just a call would have kept me from going mad.'

'You'll be all right.'

'I don't want to be all right.'

'But that's the best we can hope for each other.'

She could see in his eyes the finality of decision. She had seen it in other men. The end of a spell and their sudden remembrance of what they called conscience or freedom or family or work, or something else. And she felt tired now. Tired of the violence of love and separation. She reached for his hand again and locked her fingers in his. She looked at the floor and wept. She tried not to, but she wept. Her grip around his fingers grew fierce. She shut her eyes tight. He could barely make out what she said. 'I am not some holiday you take when your wife is away' (probably that was what she had said). She untangled her fingers from his and wiped her tears, like a child. Then she walked away.

She would return four times that day, against her better judgement, to plead with him, and each time she would go back in the humiliation of having begged for love. She would do that for another three days until Acharya would tell her, 'This can't go on. Either I should leave, or you should leave.' She pushed the heap of mail from his desk. She looked demented. But Acharya was capable of far greater rage, and in the fury of the moment that drove away the pigeons outside the window, he screamed, 'Get out, get out.'

Character, Ayyan Mani observed in the anteroom, is actually blood pressure.

Oparna did not visit the third floor for days after that. But one Wednesday she appeared. She went to Acharya and said, 'I can accept this. It's over, I know. Sorry I behaved like an idiot. I'm all right now.'

'I am sorry,' Acharya said wearily. 'I am responsible for all this. But I don't know what is the right thing to do now.'

'Don't worry about that,' she said, 'I am all right.'

'You are?'

'Yes,' she said. 'Let's finish the Mission. It means a lot to both of us. And then we shall see.'

'And then we shall see,' he said softly.

Her eyes slowly became luminous and she turned away and left the room. He stood there, feeling lonely, staring at the door that was still closing. He remembered the dwarf from another time who rode the elephant, his fate decided aeons before, like the birth of stars and the collision of worlds. Our stories, too, Oparna, were just meant to be. But this truth, there was something indecent about this truth.

PART FOUR

The First Thousand Prime Numbers

IT WAS RAINING hard and the taxi driver could not see a thing. But he was racing down the wet road, honking. There were no wipers on the windscreen, but there was one lying on his dashboard. He grabbed it, muttering something, and holding the steering-wheel with one hand, he reached out through the window to clean the windscreen. He saw, just in the time, the tail-lights of a car standing at the signal. He almost stood on the break and screamed, 'Motherfucker.' The taxi stopped inches from the car. Adi asked his father what a motherfucker was.

'Tell him,' Ayyan said to the driver, who giggled coyly.

The boy, as always, was by the left window of the back seat, his good ear facing Ayyan. Despite the freak rains, the resurgent heat of September steamed in the ancient Fiat, and their shirts were damp with sweat. But even this was marginally cooler than home. Oja had had to put a bucket of water under the fan to cool the room. Adi did not pee in it any more after being slapped for that by his mother last summer.

Adi kept removing his hearing-aid and wiping it because the streams of sweat from his oiled hair were flowing into his ears. But he did not mind the discomfort. Maybe he did not recognize it as discomfort. The torment of the weather was also a type of game for him. He was licking his sweat from the cheeks.

'Mercedes,' he screamed. A long silver car had eased to a halt by the side of the taxi. The dim figure of a man was visible in the back seat. He was sitting cross-legged and thoughtful, elbow on thigh, finger on the lower lip. Adi imitated him perfectly. The man in the car smiled. Adi smiled back. Then the signal turned green.

'How much is a Mercedes?' he asked his father.

'What model was it?'

'C-Class. 220 CDI.'

'That's a cheap one.'

'How much?'

'Thirty lakhs.'

Adi howled. 'Expensive,' he said in English.

'Not that much.'

'You should save money. We should not take the taxi to school.'

'We do this only when it rains and it is only twenty rupees.'

Adi puffed out his cheek and made a fart sound, and they both giggled.

'Now tell me Adi, what did you do?'

The boy put his hand on his head in exasperation. 'How many times do I have to tell you? Nothing.'

'Then why does the Principal want to meet me?'

'I don't know,' Adi said. 'Yesterday I didn't do anything. The day before yesterday I didn't do anything. Day before day before yesterday, I asked the maths teacher, "Is five to the power of zero equal to one, Miss?"'

'So why is the Principal calling me?'

'I don't know.'

'She had written in your handbook, "Come with the boy to my room."'

'I don't like her,' Adi said.

'We will go and find out what you've done.'

'I do only what you say I should do.'

'Good boy.'

'What if someone finds out?'

Adi's face turned serious as his father fondled his hair playfully. 'So much coconut oil your mother poured on your head.' The oil made the boy's forehead and ears shine. He was such a beautiful, healthy boy, Ayyan thought. Then he felt the lifeless hardness of the hearing-aid in the other ear.

Sister Chastity had a scowl on her face. She was sorting out some papers on her table and getting more entangled in the muddle. Behind her, the head of Jesus Christ appeared more tilted than Ayyan remembered, as if to get a better view of her. Across her table were seated two unhappy men and a young skinny woman in a cotton sari.

'Good morning Sister,' Adi said, and, turning to the three other teachers, he said quickly, 'Good morning Sir, good morning Sir, good morning Miss.'

Sister Chastity looked up with a tired face, but she brightened up a little when she saw the father and son. 'You have come,' she said. She asked the teachers to leave them, 'for exactly five minutes'. The teachers carefully gathered their share of papers from the table. The way they treated the loose sheets made Ayyan curious. All he could make out before they put the papers in a file was that every sheet contained numbered questions. The teachers gave a knowing smile to the father and son, and they left the room.

Sister Chastity pointed to the chairs and rubbed her hands in anticipation. She looked at the boy and at his father and then, in a more interested way, at the boy again. She was distracted by the stacks of paper between them. She pushed them away muttering, 'They gave me a computer saying I'd never need to file papers again. But now, all I am doing is filing print-outs. Do you have a computer at home, Mr Mani?'

'No,' Adi said.

'I am talking to your father, Adi. You must know how to behave.'

'I am sorry, Sister, I have sinned.'

'It's "I am sorry, *Father*, I have sinned". Genius and all that, and you don't know simple things?'

'I am sorry, Sister.'

'Now what was I trying to say? Yes. Mr Mani, you don't have a computer at home?'

'No,' he said.

'St Andrew's Church is selling old computers at unbelievable prices for its less fortunate parishioners,' she said. 'Just one thousand rupees for a Perinium 2.'

'Pentium,' the boy corrected.

'Yes, Pentium. Adi, I am talking to your father.'

'Nice thing the Church is doing,' Ayyan said.

'Isn't it nice? Do you know where St Andrew's Church is?'

'No.'

Sister Chastity shook her head sadly. 'The joys of Christian life are available to all but very few open their eyes before the Lord shuts them.' Ayyan looked at her meekly. 'Now, Mr Mani,' she said, 'I will come to the point. You are aware of the interschool science quiz we are organizing?'

'No, Sister.'

She widened her eyes. 'You haven't seen the posters?'

'No.'

'The posters have been up on the main gate notice-board for over a fortnight now. You must always read the notice-board, Mr Mani. In three days, we will be hosting the quiz finals. Grand Finale, it is being called. Five hundred tenth-standard students from fifty schools went through the written elimination rounds. Six teams have been chosen for the finals. For the Grand Finale.' Ayyan nodded with evident interest. 'We were, in fact, finalizing the questions when you walked in,' she said. 'That's the quiz committee waiting outside.'

'I didn't see anyone outside,' Ayyan said.

'The three teachers, Mr Mani,' Sister Chastity said, making a face of immense patience. 'They went out right now, didn't they? They are the quiz committee.'

'OK,' Ayyan said. 'Can parents come and watch the quiz?'

'Parents have to come. We are having the event in our main auditorium.' (She always said 'main auditorium' though the school had only one. She also said 'main gate' though there was only one entrance.)

'We will be there,' Ayyan said.

'There is a reason why I asked you to come with Adi,' she said softly. 'The teams from our own school couldn't make it to the finals. They were disqualified in the preliminary rounds. You know how fair we are. We wouldn't do anything shady to favour our teams. We are the host school and we have graciously accepted that our teams were not good enough. But it is sad, isn't it?'

'It is sad.'

'It's very sad. But I have an idea,' she said, now beaming. 'I can still make a place for a special participant from our school who will not compete for the prize but for the honour.'

'And you want Adi to be that special participant?'

'Obviously.'

Ayyan looked thoughtful.

'What's the problem with that?' she asked, looking at Adi. 'A small brilliant kid competing against the brightest seventeen-year-olds in the city. It will be a sight. How old are you now, Adi?'

'I am eleven. Eleven is a prime number.'

Sister Chastity imitated him fondly, '"I am eleven. Eleven is a prime number." What an odd angel this boy is.'

'He is just a little kid who is fooling around,' Ayyan said feebly.

'But he is a genius.'

'He has stage fright.'

'Stage fright?'

'Yes. He becomes frightened when he has to face a lot of strangers.'

'We will all be there to make him feel comfortable,' she said, her face now beginning to lose its pleasantness.

'But there is something we have to think,' Ayyan said carefully in English. (Sometimes he spoke to her in English. For practice.)

'You mean there is something we have to *consider*,' she said severely, and looked with sympathy at the boy.

'Yes, something we have to *consider*,' Ayyan said.

'What is it?'

'Think: Adi is sitting on the stage. Sorry, *imagine* Adi is sitting on the stage. Then the questions come. Adi begins to answer those questions, it will be great.'

'Yes. It'll be incredible.'

'No.'

'No?'

'It will be so unbelievable that people will accuse you of leaking the questions because he is from host school.'

Sister Chastity ignored the missing definite article. She saw his point. She nodded. 'I didn't think of it that way,' she said.

Ayyan looked at the stacks of papers on her table. He wondered where the quiz questions were. Probably with the three teachers who were waiting outside. Or, probably right here.

'You have a point,' she said and exhaled. 'OK, then. The classes are going to start now. Adi, you should get going.'

'How many teams in the finals?' Ayyan asked.

'Six,' she said.

'Girls and boys?'

'Yes,' she said impatiently. 'Mostly boys. But one team has only girls.'

There was something here, Ayyan knew. There was an opportunity. 'The plan to expand the computer lab – any progress?' he asked.

'Yes, parents will be notified,' she said, now overtly irritated.

'Any increase in fees because of computer lab?'

'We've not made any decision on that front. Now Mr Mani, if you'll . . .'

One of her phones rang. 'Hello,' Sister Chastity said. 'Oh dear. Where? I am coming.' She put the phone down and rushed out. 'A girl has fainted,' she muttered on her way out.

The door shut behind her, but Ayyan could hear her fading footsteps. He counted them. She seemed to have gone far. He stood up and arched towards her side of the desk, and rummaged through the stacks of paper. He did not look at the door even once, but he listened for the slightest sound. He removed whole sheets of paper from of envelopes and went through them swiftly.

There were bills and more bills and a lot of letters from the office of the Archbishop.

Adi looked at his father with his large keen eyes. 'What are you doing?' he asked.

'Shhh,' his father said.

'What are you doing?' Adi whispered excitedly.

Ayyan opened the drawers and looked in. There were invitations, rosaries and letters to the municipality. But nothing appeared to contain quiz questions. He found some mid-term question-papers though. He then threw a decisive look at the three land phones lying on her desk. He picked one and dialled his own mobile number. He took the call and put the mobile back in his trouser pocket. Very carefully, he placed the receiver slightly askew on its cradle.

He went back to his chair and waited for her. Adi looked at him with a bright smile. They heard the faint voice of Sister Chastity barking orders.

'What's wrong with girls these days?' she said, as she entered the room. She sank into her swivel chair and said angrily, 'A girl has fainted. Her mother says that after she has a meal she goes to the bathroom, puts her finger inside her throat and pukes out everything she has eaten. She is twelve you see. So Madam came to school having puked her breakfast at home. What happens? She falls down in the corridor. That's what happens. Lord, what's wrong with these girls?'

'Is she fat?' Ayyan asked curiously.

'She is a bit on the plump side.'

'She wants to lose weight?'

'Obviously.'

'So she vomits the food she eats?'

'Yes,' Sister Chastity said.

'You should give her one slap,' he said.

'She is all right now. We sprinkled some water on her face and gave her glucose.'

'You didn't understand,' Ayyan said. 'You should give her one good slap.'

'No no, we don't do that kind of thing here.'

Sister Chastity called the name of the peon, thumping the bell on her desk. The peon peeped from the doorway.

'Ask them to come in,' she said. 'OK, Mr Mani. Sorry for wasting your time. I've to sit with the quiz committee now. Adi, go to your class.'

As the father and son left the room, they saw the three teachers enter. Cordial smiles were exchanged once again. Ayyan took his son to the base of the stairway that led to his classroom. He fished out a notebook from the boy's bag and tore off several pages. Adi put his hand on his head. 'What are you doing?' he asked. Ayyan took a pencil from his box.

'Adi, now go to the class,' he said, giving him the bag. 'And, remember, all this is our secret.' Ayyan extended his little finger. Adi locked it with his.

'But what is the secret?'

'What I did in the room.'

'Why should that be a secret?'

'Adi, run now.'

The deafening sound of the morning bell startled them both. They looked at each other for a moment. And they laughed. 'Go now,' Ayyan said.

He watched as the boy made his way up the stairs. Then he put his mobile to his ear and poised the pencil against the pages he had torn from Adi's notebook. As he walked towards the black wrought-iron gate, Sister Chastity's room came alive in his ear. They were talking, and they were talking about the quiz. He stood in a peaceful back lane near the school listening to their conversation. But he could glean only six questions.

IT WAS AROUSING. Oja Mani's hair was bundled into a thin white towel. The back of her red nightgown was wet. Her silver anklets lay feebly at her turmeric yellow ankles. It was a sight that always made Ayyan look furtively at what his son was doing. In the freshness of marriage, when he used to see her like this, he would pester her to take off all her clothes, except the towel. In time, she refused to yield. But that did not cure him. This post-bath image of the woman that disturbed his peace so easily was also the most enduring symbol of a housewife. He had seen it in the Tamil soaps that Oja was addicted to. Housewives shrouded their hair in a towel. Working women used hairdryers.

Oja opened the steel cupboard, aware that he was watching. The hierarchy in the cupboard had not changed ever since she had established it. The lowest rung was for the grains. Above it were the spices and pickles and then there were special plates for guests. The top three rungs were for clothes. In a blue plastic box were her ancestral ornaments that always reminded her of her good fate. 'It does not matter if it's with me or if it's with you, my child,' her mother had said before her marriage, 'it will be his when he threatens to burn you with kerosene.'

Oja took out four of her best saris and showed them to him. He walked to her side to get a better look. She was surprised at how seriously he was taking this. He pointed to the only sari that did not shine. It was a blue cotton sari with small white squares.

'There will be a lot of rich people,' he said, 'and rich women laugh at women who wear shiny clothes in the day.'

'How do you know so much about rich women?'

'And no fat gold necklace. What you are wearing is all right. It's thin. It's good.'

'But it is an important day, you said.'

'Important does not mean gold any more.'

She frowned, but conceded. In these matters, he was usually right. She studied her man. He was in a Rin-white full-sleeved shirt, smartly tucked into grey trousers. His black formal shoes were newly polished. And he was wearing a watch. He wore that only on special occasions. And he was smelling good.

'You should wear that coat you have,' she said. 'You look like a hero in it.'

'No, no. You are not supposed to wear a coat for something like this. You are supposed to look like you don't care much.'

'Adi,' Oja screamed, 'finish your bath.'

Adi was in the stained-glass enclosure in the corner of the kitchen. And he was singing aloud, 'D-I-S-C-O. Disco, Disco.'

'Adi, get out now.'

The boy emerged in a towel. Oja went hastily into the enclosure, giving him a foul look. 'Disco, disco,' Adi told her.

Ayyan dried him, glancing at the stained-glass bathroom he had once built with love. The boy showed the hearing-aid to his father. Ayyan helped him put it on. He bound the small white box around Adi's stomach. A white wire ran out of the box. He blew into the boy's left ear to dry it. Adi giggled. So Ayyan did it again. Then he fitted the earpiece into Adi's ear.

When Oja stepped out of the enclosure, she looked at them for approval. This is a very beautiful young woman, Ayyan thought. He pouted his lips at her in a raunchy code. She smiled. She didn't mind dirty thoughts because she didn't have to do much beneath them. She went to the full-length mirror of the cupboard. Ayyan and Adi watched her closely as she bulged her eyes and drew around them with a black pencil.

They had an argument in the taxi. Oja had wanted to take the bus or walk. Ayyan wanted to take the taxi.

'It's going to rain,' he told her.

Adi was squeezed in the back seat between his parents.

'It does not rain inside the bus,' she said angrily.

'And from the bus-stop to the school?'

'We have umbrellas, don't we? And anyway, I don't think it's going to rain.'

'It's just twenty rupees.'

'Little grains make a fat man's meal,' Oja and Adi said together, and that made them laugh.

By the time the taxi approached the gates, Oja had fallen silent. She was nervous. The left side of the lane was completely taken up by parked cars. And there was a commotion near the gates. Drivers who couldn't find a parking space were trying to turn around, and that was causing a jam. The guard looked at Oja, breast to toe, and beamed at Ayyan.

'All the rich folks have come,' the guard said.

'I have to go to the class,' Adi said, extricating his finger from his father's fist. 'Parents have to go to the hall. Students will come in a line,' he said. Then he gave quick instructions. 'Parents don't have to walk in a line. They can walk anyway they want.' He pointed to the main block to his right. 'The main auditorium is here. Don't call it "hall". It is called "The Main Auditorium".'

He walked briskly down the front path towards the stairway. After a few paces he turned and gave a knowing smile to his father. Oja waved at him, and for a moment tried to decipher what the stealthy smile between father and son was about. She went quietly with Ayyan towards the main block. Two little girls in blue pinafores, much younger than Adi, were walking in front of them and talking animatedly in English. Oja laughed. 'So fast they speak in English,' she said.

Outside the auditorium's rear entrance, parents chatted above the din of the festive murmurs coming from inside. They directed occasional glances towards the students who were arriving in orderly lines and vanishing through the front door.

'Should we go in now or later?' Oja whispered to her husband.

'Why are you whispering?'

'I am not whispering,' she whispered.

They were standing a few feet away from a group of parents, about a dozen of them, who were talking about the horse-riding classes in a new international board school that had sprung up in the suburbs. The mothers were in T-shirt and jeans, and trousers that reached just below their knees, and long skirts. Some were in salwars. All of them – they looked so expensive. Oja inched closer to her husband.

Ayyan studied the fathers. His own shirt, he knew, was good. It had cost him five hundred rupees, but there was something about the shirts of these men and their trousers and the way they stood, that made him feel that he looked like their driver. In the morning, when he had inspected himself in the mirror, he was certain that he measured up to them, but now, in their midst, he was somehow smaller. And Oja looked like their cook.

'Let's go and talk to them,' Ayyan said.

'No,' Oja said, but he had already started walking towards them. She trailed behind him. They stood at the periphery of the group. Ayyan maintained a smile of being involved in their conversation and tried to make eye-contact with a man he remembered meeting earlier. The women surveyed Oja briefly. One of them looked at her feet, and Oja curled her toes.

When there was a brief pause in the conversation, Ayyan said to his acquaintance, in English, 'We have met. I am Aditya Mani's father.'

The acquaintance looked kindly at him and said, 'Of course, I remember.' He turned to the gathering and said, 'Guys, this is the father of the genius.' Oja did not realize it, but she was nodding like a spring-headed doll and smiling at the women.

'Genius?' a man asked in a whisper.

'Yes. He is what, eleven or something. And he talks about relativity and all that.'

'Really?'

'Aditya, yes,' a woman's face lit up. 'I have heard stories about him. So he really does exist.' She told Oja in Hindi, 'Your son is very special.'

Oja looked coyly at her husband and giggled. She whispered to her husband, but everybody could hear it, 'Let's go.'

Six tables were arranged in a semi-circle on the stage. On a blue background was a thermocol board that said, 'St Andrew's School. First Interschool Science Quiz'. The participants were yet to arrive but the hall was packed. On either side of a red-carpeted aisle, students sat on wooden benches. They filled most of the auditorium. Adi was somewhere in the sixth row. In the last rows, some boys had faint moustaches.

'These boys are so big,' Ayyan told his wife. 'And these girls have breasts.'

They were towards the end of the hall, on cushioned chairs, with other parents and teachers. The little group of parents Ayyan had spoken to outside were in the row in front. Oja toyed with the pendant of her thin gold chain and studied the necks of the mothers.

The lights dimmed and the murmurs of the students grew louder. On the darkened stage, six pairs of students appeared. There were two beautiful adolescent girls in olive-green skirts and white shirts. Others were pubescent boys in various uniforms. They sat at the desks and waited. The stage lights came on and the audience clapped. There were a few whistles too. Sister Chastity appeared and she walked smartly to the middle of the stage holding a wireless mike.

'Who was whistling?' was the first thing she said. That brought about an absolute silence. 'Students of St Andrew's do not whistle.' She then smiled at the gathering and said, 'Good morning parents, teachers and students. Welcome to the first Interschool Science quiz of St Andrew's.'

She spoke about the school, its recent achievements, its plans and then she introduced the quizmaster. He was the senior maths teacher of the school, one of the men Ayyan had seen in the Principal's office the week before.

There was a loud applause when he walked on to the stage. He looked happier now and smarter in a black suit and blue tie. He too had a wireless mike in his hand. He had an amiable way of speaking, and he spoke very fast as if he were reading out the risk factors in a mutual fund commercial. He laid down the rules and asked the contestants to introduce themselves. Sister Chastity went down the aisle and sat among the parents and teachers. She was in the same row as Ayyan, but on the other side of the aisle.

'Let's begin the first round,' the quizmaster said. 'The first round is the physics round.' He looked at Team A and said, 'Are you ready for the very first question of the first Annual Interschool Science Quiz Contest of St Andrew's English School?'

The grim boys of Team A did not nod.

'All right. Here goes,' the quizmaster said, looking at a card that he was holding. 'These two gentlemen wanted to prove the existence of something called ether. Instead, they accidentally discovered that light travels at a constant speed irrespective of the speed of the observer. Who are these men?'

The boys looked perplexed and thoughtful. They passed. The next team too considered the question deeply, and also passed. The third team was the all-girls team. They passed immediately, without fuss. The question was passed by all the six teams.

'Nobody?' the quizmaster asked, with a touch of triumph. He looked at the audience. 'The question passes to the audience.'

There was a silence that was heavy with embarrassment. Oja looked at her husband apologetically, as if she was ashamed she did not know the answer.

'Albert Michelson and Edward Morley,' the quizmaster said, and there were hisses of agony from the boys on the stage. One boy spread his hands in overt exasperation.

'Michelson and Morley,' the quizmaster said, 'set out to prove an old theory that the universe was filled with an invisible thing called ether. As we now know the universe is not filled with ether. But they accidentally discovered through their experiments that light travels at the same speed irrespective of how fast or slow an observer is moving.'

The quizmaster looked at Team B.

'Are you ready? All right. Here is the second question. What discovery is Sir James Chadwick known for?' A small voice pierced the silence of the hall.

'Neutron,' it said.

There was a stunned silence and then murmuring. Everybody on the stage looked confused. Team B looked angry.

'Who was it?' the quizmaster asked, looking at the audience. The parents were looking at each other with soft chuckles.

Oja's hands were trembling. She held the sleeve of her husband and asked in a frightened voice, 'Wasn't it Adi?'

Ayyan, breathing a bit hard, said, 'Yes.'

A man in the row in front of them turned and looked impassively at Ayyan and Oja. Sister Chastity's head peered from the row across the aisle and her eyes met Ayyan's.

'Who was that?' the quizmaster asked.

Children in the front rows were pointing to the boy who was sitting in their midst.

'You, Sir, was it you?' the quizmaster asked, amused and disbelieving. 'Aditya, will you please stand up.' Adi stood up, his hands folded behind his back. There were murmurs among the parents. Several heads were turning and looking at Ayyan and Oja. 'So it was you, Sir?' the quizmaster asked.

'Yes, Sir,' Adi said smartly.

'Well, I don't know what to say,' the quizmaster said, making a face of incredulity. 'You are absolutely right. Now introduce yourself, Sir.'

'Aditya Mani.'

'And how old are you?'

'Eleven. And eleven is a prime number.'

'Ladies and gentlemen,' the quizmaster said, pointing to Adi. And there was a round of loud applause. Parents stood, one by one in a standing ovation, and threw glances at the curious couple sitting in their midst. Oja had tears in her eyes as she stood with her husband and clapped.

Sister Chastity went down the aisle and stopped in the middle of the hall. The silence returned. She looked happy, but she spoke sternly. She did not need a mike.

'While I greatly appreciate the brilliance of our students I request everybody in the audience not to answer out of turn. If none of the contestants knows the answer, the question will be passed to the audience. You can then raise your hands and the quizmaster will decide who will answer the question. Am I clear, Adi?' She went back to her seat, shaking her head happily at Ayyan.

The quizmaster turned to Team B and was about to speak. Then he looked at Adi again and shook his head. 'Wait till you get your chance,' he said, and that made everybody laugh. 'Now Team B, you get another question.'

Team B was still angry. The two boys made a face to suggest that they had known the answer.

'Are you ready?' the quizmaster said, 'Here it is. What is the connection between Little Boy, Fat Man and Manhattan?'

Oja held her husband's sleeve again. 'I hope he keeps quiet this time,' she said.

'He will,' Ayyan said confidently.

The silence was heavy with anticipation. Team B threw a nervous glance at Adi. They looked as though they were anxious to answer before the boy did. Then they appeared to hope that Adi knew the answer. The quizmaster too looked in the direction of Adi. Some children in the audience stared at the boy expectantly. Parents craned their neck to see what Adi was doing. Team B passed. The girls of Team C pounced on the question. One of them answered, as the other nodded furiously: 'Little Boy and Fat Man are the names of the atom bombs which were dropped over Hiroshima and Nagasaki. The atom bomb project was called the Manhattan Project.'

'Excellent,' the quizmaster said, and there was a round of applause. He looked at Adi and said, 'Sorry, Sir, they got it.' A roar of laughter filled the hall.

Three more questions went this way, with the teams throwing

anxious looks at Adi, the audience waiting for something from the boy and someone on the stage finding the answer eventually. The tension in the hall was now easing.

'Team F, your turn now,' the quizmaster said, 'This is the final question of Round One. Are you ready? All right. An interesting one. This scientist spent his last days trying to convert ordinary metals into gold. He wasted his latter years in . . .'

'Isaac Newton,' said the voice of Adi, and the stunned silence returned to the hall. As the silence broke into murmurs, Sister Chastity stood, arms akimbo, in the aisle.

Oja's quivering fingers covered her mouth. She looked frightened. Parents turned to her with smiles of regard and envy. Ayyan got up from his chair and said a loud 'sorry' to the Principal. He went down the aisle towards his son. All eyes were on him. In the sixth row, children on the wooden bench lifted their legs to let Ayyan through. Ayyan bent towards Adi's good ear, his index finger pointed sternly, his face poised in a reprimand. And he whispered, 'Excellent, my son. Just one more time.'

Ayyan walked back to his seat looking embarrassed. Never in his life had so many eyes been on him. He apologized once again to Sister Chastity, who nodded graciously. She shouted from the aisle, 'Adi, now behave.' When Ayyan sank into his chair, a man in the row in front turned to him and said, 'Your son is unbelievable.' Oja held the sleeve of her husband again. She did not make an effort to contain her tears any more, and they smudged her mascara.

The quizmaster said, 'But was it the right answer?' He looked blankly at the audience. He began to nod. 'It's Isaac Newton, of course.' The applause was long, but nobody stood this time.

'Now I have to find another question,' the quizmaster said above the din. 'We are running short of questions. Adi, as the Principal said, you have to behave. When the question is passed to the audience, you may answer. Or we may have to ask you to leave the hall. OK? Am I clear? Team F. Are you ready?' Team F looked nervously towards Adi.

'Easy question. If you know the answer, be very fast,' the

quizmaster said, and looked towards the boy. 'Who was the second man on the Moon?'

'Buss Adrin,' Adi screamed.

The quizmaster looked down at the floor. Sister Chastity got up. Ayyan jogged down the aisle. The kids lifted their legs again to let him through. They were now enjoying this. Ayyan went to his son and led him out of the row and through the narrow aisle. Hand-in-hand, they walked towards the exit. They heard the quizmaster say, 'Buzz Aldrin it was,' and there was a standing ovation once again. Ayyan tried to look embarrassed. Adi was beaming.

They stood on the corridor outside the auditorium, laughing. Soon, Oja appeared at the far end of the corridor, crying and running. She stopped abruptly, adjusted her hair, looked to her left and right sheepishly, and walked hastily. Then she ran again. This woman's life, Ayyan told himself, is not ordinary any more. For that moment alone, he knew it was all worth it. Did she ever imagine when she was growing up as a waiter's daughter, when she walked into a humid one-room home as a new bride, or when she discovered one evening that her son could not hear well in one ear, that she would see a day like this. But he also felt the odd unnerving mix of fear and excitement. He was stretching the limits of the game. And it had to end. Probably right now. It was fun, we got away with it, but the game is over now.

Oja fell on her knees beside her son and held him by his hair, 'Adi, how do you know all this?' She hugged him and then pushed him back, holding his arms tight. 'You are so bright, Adi. You are so weird,' she said, kissing his nose fondly. She looked up angrily at her husband and said, 'I am going to put an evil-eye on his cheek.'

'Nobody does such things any more,' Ayyan said.

'I don't care. Did you see how those women were looking at my son?'

'How did they look?'

'They were such diabolic women, all of them. Did you see? They coloured their hair.'

'What's the connection?'

'I don't know. All I know is that my boy is going to get a black dot on his cheek every morning when he goes to school.'

'All I know is that my boy is not going to have any silly dot on his cheek. We don't believe in superstitions, do we, Adi?'

A man appeared on the corridor. Oja rose from the floor and eased the large wrinkles on her starched sari. She joined her palms and smiled at the man as he stood beside them. He was a stout, harrowed-looking man with thick muddled hair, and his shirt was slipping out of his trousers. He shook hands with Adi.

'You were brilliant,' he said. 'I am Anil Luthra,' he told Ayyan, as he extended his hand. 'My son is in the tenth standard. Amit, his name is. I had only heard about your son. Today, I saw him in action.'

'He is just a little boy fooling around, really,' Ayyan said.

'Don't be modest . . . sorry, what is your name?'

'Ayyan.'

'Ayyan, you are a very lucky man. For a moment out there I thought the school had leaked the questions to him,' he said, and started laughing to emphasize that it was only a joke. Ayyan laughed sportingly. Luthra gave him his card. It said: 'Metro Editor, *The Times of India*'. When Ayyan's card was not forthcoming, he asked pleasantly, 'And what do you do, Ayyan?'

'I work in the Institute of Theory and Research.'

'Oh,' Luthra said. 'Jal is a good friend. Jana Nambodri too. I have met Acharya once. Difficult man, isn't he?'

'Yes. But he is a good man,' Ayyan said, because he did not trust strangers.

'He is, he is,' Luthra said without conviction. He studied Adi. 'I am sure this boy is going to be famous very soon. What did he say out there? "I'm eleven. And eleven is a prime number"?' Luthra laughed.

'He is obsessed with prime numbers,' Ayyan said. 'You know something. He can recite the first thousand prime numbers.'

Oja looked at her son with a grimace.

Luthra became serious. 'Really?' he asked.

'Really. But he is so shy with strangers. I can try to get it out of him though.'

'This is what I am going to do,' Luthra said excitedly. 'Take my mobile number. When you think he is ready to recite the first thousand prime numbers, call me. I will send a reporter. What do you say?'

'That's very kind of you.'

In the taxi, Oja asked, 'What is this pime number?'

'Prime number,' Adi corrected, putting his hand on his head. 'A prime number is a number that is divisible only by itself or one and no other number.'

'So?' she asked, looking worried.

'So nothing.'

'I don't understand all this. Tell me, Adi. You know the first thousand prime numbers?'

'No,' Adi said.

'He knows,' Ayyan said. Adi looked at him and they smiled.

'What is this sign language you both have?' she asked angrily. 'Sometimes you make me feel like a stranger.'

'I am hungry,' Adi told his mother. Somehow that consoled her.

HER LARGE INSECT eyes were popping out of their sockets. Her hair was brown in patches, her cheeks puffy and, for some reason, Ayyan was certain that her double chin would feel cold if he touched it. She was in a thin red top through which he could see at least two layers of slips, and that her bra strap was astray. Her light blue jeans were stretched taut over her large tree-trunk thighs. The Feature Writer, as her card proclaimed, was in the discomfort of the peculiar humidity of BDD. She was wiping her face constantly as she sat on one of the two red plastic chairs in the house. Adi was on the other. Oja was not at home. She had gone to see the fourth baby of an aunt. The reason why this was even possible.

A pale, somewhat detached photographer hovered in the background holding a camera.

'Can we begin?' Ayyan asked.

The Feature Writer nodded.

Adi was in a smart full-sleeve shirt and black jeans. His lush oiled hair was neatly combed. He looked intelligent and beautiful. The earpiece of the hearing aid was fixed to the right ear. A white wire ran from the earpiece and disappeared inside his shirt. Ayyan went to his son and playfully ruffled his hair. And gently eased the creases on his shirt. It was then that Ayyan felt a stab of cold fear. What am I doing? This is foolish. Everything is going to go wrong. He felt those familiar acidic vapours rise in his stomach. Until a few moments ago he was so certain that it was all going to be easy. Even when the reporter and the photographer had arrived he had not felt nervous. But it now struck him that what he was about to do was crazier than he had imagined. The world was stupid, of course, but not so stupid. It was not too late yet to withdraw. He could end it right now. He could tell the reporter that Adi was not feeling very well.

But the fear somehow subsided and the chill in his throat was now the chill of excitement. He had thought carefully about this for many days and he knew in his heart that nothing could go wrong. 'You look so smart, Adi, Ayyan said. 'Now show them what you know.'

Ayyan took a few steps back. Adi waited for a little while, and began the recital: 'Two, three, five, seven, eleven, thirteen, seventeen, nineteen, twenty-three . . .'

The Feature Writer listened with a keen face. The photographer took some pictures. Ayyan made a gesture to the photographer to suggest that he should not take pictures now. It was very important that the pictures were not shot at this point. Ayyan had not considered the possibility of the photographer jumping the gun, and he kicked himself for overlooking that. It could lead to disaster, Ayyan knew.

Adi went on, occasionally swallowing his saliva but without disrupting the pace of the recital: 'One seventy-nine, one eighty-one, one ninety-one, one ninety-three, one ninety-seven, one ninety-nine, two hundred and eleven, two twenty-three, two twenty-seven, two twenty-nine . . .'

The reporter referred to a printed paper. It was a list of the first thousand prime numbers. She was checking if Adi was on the right track. Ayyan heard the clicks of the camera again, but when he turned, the photographer stopped.

Adi went on: 'Six sixty-one, six seventy-three, six seventy-seven, six eighty-three, six ninety-one, seven hundred and one, seven hundred and nine, seven hundred and nineteen, seven twenty-seven, seven thirty-three . . .'

The reporter looked at Ayyan and raised her eyebrows.

Adi went a bit faster now: '4943, 4951, 4957, 4967, 4969, 4973, 4987, 4993, 4999, 5003 . . .' He went on and on like this and raised his voice as he finally said, '7841, 7853, 7867, 7873, 7877, 7879, 7883, 7901, 7907, 7919.' And he stopped.

The reporter lifted her head from the sheet and clapped.

Adi removed the earpiece and threw a quick glance at his father when he realized his mistake. He put it back. The photographer started clicking.

'Actually,' Ayyan said, standing between the photographer and his son, 'Can I make a request?' He removed the earpiece from Adi's ear and pushed it inside the boy's shirt, 'Can you take pictures of my son without the earpiece? You see, we don't want him appearing as though he is handicapped in any way.'

'I understand,' the reporter said.

'Could you please ensure that he does not appear in the paper with the hearing-aid?'

'Don't worry about that,' she said, kindly.

The photographer asked Ayyan to stand by his son. And he started clicking.

'How many pictures are you going to carry?' Ayyan asked, somewhat amused.

The photographer did not respond. He continued to click and then stopped abruptly. He put the camera back in his bag and left without a word.

The reporter set her scribbling-pad on her lap, poised a pen in the air and smiled at Adi.

'You are really brilliant, Aditya,' she said in English. 'Can I ask you some questions now?'

Ayyan put the earpiece back in the boy's good ear. It was a Walkman earpiece, fixed to the shell of the hearing-aid. The Walkman was inside the boy's shirt, taped to his stomach.

'Can you hear?' Ayyan whispered to his son. The boy nodded.

'I'd like to ask you some questions now, Aditya,' the reporter said.

'OK,' Adi said, gulping down a glass of water.

'Why are you interested in prime numbers?'

'Prime numbers are unpre . . . unpredictable. So I like prime numbers.'

'How are you able to recite all these numbers, so easily, from memory?'

The boy lifted his finger as though to point to the earpiece. Then he started giggling. 'I don't know,' he said.

'What are your future plans?'

Adi shrugged and looked at his father. 'He is very shy, you know,' Ayyan said.

'What do you want to become?' the reporter asked, ignoring Ayyan.

Adi looked at his father again and giggled coyly.

'He is not very easy to talk to,' Ayyan said. 'I can answer for him, if that makes it easier for you.'

She considered the offer.

'About a year ago,' Ayyan said anyway, his voice soft and conspiratorial, 'When I was teaching him numbers, I observed that he was seeing patterns. He would select numbers like three, five, seven, eleven and tell me that he liked them. I later realized that he felt that way about all prime numbers. How he began to identity prime numbers is a mystery to me.'

IN THE GLOW of the morning light that illuminated the flies, people stood with their little buckets in two silent lines. Even though they never spoke English here, when they stood like this every morning, they regarded themselves as Ladies and Gents. The two arched windows high above the common toilets, some of their glass broken long before the memories of these people began, were ablaze in a blinding light as if God were about to communicate. Ayyan arrived at the end of the gents' line, in loose shorts and an oversized T-shirt, holding a blue bucket and *The Times of India*. A man who was ahead in the line spotted him and said, 'I saw the article today.' Slowly, heads turned, and the news went round that Adi had now appeared in *The Times of India*.

Portions of the toilet queues disintegrated and people gathered around Ayyan whose copy of the newspaper was now unfurled. At the bottom of the ninth page was an article that said, 'Boy Genius Can Recite First Thousand Primes'. There was a striking photograph of Adi, beaming. In the picture, he was wearing what looked like a hearing-aid. When Ayyan had seen the item in the morning he had silently cursed the reporter and the photographer. But nobody noticed that Adi was wearing the ear-piece of the hearing-aid on his right ear, the good ear. Not even Oja. It was not an easy thing to spot.

Some women set their buckets on the floor and jostled to get closer to the paper. 'But I don't understand what the boy has done,' someone said.

So, in the faint stench of urine, shit and chlorine, and in the enchanting illumination of morning light, Ayyan explained what prime numbers were. And the people of the toilet queues looked at the father of the genius with incomprehension, affection and respect. Mothers asked him what they should do to make their children half as bright, what must they teach, what must they feed? Was Lady's Finger really good for maths? Should boys be allowed to play cricket? Then matters moved beyond Adi.

'Another offer has come from a builder,' a man said. 'What is your suggestion, Mani? Should we sell?'

'How much?'

'I hear he is offering twelve lakhs for a flat.'

'We should sell,' Ayyan said. 'We should sell and leave this place. We should live in proper flats. How long must our children live in this hell?'

'But we are used to this, aren't we?'

'Our lives, my friend, are over. For our children, we must move.'

Ayyan stood in the porch of the Institute, facing the blackboard near the main stairway. He wrote the Thought For The Day: *If you want to understand India, don't talk to Indians who speak in English – Salman Rushdie*. Adi was standing at a distance, near the lifts. He was in his favourite outfit – a blue half-sleeve shirt, white jeans and fake Nike. The Brahmins had summoned him. They had read the article in *The Times* and they had called Ayyan on his mobile. They wanted to see for themselves a Dalit genius, though they had put it differently. Ayyan could not resist the entertainment of watching those great minds mill around his boy, expressing their grand acknowledgement of his infant brilliance. Genius to genius, they would make it all seem. But he was certain that this was the last day of Adi's genius. He had told his son last night on the tar-coated terrace of BDD, the game was now over. He would not be given clever things to say in the middle of the class any more, quiz questions would not magically land on his lap, articles about him would not appear in the papers.

Adi had nodded, a bit sadly, but he had understood. The game, his father made him repeat, was over.

Adi liked his father's office, even though he found the word 'Institute' terrifying. The sea was so close here and only people with special passes could go to the black rocks. The garden was flat and green, and nothing happened there. Crows chased coloured birds in the sky. And everything was far from everything else. But what Adi liked the most was the lift. He loved the way the lights crept across the numbers. And he loved its hum, like an old man about to sneeze. His father said that the lift was a robot, which made him like the lift even more. He had been here many times. His father often brought him and his mother on Sundays. They sat on the rocks by the sea or walked around the building, or went up and down in the lifts. On Sundays the place was empty. But today was a working day. So it was full of people. That's why he was silent in the lift though some people were smiling at him. They smelled very good. They smelled like the inside of a car. Not a taxi but a real car. He had been inside L. Srini's car once. He liked the smell of a car.

They were on the third floor. The door opened and a lot of people waited outside to get in. He wanted to spend his entire life going up and down in the lift. But his father held his hand and they went down the longest corridor in the world. He had seen it before, on Sundays. He preferred the corridor dark and empty. Then it looked like a road in the comics. People on the corridor looked at him and smiled.

'He is the guy, isn't he? The genius,' one man said.

Adi smiled. He liked being called a genius. It was different from being called special. All handicapped children were called special and he did not believe he was really handicapped. He could hear without the hearing-aid but only in the right ear. He was worried that if the game was over, as his father said, people would begin to call him special again. At the end of the corridor, his father stopped at a door on the left side that said 'Deputy Director – Jana Nambodri'.

'Ready?' his father asked.

'Ready,' Adi said.

He saw Ayyan knock twice and then open the door. A man with a lot of white hair looked surprised to see them but he rose from his chair smiling. He was with three men who were younger and had black hair. They were all wearing jeans. They were standing now and smiling at him. He liked it when people looked only at him and nothing else in the room. They made him sit on the table though he wanted to sit on the chair.

'Aditya Mani,' someone declared to the room, without looking at him.

'But that's *my* name,' Adi said, and the men laughed.

'Tell me, Adi, why do you like prime numbers so much?' the short man with white hair asked in English.

'It's unpredictable,' Adi said.

'What are the other numbers you like,' the man asked.

Adi smiled coyly because that was what his father said he should do if he did not understand the question.

'He is shy,' his father said. 'He doesn't talk much at all.'

'What do you want to be in the future, Adi?'

'Scientist.'

'Of course. But which field interests you the most?'

Adi smiled coyly.

'You like maths or physics more?'

'Physics.'

'Physics,' the men said happily, all at once.

Arvind Acharya was relishing the moment. He was imagining a giant balloon, twenty storeys high, soaring against a clear blue sky. The gondola that was carrying the four sealed samplers was such a meagre tip dangling at the bottom of the balloon. It was absurdly disproportionate, he thought, for the basket that was the very reason why the balloon existed, to be a few hundred times smaller than the balloon itself. It was not an aesthetic image. He had always loathed such disproportion. That's why he had once despised the Zeppelins, and the sight of little white women driving long sedans. The device and its purpose had to be in proportion. But then he wondered if it was a reasonable demand. The device was physical and so it had a size. The purpose was actually abstract and so could not be described by size. The little white woman was not the purpose of the sedan. The sampler in the balloon's basket was not the purpose of the hot-air balloon. The purpose of the sedan was that the little woman had to go somewhere, say, to a funeral. The purpose of the balloon was to confirm that there were aliens in the sky. So where was the question of disproportion? Also, if the goal of the universe were to manufacture life, as he secretly believed, then the universe was a giant device containing unimaginably vast nebulae and star systems that caused unimaginably large-scale cataclysms to make minuscule pieces of life here and there. So, even in his own version of the truth, the device was physically disproportionate to its purpose.

It was inevitable that he would then wonder, not for the first time of course, if the universe needed a goal. But he liked the idea. A whole universe churning violently inside to create the seeds of what would eventually become a state of being: little disjointed minds that would look back at the sky and acknowledge that yes, it is there, there is a universe. Why must the universe do it? It had enough real estate to create large lifeless bodies. Why must it pack enormous amounts of energy in a type of electricity called consciousness? It was simpler for the universe to make a Jupiter than a frog, or even an ant. All this was leading to an unavoidable question, but he tried to delay it because its philosophical nature embarrassed him, and philosophers were such third-rate bastards. But he asked anyway – So, why is there life? What's the whole game? It was the sort of moment that frustrated him and made him wish that someone had left the answer in his drawer on a neatly typed piece of paper, so that he could just read it and say, 'Oh yes, I thought so,' and go back home for a nice long nap.

The door opened and he was annoyed to see his secretary. For some reason, he was more annoyed at the sight of him today than ever before. Such a terrible apparition Ayyan Mani was. So fresh, so eager, so much of an insider in this world. So hopelessly obsessed with living. Always busy, always up to something. Acharya found it funny that he must think a man was an insider in this world, because he did not know the function of an outsider. But he knew there were the insiders and there were the outsiders. He asked himself where he himself truly belonged.

'Sir,' Ayyan said, for the third time.

'Yes.'

'I've brought my son.'

Adi had by then appeared at the door, and he was looking curiously at Acharya from behind his father's back. A pleasant smile appeared on Acharya's face and that surprised even Ayyan. After the end of the Oparna affair, Acharya had become more moody and introspective than ever. Some days, he rocked in his chair excitedly for no apparent reason, but on the whole he had simply withdrawn into himself. He was once again the mammoth ghost that was either arriving or departing.

'There you are,' Acharya said. 'Come in.'

Adi did not move. He opened his mouth wide, put out his tongue and gave a silly laugh.

'Put your tongue, in Adi,' Ayyan said sternly. 'And come in.'

The boy walked in gingerly. Acharya stood up and went to the white couches in the far corner.

'Let's sit here,' he said.

Adi, now more confident, sat facing him across the small centrepiece where the glass jar that was once an accomplice in illicit love now lay bearing fresh orchids. The boy looked at his father and tapped the couch asking him to sit. But Ayyan did not move.

'Sit down,' Acharya said impatiently. And for the very first time Ayyan Mani sat in the chamber of the Director.

Acharya studied the boy carefully and said, 'He is wearing it in the other ear.'

'What, Sir?' Ayyan asked.

'In the picture that they carried in the paper today, he was wearing the hearing-aid in the right ear. But now he is wearing it in the left ear.'

'Oh, that,' Ayyan said with a chuckle. 'By mistake, they flipped the picture in the paper, Sir.'

Acharya did not suspect anything. He was merely struck by the visual anomaly. He did not pursue the matter further. He was more interested in the boy. 'He seems completely normal. Is this how geniuses are made these days?'

'He is just an ordinary boy who is fooling around, Sir,' Ayyan said.

'I am a genius,' the boy said defiantly.

'You must be,' Acharya said. 'Tell me, Aditya, how do you remember so many prime numbers?'

'They are unpredictable.'

'Adi,' his father said, with an edge in his voice, 'he is asking how you remember the first thousand prime numbers.'

'I hear it in my head.'

'You do?' Acharya said with a look of amusement. 'You like prime numbers?'

'Yes. They are unpredictable.'

'They are, they are. But I always found prime numbers ugly. When I was your age I used to love even numbers. Do you like even numbers more than odd numbers?'

Adi shrugged.

'You should say "yes" or "no", Adi,' his father said. 'Don't just sit there and make a face.'

'What do you want to become, Adi?' Acharya asked.

'I want to join the Institute of Theory and Research.'

'You should then. Maybe you should take our entrance test,' Acharya said jovially.

'OK,' said Adi.

'Ten thousand students from all over the country take the test. But only one hundred pass. Do you want to take it?'

'OK.'

'Grow up fast then.'

Acharya's keen twinkling eyes then surveyed the boy through a comfortable silence that to him was always a form of conversation. Adi turned nervously towards his father and raised his eyebrows. Acharya's eyes then slowly became lost and distant. 'Of all human deformities,' he said softly, 'genius is the most useful.'

PART FIVE

Aliens Used Aliens To Make Curd

THE SCHOLARS OF the Institute, too, agreed that news travelled fast. But this evening there was a dispute over how fast. Ayyan Mani was at a corner table of the canteen when the argument broke out between two middle-aged mathematicians who were in a large group. They were near the window that opened to the undulating backyard and ancient solitary trees. In the sedative sea breeze and the hush of the calm sea, the debate unfolded as part banter and part science. It slowly escalated into a serious quarrel. One of the mathematicians angrily ordered a paper plate and appeared to scribble a long string of formulae to suggest that if various probabilities were known, it would be possible to calculate how fast a piece of news, like say the death of a colleague, would travel. The other mathematician angrily ordered another paper plate and wrote down something to show that even if various probabilities were known, the speed of news can never be predicted. Velocity was a function of distance, he said. Though news did travel, he said, it did not travel through a physical space, and so where was the question of speed? The first mathematician shook his head many times and said that there was a 'nonlinear' distance involved, and thus news indeed travelled through physical space. Ayyan did not fully understand what they meant by probabilities or nonlinear distance. But he did not have the heart to leave the canteen. After about an hour, both the mathematicians amicably agreed on the third paper plate that bad news travelled faster than good news. That, Ayyan already knew.

He was reminded of the episode a month later, one tense

December afternoon, as he sat among his phones waiting for all hell to break loose. But nothing happened. Two hours had passed since the Press Officer had declared, in a release which was faxed to every newspaper and television channel: 'A stunning breakthrough has been achieved.' That morning, Oparna Goshmaulik had emerged from the isolation of her basement lab along with two American scientists who were supervising the analysis of the cryogenic sampler. She was holding a bundle of papers in her hand: a collection of handwritten material bound together by a cord. On the last page she had concluded, somewhat inappropriately in thin unremarkable handwriting, 'The results prove without dispute that living cells have been found at the altitude of 41 kilometres. Spores of rod-like bacillus and engyodontium albus de hoog, a fungus, have been found.'

In the first week of November, Arvind Acharya's mammoth balloon had flown over Hyderabad carrying four samplers to capture air. Three of the samplers were sent to labs in Boston and Cardiff. The last sampler had arrived at the Institute in a Toyota Innova. Oparna's team of research hands and the two American scientists, old friends of Acharya, had since studied the sampler. They were completely cut off from the rest of the Institute, and there had been no word from them until this morning. They had walked silently down the third-floor corridor, and without waiting for Ayyan's rituals of passage, they had gone inside Acharya's room. It would be recounted later, several times, that when Acharya heard the news he shut his eyes, and did not open them for so long that the visitors left without a word, smiling.

It was now confirmed. There were beings that were falling from the sky. Acharya had become the first man to discover aliens. And the theory that all life on Earth first arrived as microscopic living organisms from space had found support. The line between what was alien and what was terrestrial was now forever blurred. When Acharya came out of his trance, he summoned the Press Officer, a portly hectic man who frequently wiped his forehead with a kerchief.

Ayyan Mani heard the entire dictation on his spy-phone.

'We have been living with aliens,' Acharya told the Press Officer, who first thought he was being scolded. 'It is probable that all these years,' Acharya had then said happily, 'aliens used aliens to make curd.'

Five minutes later, Ayyan had seen the Press Officer almost run out. He returned with a printed release, headed (in large capital letters), 'EXTRATERRESTRIAL LIFE FOUND'. Acharya reprimanded him for the hysteria of the huge fonts, but the rest of the release was approved.

It was around two in the afternoon when Ayyan began to get calls from the exceptional faculty of the Institute asking for more information. Phones began to ring in almost every room, especially the sanctified third floor where the senior scientists worked. The news began to travel. Old men pressed the phone receivers to their hairy ears and raised their eyebrows in incorruptible fascination as they heard from their peers what Acharya had discovered. The younger scientists fired questions at their informers to crosscheck their disbelief. Then the many doors on the long finite corridors of the Institute opened. Scientists walked from their nooks to the office of Arvind Acharya. They went without invitation because it was a tradition here that an appointment need not be sought to congratulate a scientist.

They went to Acharya not in friendship, not in the secret mourning of someone's good fortune, not even with the foresight of sycophancy. They went as scientists. They wanted to celebrate a moment in time – a rare moment in time – when man was about to learn something more about his little world. That there were living things in the cold reaches of the stratosphere; that they were coming down from space not going up from Earth. That we were not alone, we were never alone. For the first time in the history of rationality, the nature of alien life was going to be explained. So they went to hold the large chubby hand of a difficult man, an arrogant man, who more than everything else, was now a discoverer.

When they began to trickle into the waiting-room, the moving honesty of the silent concourse gave Ayyan gooseflesh. He accepted for the very first time that there was, in fact, such a thing called the pursuit of truth and that these men, despite all their faults, held this pursuit very close to their hearts. That day, just for that day, he conceded that there were things far more important in the universe than the grievances of an unfortunate clerk. He kept Acharya's door open. It did not have a door-stopper, so he shoved a glossy newspaper supplement that spoke of hair-care, meditation and relationships under the crack beneath the door. He went to a corner of the waiting-room and stood in a funereal silence as the men went in to whisper compliments, or to give a pen in appreciation, or to just stand beside him. From where Ayyan was standing he could see Acharya. He looked happy and graceful, as he stood by the large sea window with the old guard and the young. Jana Nambodri too arrived eventually, though his office was the closest to the Director's. He went into the open chamber and said, 'Something in me dies when a friend does well.' And they hugged.

Later in the evening, the Press Officer sombrely surveyed the ground-floor media-briefing room. There were about twenty journalists. Photographers were taking up positions near the dais. Large men at the back were setting up their cameras. The Press Officer searched the faces of the journalists. He knew most of them. They were seasoned science reporters. He looked with concern at some young fresh faces. He asked their names and said sternly, but with the occasional servile smile, 'Please read the release very carefully. Everything you need to know is in it. I hope you are aware that the Director is extremely short-tempered.'

A photographer came to him and asked if the aliens could be photographed.

'No, no,' the Press Officer yelped. 'They are microbes, they are microbes. And right now we are not in a position to release their visuals.' He looked worried now. 'Listen, don't ask him anything directly. Ask me. And be very careful when you take pictures of Dr Acharya.'

'Careful, meaning?'

'Don't get too close. Don't use flash. Just make sure he is not annoyed, OK? I don't know what will make him go mad.'

The memories of what had happened when Stephen Hawking had last visited Bombay were vivid in his mind. A horde of photographers had surrounded the crippled physicist. Hawking's delicate face could not take the explosion of flashes all around. He had looked frightened in his wheelchair, unable even to beg them to stop. Acharya had come to his rescue, charging towards the photographers with clenched fists. 'He deserved better treatment,' he later said, 'even though he is an ambassador of the Big Bang.'

The Press Officer inspected the dais. There were four chairs. He asked a peon to remove one of them. And he said aloud, hands on hip, 'Dr Arvind Acharya and the team will arrive any moment. I want briefly to tell you what this is all about though I am sure you are aware of it. Everything is there in the printed material I have given you. Please read it carefully. Four weeks ago, the Institute of Theory and Research, under the direct supervision of Dr Acharya, sent a hot-air balloon from our Hyderabad launch facility. The balloon went up with four samplers. Samplers are sterilized steel devices that are opened by remote control at a particular altitude. The samplers captured air at the altitude of forty-one kilometres. The objective of the balloon mission was to see if there is any life forty-one kilometres above the Earth. At this height, if there is life, it would mean that it is coming down, not going up. Out of the four samplers, two have been sent to Cardiff and one to Boston. They are being studied there right now, even as I speak. We studied one sampler right here in our Astrobiology lab. And we have discovered a rod-like bacillus and a fungus. This is an astonishing discovery because this is the first time anyone has even come close to discovering aliens. Also, this reopens the debate on whether some diseases which appear suddenly, like SARS, are actually extraterrestrial in nature. And of course, it makes us question whether all life on Earth, too, originally came from space.'

He wiped his forehead. His face did not suggest that mankind was at a significant junction. He was more concerned with the little matter of the press conference proceeding smoothly without any mishap.

'There they are,' he yelped.

Acharya walked in with his two American friends who were as tall as he was.

'Where is Oparna?' Acharya asked the Press Officer, who whispered, 'She did not want to come, Sir. She wanted to be low-profile. She insisted, Sir. I tried.'

Acharya took the centre chair on the dais. He was flanked by the two white men.

'Dr Arvind Acharya,' the Press Officer said grandly, adding, more softly, 'Dr Michael White is to his right and Dr Simon Gore is to his left. They are astrobiologists from Princeton. They assisted our research and independently supervised the analysis of the contents of the sampler. I leave the floor to the scientists.' He went to a corner of the room and studied the journalists with a harrowed face. (He hated journalists.)

'I'm sure you have been briefed,' Acharya told the audience. 'I've nothing more to add except this. Oparna Goshmaulik was the project coordinator. She was involved in the project before the launch and she was in charge of the analysis of the sampler. Unfortunately she could not make it today. Now, you may ask questions.'

There was a silence for a few seconds. Then a man asked, 'What exactly has been found?'

Acharya shot a glance at the Press Officer, but answered patiently: 'A rod-like bacillus and a fungus called engyodontium albus de hoog.'

'Can you spell it?'

'No.'

There was a brief silence which was broken by the squeaky voice of the Press Officer. 'The exact spelling is in the printed material I've given all of you. If you can't find it I will give it to you after the conference.'

A woman asked, 'Dr Acharya, why have you concluded that this living matter has come from space?'

'I have not concluded this. It is a reasonable guess supported by several facts. For example, it is difficult to see how the living matter got there because until now it was believed that bacteria and fungi do not exist at such heights. The chances of bacteria living at such heights due to space debris of defunct satellites are very, very small.'

'Maybe the sampler somehow got contaminated in the lab?' someone asked.

'All precautions were taken to secure the samplers,' Acharya said. 'The bacteria and fungus we have discovered are very rare and difficult to culture in a lab environment.'

'If these organisms really came from outer space,' a voice asked, 'how did they survive the extreme temperatures?'

'In the spore form, microbes not only survive extreme conditions but are almost immortal. It is believed that in the hibernated state they can even live for millions of years.'

'Dr Acharya, where do you think these microbes come from?'

'I don't know,' he answered with a chuckle. He looked at his two friends and they smiled too.

'Dr Acharya,' someone asked, 'what about the other three samplers?'

'They are being studied in Cardiff and Boston. The results will be out in two or three months. Their processes are slightly different and so will take more time. We hope to find more interesting stuff in those samplers. In fact, we hope to find organisms that have no history on Earth.'

In the back lanes of the academic world the news of Acharya's discovery was greeted with joy, and with the inadvertent compliments of scepticism. But in the real world of regular people, for which science pretended to toil, the event went across the day like an invisible epoch. Between the news of the stockmarket upsurge and Islamic terror and a man stabbing his lover twenty-two times, *The Times* hurriedly summarized an epic scientific labour. Rather as an epitaph tells the story of a whole life in the hyphen between two dates.

Ayyan Mani felt a soporific gloom in his heart that reminded him of the widows of the BDD chawls who sat in the doorways, their cataract eyes baffled at the sheer length of time. These days, there was an excruciating stillness in his world too.

From behind the phones and heaps of transient mail, he stared at the ancient black sofa. Its leather was tired and creased. There was a gentle depression in the seat as though a small invisible man had been waiting there forever to meet Acharya and show him the physics of invisibility. The faint hum of the air conditioner made the room seem more silent than silence itself could have done. A fax arrived. One of the phones on his glass table rang for a moment and stopped abruptly. Voices outside grew and receded. A still lizard, high up on the stark white wall, looked back, needlessly stunned.

Ayyan felt like a character in an art film. Nothing happens for a while, and nothing happens again, and then it is over. There was no goal any more in his life, no plot, no fear. It was a consequence of choosing to be a good father. He had put an end to the myth of Adi's genius. It had to end before the boy went mad. The game had gone too far. In the place of its nervous excitement was now the ordinariness of the familiar flow of life, the preordained calm of a discarded garland floating in the sewage.

Every morning he woke up in the attic, and went to stand in the glow of the morning light, among people and buckets that inched towards the chlorine toilets. He then bathed by the kitchen in the fragrance of tea and soap, and went to work in a melancholy train, stranded inside an unmoving mass of bleak, yawning strangers. All that to come here and bear the austere grandness of the Brahmins and their marvellous incomprehension of the universe, and take phone calls for a man who did not want to be disturbed. And finally to go home in the shadows of rows and rows of large grey tenements and eat in the company of a half-deaf boy who had lost all his ill-gotten glory, and a woman whose only hope was in the delusion of her son's mythical genius. Then, in the morning, to wake up in the attic, again.

This, Ayyan accepted, was life. It was, in a way, a fortunate life. It would go on and on like this. And one day, very soon in fact, Adi would be an adolescent. An adolescent son of a clerk. A miserable thing to be in this country. He would have to forget all his dreams and tell himself that what he wanted to do was engineering. It's the only hope, everyone would tell him. Engineering, Adi would realize, is every mother's advice to her son, a father's irrevocable decision, a boy's first foreboding of life. A certainty, like death, that was long decided in the cradle. Sooner or later, he would have to call it his ambition. And to attain it, he would compete with thousands and thousands of boys like him in the only human activity for which Indians had a special talent. Objective-type entrance exams. Very few tests in the world would be tougher than these. So, in the enchanting years of early youth, when the mind is wild, and the limbs are strong, he would not run free by the sea or try to squeeze the growing breasts of wary girls. Instead he would sit like an ascetic in a one-room home and master something called quantitative ability. '*If three natural numbers are randomly selected from one to hundred then what is the probability that all three are divisible by both two and three?*'

He would have to answer this probably in thirty seconds in order to stand any chance against boys who were barely seven when they were fed iron capsules and sample-question papers for this very purpose; who had attended tuitions and memorized all the formulae in the world before they learnt how to masturbate; whose parents whispered into their ears every day of their lives the answer to the decisive question: 'What do you want to become in life?' Adi would have to fight them for a sliver of the future that men of God reviled without conviction as the 'material world', exactly the place that a father wishes for his son. Adi, despite the misfortunes of poverty, would somehow have to find a way to get into an engineering college. And then ensure that he did not spend a single day of his life as an engineer. Because everyone would tell him then that the real money was in MBA.

And so, even before the engineering course was over, he would start all over again, and prepare to battle thousands and thousands of boys like him in yet more entrance exams. When he finally made it and became a zombie who had entirely forgotten what he really wanted to do with his life, the light-skinned boys in the dormitory would look at him with a sad chuckle and whisper among themselves that he was a beneficiary of a 15 per cent reservation for the Dalits. 'Lucky bastard,' they would say.

Ayyan rose from his chair and considered his decision one more time. It was insane what he was about to ask Acharya, but it was less insane than life. One last game, he told himself. One final flutter in his one-room home before they all succumbed to the inevitability of a future he had just seen so clearly.

Acharya was sitting like an emperor, huge hands resting on the arms of his throne, eyes lost in the glow of celestial orbs that probably tilted gently at the honour of being invoked by such a mind.

'Sir,' Ayyan said.

Acharya nodded, staring at a vacant wall.

'I wanted to ask you something.'

'Ask fast.'

'My son Adi has been talking a lot about you. Ever since he met you he has gone crazy. He has been talking about the Institute even in his sleep. He wants to get admission into the Institute.'

Acharya nodded faster now, growing impatient already.

'You had told him that he should take the Joint Entrance

Test,' Ayyan said. 'I know, Sir, it was just a joke but he has taken it very seriously. He says he wants to take the test.'

'He should then,' Acharya said.

'This year, he wants to take it.'

'In April?'

'Yes, Sir.'

'Are you crazy?'

'I know it sounds like that, Sir. But he says he will pass the test.'

'And what does he want to do after he passes the test?'

'Maths, I think.'

'He said that?'

'Yes.'

'Ayyan, are you seriously suggesting that I allow a ten-year-old boy to take the JET?'

'He is eleven, Sir.'

'It's still crazy.'

'It's entirely your decision, Sir.'

'He might be an exceptional boy, Ayyan, but ten thousand not-very-dumb graduates take the test. Only a hundred make it.'

'I know, Sir. I just thought I would ask. I also know that, according to the rules, a candidate has to be at least a graduate to qualify for the exam.'

'Forget the rules. It's just that I find it ridiculous that a boy of eleven should be allowed to take the test.'

'I thought I would ask because he is so keen.'

'No way,' Acharya said, a bit amused now at the thought of a little boy having a shot at the Institute's entrance exam. 'The Joint Entrance Test is not some joke meant to entertain a boy,' he said.

'I know what you mean, Sir.'

'And what's wrong with the coffee these days? It tastes chemical.'

'I will ask the peons to be careful, Sir.'

As Ayyan was about to leave, Acharya said, 'Wait.' He toyed with the meteorite paperweight and appeared to consult his reasonable conscience. He asked, in a soft voice, 'The boy will be disappointed?'

'That's all right, Sir.'

'That, of course, is all right with me too. What I asked was, will he be upset?'

'A bit, Sir, but that's all right.'

'I'll write a letter to him personally explaining why he cannot take the test. I will write to him saying that he is too young to take the test. OK?'

'Thank you so much, Sir.'

'So don't break the bad news to him now,' Acharya said in a soft conspiratorial tone, 'Wait until I give you the letter. You understand?'

'Yes, Sir.'

Ayyan went back to his desk and exhaled. He had thought that the maverick mind of Acharya might see the charm in a little boy asking for a chance, but the absurdity of his request had just sunk in and he felt a bit foolish. In fact, Ayyan did not really want Adi to take the test. The boy, obviously, would not have the faintest hope of passing it. What he wanted was the news of the juvenile being allowed to attempt one of the toughest tests in the country to travel for a day in the newspapers, and probably on the television channels, and create one last festive commotion in his home and in the toilet queues.

The Joint Entrance Test (also called JET) exuded the terror of an excruciatingly selective screening process. But it also had the peculiar aura of art. It was a three-hour, objective-type test that carried about a hundred questions, broadly divided into physics, chemistry and maths.

Of the ten thousand candidates who sat the JET every year, two hundred would be shortlisted for interviews, half of them fated to make it – fifty in the postgraduate courses and fifty in research positions. How the JET question-paper was set, how it was printed, stored and eventually distributed to the exam centres, was a closely guarded secret known only to the old hands. Ayyan knew some bits of the secret. He even knew how to make a small hole in the fortress of security systems that were built around the question-paper. The weak brick in the otherwise impenetrable walls was, improbably, a modest bill-file stored in a lockless steel cupboard in the accounts department. Unknowingly, Ayyan began to doodle the ramparts of a fort on his scribbling-pad and then the images of a siege. Finally, he drew a crow flying away from the fort holding something in its beak. A phone rang on his table, and he was shaken out of his daydream. As he took the call, he wondered why he was thinking of the JET question-paper.

It preoccupied him the whole afternoon and made him fear that he was getting obsessed with an insane idea. But in the evening, when Acharya gave him the handwritten letter for Adi, his fever began to subside. It was now confirmed. Adi would not take the test. By the time Ayyan entered the perpetual laments of the BDD chawls, his nefarious excitement had died away without a trace.

In the inner reaches of BDD, there was a festive spirit that evening. Ayyan realized that all heads on the broken cobbled pathways were turned in one direction. Children were sprinting to where the elders were gawking. Near Block Thirty-Three, a crude stage had been erected. A small crowd was gathering near it. Huge speakers were piled on both sides of the stage. Some men were stringing fairylights between two lamp-posts. There was a sudden roar from the crowd. A thin, spirited boy had just walked on to the stage. He was wearing black leather trousers and a black shirt with gleaming silver dots. He took his position at the centre of the stage. His back was to the audience and his legs were parted. That suggested breakdance.

The boy stood waiting for the music to begin. The crowd grew. The boy turned and looked unhappily at his friends near the stage who were having a problem with the sound system. They somehow always did before a breakdance. Ayyan had seen this a thousand times – a boy in leather trousers standing with his back to the audience, legs parted and waiting sheepishly for the music to start. But this time, the wait was brief. Portentous drum-beats filled the night. The boy's hips began to sway. And he stretched his hands sideways. From the tip of his left hand, a wave began and moved like a violent fit towards his shoulder and then to his right hand, and was about to return the same way when the music died abruptly. His hands fell. He parted his legs again and waited.

Ayyan resumed his walk home. From the shadows emerged a drunkard in loose shorts and a T-shirt that said 'Smart', and loose shorts.

'Mani,' the drunk said. Even though the man was swaying in a personal gale that only a mixture of rum and egg-roast could unleash, there was something deep and strong about his voice. It was an authority that came from another time, when they were just boys and so close and their simple fates seemed interwoven. Ayyan, who usually handled such defeated friends by continuing to walk with nods and murmurs, was forced to stop. 'Mani,' the man said, 'You know what happened to Pandu?'

Ayyan shook his head. Pandu was the fastest underarm bowler Lower Parel had probably ever seen. That was a long time ago, when he was an unreasonably happy boy who used to draw erotic images of girls with their little buckets, all waiting in the toilet queues beneath a providential sunbeam. In time, the unhappiness of adulthood and the slave job as a driver for Balaji Car Hire transformed Pandu. He grew silent and never found the time to sketch, and drank like a fool every night.

'He is dead, Mani, he is dead,' the man said with a chuckle. 'Police picked him up last night. His owner said that he stole some money. This morning the police came to his house and told his wife that he had hanged himself in the lockup.'

Ayyan's temples moved in a silent rage, because here everyone knew what it meant when the police said a man had hanged himself in custody.

'They beat him to death, Mani, they beat the life out of him,' the drunk said and walked away muttering that Pandu, the greatest painter whom no one knew, was dead.

Oja Mani opened the door in annoyed haste and went back to sit transfixed in front of the television. Ayyan surveyed the dramatic wailing of the women in the soap. It somehow comforted him.

Pandu deserved the tears of all. Ayyan imagined the prime-time tears in every home in the nation, in every distraught character and in every woman enthralled by the soap, and dedicated the million melancholies to the memory of a boy who once found freedom in art. But then the drama ended abruptly, and there was this sudden gaiety of Red Label Tea. A woman with long flowing hair was serving tea to her family and everybody was becoming ecstatic after a single sip. It was cruel that on the night when the broken body of Pandu was still lying in a morgue, his woman running her frail shivering fingers on the wounds of his chest, and the cops instructing her to accept that the wounds were caused by his cowardly suicide, the wails of the mourners in Oja's serial must be interrupted by the joys of tea.

Oja sprang to life and began magically to put together a meal.

'Adi,' she screamed. It was just a word, but the way she said it meant different things at different times. The boy was sitting near the fridge, turning the pages of a textbook. He was a bit dejected these days because the game had ended. Teachers were still wary of him at school, his classmates still called him 'brains' and the neighbours continued to beg him to teach their children, but he knew his heroic status would soon be forgotten if it were not replenished with fresh achievements. He threw the book away and slid to the centre of the room for dinner. Ayyan wanted the attention of his wife who was setting the plates on the floor.

'You know, Oja,' he said, 'there are tea cups that cost five thousand rupees.'

'A single cup?' she asked.

'Yes. Five thousand rupees.'

'I would be so scared to drink from it,' she said, sitting down to eat.

'If you could buy it, you wouldn't be scared,' he said.

The commercials ended and Ayyan slowly drifted into the trauma of the soap. He felt a peaceful grief in his heart that numbed all his muscles. And this gloom would stay with him for many days, long after he ceased to mourn a lost friend.

The tired face of Oja, the despondence of Adi, the thousand eyes that gaped vacantly in the grey corridors, the widows who sat and sat, the nocturnal love songs of the drunkards, and the youth who stood impatiently in the toilet queues to go seize the day, and of course fail – all this and more, Ayyan was finally willing to accept as home because the other life, the bewitching life of creating a whole myth, was dangerous. And only bachelors had the fortune to be foolish.

THESE DAYS, HIS thoughts of Oparna Goshmaulik reminded Acharya of an ancient scar in the centre of his huge forehead. The scar was inflicted over three decades ago by a young Belgian astronomer named Pol Voorhoof who threw an unopened beer bottle at him. That night, they were with friends in a New York pub called Zero Gravity. Acharya, who by then was convinced that the wide acceptance of the Big Bang theory was influenced by a Christian compulsion to believe in a beginning and an end, accused the Belgians of starting the whole fraud. It was a Belgian Catholic priest named Georges Lemaître who in 1927 had come up with the idea that the universe began from the explosion of an atom. Unable to bear Acharya's long unprovoked polemic against Belgians, Voorhoof responded by calling Indians half-naked imbeciles, and even accused their goddesses of being topless tribals. In the happy stupor of inebriation, Acharya stood on the table and declared to the pub that he was smarter than all the Belgians in the world and challenged them to a round of blindfold chess. Voorhoof, of course, accepted the challenge.

They were blindfolded with the kerchiefs given by cautiously excited girls who were confused by the intellectual duel of two foreign men. Acharya and the Belgian spoke their moves, and a drunken friend offered to move the pieces on a chessboard that a waiter had produced. Acharya won in five minutes and let out a long operatic laughter with his blindfold still on. Voorhoof, who was also blindfolded, took an unopened beer bottle and flung it in the direction of the laughter. The bottle found its target but, fortunately for Acharya, it broke only after it hit the ground. But it left a deep gash in his forehead, and for the first time in his life he tasted blood. The gash hurt so much in the coming days that he refused to believe a time would come when he would no longer feel the pain. Long after the wound healed, every time he felt sad, he would think of the scar and remind himself not only of the fleeting transience of pain but also of convictions, friends, love, daughters and everything else that men held so dear.

The memory of Oparna too was no longer an open wound. To each other, he believed they had become endearing scars that in solitary moments would open the magical windows of remembrance. That was how he wanted her to remember their brief love. And this hope was reaffirmed when she walked into his room that Wednesday with such tranquillity and with the other deceptions of woman's amnesia.

'I called you to discuss the bad news from Boston,' he said, rocking himself in the chair consciously to reassure her that it was not a tragic matter and that she should not be disappointed. 'I believe you got a copy too?'

'Yes,' she said. 'Sad, isn't it.'

Boston University had confirmed that it had finished studying the sampler and had found no sign of life in it.

'There are still two samplers and Cardiff will be getting back soon,' he said cheerfully.

'Let's hope there is something interesting in them,' she said, looking at her fingernails.

'Let's hope,' he said, and looked at her fondly. 'I was thinking, Oparna, Astrobiology has to be made one of the main streams in the Institute. What do you say?'

She said, in a somewhat lifeless way, that it was a good idea.

He mistook her response for the boredom that so often fills researchers after the excitement of a big project. The hired hands in her lab had been asked to leave, most of the equipment was shrouded in protective covers, and she was left alone in the basement once again with ghostly peons, and the uncertain wait for another worthy assignment.

'You will be part of the faculty then?' he asked pleasantly.

'I don't know,' she said, and looked away.

That introduced a silence which ended with Oparna asking if there was anything else he wanted to discuss. When she was at the door, she turned to look at him for a passing moment. Just for an instant, he thought, they were once again in that abstract doorway of love where they did not know if they were reuniting or growing apart.

Their next meeting, three weeks later, was more grim. It was in the company of the Press Officer who wiped his forehead out of habit, even though he was not sweating. Cardiff too had said that the study of the two samplers was complete and no form of life had been detected. Acharya looked sombrely at Oparna, and then at the Press Officer, who straightened his back.

'We have a moral obligation to go public with this news,' Acharya said. 'We have to state clearly that two external labs have detected nothing in the samplers.'

After the Press Officer left hurriedly to type out the release, Acharya and Oparna maintained a deep thoughtful silence that both of them understood as a form of professional conversation and not as the discomfort of defeated lovers.

Finally he said, 'Considering the fact that Cardiff and Boston have not detected anything while we have, it is natural for people to question whether the sampler that was studied here was accidentally contaminated in the lab. I know such a thing could not have happened under your watch. But we must reassure people that our lab maintains the highest standards.'

Oparna nodded, but he could see that her mind was drifting.

He leaned forward and asked her with affection, 'I hope you are not disappointed with the news from Cardiff?'

'I am not,' she said.

'I am,' he said. 'But this is just the beginning. We are going to send many, many balloons up there. And all those things that are falling down, we are going to trap them in our samplers and show beyond any dispute that there are aliens among us.'

Oparna rose from her chair and went around the desk to his side. She held his face with her two warm hands and kissed him on his forehead. She had the peace of a mourner. There was something morbid about her face. It looked as if he had died and she was bidding him farewell. He felt a stab of such a cold fright that he thought of Lavanya, and wanted to complain to her that he was dead.

MANY YEARS LATER, several scientists would still recall that Tuesday morning with the minute details of where they were and what they were doing when they first heard the news, like the word of an assassination freezes the memory of a whole generation.

Jana Nambodri was with his usual company of radio astronomers when the phone rang. He held the receiver to his ear, and after making the first perfunctory noises he listened speechless. The radio astronomers, greatly dispirited after the failed mutiny to erect Search for Extraterrestrial Intelligence as an autonomous department, gathered in Nambodri's office more often than before with lament masquerading as hopeful conspiracy. That morning, there were six of them, including Nambodri, in the room.

It was the portly professor called Jal, with a Gorbachev bird-dropping stain on his bald head, who first noticed that Nambodri's hand was trembling. Jal nudged others to look at their ringleader. Nambodri's left hand, which was holding the receiver, was shaking, and his right was drawing concentric circles on a discarded envelope. He finally said into the phone, 'This is . . . I don't know what to say . . . This is unbelievable.' He put the phone down and stared blankly.

'What's happened?' Jal asked.

'I can't tell you,' Nambodri said. 'You've had a bypass.'

'Tell me, Jana. What happened?'

Nambodri, whose mind had not fully returned from the phone call and the train of thought it had inspired, banged the table with his fist, and winced.

'Stupid girl. Stupid girl,' he said. Then he stormed out of his room, into the long corridor. Halfway down, he turned and looked at the door that said 'Director'. Even to the unpoetic mind of Nambodri, the austere wooden door was beginning to resemble the lid of a coffin.

Ayyan Mani looked at the courier letter on his table that the morose peon had dropped, as he always did, like a grievance from his heart. It was an unremarkable courier letter from the Ministry of Defence, and Ayyan knew he was going to open it. He looked furtively to his right, in the direction of Acharya's door, and to the left where the main entrance was. The letter was from Basu.

Dr Arvind Acharya,

This is to inform you of an extraordinary development. We have a letter with us from Dr Oparna Goshmaulik, Head of the Astrobiology lab and the project coordinator of the Balloon Mission. We have independently verified with Oparna that she was, in fact, the author of the letter. She has declared, with a detailed chronology of the events, that she was pressurized by you into contaminating the contents of one sampler with the purpose of claiming that microscopic life has been detected at the improbable altitude of 41 kilometres above the Earth.

She has claimed that when she first informed you that no life had been detected in the sampler, you instructed her to contaminate it and fabricate a report. And that you threatened her with severe professional consequences if she did not go with the flow. Taking moral responsibility for her actions, she has offered to resign. This is an extraordinary allegation and I'll be in the Institute on Wednesday, by noon, to see how we can resolve this. I'll be joined by an empowered committee for an internal inquiry into the matter. All senior faculty of the Institute have been instructed to be available to be called upon. You are hereby asked to present yourself before the empowered committee.

Bhaskar Basu

Only after he had read the letter twice did Ayyan realize that he was standing. A corner of the letter was quivering in the breeze of the air conditioner. It was as if the note were shaking in the first tremors of the news. He sat down and repaired the letter with the supply of official envelopes he had in the bottom drawer. He tried to recall when he had last felt this familiar fear in his heart which was a cruel mix of sorrow and anticipation. As he entered Acharya's room, Ayyan recognized the fear. Many years ago, when he had to wake up the aged father of a friend to inform him that his only son had drowned in Aksa, he had felt this way, as if his heart were turning into ice. He put the letter on Acharya's desk.

Acharya regarded the letter without interest. Then he returned to *Topolov's Superman.*

In the peace of the dormant equipment, shrouded in their plastic covers, Oparna sat on the main desk swinging her legs. She was staring at the phone. The murmurs of subterranean machines filled the room as the door opened. As it slowly shut, the haunting silence returned. Nambodri walked in delicately, like an explorer. He looked up at the ceiling and in other directions, and smiled. He stood by Oparna's side and looked at her without a word. Unable to bear his phoney intensity any more, she turned to the phone and resumed her vigil.

'Why are you doing this?' he asked. She removed her hairband, held it in her mouth, and tied her hair in a fiercer knot.

'You must ask the man, don't you think?' she said.

'The victim, are you?' he asked.

'Yes.'

'He would never even think of doing something like this. Oparna, why don't you tell me what this is all about?'

She began softly to hum a rhyme, probably a Bangla rhyme. She was suddenly scary.

'I've heard some stories about you and him,' Nambodri said. 'Something happened? And this is some kind of a revenge? Woman scorned, or some rubbish like that?'

'Why don't you come later, Mr Runner-Up?'

That disturbed his poise but just for a moment. He told her, almost fondly, 'You're being stupid, Oparna. This is not the way to do it. You're almost there but you have to be careful. Acharya is not easy to destroy.'

He could see clearly, in the nonchalant way that she was sitting, the way she was swinging her legs, her nervous hum and her paranormal expectation of the phone to ring, an insanity that he might never have suspected before. He felt afraid, not only to be standing there in the deserted basement lab, but for the times when he had tried to flirt with her, because if she had granted him the possibilities, his fate would probably have been far worse than Acharya's.

'You must listen to me carefully, Oparna,' he said.

She slouched a bit and yawned. 'This is not the time for desperate mentors to come,' she said. 'What is done is done.'

Nambodri leaned on the desk and said, almost in a whisper, 'Oparna, there is something you must understand. Even before you were born, Arvind Acharya was a name that floated once every year as a probable Nobel recipient. He is big. He is very big. Nobody is going to believe you. He has to just say he was framed and your game is over.'

'There are people who'd like to believe me. I know that much,' she said.

'That's true,' Nambodri said thoughtfully. 'But writing a letter to the Ministry is not the way to do it. You've got to understand. There are people who hate him but there are also very powerful people who love him. The game now could go either way. So you must go to the press right now. It has to be all over the papers before the internal inquiry even begins. People have to see this news, not hear it from their friends. Do you understand? It has to be news, not gossip. People believe news. You've got to go public with this story, Oparna.'

She looked at him innocently, almost like a child, and said, 'But isn't that unethical?'

Then the phone rang, and a fond smile appeared on her face.

Ayyan Mani said two soft 'hellos' to the dictaphone and played his voice back to check an instrument he had never held with so much reverence before. It was, until this day, an enduring symbol of his plight, a reminder that he was nothing more than a large Indian recorder appended to a small Japanese one. But that morning, his unfailing instinct told him that this small silver thing was going to produce a treasure which he could somehow encash in the decisive war of the Brahmins that was now unavoidable. He did not have a plan, but he knew he would soon find one.

Oparna arrived without the discomforts of sanity. It was almost the same face that Ayyan had seen one morning, many months ago, when she had come with her hair untied and dressed in clothes that seemed to have a purpose. She had come to propose then. Now, there was a deep wound inside her and it showed on her face in a slanted smile. It was a misery that he recognized as a fate of love. He had seen this many times from very close, very close – that perilous distance from where the face of any woman would look ugly, and in the agony of being spurned must quickly choose to either kiss or spit. In the pale rooms of the lodgings where he used first to soften his aspiring wives with caresses, and then bid them a final farewell with a clear head – which is another form of cruelty in love – he had seen this face of Oparna. And that made him grin. At how he had escaped from the treacherous minefields of freedom unscathed, into the safety of marriage. While one of the most intelligent men alive was about to be mutilated.

Free love, Ayyan knew in his heart, is an enchanting place haunted by demented women. Here, every day men merely got away. And then, without warning, they were finished. The girl would come and say, like a martyr, that she was pregnant, or would remember that all the time she was being raped, or her husband would arrive with a butcher's knife. Such things always happened in the country of free love. Ayyan Mani had fled in time from there into the open arms of a virgin. But Acharya had fled the other way.

Oparna found her man exactly the way she had imagined. Acharya was sunk in his massive black chair, his beautiful face staring in blank confusion, like an infant's. She sat across the table from him and smiled.

He asked in a voice that was without force or expectation, 'Why, Oparna?'

She made an exasperated face as if she had hoped to talk about more interesting things.

'What did you expect, Arvind?' she said, almost with compassion. 'You sleep with me till your wife comes back from her vacation and then ask me to get out of your life.'

'I thought you understood,' he said, and at that moment, when he said it, he conceded to himself that he didn't know what he meant by that.

'No, Arvind,' she said, her words hurried and angry now. 'I did not understand. And I've never understood it when men tell me "it was fun but now we have to get rid of you".'

'So you do this?'

'Try to understand. All my life, men have humiliated me. I don't know why but that's what I remember of men. Then I go mad over an old man. And he too dumps me. I wanted to kill you. I really did.' She studied her palm and the slender fingers which she thought looked a bit too bony and aged.

He did not recognize this woman who was sitting in front of him. He felt an excruciating sympathy for her, and then he remembered that it was he who was on the verge of being destroyed. 'What do we do now?' he asked feebly.

'We are finished. That's all. Together. Your reputation is now over. And no one will hire me again,' she said in an informative way. 'It's a mess, Arvind. Even if you scream from the top of the water tank that you are innocent, you're finished. And there are enough vultures here who want you out. They already know what they must do.'

'So there was nothing in the sampler?'

'Is that what you are worried about? If there were aliens in the sampler? That's very rude, you know.'

'Tell me, Oparna, was there anything in the sampler?'

'There was nothing in it. Just air.'

He found it ridiculous that what pained him more at the moment was that the Balloon Mission had completely failed. He turned to the window and tried to accept the shock of the failure. He had the courage to accept the punishment of Oparna, and the wisdom to understand that it is in the nature of love to be disproportionate with both rewards and retributions. But he was shattered by the fact that he had to now forsake the joy and relief of having found aliens in the stratosphere. He suspected that he might not get another shot. And for the first time in his life he understood the fear of a bleak, vacant future.

He went to the window and stood looking at the calm sea. He felt the presence of Oparna beside him. He did not find it strange that they stood there like that without a word, like an ancient couple who had no need for language. They stared through the window with unflinching eyes, but never before, not even during their first naked gazes in the basement, had they looked so deeply into each other.

When she finally spoke, it was another form of silence, like the sound of the sea, and the songs of the birds. He heard her tell him dreamily how excited she was when the sampler arrived, how she hoped there was something in it that would make him happy.

'We ran all kinds of tests, Arvind,' she said. 'Then, when I began to realize that there was nothing in it, you know what I did? I did not leave the lab for four days. Four days and four nights, at a stretch, I ran test after test because I did not want to see you sad. I don't know what happened on the fourth night. Something hit me. It was as if I had woken up from a stupid dream. And I was so ashamed. I asked myself why am I such a sucker for men. Here is an old bastard who hurt me so much and I was going mad trying to make him happy, trying like an idiot to find something in a stupid steel box. I was so angry with myself Arvind, and at you, and at everything.'

So, in the stealth of dawn she had contaminated the sampler with microbial cultures that were available in the lab. It consoled her. The idea of taking him to absolute ruin, she said, made her feel powerful and, finally, smart.

They resumed the patient silence of an unnatural belonging. Then he heard her light footsteps leave the room. For hours after that he stood by the window. Pigeons that came in the excitement of landing on the ledge were stunned by his ghostly stare. Down on the pathways around the main lawn, small groups of scientists were gathering. In them there was an unmistakable excitement that masqueraded as shock, just like the entertainment of death fills funeral guests with grimness. Acharya began to understand the mysterious composure of men who are led to the gallows. Their even gait and the strength of their legs that took them unwaveringly to the hollow wooden pedestal had always fascinated him. Now, he almost experienced their condition. He felt a sick enfeebling fear inside him that had the smell of pus. But he too could walk.

By evening, the phones began to ring. Acharya let them ring. Ayyan walked in several times to say that old friends and journalists were on the line begging to know what had happened. Visitors were gathering in the anteroom and their murmurs began to grow in the first hums of a huge impending storm.

'What must we do, Sir?' Ayyan asked.

The news of Oparna's letter quickly spread across the world infecting everyone who was remotely interested. Copies began mysteriously to fall into the inboxes of journalists and scientists, with a subject message that said 'India's Woo-Suk', comparing Acharya to the disgraced South Korean scientist Hwang Woo-Suk, who had fabricated breakthroughs in stem-cell research. Blogs were besieged by self-righteous laments at the increasing fraud in science, and more compassionate analyses of why a great scientist might have stooped so low, and the impassioned defence of old hands who refused to believe Acharya was capable of such deceit. They saw in Oparna's letter the obvious revenge of an enraged woman. But the story everyone wanted to believe was that Arvind Acharya had fallen. Sombre television reporters stood outside the fortified gates of the Institute and spoke of how the scientific community was in a state of shock.

An astronomer in the glory of having discovered aliens, now interrupted by a beautiful associate who claimed she had falsified the research on his instructions. It was a great story.

THE TRIAL WAS arranged in a windowless room. It had a beige carpet that was somehow perfect, and there was an air of silent estrangement. Unlike the other conference rooms in the Institute of Theory and Research where large oblong tables conveyed the intention of equality to all chairs, at least before they were occupied by incurable egos, this one was designed for the unambiguous purpose of lecturing. Behind a reddish-brown oak table with a solitary rose peeping out of a narrow white vase, five men sat in a solemnity they had granted themselves. All the chairs in the room had been removed except for two that looked particularly austere without armrests, and they bleakly faced the jury.

Oparna entered with a premeditated smile that was poised between gloom and courage. She was in a sky-blue salwar kameez. Her hair fell in languid curls. When she saw the men behind the table, all seated like a diminished Last Supper gathering, she felt an irrepressible urge to laugh. Basu, in a black suit and red tie, was at the centre; Nambodri was to his right. She did not know the other three men. They must have been in their fifties.

One by one, the men rose to greet Oparna.

'Please sit,' Basu said graciously. She sat in one of the two austere chairs, wondering how these men knew this was the way it had to be done. Such an inquiry had no precedence, yet they knew they had to arrange the table that way and the chairs this way. She tried to imagine what would happen when Acharya arrived. She and he, together in this room on these chairs, would look like a terrible couple undergoing counselling. She tried, once again, not to laugh.

She wondered how women would have handled this situation. What if the jury had been comprised of menopausal women? That was a disturbing thought. They would have butchered her in a minute. But this jury of ageing men was going to be easy.

'You, of course, know Dr Jana Nambodri,' Basu said smartly, and introduced the other three as senior scientists who were attached to various institutes in Delhi. From the way they looked at her, almost in appreciation or gratitude – she could not tell – it was evident to her that the jury shared a common grievance.

The men examined some papers in front of them. Basu said, without looking up, 'You have stated everything very clearly in your letter. Is there any change in your statement?'

'No,' she said.

'When Acharya arrives you will have to repeat your statement in front of him. Is that all right with you?'

'Yes,' she said.

The jury appeared a bit lost now, as if they had nothing more to say.

'Are there any other statements you would like to make?' Nambodri asked, one hand on the table, leaning back a bit in what he imagined was a charming way.

'No,' Oparna said, trying to think of the day her grandmother died so that she did not burst out laughing.

'Acharya had considerable power over you,' Nambodri said, trying to remind her gently of something she might have missed. 'Did he misuse his power in any way apart from instructing you to falsify the report?'

'No,' she said, offering not even the curiosity of confusion.

'What I am trying to say is, you are an attractive woman, a very attractive woman, and he was a powerful man who forced you to do something unethical. There must have been other moments when he used his position and made you feel vulnerable? Something that you were embarrassed to mention in your letter?'

'If you are talking about sexual harassment,' she said, 'it is not he who I have a complaint against.'

That inspired Nambodri to fall silent. The other men, too, had nothing more to say to her. They whispered among themselves. Two men looked at their watches. Basu pressed a bell and a clerk appeared at the door.

'Has he come?' Basu asked.

'No, Sir,' the clerk said, and vanished.

The jury stared at Oparna with the embarrassment of having to wait for the accused. It was an awkward pause that began to disturb the confidence of Nambodri. He imagined the unrelenting presence of Acharya in the room and what it might do to the composure of everyone. Oparna might not be able to sustain the lie. He wanted her to be strong and play a decisive role. But he suspected that she did not fully understand the seriousness of the trial. He tried to draw her into the mood of the moment.

'There were two American professors in the lab when you were studying the contents of the sampler,' he said, 'Michael White and Simon Gore. We spoke to them on the phone this morning on a conference call. They expressed their shock, and refused to believe that Acharya could have instructed you to tamper with the sampler. How did you manage to contaminate the sampler when they were around?'

'They were not around when I did it,' she said. 'I did it around four in the morning.'

'You were in the lab that early for the purpose of contaminating the sampler?' Nambodri asked in an educative way, like a lawyer preparing the client for trial.

'Yes.'

'Acharya asked you to do it around that time, before the professors arrived?'

'Yes.'

'Do you think it's possible that the Americans too were involved in Acharya's conspiracy?'

'I don't think so.'

'What proof do you have that Acharya asked you to tamper with the sampler?' Basu asked.

'I don't have any proof,' she said. 'But, obviously, I have no motivation to make this revelation. Except on moral grounds.'

'Obviously,' Nambodri said. 'But why are you making it now? Why not before?'

'I was aware of the implications. I needed time to decide.'

'We understand that,' he said kindly, and then looked surprised to see the man at the door.

Ayyan Mani was holding a note in his hand.

'Dr Acharya asked me to give this to you,' he told the jury, and held the folded letter in the air. He had started walking in when Basu said ceremoniously, 'Come in.' That made Ayyan stop for a moment before resuming his entry.

He handed the note to Basu who read the contents to the gathering: 'It's beneath my dignity to react to an allegation of this nature or to present myself before a committee of this composition. I will not be interrogated by bureaucrats and subordinates. In my defence, I present my whole past – Arvind Acharya.'

For a brief moment, Oparna thought Basu was an endearingly formidable man. Then she realized that she felt that way because he was reading out the words of a man who really was.

Basu tore up the letter and handed the shreds to Ayyan.

'You may give this to him,' he said, and threw a look at Oparna to see if she was impressed. 'I interpret this as a direct challenge to the Defence Minister himself,' Basu said. Ayyan left the room holding the shreds in a tight fist. He looked forward to giving the shreds to Acharya.

Basu studied Oparna with what must have been wisdom, and said, 'What you did, even though you did it under duress, was wrong. It has brought disgrace to the Institute. But you have done the right thing by offering to take responsibility and resign.'

Oparna, once again, forced herself to think of the sudden demise of her grandmother.

He paused and nodded at the other members. 'We have

nothing more to say to you except that without your courage this matter would never have surfaced. Would you reconsider your offer to resign?'

'No,' she said. The briskness with which she replied surprised him and he forgot what he wanted to say.

Nambodri narrowed his eyes and looked sideways at her. 'Maybe we can find a post for you in one of the other institutes run by the Ministry of Defence?'

'I am not in a position to think about my future right now,' she said, standing up. The men rose to bid her farewell. She collected her handbag from the floor and walked out without a word.

Ayyan Mani was certain that after this day Oparna would never be seen in the Institute again. In the tumult of the coming days as the scandal unfolded on television screens, she would be missing. And she would be missing long after people stopped trying to find her. She would become a distant memory to be invoked with mirth – 'Remember Oparna?'

She would wander through life beseeching men to love her, frighten them with the intensity of her affection, marry one whose smell she could tolerate, and then resume the search for love. And she would suffer the loneliness of affairs. And on some mornings, in front of men who thanked their luck for such an easy fling, she would endure the shame of putting on her clothes, somehow more demeaning than undressing for them. She would wander this way every day of her life until she found shelter in the peace of age.

Ayyan saw this in his mind and waited to feel the glee. But it did not come. There was only an unfamiliar ache in his heart. For a beautiful woman whose hurt nobody fully understood, whose anguish the vultures now used in their larger game.

The trial lasted only a day. After the departure of Oparna, post-doctoral students who were part of the Balloon Mission walked in nervously and walked out without taking the case forward. The jury set aside the sampler scandal and decided to hear the complaints of thirteen scientists who said that they were mentally tortured by Acharya. This was Nambodri's masterstroke.

The evidence against Acharya was always going to be thin. And the revenge of a woman, Nambodri knew, could not be fully depended on. But he had full faith in the revenge of men and their natural brutality that would land death-blows on a venerated and arrogant person when he was down. The war of the mediocre, in the world according to Nambodri, was a battle that raged in every office. And it was a battle that they always won in the end. It was the right of simple people to survive in their little nooks and do their little things. But the geniuses did not let them. They came with their grand plans and high standards and the proud inability to offer false compliments. Even in the Institute of fantastic pursuits, where there was an imagined regard for absolute brilliance because that lent a glow to all, this rebellion had always been brewing. It was subdued, but it was there. Worse, the old man had won Oparna, the infatuation of all. So it was not only the foes of Acharya who despised him but also, secretly, his many fans. That, Nambodri knew, was the nature of men.

String theorists arrived and told the jury how they were humiliated by Acharya for their mathematical structure of the universe, for heading nowhere with the Theory of Everything and for the crime of believing in the Big Bang. Radio astronomers complained that Acharya had unfairly denied them the science of the search for extraterrestrial intelligence, and that they were not allowed to attend Seti seminars because he wanted to siphon every rupee into the Balloon Mission. Others who did not have specific complaints said that it was ridiculous that the administrative head of the Institute was so pompous and eccentric. Outside the room, on the corridors, in the library, in the canteen, and on the pathways that ran through the undulating lawns, there were passionate debates on whether Acharya was indeed a fraud. The community had to choose between the entertainment of believing that he was guilty and the dull nobility of having faith in his character. It was the sort of day when a man needed goodwill more than genius. By evening, the word spread with the decisive force of common truth that Acharya had owned up to the jury, that he had confessed. The origin of the news, everybody attributed to the other.

At the closed gates of the Institute, the guards stood amused. The crowd of reporters was swelling. Television crews were landing and the line of OB vans on the narrow lane outside stretched for a hundred metres. A few hours ago Arvind Acharya had walked out through the gates, cutting through the reporters like a silent ship. They had chased him and asked their questions, but he told them nothing. Now they waited in the hope that something big was about to be announced. The invisible machines of Jana Nambodri's public relations genius sent a steady supply of mineral water to the gates, and bits of information through scientists who would be quoted later as reliable sources and people-in-the-know.

The murmurs outside the gates grew louder when they saw Basu and Nambodri walk towards them. The guards opened the gates. The reporters rushed in and swirled around the two. Basu touched his newly combed hair. Nambodri stood with a wise smile and nodded to acknowledge some of the reporters he knew by name. His role for the evening was that of a silent and reluctant incumbent forced to take the reins of power in the midst of the Institute's disgrace. The Press Officer arrived and raised both his hands.

'Questions later,' he screamed.

Basu showed his palms to the journalists and asked them to calm down. 'I've an announcement to make,' he said, and that brought about a hush. 'The internal inquiry is over. Dr Arvind Acharya has confessed that he ordered Dr Oparna Goshmaulik to falsify the research in an attempt to fraudulently prove that he had discovered life at the altitude of forty-one kilometres above the Earth.'

There was a precarious silence for a moment which collapsed in a roar of questions.

'And, and,' Basu said, trying to reclaim the attention, 'I regret to say that we have found other instances of unacceptable conduct. He misused the funds of the Institute to feed his ambitious Balloon Mission. His general behaviour has, for long, humiliated the brilliant minds that work here. It has also come to our notice that he used the basement for some activities that we are too ashamed to disclose. It was unbecoming of the Director of the Institute of Theory and Research, an institute of excellence, to use the premises for such activities. In the light of these extraordinary circumstances, Arvind Acharya has been suspended until further notice. Dr Jana Nambodri, one of the founding fathers of radio astronomy in this country, has been elevated as the acting Director.'

In the coming days, Acharya would fervently deny that he had confessed to contaminating the sampler, but his disclaimer was lost in his silence over what Oparna meant to him and whether he had indeed used the basement as a love-nest. The uncontrollable force of public perception would, inevitably, decree that a man who could seduce a woman almost half his age in a basement lab was probably involved in other nefarious activities. Even his powerful friends who were once flattered to serve him when he deigned to call for their help, now distanced themselves from him. Some would not take his calls; others said that he should fight his battles (probably till eternity) in court. Scientific bodies that had once begged him to endorse them with his name would tell him, with formal regret, that his association was not necessary any more. Friends and fans would write to him from all corners of the world affirming their faith in him, but even in those letters he would see the strength of old boyish love and not the conviction that he was innocent.

After the declaration at the gates, Nambodri and Basu went to the third floor. As they walked down the long corridor, doors opened. Some scientists nodded in appreciation. Many stared bleakly. An old wizard of Number Theory handed an envelope to Nambodri and said he was quitting. But the mood was somewhat festive. As the two men walked, a swarm of speechless scientists began to follow. And this swarm grew until they stood outside the door that said Director. Basu opened the door and in a ritual that had no tradition, he extended his hand graciously asking Nambodri to walk in first. The applause shook the furtive labour of Ayyan Mani.

Ayyan was trying to stick together the shreds of Acharya's letter to Basu. He believed it might have a use in the future. He hid the almost-repaired note in the drawer as the crowd entered the anteroom, like the Pathans who followed John Simpson during the BBC's liberation of Kabul. Basu opened the inner door and the swarm moved in. Ayyan followed them inside to watch the rare physical gaiety of the Brahmins. He planted himself in a corner.

Basu stood at the desk and said amidst laughter and applause, 'All yours.'

Nambodri sat in the huge black leather chair and said in a deep voice, 'There was no Big Bang. There never was.' And everyone laughed.

He spotted Ayyan, who quickly laughed in a belated appreciation of a joke he was not expected to understand. 'Would you like to work with me, Sir?' Nambodri asked.

'It'll be my honour, Sir,' Ayyan said.

'How is your son, the genius?'

'He keeps talking about you, Sir,' Ayyan said. 'He loved the posters in your room.'

Those framed film posters would soon move in a procession in the feeble hands of dark peons. From the office of the Deputy Director they would pass the corner fiefdom of Ayyan and vanish through a door that was now stripped of the gold-plated mascot of the old world – Arvind Acharya. The blank textured walls of what used to be Acharya's office were now adorned with the visuals of *ET*, *Men in Black*, *Superman*, *Mars Attacks*, and a blow-up of an introspective Carl Sagan captured before he began to die.

Acharya had left everything behind except Oparna's photographs, some journals, his collection of *Topolov's Superman*, and the piece of meteorite that he used as paperweight. Nambodri threw most of his things out and altered the look of the room. He shifted the snow-white sofas to the window and arranged the desk in the corner that was diagonal to the door. The only time Ayyan had seen Acharya on the sofa was when he had met Adi. But the new regime was run from the sofas, and in the boisterous chatter of radio astronomers who spent the whole day against the backdrop of the Arabian Sea, plotting their future. They did not have to wait with Ayyan any more in the anteroom, and it was inevitable that they would throw a glance of simple triumph at the man every time they bypassed his clerical authority and went straight in to meet the new Director.

One evening in the changed world, Professor Jal rushed in barefoot and almost sprinted through the inner door. He stood by the window and told Nambodri's happy caucus, 'Look outside.' The astronomers came to where he was standing, and looked. On the tarred driveway that meandered to the sea went Arvind Acharya. His trousers lay precariously at the lower waist, one sleeve of his shirt was folded and the other was not. He stumbled on a small pothole and one of the bathroom slippers came off. He flipped it over with his foot and slipped into it. He appeared to contemplate his feet for a moment. Then he resumed his slow, laborious walk. Scores of still figures looked from the other windows and from the lawns. But Acharya went on his way unseeing, his head slightly bent. He opened the wooden beach gate and went down to the black rocks. He sat there long after the figures behind the many windows vanished, one after the other.

He began to arrive every day. He would wander around the lawns or sit on the sea rocks. The guards did not know how to stop him. He would look at them like an infant, and they would silently open the gates. Late in the evening, they would open the gates again for him to leave. He would cross the road without looking and vanish into the Professors' Quarters.

This was a fallen man, people said, who was in the misery of disgrace, but in reality Acharya was in the confusion of feeling nothing at all. He felt no pain, no shame, no anger. His eyes were always transfixed, but at nothing. They had lost the power to see even memories. Lavanya tried to console him, but she did not know how she should reach out to a man who was on the far shores of a living death. She allowed herself the mild cruelty of not trying too hard to reclaim him because his disgrace had advertised her own defeat at the hands of a younger woman. Also, his suspension had diminished her authority among the ladies of the Quarters. Her power would have completely perished had it not been for her beauty and unusual height. But she was also a beneficiary of the sympathy of the wives because, in their perennial conviction that they were all victims of men, they had a special place in their hearts for a real one. Mrs Nambodri, now bearing the charming discomfort of being called Mrs Director by the peons and guards, had arrived last week at Lavanya's door like a visiting stateswoman. And they spoke about the disparities between Vietnamese Buddha heads and Thai.

Lavanya was certain that her husband would soon rescue himself from the trance of his new abnormality and return to the old. She was more concerned about her daughter. Shruti did not talk to her father any more. She had called him a month ago to say that he must be brave, but when she read about the affair on a website, she first asked her mother if it was true, and did not speak to him after that.

Shruti's anger did not affect him. He was grateful to anyone who would offer him silence. But every day, he tried to understand what had happened to him. He wandered inside the Institute in that confusion. Old friends smiled at him. He would look at them with feeble eyes and nod. Young postdoctoral students called him names. He would nod at them too. Sometimes on the pathways, he would stop walking and just gape at his feet.

One Monday all this changed, for no reason at all.

He was sitting under a solitary palm in the backyard of the Institute when he thought of something that made him so happy that he felt his life and its many memories return to him. He had been briefly estranged from himself, but now he was all right. He got up and walked briskly towards home.

Acharya let himself in. Lavanya was asleep on the couch with *Digging to America* on her lap. He stood beside her and looked at her tired face. Her eyelids quivered and opened. She was surprised to see him standing like that.

'I want to talk to you,' he said.

'Talk then,' she said, sitting up. She was relieved to hear him speak finally.

'Lavanya,' he said, 'you may not know this, but I've thought of you every single day of my life, and my life was very good because of you. Does that make sense to you? What I just said, does that make sense you to?'

She looked worried. 'Are you all right, Arvind?' she asked.

'I also have a confession to make,' he said. 'During a Cosmic Ancestry seminar, I said, "Ladies and Gentlemen, it's my deepest belief that all life on Earth came from outer space, not just my wife."'

Lavanya burst out laughing. 'It's OK,' she said, standing up. She tried to understand what could have happened to him, but she was too amused to solve the mystery. 'Sit down, I will get you a cup of coffee,' she said.

Acharya went to the balcony. He looked at the concrete driveway, nine floors below, and calculated that it would take him no more than two seconds to hit the driveway. He inspected the wooden railing and hoped it would take his weight. He did not want to break it. That would be inelegant. The suspended shrubs were too far back to get in the way. Two shirts hung from the clothes wire and they looked like orphans, already. He sat on the railing and slowly rose on his feet. He balanced himself with his hands in the air. He felt a bit ridiculous, and it struck him how unaesthetic the process of suicide actually was.

As he stood perched to jump, it was inevitable that he would think of his whole life. 'It was easy,' he summarized. He wondered why he did not feel the intensity of death, the final ache of the very end of memories, and the indestructible peace of liberation. Instead, his mind was filled with too many thoughts that reminded him of his old desperation to live every moment. He was thinking of the frustrating problem of gravity at the moment of death, standing on a railing nine floors above the ground. He was even embarrassed on behalf of humanity for not solving the elementary question – What exactly is gravity? It was shameful that man did not know what gravity actually was. How pathetic. And he felt a wild rancour towards theoretical physicists who said that gravity was made up of gravitons. What rubbish. He wanted to understand why there was life, what was the true nature of Time, and he wanted to comprehend the beautiful absurdity of infinity which was the only real evidence mankind had to prove that maths was fundamentally moronic. There was so much to do, he thought, on either side of the wooden railing. Then he felt an inglorious fear. That, he recognized, was not the trivial fear of falling. But it was the memory of the devious friends of Lavanya, and how their faces began to glow after the death of their husbands. He wondered if Lavanya, too, would find happiness in the relief of widowhood, choosing to love him more as an enhanced memory in a photo frame than as a giant living slob. He felt an intense bitterness that only a husband can feel for his wife. And in a moment of pristine jealousy he wanted to deny her the pleasure that she might derive at his expense. He slipped on the railing, but found his balance in time.

Beneath the solitary palm when he had prescribed to himself the simplicity of death, he was certain that he had arrived at an obvious solution. His mind was dead, his spirit was dead, and they were beseeching from another world to relieve the body too. But now he understood what had happened to him since the day of the trial. He understood why he did not feel anything after they consigned him to the short blacklist of fraudulent scientists. The truth was, as always, simpler than he thought. What they had killed was not his mind, or spirit, or other things that might not exist at all. What they had killed was his stature. The great Arvind Acharya, the Nobel laureate who did not win a Nobel. The Big Bang's Old Foe. The lone discoverer of aliens. That being had been slain. And the confusing numbness of death inside him was actually the paradise of relief. All his life he had tried to hide the torments of one paranormal boyhood experience. He had hidden them behind the manly grandness of science. His cerebral deformity which others called genius had made it easy for him to understand the mathematical pursuit of truth and it had quickly shrouded him in an inescapable glory when he was very young. He was entrapped in a fame that he feared he would lose if he tried to explain that every single action in the world was preordained, or if he attempted to investigate the purpose of life. Now that he was stripped of his reputation, he was free. He could now become the prophet of a new form of science that would not try to understand the universe through particles and forces but through the great game of life.

The decision of a woman in the market to buy cabbage instead of brinjal, the decision of a man at a junction to turn left instead of right: what if these events were as preordained as the birth of a star and its inevitable death? If the flutter of a butterfly or the shudder of a flower in the breeze was preordained aeons ago, he would now find a way to understand it. There would be no shame in that. Because every man grants others the power to shame him, and Arvind Acharya decided to withdraw that privilege from the world.

He walked into the hall, dusting his trousers. He sat with his elbows on the dining-table. Lavanya came with a tray. She watched him curiously. 'Are you all right, Arvind?' she asked.

He did not reply. He sipped his coffee and looked around the house as though it were the first time he was here.

At that moment, she was reminded of her mother's prophecy, a day before her wedding, that he would go completely mad one day.

'But he seems so happy,' she had told her mother.

Her mother had stopped scrubbing the copper plate, and said, 'It's not only the sad who go mad, my child, it is also the happy.'

Acharya set the cup on the table and stood. He steered his trousers around his waist and walked out of the house. He began to see things in a way he had never seen them before. The corridor that led to the lift was grey and it had pieces of splintered tiles arranged in concentric circles. The liftman was dark and lost, and he had a mole at the edge of his lip and another one at the edge of his nose, and there was a strand of hair sticking out of both. That reminded him of Lavanya's hypothesis many years ago that the cure for balding might be in the mysteries of melanin because the longest strand of hair on the limbs and the face, she said, always rose from the moles. The little girl who was playing in the driveway where she might have seen him fall, had he not tried to understand himself in time, was wearing a frock with fractal motifs. And she looked so beautiful that he hoped she would never ever hear the word 'fractal' in her life. There were four guards at the gates of the Institute and they were in ash-grey shirts and black trousers, and black caps with two red streaks that were parallel to each other. He looked at the fork of the pathway and the square lawn and the L-shaped main block and the people going about. He felt as if his vision had improved. Like that evening on the Marine Drive where he had once gone to escape Oparna's love. The grey fog of rain had vanished and a strange light had filled the city.

He sat on the black rocks and told the sea his version of the universe. A group of young doctoral students were gathered at a distance. They threw cautious looks at him. It was a tradition here to accept that sometimes men spoke to themselves. But Acharya had never been known to seek his own phantoms. They stared at him for a while, then they resumed their animated discussion about supersymmetry, occasionally glancing at him.

The breeze brought him the rudiments of their debate. He listened, his head inclined. Then he went to them and stood with his hands in his deep trouser pockets. They looked at him nervously. One boy tried to infect others with the smile of contempt.

'Don't look at me like that, son,' Acharya told him. 'When I was your age I was so smart that if you wanted to kiss my arse you would've had to take an entrance exam.'

That made the other boys laugh. Acharya laughed too. And he told them what he thought of supersymmetry. They listened, rooted to the ground. They asked him questions and he answered with deeper questions and an excited banter began to flow. His audience began to grow.

He started arriving every day, like a wandering bard. By the sea rocks, on the pathways and in the undulating backyard, students and scientists milled around him, and listened to the tales of his life, the day he met the Pope and how he was banned forever from the Vatican for whispering abuse in the pontiff's ear, the hilarious insanities of great minds, their private chauvinism and how they believed wives were conspiracies, the temper of Fred Hoyle, the encounters with Hawking who was a cunning man, the impending shocks that would emerge from the Large Hadron Collider, and the bleak future of theoretical physics. The swarm around him began to grow with every passing day and their banter beneath the skies became a sudden culture.

It was a sight that Jana Nambodri caught every evening from his new window. And this evening, as he surveyed the resurrection with a face that was always a mask, he held his mobile to the ear and asked when the formal dismissal of Acharya could be arranged. He put the phone away and stared with such meditative forbearance that his mutant ears, which could gather even the voices of thought, did not hear the door open.

Ayyan Mani stood in the relief of finally catching this man alone. For several days he had been waiting for a quiet moment like this, but Nambodri was always surrounded by his inner circle of liberated radio astronomers.

'Sir,' Ayyan said, enjoying the startled jerk of his new master. 'I wanted to have a word with you, Sir.'

Nambodri nodded without turning.

'That day Oparna Goshmaulik had come here, Sir.'

'Which day?' Nambodri asked, now looking at Ayyan.

'The day when everybody started talking about what Dr Acharya had done. She came here and told him why she contaminated the sampler. The door was not shut properly, Sir. So I heard everything.'

'Why wasn't the door shut?'

'Her hairclip had fallen on the floor when she was entering and that jammed the door, Sir. She didn't know that.'

'She contaminated the sampler of her own free will? Arvind didn't ask her to do it?'

'Yes, Sir.'

'She said that?' Nambodri asked, sitting on the sofa.

'Yes, Sir.'

'And you heard it?'

'Yes, Sir.'

'Why did she contaminate the sampler?'

'Love problem, Sir.'

'Why are you telling me this, Ayyan?' Nambodri asked, collecting a newspaper from the centrepiece, and turning its pages casually. Ayyan interpreted this as a calculated move to make him feel that it was not a big issue. He knew the tactics of the Brahmins. They called it management.

'I'm telling you this because I think you should know, Sir. What I am trying to tell you, Sir, is that even if I was called by the inquiry committee I would not have told them what I'd heard. I thought, for the good of all, the man has to go. I wanted you to be here in this room, Sir.'

Nambodri pointed to the sofa that was facing him and Ayyan sat down feeling strangely impertinent. Nambodri threw the paper away and asked with dead eyes, 'What do you want, Ayyan?'

'Nothing, Sir.'

Nambodri studied the floor. 'I am so touched by your gesture,' he said. 'A personal secretary's deposition would have meant nothing to the inquiry committee. We were interested only in the statements of scientists. But still, I am deeply moved.'

'Shall I get you some coffee, Sir?' Ayyan asked cheerfully,

standing up. Nambodri shook his head. Ayyan went to the door. 'Dr Acharya was a good man, Sir,' he said from the doorway, 'but sometimes he was very rude.' He walked back into the room and said, 'I will give you an example. My son loves the Institute. He talks about it every day. He wants to take the JET, Sir. He is only eleven but he says he will crack the entrance test. He is mad, my son. I asked Dr Acharya if Adi can sit for the entrance exam. He asked me to get out. He said the entrance exam is not a game. I thought that was very unfair.'

'Your son wants to take our entrance test?'

'Yes, Sir. People call him a genius, but I know he doesn't have a chance to make it.'

'He does not have a chance,' Nambodri said.

'I know, Sir. But Sir, do you think, you'll let the boy take the test?'

Nambodri's eyes studied his secretary with a mix of cunning and new respect. 'Ayyan, how many people know about it?' he asked.

'About what, Sir?'

'About what Oparna had told Arvind.'

'No one, Sir.'

'Are you sure?'

'No one. Except me, Sir.'

The news of Adi's application to the Institute of Theory and Research was covered in the English papers with a happy photograph of Jana Nambodri accepting a form from the boy. Two television channels interviewed them in the Director's chamber.

'He is a genius, so I thought, why not give him a chance?' Nambodri explained.

'I'll pass,' Adi said.

It was a fitting end to a great game. But three days later, the Marathi papers would tell this story with the picture of a man whose arrival on the scene unnerved Ayyan Mani. The game, he feared, had now gone too far.

PART SIX

One Last Shot

NOT EVERYBODY IN the crowd knew what they were waiting for, but they stood in a festive murmur outside one of the many exits of the BDD chawl. Some people asked what was going to happen. Many did not bother to ask. Excited boys ran through the assembly, and little girls played a conspiratorial game among themselves, all hopping on one leg. At the head of the crowd was Ayyan Mani, and a man bearing a massive rose garland that could break the neck of the beneficiary.

On the pavement by the side of the road was planted a banner two storeys high. Even in the blow-up the celebrity appeared stunted. He stood in a safari suit, his palms joined in greeting. His face was a light pink because poster artists did not have the freedom to paint his face black. His little mop of hair was spread thinly over an almost flat scalp. And his thick moustache had sharp edges. Just above his head was an English introduction in large font – DYNAMIC PERSONALITY. A thinner line that followed said he was the honourable Minister S. Waman. It seemed appropriate that it was at Waman's black shoes the author took credit, in Marathi and in diplomatically chosen small font – 'Billboard Presented By P. Bikaji'. Bikaji was the man who was holding the massive garland. His white kurta had become transparent in his own sweat and he was almost trembling under the weight of the garland.

'When he comes,' he told Ayyan, 'I will give him the garland first and then you speak.'

'Why do you want to waste your time?' Ayyan said. 'He is not even going to look at you.'

Someone screamed, 'He is here.' The crowd surged into the road. A pilot jeep screeched to a halt and behind it stopped a light-blue Mercedes, which was quickly surrounded by people. From the jeep, four bodyguards with machine guns ran to the Mercedes. (They guarded the minister at all times from the danger of being considered unworthy of such security.) They had to jostle and push to open the door of the car.

Waman, in a starched white kurta, emerged with joined palms.

Bikaji shouted, 'The Leader of the Masses,' which was repeated by the crowd.

Then they heard Bikaji scream, 'Motherfucker,' because an intrusive friend was now sharing the burden of the garland.

'I am just helping,' the friend said, offended.

Bikaji pushed him away angrily and advanced to the leader to garland him before others tried to benefit from his roses. Waman held the garland over his shoulder until a bodyguard extricated him.

'I made that banner for you,' Bikaji said, pointing to the illegal billboard on the pavement.

'Nice, good,' Waman said, and asked, 'Where is the boy's father?'

Men began to yell, 'Ayyan, Ayyan.'

Ayyan emerged from the crowd, held the hand of the minister with both his hands, and then touched his chest.

'Let's go,' the minister said.

Ayyan and Waman walked down the broken, cobbled ways of the chawls with at least three hundred people following them. Photographers ran in front to take their pictures, and in-between the shots they jogged backwards. The minister looked around at the rows of grey identical buildings.

'I know that you too lived in a chawl once,' Ayyan said.

'Yes, in Grant Road. A long time ago,' Waman said, with a smile that was proud of its old sorrows.

'We have been trying to sell,' Ayyan said. 'Builders are interested.'

'Of course they will be. This land is worth its weight in gold.'

'I want to sell too,' Ayyan said, 'but a lot of people are resisting. There are eighty thousand people who live here. It's hard to get everybody to agree. Builders want all or nothing.'

'Obviously,' Waman said, shaking his head, 'People are afraid, aren't they? They have lived here all their lives. They are comfortable with the things here.'

'Yes. They want the same neighbours, the same lives.'

'How much are the builders offering, Mani?'

'Twelve lakhs for a 150-square-foot flat,' Ayyan said.

'Drive it up to fifteen,' Waman said confidently. He looked at the vast real estate and appeared to make some calculations in his head.

The entourage went to the terrace of Block Number Forty-One, where a hundred others were already gathered. A table shrouded in a white cloth was at one end of the terrace. Waman made his way through the assembled crowd, smiling and bowing, and naming one hoisted baby who was already named.

When he sat at the table, Bikaji and his men formed a human cordon around the minister. The cordon parted to admit Ayyan, with his son and wife. Oja joined her palms and gushed.

The minister asked, 'And this is the great Adi?'

The boy was more absorbed in the machine guns of the guards.

'Can I hold?' he asked a guard who shook his head.

'Lock it and give it to the boy,' Waman ordered. 'It's very light,' he said with affection to Adi.

The guard did as he was told, and Adi felt the magic of holding an AK-47.

The family sat down next to the minister. The audience was on the floor or on the chairs they had dragged from their homes.

The minister gave a speech in which he narrated how when he was as old as Adi he was tied to a tree by Brahmin priests because he had committed the crime of entering a temple. 'They left me like that the whole night,' he said. 'Next morning, I ran away from my village and came to Bombay with nothing, not even ten rupees in my pocket. Not even a pocket actually.'

Ayyan had heard this story before, and many more that the minister would not recount. How he had once sold vegetables on a wooden cart near the Crawford Market and slowly become a thug, despite his small stout frame. He pelted stones and broke shop windows to protest against matters he did not understand and to mourn the deaths of leaders he did not know. He grew to become a coordinator of freelance goons and, in time, joined politics. His art lay in raising armies of angry Dalit youth at short notice who could turn very violent at times. The Untouchables, in modern times, had won the useless right of being touched by the high caste, but they remained the poorest in the city. Every time they felt slighted, as for instance when miscreants once garlanded the statue of their liberator Ambedkar with slippers, men like Waman used to lead a battalion of angry youth and loot whole lanes.

'They go in rage and return with Adidas,' Ayyan had told Oja on a day when from the kitchen window they had seen looters going home happily with huge cartons.

'Who is Adidas?' Oja had asked.

The entry of such a man into the innocuous game of erecting a boy genius made Ayyan feel afraid. He stared at the profile of this fierce orator whose panegyric of Adi now erupted in spangled silver spit that glowed momentarily against the twilight sky, like minuscule fireflies.

'Such a boy, is a rare boy,' the minister was saying, 'Adi is a rare boy.'

The way the minister said 'Adi' sounded morbid to Ayyan. A man capable of murder now knew the name of his son and there was something disturbing about it. But Ayyan calmed his fear by the other stories he had heard about the minister which made him seem more endearing. When Michael Jackson had visited the city a few years ago, Waman had been part of the group of politicians who met him. The minister had later told the press, 'He is a very polite man. There is not a trace of arrogance in him. You don't get the feeling at all that you are talking to a white man.'

Waman finished his speech by hailing Adi as the future liberator of the Dalits.

'I've been hearing about him for so long,' he said. 'He is so bright that he has now been given the permission to take one of the toughest exams in the world. And he is just eleven. May we have many more like him. Let's together show the world, the power that is locked inside all of us.'

The audience clapped and the minister sat down, wiping his face with his fingers. A guard advanced with a huge cardboard box.

'It's a computer,' Waman declared to the crowd, which applauded again. Some women in the audience looked at each other, raised their eyebrows and curled their lips.

The minister presented the box to Ayyan with the boy standing in-between them as the nominal recipient. Photographers clicked through the din of ovation and Bikaji's hysterical screams: 'The leader of the masses.'

As the minister left the terrace, cutting straight through the unmoving crowd, desperate voices filled the air, asking for jobs, money and welfare. He nodded many times, looking all around but never meeting an eye. 'Go home. Have faith in the government,' he said.

Before he got into his car, he turned to Ayyan and said, 'Come and meet me sometime in my office. We will figure out a way to sell this place.'

Ayyan went back home, accepting a thousand greetings on the way, and the heavy gazes of appreciation and envy which wore the same face here. Adi was alone at home. He was trying to yank the monitor out of its carton. He smiled brightly at his father and said, 'Now I have a computer.'

'Yes, you do, but don't break it. Let's read the book and fix it. Where is your mother?'

'Some women came and took her away.'

Ayyan latched the door and sat on the floor beside his son. 'Adi, now I want you to listen to me carefully.'

The boy was trying to pull the monitor by its plastic hood.

'Adi, sit down and look at me,' Ayyan said sternly.

Adi sat on the floor and looked at his father.

'It was fun, wasn't it?' Ayyan said.

'It was fun,' Adi said.

'Now, it's over. I know I've said this before, but now it's definitely over,' Ayyan said.

'OK,' the boy said.

'You're not going to take the exam. You're not smart enough for that. You and I know that.'

'OK,' Adi said.

'Do you understand?'

'Yes.'

'All this will not happen again, Adi. Now the game is over. You'll be like other boys and it'll be a lot of fun too.'

'I am not like other boys. They call me deaf.'

'If anyone calls you deaf, tell him, "But I can hear you, but I can hear you." Keep saying it till he stops talking. OK?'

That made Adi smile. 'I can hear you, I can hear you, I can hear you,' he said.

'If he still calls you deaf,' Ayyan said, 'tell him, "But I heard your mother fart, but I heard your mother fart".' That made Adi roll on the floor laughing. He went breathless for a second and only the fear of dying made him stop laughing.

There was a knock at the door. When Ayyan opened it he found Oja caught in a moment of self-important haste. She was standing at the doorway, about to enter but hurriedly imparting final instructions to four women who stood meekly in the corridor.

'People can't keep throwing garbage from their windows,' Oja was saying. 'We have to introduce fines to control this. Or, we should collect the garbage and throw it back into the house of the person who has flung it. If we don't take care of our chawl, who will?'

Then she walked into her house and shut the door. Ayyan noticed that she was holding a wedge of lemon. She went straight to Adi and squeezed it on his head. He tried to run but she held him tight and said a quick prayer. And she ran her palms over his cheeks and cracked her knuckles on her ears.

'Evil eyes, all around,' she said.

THE LIGHTS DIMMED and a hush fell over the auditorium. Every seat was taken. There were people sitting on the edges of the aisles. The blood-red curtain went up in somnolent folds and revealed seven empty chairs on the stage. 'There is a seat, grab it,' someone in the aisle said, and the hall erupted in laughter. A banner on the black backdrop of the stage said 'Indian Search For Extraterrestrial Intelligence'. Ayyan was standing at the foot of a short flight of wooden steps that led to the stage. His hands were folded and he surveyed the audience. He had decided to disregard his assignment, which was to ensure that the special dignitaries in the front row – mostly scientists, bureaucrats, one failed actor and other friends of Nambodri – were given a steady supply of whatever they wanted.

A girl who was preoccupied with her own glamour arrived at the podium in a dark-blue sari that fluttered in the gale of the ceiling fan. She looked at the audience with one eye, the other was hidden behind her cascading hair,

'A mysterious character of UFOs is that they are sighted only in the First World,' she said, 'and no alien conquest of Earth begins until the Mayor of New York holds an emergency press conference. When Mars attacks, it attacks America.'

She then asked very seriously, with a faint tilt of her head that partially exposed her other eye, 'Is this because of an intergalactic understanding of the balance of power on our planet?' She smiled modestly when she heard some chuckles. 'Whatever the reasons are, "we are not alone" is a western anthem. But today, we present the first attempt of our country to formally understand what extraterrestrial life is all about.' She invited seven men to the stage.

The first was a very old man whom Ayyan had to help up the stairs. He had a thick mop of furious silver hair, bushy bristles peeped through his nostrils and ears, and his hands were trembling as Ayyan held them. Then came a mountainous white man. There always had to be a white man in such a gathering. 'The whites are the Brahmins of the Brahmins,' Ayyan often told his wife. And every year, they grew taller. Jana Nambodri followed, in a Chinese-collar black shirt and black trousers, and with four of his satellites.

Ayyan stood in his dark corner and listened to these men as they heralded, as they always had for centuries, 'a new dawn'. Nambodri spoke about how the array of radio telescopes called the Giant Ear was finally liberated. He announced, in the midst of a great applause, that the Ear would now scan the skies for signals from advanced civilizations.

The white man came to the podium, and joined his palms together. It was his first visit. 'Namaste,' he said. He welcomed India to 'mankind's search for company'. Later, other radio astronomers spoke about the importance of youth in Seti. After them came the old man. He was introduced by the announcer as a retired scientist from Bangalore. He arrived feebly at the podium and was startled by the squeal of the mike. When he recovered, he began to talk about the greatness of ancient Indians. The crowd applauded every compliment he gave their imagined ancestors. Ayyan laughed. Yes, yes, Indians were the oldest civilization on Earth, the greatest, the best. And only Indians had culture. Others were all dumb nomads and whores.

Ayyan detested this moronic pride more than anything else about the country. Those flared nostrils, those dreamy eyes that people made when they said that they were once a spectacular race. How heaps of gems were sold on the streets, like berries. How ancient Brahmins had calculated the distance between the Earth and the Moon long before the whites; how ayurveda had figured everything about the human body long before Hippocrates;

how Kerala's mathematicians had discovered something close to the heliocentric theory long before Copernicus. In this delusional heritage of the country, his own ancestors were never included. Except as gory black demons in the fables of valiant fair men.

The old man now began to speak about the mysteries of the cow, and the wisdom of Indians in granting the creature an enduring holiness. He attributed his longevity to the consumption of a glass of cow's urine every morning. That brought about a polite silence. But Ayyan saw some aged people in the audience nod wisely.

'Ghee, it has been proved, is good for the heart,' the man said. 'And in Jaipur, scientists have proved that a paste made out of cow dung, when spread on the walls and roofs, blocks nuclear radiation.' He cited the work of an astrophysicist who had investigated the effects of cow slaughter. 'The cries of the cows go down to the core of the Earth through Einsteinian pain waves and cause seismic activity, especially after Muslim festivals when there is a mass slaughter of cattle. That's why, a few days after every Muslim festival, somewhere in the world there is always an earthquake.'

Finally, he came to the point: 'How did the ancient Indians know so much? How did they know about the secrets of the cow, about the human anatomy, and the distances between heavenly bodies? I believe, very early in the life of the Indian civilization, in the vedic age, there was an alien contact.' Mahabharata's great war, with its flying machines and mystical missiles, he said, was fought using extraterrestrial technologies that were later mistaken as the hallucinations of poets. 'Sometime in the great past of our country, there was a technology transfer from an advanced civilization. Our gods are, in reality, artistic representations of extraterrestrial visitors. I really don't care what you think, but I know that Krishna was an alien.'

The audience erupted and gave him a long round of applause. The men on the stage rose, one after the other, yielding to the force of the moment, and clapped somewhat sheepishly. In the din, Ayyan felt a strange affection for Arvind Acharya. He missed him. This was the kind of rubbish Acharya had fought against all his life. The pursuit of truth seemed less ridiculous when he was at the head of the quest. And Ayyan felt the impoverishment of serving a lesser regime.

In the days that followed, the search for extraterrestrial intelligence assumed the character of a revolution whose time had come. Scientists from other institutes landed in the euphoria of finally being granted rights over the Giant Ear. There were seminars and lectures. Journalists, who did not have to wait in the anteroom any more, came to learn about the exotic future of Seti. School teachers, who had to wait, came to ask for excursion trips to the array of giant radio telescopes.

One morning, at the height of the carnival, Ayyan was surprised to see the silent wraith of Acharya enter the anteroom with a twinkle in his small eyes and a grin that appeared to condemn the visitors on the crowded couch. Ayyan got up in his customary half-stand.

'So your son is taking the entrance test, I hear,' Acharya said.

Ayyan nodded without meeting his eyes.

'I am going in,' Acharya said.

'They are having a meeting,' Ayyan told him, 'but I think you should do as you please, Sir.'

The radio astronomers felt a familiar terror, before they remembered that the apparition at the door was merely a wandering memory of a monster they had slain. They were grouped on the white sofas, around the centrepiece which was cluttered with teacups and biscuits. Acharya did not understand the room. The furniture which he had always presumed was immovable had magically shifted, and the walls had framed posters. He threw a look of affection and misgiving at the poster of Carl Sagan, and Sagan returned his gaze.

Ayyan appeared at the doorway in a farcical scramble and said, 'I am sorry, I could not stop him.'

'Nobody can,' Nambodri said, rising graciously and ushering Acharya to a vacant portion of the sofa.

Acharya sank down comfortably and looked carefully at the six faces around him. He said, taking a biscuit from the tray, 'My friends say that the letters they send me come back to them these days.'

'That's because the Earth is round, Arvind,' Nambodri said.

'The Pope said that before you.'

'Yes, I think he did. Arvind, it just struck me, you still have friends?'

Professor Jal let out a deep impulsive laugh which stopped abruptly when he heard his mobile ring. He muttered 'yes' and 'no' into the phone before he disconnected. He looked around the room somewhat puzzled, and said, 'Every time I get a call here, there is a disturbance on the line. It's as if there is always a live phone somewhere nearby.' But the others were too distracted by the presence of Acharya to consider Jal's problem.

'So, Arvind,' Nambodri said, 'What can we do for you?'

'Can we talk alone?'

'That won't be possible,' Nambodri said. 'We were in the middle of a budget meeting. Anyway, we make all decisions together. So if you have something professional to discuss you should tell us all.'

'Six men, one mind?'

That annoyed Nambodri, but he smiled. 'We are a bit busy, Arvind. If you would like to, we can meet later.'

'Six men, one mind. That reminds me of something,' Acharya said, taking another biscuit. 'When America decided to finish off Afghanistan, remember the Taliban council that used to hold desperate press conferences in Kabul? Remember those guys? One chap did not have a nose. Another guy did not have an ear. Their chief was one-eyed. But taken together they had one complete human face.'

'Arvind, do you want to come later?'

'Let's finish it now. I suppose it really does not make any difference if these guys are around,' Acharya said. 'What I want to say is, I feel a bit incomplete these days. There is a sort of hollow inside me.'

'That's because you are dead, Arvind. It's called retirement.'

Acharya munched the biscuit thoughtfully and said, 'You got want you wanted, Jana. I am OK with that. But we need to figure out my immediate future.'

'Your future?'

'You see, I want to continue working here.'

'And do what?'

'I want to plan more balloon missions. And there is something more. There is no deep way of saying it, I suppose. I am sure you know Benjamin Libet.'

'Libet? Yes, yes. Libet.'

'I want to continue his experiments here.'

Nambodri looked at his men. The spectacles on the nose-bridge of Jal began to tremble in his soft chuckle.

'Arvind, you want to continue searching for falling aliens and you want to find out if every single human action is predestined. Is that correct?' Nambodri asked.

'Exactly,' Acharya said, pouring himself coffee from a jug.

'What do you want from me, Arvind?'

'A lab, some funds, some office space. That's it.'

'Really?'

'Yes.'

'Did you know, Arvind, that a man no less than Galileo Galilei once gave a lecture on the size, dimensions and even the location of hell? And more recently, a scientist called Duncan MacDougall revealed the weight of the human soul. He said it was about twenty grams.'

'Why are you telling me all this, Jana?'

'You're getting there, Arvind,' Nambodri said standing up. 'You're getting there, my friend. Nice of you to drop in.'

Acharya rose with his coffee cup and drank it with urgent enthusiastic sips. 'I'll come back later,' he said and marched out.

Ayyan Mani was holding the phone receiver to his ear, listening. The new regime could not terminate his espionage, but it did force him to change his methods. Nambodri was a man who would notice if his phone were off the hook. So, every morning, before Nambodri came to work, Ayyan called his own mobile and hid it in the new Director's desk, and listened from a landline. He half stood as Acharya walked past cheerfully.

On the sea rocks, Acharya stretched his legs. He followed the low flights of the seagulls as they were chased by predatory crows, the laborious journey of a distant cargo ship, the fall of a solitary leaf down the rocks. He sat this way for probably over two hours. Then he heard the voice of Ayyan Mani.

'Would you like some coffee, Sir?'

Acharya nodded, without turning. A few minutes later, a peon walked down the winding pathway to the sea holding a cup of coffee, fruit and three unopened biscuit packets on a tray.

This soon became a common sight. Acharya would be sitting on the rocks, alone or in the company of animated students and scientists, or ambling in the lawns or lying beneath a tree with a book, and a peon would walk towards him with a tray.

On days when Ayyan found Acharya sitting by himself, he would go to him and talk. In the tone of banter between old friends who had gone through life together, Ayyan would ask how scientists knew that the universe must be so big and no more, or how they could say so confidently that a planet that was an unimaginable distance away had water, or how they could claim from a single bone of an ancient beast that it used to fly. 'It's like this,' Acharya would always begin. On occasions, he defended science and insisted that it had no choice but to make very smart guesses from little information. On other occasions he would laugh with Ayyan at the absurdity of scientific claims.

'Sir,' Ayyan asked one late noon when Acharya was sitting beneath a tree and studying the progression of red ants. 'How many dimensions do you think there are?'

'Four,' Acharya said, without taking his eyes off from the ants.

'Up–down, left–right, front–back,' Ayyan said. 'Then?'

'Think of time ticking away as these ants try to go somewhere in a universe that has length, breadth and height. That's another dimension,' he said.

Ayyan tried to imagine it, and reluctantly ceded the point. 'OK, four. But why do they say there are ten dimensions?'

'I don't know, Ayyan. I used to know but I don't any more.'

'Some men have been working on that for twenty years, Sir.'

'You're right.'

'And that's their job? To prove that there are ten dimensions?'

'Yes, that's their job.'

A peon arrived with coffee and said to Ayyan, 'You are here? Director is looking for you.' He stuck his tongue out like a terrified little boy and glanced apologetically at Acharya for using 'Director' in reference to another man.

Acharya simply asked, 'No biscuits today?'

Ayyan knew there was trouble when he saw the face of Nambodri, who was sitting with the grim inner circle on the white sofas.

'Who writes the Thought For The Day?' Nambodri asked.

'What thought, Sir?' Ayyan said.

'The daily quote on the blackboard. Who writes it?'

'Oh, that. I write it sometimes, Sir.'

'Not every day?'

'Most of the days, Sir.'

'Did it you write it today?'

'Yes, Sir.'

'Today's quote was, "A greater crime than the Holocaust was untouchability. Nazis have paid the price, but the Brahmins are still reaping the rewards for torturing others." Is that correct, Ayyan?'

'Yes, Sir.'

'The blackboard says Albert Einstein said this.'

'Yes, Sir, that's what was written on the chit.'

'What chit?'

'I get the Thought For The Day every morning from Administration, Sir.'

'Who in Admin sends it to you?'

'I don't know, Sir. A peon leaves it on my table.'

'What is the name of the peon who leaves it on your table?'

'I don't know his name, Sir.'

Nambodri folded his hands and crossed his legs. 'A week ago,' he said with a smile, 'the Thought For The Day read, "If souls are indeed reborn as the Brahmins say, then what accounts for population growth? Rebirth is the most foolish mathematical concept ever." Apparently Isaac Newton said that.'

'That's what the chit said, Sir.'

'Ayyan, how long have you been writing the Thought For The Day?'

'A few years, Sir.'

'And who asked you to write it?'

'Administration, Sir.'

'Who exactly?'

'I don't remember, Sir.'

'Stop this bullshit,' Professor Jal said rising angrily. Others asked him to calm down. Jal sat down breathing hard, glasses trembling on his nose-bridge.

'You know Professor Jal, of course,' Nambodri said kindly to Ayyan. 'And you know what BBC *Mastermind* is?'

'Yes, Sir, I used to watch *Mastermind*. My wife would fight with me. Because, you know, she wanted to watch . . .'

'Jal once won *Mastermind*. His area of specialization was Einstein. He knows every word that man ever wrote, every word that man ever said. Einstein never said anything about Brahmins. And Newton, my friend, probably did not know what a Brahmin was.'

'That's shocking, Sir.'

'Is it, Ayyan?'

'Yes, Sir. Someone has been giving me fake quotes.'

'You don't like Brahmins very much?'

'Sir, I'm going to find out who has been giving me the fake quotes.'

'Shut up,' Nambodri screamed, which shocked the others.

They had never seen him angry. Ayyan loved the sight. He gave a benevolent smile to Nambodri.

'Stop, stop, stop fooling around,' Nambodri said. 'Stop this, this rubbish. You're talking to men with IQs that you cannot even imagine.'

'My IQ is 148, Sir. What is yours?'

A silence filled the room. Nambodri looked intently at the floor. A foolish pigeon banged into the window glass and banged one more time before changing direction. A phone rang somewhere far away.

'I got into Mensa when I was eighteen,' Ayyan said.

'Was there a 15 per cent reservation for Dalits?' Nambodri asked. The astronomers burst out laughing. Nambodri walked a few steps and stood a foot away from Ayyan. 'I don't want you ever to touch that blackboard again, do you understand?' he said.

'Yes, Sir.'

'And I hear you have been asking the peons to get coffee for your master.'

'And fruit and meals too, Sir.'

'I see, I see. You're good at that kind of thing, aren't you? We all should stick to our strengths, Ayyan. What do you say? We will figure out the universe. And you will bring coffee. Let's stick to that for the good of everyone. What are you waiting for? Go and get us some coffee, Ayyan. Right now.'

Ayyan went to his desk and took out the silver dictaphone from the top drawer of the table. He turned on the speaker mode of one of the landlines.

'IQ of 148,' the voice of Nambodri was saying. 'If Dalits can have that sort of an IQ, would they be begging for reservations?'

'Did you see the way he was talking?' Jal said. 'I can't believe this. That's what happens when you put someone who is meant to clean toilets in a white-collar job.'

'He was in Mensa,' Nambodri said, and there was a crackle of laughter. 'Just because his son is some kind of a freak, he thinks even he is.'

'Something fishy about his son,' someone said. 'I have never come across a Dalit genius. It's odd, you know.'

The astronomers continued in this vein. They spoke of the racial character of intelligence and the unmistakable cerebral limitations of the Dalits, Africans, Eastern Europeans and women.

'If there are clear morphological characteristics that are defined by the genes, obviously even intellectual traits are decided that way,' Nambodri said. 'Look at women. They will get nowhere in science. Everybody knows that. Their brains are too small. But our world has become so fucking politically correct, you can't say these things any more.'

They spoke about the debilitating influence of reservation in education and the dangerous political resurgence of the Dalits. There was a pause in the conversation and Ayyan was about to turn off the speaker mode. He thought the men were about to walk out. Then Nambodri made a comment about Ambedkar which stunned even Ayyan. What Nambodri had said about the liberator of Dalits was so damning that the silver dictaphone in Ayyan's hand was a weapon that could consign to flames not just the Institute but also the whole country.

Ayyan went down the corridor trying to calm the tumult within. Midway down the corridor, he veered left towards the small pantry. A peon was washing the cutlery in the sink. Two others were making coffee. Ayyan played the recorder and put it on the kitchen platform. The peons did not understand the voices at first, but soon their faces began to change. They stopped what they were doing and listened. As the voices spoke, Ayyan translated some difficult portions into Marathi.

'Genes are things that parents pass on to their children,' Ayyan told them. 'You are black because your parents were black. They are saying that you are dumb because your parents were dumb. And the Brahmins are smart because their parents were smart. And they are saying about me that I am only fit to be a toilet-cleaner because I am a Dalit.'

When the recording ended, he put the dictaphone in his

pocket and said, 'They want coffee. They said they want coffee right now.'

One of the peons filled a jug. He stared at the other peon and at Ayyan in the fellowship of the moment. He opened the lid of the jug and spat into it.

Later in the evening, as Acharya was dozing somewhere near the lawn, Ayyan knelt beside him and said, 'Sir, do you want some office space?'

Acharya opened his eyes and looked confused.

'Do you want an office, Sir?' Ayyan asked again.

Acharya followed him. They went down to the basement. The stark white walls and the hum of subterranean machines brought back to Acharya the memories of nocturnal love. Somehow it was always night here. It felt like night. He saw in his mind the face of Oparna, and the way she used to look at him. He remembered the way she used to sit, her melancholic smoking, and her insolence that seemed then to be the right of every naked woman. He felt a nervous anticipation in his stomach as if she would appear at the end of the walk, waiting for him on the cold floor in the fragrance of lemon.

The board that said 'Astrobiology' was still there, but the lab door was locked. Ayyan took out a key from his pocket.

'How do you have the key?' Acharya asked in a whisper because he was still in the fragile delusion that Oparna was inside and that this dark man was an accomplice of love.

'Keys are easy to find, Sir,' Ayyan said. He opened the door and switched on the lights.

'You're going to get into trouble for this,' Acharya said.

'Yes,' Ayyan said.

'Why are you doing this, Ayyan? Jana is a very mean man. He is the practical sort.'

'So am I,' Ayyan said.

Acharya looked around the lab for the memories of a girl. But there was no life here. The air had no smell. The equipment on the main desk was shrouded in its covering. The chairs were in a perpetual wait. The phone was still there, on the same wooden stool. Everything was as he remembered. Like the abandoned rooms of the dead.

Ayyan turned on the computer and inspected the air-conditioning vents. 'There is internet,' he said. He held the phone receiver to his ear. 'This is still working. I'll give you a number you can call if you need anything.' And he left.

Acharya sank to the floor holding a knee. He leaned his back on the wall and stretched his legs. In the desolation of the lab, he saw the face of Oparna and heard her say this and that. And he remembered a love so light, like the sack of that eloping girl from another time whom he had seen as a boy from the footbridge over the railway tracks. He wondered how the life of that girl had turned out. Maybe she lived happily with her man and recounted her elopement to her grandchildren with delirious exaggerations. He would confirm all her lies, if she so wished.

IT WAS TRUE that Administration had the mystery of God in the Institute, but very few realized that on the second floor there was, in fact, a board that said 'Administration'. The mystical department was a maze of wooden partitions where laypeople looked soberly at their computer screens, silently sustaining the pursuit of truth in the higher floors. At one end of the room, the maze became more intricate and the cubicles became smaller and numerous. This was the Accounts Department which Ayyan Mani always remembered for the striking ugliness of its women, and the old bonds of friendship he shared with its mostly Malayalee men.

He saw Unny at the end of a narrow way that ran between the cubicles. He was kicking the base of an enormous printer.

'The great man comes to the abode of the poor,' Unny said, throwing a glance at Ayyan. He kicked the printer one more time. 'One day, someone will make a printer that works,' he said. 'A lot of paper is jammed inside.'

Ayyan kicked the printer a few times.

'Forget it,' Unny said. 'How is the boy genius?'

'He is all right. Now he wants to know if underwear is important in life,' Ayyan said.

'That's strange, even my son asked me that. Come, let's go to my desk.'

'I'm in a hurry,' Ayyan said. 'Your Malayalee chief wants something urgently.'

'Who? Nambodri? What does he want?'

'He said he wants some copies from the payment files of Aryabhata Tutorials. Do you know what that means?'

Unny nodded and went to an open steel shelf that was stuffed with files. As he was searching, he asked, 'Adi is studying hard for the test?'

Ayyan did not show his impatience, but he wanted to finish the job quickly, and as discreetly as possible.

Unny screamed to someone across the room, 'Where is the Aryabhata file?' That made Ayyan nervous. He looked around the room for any suspicious faces. 'It's in the petty cash shelf,' a woman's voice said.

Unny went to the adjacent shelf, muttering how disorganized the place was.

'Tell me, Ayyan,' he said, standing on a stool and tapping the spines of files with his index finger. 'How did Adi become so bright? Do you feed him something we don't know about?'

'He was born a bit strange,' Ayyan said.

'There it is,' Unny yelped, and pulled out a thin file. He went through it with a confused expression and handed it to his friend. 'I've always wondered what exactly is this Aryabhata Tutorials,' Unny said.

'Only God knows what it is,' Ayyan said, trying to look as if he had no interest in the file, but his hands were trembling.

'It is a separate company owned by the Institute,' Unny said. 'Why would the Institute own a tutorial? And where is this place? What does this tutorial do? I don't understand. I've not seen a single board in the city that says Aryabhata Tutorials. I don't know a single student who goes there. It's very strange, you know.'

Ayyan leafed through the file. His heart was pounding, but he tried to look relaxed, even bored. He photocopied three bills and gave the file back.

Unny went through the file again and shook his head. 'These last twenty years, Aryabhata Tutorials has made payments only to printers. Nothing else. It only makes payments and it pays only printers. It does not earn.'

'God knows what these guys do,' Ayyan said. 'I never understood them anyway. I will see you in the canteen soon?'

Ayyan went to his desk and collected the late courier mail and the faxes, opened the inner door and walked in. As usual, the astronomers were sitting on the sofas by the window. Some of them stared unpleasantly at him. Eyes followed him as he went to Nambodri's vacant table in the far corner. Normally, they did not register his presence but that had changed after their last encounter. He pretended to sort the courier mail and the faxes on Nambodri's desk. His left hand slowly reached for the small gap between the table top and drawer compartment where he usually left his mobile phone. He put the phone in his pocket and walked out.

He went down the corridor of the third floor and as he walked he took out the copies of the three bills he had made in the Accounts Department. He dialled the number on the first bill. A woman's voice came on the line. Ayyan said, 'I am calling from Aryabhata Tutorials. I want to know when we can expect the consignment?'

The woman's voice asked, 'You said you are from Aryabhata Tutorials?'

'Yes.'

'Hold on,' she said.

A man's voice came on the line. 'Who is speaking?'

'Murthy,' Ayyan said.

'Which job are you talking about?'

'There was only one.'

'But the sample papers were sent a month ago,' the man's voice said with concern.

Ayyan disconnected the line and called the second number, and then the third. The other two printers too said that the consignments had been dispatched a month ago. Ayyan had feared this. He was too late.

The question-paper of the Institute's Joint Entrance Test was a jewel and it was guarded not through the frailties of a written code, nor the dangerous inconsistencies of loyalty, but by the force of tradition. Its annual creation was a highly secretive process known to very few. Ayyan was not supposed to be among those few. He had learnt its rudiments over the years, listening carefully to the walls and piecing together bits of information.

Every year, five professors and the Director met discreetly over three weeks to create the questions of the entrance exam. They never used the computer. They always wrote down the questions by hand in a single notebook. They made three question-papers and gave them to three different printers. Every year, one of the professors in the JET panel went personally to the printers, posing as a representative of Aryabhata Tutorials. So, even the printers did not know what they were printing. They probably thought that they were printing the study material of one of the thousands of tutorials in the city. Sometime before the entrance exam, the Director would choose one of the three printed versions of the question-paper.

Ayyan had just learnt from the printers that the question-papers had been delivered. They were somewhere in the Institute, he was certain. The entrance exam was eight weeks away and he believed he had enough time to find out where the papers were stored. Three versions of a question-paper meant for ten thousand candidates, he calculated, would require at least three big cartons. Such a delivery could not have gone unnoticed. He began to wander around the various floors and identify rooms that were mysteriously locked. He found three. They were not sealed. Just locked. And keys were never a problem. But a search in those rooms yielded nothing. He enquired of the guards if they had seen anything, and asked his army of peons if they had ever been sent to a press to collect a consignment, or if they had seen the improbable sight of huge cartons being brought in personally by a professor. But they could not help him.

For two weeks, Ayyan spent the nights searching almost every room in the Institute for the question-papers. The Accounts Department, he learnt, had a safety vault but it was not big enough for even a single carton. It confused him that a massive consignment of three huge cartons could be so invisible. As the days went by, he realized that only one man could help him.

IN THE RELENTLESS night of the basement, Arvind Acharya became infatuated with his own shadow. He wandered through the space feeling the entertainment of being a one-dimensional ghost. He arranged the table lamps on the main desk in different ways to see himself on the walls and on the floor in disproportionate sizes. Most of the time he could not take his eyes off his shadow because he was enchanted by the thought that these illusionary images had the same memories and the same theories as he did. And the same wife. The shadows even asked him deeply why they should not be granted the status of real creatures since reality anyway was merely the perception of the eye. So he granted them that. He multiplied himself through his shadows and sat among them in the peace of knowing that there were at least some men who were exactly like him, who understood him and who even loved him.

He was preoccupied by the joy of a liberation he could not name but he was also tormented by a pubescent love. It was a love that was far more terrifying than what he had felt for Oparna. Because it was dedicated to his wife who had abandoned him five days ago.

Lavanya had told him that she could survive him so far because he had always tried his best not to appear mad, even though he was. But now, she could not bear his unreasonable joy at nothing at all, and the way he spoke to objects as though they had asked a question. She said his perpetual happiness made her feel that she was not required. He had asked her if the truth was that she was just embarrassed by him. She had held his hand and said,

'Why would a woman be embarrassed by you? You are too beautiful, Arvind. It's just that I can't handle what you've become. It hurts me even though I know you are very happy.' Then she gave clear instructions to the maids, packed her things in a suitcase, and left for Chennai to be with her interminable family.

So Acharya began to spend all his time in the basement. And he metamorphosed from a sudden cult on the pathways into a subterranean legend. It was not just the scholars of the Institute who began to seek him out but also scientists and students from other such places. They sat on the floor, or on the tables and chairs, and they talked about the philosophical future of physics, the ceaseless descent of eternal aliens, Stephen Hawking's claim that the question *why* there was life in the universe would soon be answered, and about a lot of other things.

One evening in this basement world that was filled with over forty scientists and students, a strange figure walked in nervously.

'I'm from the security department,' the man told Acharya, casting glances at the others. 'This is to inform you that a decision has been taken regarding your illegal stay in the Institute. You've been asked to vacate the premises immediately and stop using the basement as your office.'

'But I like it here,' Acharya said.

'These are the orders from the management, Sir.'

A man in the audience who was a senior scientist from the Institute asked the informer to be reasonable.

The informer said helplessly, 'I do not own the Institute, Sir. I am only informing him about a decision taken at the highest level.'

The congregation became silent and gloomy, and it slowly dissolved. Some reassured Acharya that they would think of a way to help him; others shook hands with him sombrely. When the last of the visitors, a scrawny boy with a shoulder bag strung on his back, was about to leave, Acharya commanded: 'Boy, get me some clothes and a lot of chocolates. And a lot of bananas.'

★

For twelve days after that evening, Acharya did not stir from the basement. He feared that if he left the lab even for a walk on the lawns, someone would lock the door and he would be thrown out of the Institute. Visitors now began to arrive in greater numbers than before, bearing food and clothes. And soap. It became a spontaneous basement rebellion. Nambodri was flooded with polite calls to reconsider his decision. But he did not relent. In his calculation, the ill-feeling against him would be forgotten once Acharya vanished not only from the Institute but also, after his dismissal was formalized, from the Professors' Quarters.

Acharya, for his part, did not budge. Security guards, ordered to throw him out, arrived and stood by his side, not having the courage to touch him. He would offer them bananas or ask them to get him some more. Then something changed. Late at night and early in the morning, the guards became accomplices, because that was the wish of Ayyan Mani. And Acharya went for quick walks on the campus.

One night, when he returned from his walk, he saw a figure sitting on a chair near the main desk. His first reaction was that one of his own shadows had been liberated from the walls. But he soon realized it was Ayyan. 'Did I scare you, Sir?' he asked.

'No, Ayyan. You did not scare me. I hear you are the one who is taking care of me. Is that true?'

'That's my duty, Sir.'

'What are you doing here so late?'

'I came to talk to you.'

'Come here, let's sit on the floor and chat,' Acharya said.

They leaned on the wall and stretched their legs. They could see each other in the dim light of a solitary bulb. Acharya never switched on all the lights because he did not want to abolish his shadow.

'I hear your wife has left you, Sir,' Ayyan said.

'Yes. She went away. Everybody told her that I'd gone mad. She didn't want others to know, you see.'

'She will come back,' Ayyan said. 'Wives of an age are like evicted hawkers. They return in time.'

'I don't think so.'

'I am very sure, Sir,' Ayyan said. 'You must go and get her. But you must now start pretending to be normal, as you used to before. A man cannot be exactly the way he wants to be and also dream of keeping his wife. You must control yourself a bit, Sir. And start thinking about your future.'

'But I don't have a future, it seems.'

'You do, Sir. I have come with it,' Ayyan said, and he asked casually, 'Will you tell me where the JET question-papers are stored?'

'Why do you want to know?'

'Because I know the rest. I know about Aryabhata Tutorials and the names of the three printers.'

'That's impossible. You know the printers?'

'Magna, Lana and Scape.'

Acharya peeled a banana thoughtfully. 'You want to steal the JET?'

'Yes, Sir' Ayyan said.

'Because your son is no genius?'

'He is, but the JET is too tough for him.'

'So let him fail,' Acharya said, eating the banana with swift bites.

'That is not a good idea, Sir.'

'But obviously, Ayyan, I can't help you.'

Ayyan took out the dictaphone and played the conversation between Acharya and Oparna when she had come to tell him why she had contaminated the sampler.

'Why, Oparna?' the sad voice of Acharya asked.

'What did you expect, Arvind?' the voice of Oparna replied. 'You sleep with me till your wife comes back from her vacation and then ask me to get out of your life.'

The conversation moved on with long excruciating pauses which Acharya recognized as the painful language of final separation. He then heard the voice of Oparna clearly explaining how, very early one morning, in a fit of love and vengeance, she had contaminated the sampler.

Acharya did not realize that he had been holding a half-eaten banana near his mouth for over five minutes. When Ayyan put the dictaphone back into his trouser-pocket, Acharya asked softly, 'How did you get this?'

'I used to listen,' he said.

Acharya started laughing. 'I always knew you were some kind of a bastard,' he said. 'Why didn't you show this to the inquiry committee?'

'We did not have a deal then.'

'And we do, now?'

'Let's talk about your future, Sir,' Ayyan said. 'Wouldn't it be nice if you got your old job back? Don't you want to send balloons up and carry out all the other experiments? I know how we can do that.'

'How?'

'You leave that to me. I know what I must do. But you have to help me. I want the question-paper. Are you going to help me?'

Acharya ate the rest of the banana without uttering a word. Then he said, 'There are three versions of the question-paper.'

'I know. Where are they?'

'And this time, the questions are really nasty,' Acharya said, chuckling.

'Where are the question-papers?'

'We had just sent the questions to the printers when all the shit began to happen. All the three question-papers, they are classics. Jana may have already decided which of the three will finally go to the test centres.'

'Where are the question-papers?'

'You can't get them, Ayyan.'

'I can. Just tell me where they are.'

'They are not here,' Acharya said, with a triumphant chuckle. 'They are never stored at the Institute. They are in a sealed and secured room in BARC. You can't get there.'

The Bhabha Atomic Research Centre was a fortress that was beyond the methods of a clerk. And Ayyan knew that.

'What do we do now?' he asked.

'Why do you need to see a question-paper,' Acharya said, pointing a finger at his head, 'when it's all here?'

'You remember all the questions?'

'Most of them.'

Ayyan sprang to his feet and rummaged through the drawers of the main desk. He grabbed a bunch of blank sheets of paper and a pen, and put them in front of Acharya. 'Write then,' he said.

'Tell me, Ayyan. Is your son a genius?'

'He is, Sir.'

'Really?' Acharya said, looking amused. 'Did he ever win that science contest? Can he really recite the first thousand primes? Is he really what people think he is?'

'That's not important to your future,' Ayyan said. And that made Acharya laugh.

Acharya sat by the main desk and wrote down over two hundred questions from the three versions of the question-paper, occasionally exclaiming at the sheer brilliance of some of the questions. When he finished, he gave the sheets to Ayyan.

'Write down the answers too, Sir,' he said.

Acharya laughed. 'I'll do that,' he said, 'But there is something very important you must know. Forty correct answers out of hundred questions is a very, very good score. So your boy must attempt not more than forty. Anything more than that would be suspicious.'

On the day of the exam, Oja oiled her son and scrubbed him with a fistful of coconut husk. He wore the new clothes that she had bought a week ago. 'Full pants', as she called them, and a long-sleeved shirt. She gave the hall ticket to Ayyan, and in the same manner gave the boy's hand to him. At the door, she hugged and kissed her son, and began to cry. Adi looked at his father with an exasperated expression. But when she bid a final goodbye and shut the door, the boy felt a pang of gloom. He could hear her crying inside and he did not like it when she cried like that, alone and for no good reason.

'Can she come with us?' he asked his father.

'She has a lot of work,' Ayyan said.

As they set off down the dim corridor, people standing in their doorways looked. Some smiled; some conveyed their best wishes. When he was halfway down the corridor Ayyan realized that a small group of men, women and children was following them. And this swarm grew as they went down the steps and into the broken stone ways of the chawls. By the time they reached the road, there were at least a hundred neighbours shadowing them in silence. From the windows of buses and cars, people stared curiously, trying to understand the sight.

Someone stopped a passing taxi.

'Shouldn't we save money?' Adi asked his father.

'Not today,' Ayyan said.

PART SEVEN

The Riot

THEY STOOD CLOSE together, looking blank, as if they had become a photograph. Ayyan Mani was in the best shirt he had ever worn. His feet were bare because he wanted to appear indifferent. Oja was in the sari she had worn for the quiz. She was once again forced by her husband to sacrifice lustre for the unreasonable requirements of elegance. Adi was in-between them, unhappy that he had to wear long trousers again. They were standing near the kitchen platform and staring at the door. There was a faint murmur in the air, which slowly grew. A crowd was approaching. Oja surveyed her home nervously. She spotted a strand of a cobweb under the wooden attic.

'Is there time to clean?' she asked.

'Are you mad?' Ayyan said.

'At least the milk is boiled,' she said, easing the creases of her sari. Ayyan tried to understand what she had said.

'Why did you boil the milk?' he asked.

'I don't know,' she said. 'When I don't know what to do, I boil the milk.'

Outside, on the corridor, a girl in a fitted shirt and jeans walked with an enormous man who was carrying a camera on his shoulder. Behind them was a mob. The corridor was so packed that the men and children at the edges were squeezed against the pale walls, and some fell festively into the open homes.

The girl was escorted by about a dozen men to the only shut door on the corridor. They knocked. It opened partially and the face of Ayyan tried to evaluate the situation. But the force on the door was too much for him and he yielded. The reporter and the cameraman were taken into the house by a tide of happy neighbours.

'Not everybody,' the girl screamed. 'Who is Ayyan Mani?' she asked.

Ayyan began to push the people out. 'This is crazy. Let them do their jobs,' he said.

'You've already forgotten us, Mani,' a tiny man said angrily, as he was being shoved outside. 'You have become a big man, have you?'

'You come inside then, I will go out. OK?' Ayyan told him, with a playful slap.

It took five minutes to evict all the neighbours and shut the door. In the sudden calm, the girl turned to Oja and smiled. The cameraman looked around and decided to squeeze himself between the cupboard and the fridge. He wore a headphone and turned on a light that blinded everyone for an instant.

'Are you ready?' the reporter asked the family.

They nodded.

'Answer only in Hindi. Don't use too many English or Marathi words,' she said.

She turned to the camera. Her face transformed. She looked alert, smart and excited. She told the camera, 'We are inside the humble one-room home of Aditya Mani, the wonder-boy who has cleared one of the toughest exams in the world. The eleven-year-old is only an interview away from joining the postgraduate course at the Institute of Theory and Research.'

'Stop,' the cameraman said. 'Too much noise outside.' He opened the door and screamed, 'Keep quiet.'

The crowd fell silent for an instant. Then the murmurs grew about how a stranger whom they had helped find the way was now asking them to shut up. But they calmed down eventually.

The girl repeated what she had just said. She knelt down beside Adi.

'How do you feel?' she asked.

'I feel hungry,' he said.

She smiled kindly at him and asked, 'How did you manage to do this, Aditya? At such a young age. How did you do it?'

'I knew all the answers,' he said, and smiled at his father.

'Of course you did,' she said.

'What are your future plans?'

'I don't know.'

After a few more questions to Adi, the girl turned to Ayyan. 'Sir, it must be a very special day for you.'

'It obviously is,' he said. 'I cannot believe this.'

'What are your plans for him?'

'It's too early to say.'

'When did you know that he was a genius?'

'He was always a bit different. He thinks differently.'

'Will he be wearing shorts or trousers to college?' she asked.

'That has not been decided,' he said, without a smile. 'Actually, he has not got in yet. There is an interview process.'

The girl turned to Oja Mani and said, 'You must be a very proud mother.'

Oja laughed coyly and looked at her husband. After a brief silence, she moved closer to the mike and said, 'I want my son to be a normal child.' She fell silent again. Then she asked, 'Do you want some tea?' That made the cameraman wince.

The girl tried to extract more information from the family, and when she was satisfied she signalled to the cameraman that the session was over. Ayyan told her that he was going to hold a press conference in Minister Waman's office on Tuesday. 'I am making an important announcement,' he said. 'You will not want to miss it.' That made her curious, but he did not divulge anything more.

The girl walked out, followed by the cameraman who had resumed shooting. The crowd, which had grown further, greeted her with a roar, and a few whistles. She was quickly engulfed by giggling men. She shoved her mike at one of them, who turned serious. She asked, 'What do you have to say about the boy's achievement?'

'He has made us all proud,' the man said, swaying in the tugs and pushes of the crowd.

The girl suddenly yelped and jumped. Someone had pinched her.

AYYAN MANI SAT behind a table crowded with mikes. Waman was by his side. The conference room of the minister's office was packed with journalists. Photographers were kneeling in the front, near the table. Cameramen at the back were screaming at some reporters who were standing. 'Sit, sit,' they were saying. A disconsolate girl was telling a man who did not stop nodding, 'You should have separate press conferences for the press and for the TV. These cameramen are animals. They are not journalists.'

Ayyan searched for a hint of fear inside him, but he felt nothing. What he had done, he himself could not believe. Adi was in every paper and on every channel. So too was Sister Chastity. And she was tirelessly recounting the boy's extraordinary state of mind. Parents who had witnessed the quiz recalled the episode on news channels with happy inaccuracies. The whole country, it seemed, was in the trance of the Dalit genius, the son of a clerk, the grandson of a sweeper. 'At the end of the oppressive centuries, at the end of the tunnel of time,' Ayyan was quoted by newspapers, 'my son has finally arrived at the edge of an opportunity.'

Waman clapped his hands and asked for attention. The room fell silent. Without a word, Waman handed a mike to the father of the genius.

'I will certainly make a speech,' Waman told the gathering, 'but you will understand what I have to say only after you hear this man.'

Ayyan inhaled. The image of Oja sitting with a baffled face in front of the television crossed his mind.

'Adi is not here because I thought his presence was not required,' he said in Hindi. 'My boy applied to the postgraduate course in maths in the Institute of Theory and Research. He wrote the Joint Entrance Test and he passed it. Only the interview is left. I am here to tell you that he will not be appearing for the interview. He will not be joining the Institute.'

A faint murmur arose, but it died fast.

'There are reasons,' Ayyan said. 'One is that he might be very bright, but I think he has to finish school first like other boys. I think it was a mistake to let him sit the entrance exam. The other reason is . . .' Ayyan looked at the minister, who patted him on his back.

'I've worked as a clerk in the Institute for fifteen years,' he said. 'I started as an office boy and made my way up. I worked for a man, a great man called Arvind Acharya, who has now been shamed, as you all know. His life has been destroyed. He has almost gone mad. What actually went on there, most of you do not know. But I know. I have with me a CD of a recording I made which will explain exactly what happened. I was just a clerk and so nobody would have taken me seriously until this day. That's why I have never revealed this before. I have another recording which is more shocking. Once you listen to that you will understand why I don't want my son to be part of such an institute. It's a scary place.'

The radio astronomers were in a sombre huddle around the low centrepiece. They were staring at the flat-screen TV on the wall near Nambodri's desk. Someone was flicking through the news channels. They were no longer airing the poignant conversation between Oparna and Acharya. All the news channels were now playing the voices of the men in that room – their plebeian views about the intellectual limitations of Dalits, and of women, which made female reporters and presenters, of whom there were suddenly many, pass snide remarks about the kind of men who were running Indian science. Nambodri had grown silent during the last hour. The phones on his table were ringing incessantly. He had long switched off his mobile.

These men were in the misery of two distinct fears. The Oparna tape would exonerate Acharya. His return was probably imminent. Nobody was in doubt that it was her voice, though Nambodri had said earlier, before he had lost the power of speech, that they could attack the credibility of the recording. The other fear was the fear of death. Whole cities had burned when Dalits felt slighted. In a matter of hours, the Institute would be under siege. Police vans were standing sentinel at the gates, but that only made the astronomers more nervous. The first wave of protest had already arrived. The peons had gone on strike. They had stopped working and were now gathered near the main lawn. Before that they had left all the taps on and had clogged up the toilets with broken cutlery.

As the regime sat in uneasy calm, Jal steamed in holding loose sheets of paper, an envelope and a newspaper. His excitement seemed unreasonable.

'Where have you been?' someone asked him. 'You know what has happened, right?'

'I know a lot more than that,' Jal said, stopping for an instant when he heard his voice on the television describing Dalits as genetically handicapped. He put the things he was holding on the centrepiece and rubbed his hands. 'You will not believe this,' he said. 'You will not believe this.'

'What has happened?' Nambodri asked. There was a faint ray of hope on his face.

'Cheer up, my friend, we are going to war. These last few days, I've been checking up on that guy and his son. And what I've found is very, very strange. Here is Adi's answer-sheet. It's unbelievable. He got thirty-nine.'

The answer-sheet passed from hand to hand. Jal's enthusiasm now infected everyone in the room.

'This means he is in the top five. A boy of eleven in the top five. Now, let me try to be coherent,' Jal said. His glasses quivered on his nose-bridge. 'Let me begin at the beginning. Do you remember the day when Ayyan showed us a clipping of his son winning a science contest hosted by the Swiss Consulate? I checked with the Consulate. They have never held such a contest. Never. I managed to call the reporter. His name is Manohar Thambe. He said that the news was given to him by Ayyan. Apparently, some language newspapers officially take money to cover news.'

Nambodri began to pace the floor.

'Are you listening, Jana?' Jal asked.

'Go on,' Nambodri said, beginning to understand.

'Then I noticed something strange,' Jal said. He looked at the television screen. A commercial was underway. So he took the remote and started flipping through the channels until he arrived at one which showed the face of Adi.

'Look, look. Look carefully. He is wearing the hearing-aid in his left ear.' Jal then showed the picture of the boy in *The Times*. 'This picture went with the article about how he could recite the first thousand primes. His hearing-aid is in the right ear. The article clearly mentions that the boy is deaf in his *right* ear. But in every other image I have seen of the boy, he is wearing the hearing-aid in his *left* ear.'

'What does that mean?' Nambodri asked.

'Think, Jana, think. How can a boy of eleven recite the first thousand primes?'

'I don't believe this,' Nambodri said, sitting down slowly.

'But what about the quiz?' someone asked. 'Hundreds of people saw the boy.'

'Maybe his father had whacked the questions. Like he probably did with JET?'

'He stole the JET, didn't he?' Nambodri said softly.

'But that's impossible,' one of the astronomers said. A supportive murmur followed.

'Listen to me. Listen to me,' Jal said impatiently. 'I called up our printers and asked them if there had been any enquiries from Aryabhata Tutorials recently. Two of them said that they didn't know, but one of them distinctly remembered someone calling less than eight weeks ago asking when the consignment was expected to be delivered. I don't know how he got the JET, but I tell you, he did. An eleven-year old boy cannot score thirty-nine. Come on, we have seen geniuses; we know them. We know what is possible. Put it all together, Jana. Ayyan Mani is a con. His genius son is a fraud.'

Jal then appeared thoughtful. He chuckled.

'What is it?' Nambodri asked.

'But that bastard did get into Mensa.'

The door opened. The astronomers looked with the eyes of the dead as Ayyan Mani entered with some faxes. He went to Nambodri's desk and laid them out neatly. As he walked back to the door he told Nambodri, 'I am sorry I'm late, Sir. I had to attend a press conference.'

'That we know,' Nambodri said.

'I wish I could get you coffee, Sir, but I think the peons are missing.'

'We know that too.'

Ayyan was about to leave the room when Nambodri asked, 'Is your son deaf in the right ear or the left?'

The astronomers held their breath. They waited to see fear on the face of Ayyan. But he smiled.

'Both the ears, Sir,' he said. 'But Adi likes wearing only one hearing-aid at a time.'

Nambodri put his hands on his hips and studied the floor. 'I see,' he said. 'Ayyan, how did you steal the JET?'

'I don't know what you are talking about, Sir.'

'We know that he did not win any science contest. We know that your son cannot recite the first thousand primes and we know that he is no genius. If you cooperate, we will ensure that you don't go to prison.'

'I forgot to tell you, Sir,' Ayyan said, looking towards the window. 'It is not safe for you to be here. Anything can happen. I suggest you go home.'

'We will manage, Ayyan.'

'Do you know what is happening at the gates, Sir? I think you should look.'

Nambodri first raised his eyebrows in defiance but the defiance slowly, inexorably, became curiosity. He went to the window and looked. A mob was standing outside the gates with metal rods, sticks and banners. They were standing calmly, as if waiting for a decisive sign.

Nambodri walked back to the sofa and said, 'We will manage this, Ayyan. Why don't you think of yourself?'

'I've always thought of myself, Sir.'

'Let's make a deal, Ayyan. You confess that you have cooked up these recordings and we will not press charges against you.'

'What charges, Sir?'

'Listen, Ayyan. If the boy is interrogated for one minute by any science graduate, it will become clear that he is no genius. I can publicly challenge him to recite the first thousand primes. The Swiss Consulate is going to make a statement this evening saying that it did not hold any contest. Your reporter Thambe has agreed to give it in writing that he was paid for the article about your son. The game is over, Ayyan. But we can help you, if you are willing to make a little confession.'

Ayyan left the room. The radio astronomers looked at each other. They were tense, but they could now see the first signs of hope. The way Ayyan had fled the room was consoling. Then he returned.

'The minister wants to talk to you,' he told Nambodri, handing the phone to him.

Nambodri held the instrument to his ear and said, 'It's a pleasure talking to you.' He listened. Finally, he said, 'I am sorry, this is not agreeable to me, Minister.' He gave the phone back to Ayyan and said, 'Ayyan, you have another five minutes to decide.' Ayyan laughed and left the room, shaking his head in private mirth. That unsettled the astronomers.

'He seems to know something we don't,' Jal said. 'What did the minister say, Jana?'

Nambodri rubbed his nose and said, 'He told me that if we don't go public with what we have found out about Adi, he will promise us safety.'

'Safety?' Jal said nervously. 'What did he mean by safety?'

'Relax,' Nambodri said. 'I know how to play this game.'

He took out his phone and was about to dial a number when they heard a sound. The glass of the huge square window had cracked. The astronomers fell on the floor and lay on their stomachs. There was another sound and this time the window crashed. They could hear the roar of the mob down below. Five more stones landed in the room. They could hear other windows break and the sound of things being beaten to pulp, and the shrieks of women. They lay on the floor without moving. Then they heard the riot come closer. Things were exploding, men were screaming. The astronomers crawled closer to each other and stared at the door as the sound of death grew louder and louder.

The door finally burst open and about two dozen men rushed in with iron rods. They began to break everything in the room. Then they began to beat up the astronomers with the rods. The scientists screamed in mortal fear as they had never screamed before.

'Not on the head,' one of the goons screamed. He observed the assault keenly, academically and looked somewhat disappointed. 'Stop,' he screamed. The thugs stopped. There was the sound of men groaning and weeping. The leader of the raiders then placed his rod below the knee of Nambodri and told his men, 'This is how you must do it.'

It took three hours for order to be restored in the Institute. Police carried away happy rioters who waved to the cameras. One car burned in the driveway. The windscreens of the other cars were broken. Windows dangled from the main block. Stunned inmates walked out in a silent file escorted by the police.

Across the city there were protests, but they were less violent. Later in the evening, outside the Bombay Hospital, mobs paraded an effigy that was named after Nambodri. They beat it with slippers and finally burnt it. There were reports of stray violence in other parts of the country but after two days the riots receded.

LAVANYA ACHARYA SURVEYED the room with the autocracy of a wife. The last two weeks she had supervised the resurrection of her husband's office. The textured walls seemed too empty, but he refused to allow any adornments except the framed poster of Carl Sagan.

'They broke everything but this?' she asked, looking at Sagan's charming face. 'Arvind, can't you let me put up at least one painting? After all, you begged me to come back.'

'I like the walls blank,' he said stubbornly, looking at the sea through the new window.

'OK, then,' she said. 'I'm too tired to argue.'

On her way out she smiled at the clerk, who was half standing, and she said to him in Tamil, 'Take care of him, Ayyan.'

'I always will,' he said, touching his chest with the tips of his fingers.

That evening, Ayyan Mani and Adi were sitting on a pink concrete bench, one of the many benches on the Worli Seaface that were dedicated to the memory of a departed member of the Rotary Club. Adi was peering into the paper cone searching for hidden peanuts at the bottom. Ayyan studied the walkers. Young women in good shoes walked in haste, as though they were fleeing from the fate of looking like their mothers; proud breasts bounced and soft thighs shuddered. Newly betrothed girls went with long strides to abolish fat before the bridal night when they might have to yield on the pollen of a floral bed to a stranger bearing K-Y Jelly. Old men went with other old men discussing the nation they had ruined when they were young. Their wives followed, talking about arthritis and other women who were not present. Then came Oja Mani, walking swiftly in slippers.

Adi started laughing. He could not bear to see his mother like this. Ayyan laughed too. She gave them a foul look and marched towards the other end of the promenade.

Adi was muttering something to himself and looking at the fluorescent shoes of the boys who were passing by.

'Adi,' his father said, 'look what I have in my hand.'

The boy looked up. His father was holding a spoon.

'Do you know that some people can bend a spoon with their minds?'

'Really?' Adi said.

'Do you want to bend a spoon with your mind, Adi?'

'Yes,' the boy said.

'OK, then listen to me carefully,' Ayyan said, 'but this is the last time. The very last time we do something like this. OK?'

They looked at each other for a moment. And how they laughed.